"Am I to go free?" Arissa asked, hardly daring to hope. After all, Colonel Haskill had wanted her dead.

"In a sense," Phillip answered. "I've assumed responsibility for you. You are released into my custody. Should you behave yourself in a fit manner, until we march to Quebec, you will be allowed to remain at the Chateau Royale . . . under supervision."

He picked up her bag and put it on the table. He seemed to be groping for words, as she met his gaze. Finally, he spoke. "We're going to be married, Arissa."

"What?"

"Arissa . . ." Phillip grasped her arms and pulled her to him. "If I am to be responsible for you night and day, I intend to make it honorable."

"But . . . that's an absurd reason to marry!"

"This isn't." Phillip captured her lips before she could turn her head. With his arms wrapped about her, pinning her own arms against her side, there was no retreat. But this was absurd, indeed, she thought, fighting to remain detached from the passion that leapt to life within her. When she married, it would be for love, not for this dizzying reaction Phillip Monroe could invoke at whim. This rapture was what kept brothels in business, not a solid foundation for a life together. . . .

"This is not fair, Phillip . . ."

He held her closer. "All's fair," he whispered, "in love and war."

WINTER ROSE

Linda Windsor

Zebra Books
Kensington Publishing Corp.
http://www.zebrabooks.com

ZEBRA BOOKS are published by

Kensington Publishing Corp.
850 Third Avenue
New York, NY 10022

Zebra and the Z logo Reg. U.S. Pat. & TM Off.

First Printing: December, 1997
10 9 8 7 6 5 4 3 2 1

Printed in the United States of America

One

Phillip Monroe stood in the dormer of the upstairs room he shared with three other travelers, and stared through the casement window at the inn yard below. The young Canadian he had contacted earlier that evening took his steed from the stableboy and mounted it clumsily. The lad had a good night at the tables and a good number of flips, he thought, one corner of his mouth curling in mild amusement. Hopefully, the horse would know the way home and get him there, before the bottom dropped out of the clouds overhead. In hope of the lad making it home—at least dry from within—Phillip and he traded cloaks earlier, after Conway accidentally bumped into one of the tavern wenches carrying a pitcher of beer and gotten himself soaked.

The lad, Phillip reflected wryly . . . he was but a year Stephen Conway's senior, but Phillip felt at least ten years older. With the seasonal dampness, he'd opted to remain at the inn, rather than ride the twelve miles to Conway's place tonight and risk setting off his game leg. That alone was enough make him feel older. A surge of bitterness rose from nowhere, choking and painful.

He wouldn't think of Deborah, he resolved, staring all the more fiercely at the lantern-lit inn yard to keep his eyes from glazing. Feelings all too familiar started to flow untapped, despite his efforts to quell the memory of his wife's death: fire, burning with a heat from hell, consuming their home; Deborah screaming from the second story window for him to catch their baby. He did manage that, but that was not enough.

He'd tried, God knows he had. He'd felt his clothes afire and his lungs singe with each breath, as he forced his way into the inferno to reach her. Then, suddenly, there was pain beyond imagination and a scream. Had it been his own? The blackness erased it all, the horror and the pain, until he'd regained consciousness two days later, his leg broken and badly burned.

Subconsciously, Phillip rubbed his leg. He was tired, and yet he was reluctant to leave the window. One of his roommates was snoring loudly. Was his reluctance because he thought he'd have trouble going to sleep, or was it that he feared another night of hellish dreams. He started away, when another movement in the inn yard caught his eye.

Three men were coming out of the stable leading horses—the same three he'd seen leave before he and Conway parted company in the taproom below. Except that they obviously hadn't left. They'd been waiting in the barn.

With a muffled curse, Phillip swung away from the window and groped in the semi-darkness for the cloak he'd exchanged for his own earlier. It didn't take a genius to figure out what was going on. Conway's purse was fat with winnings, and he was hardly in any shape to fend off one thief, much less three. Phillip slung the cloak over his shoulders and fastened it, he grimaced at the stench of the cheap beer. Perhaps a fast ride to Montreal would air it sufficiently, he mused, for that was exactly where he was about to go, regardless of the previous plans made with his Canadian contact.

The stableboy was outright shocked when yet another guest who'd paid for his night's lodgings took his horse from the barn and left in seeming haste, but Phillip's handsome tip at least left the lad smiling. As he rode off, Phillip checked the pistol he'd tucked in his belt, subconsciously, as if to insure its exact whereabouts, should the need for it occur. He'd have one good shot and the rest would have to rely on his skill with the saber—and a knife, he mused, reaching down to his boot, where the hilt of the dagger Deborah had given him on their first anniversary was hidden.

Thankfully, every once in a while, a sliver of moonlight managed to sift through the thickening clouds, helping Phillip keep to the road. He pushed his dapple grey as much as he dared, considering his lack of knowledge of the lay of the land. A crippled horse would do neither him, nor Conway, any good.

It seemed as if he'd ridden for miles, when he finally heard what appeared to be a confrontation of sorts. A horse whinnied in panic and curses filled the otherwise still air. Around a bend in the road, Phillip finally saw them, three wolves darting in and out on horseback at their beleaguered prey. He drew his pistol from his belt and urged the grey forward with a loud yell.

His hand steady, he took aim at the man closest to Stephen Conway and pulled the trigger. Silently, Phillip gave a grateful prayer for all the marksmanship contests he'd taken part in at the Monroe country home in Albany, during the summers of his youth. The brigand lurched backward with the impact of the ball, as if to lie down on his mount, and then toppled sideways. Startled, the other two men drew away momentarily, but upon seeing only one man approach them, they regrouped.

"Forget the bloody purse, just do 'im in and be off!" one of them shouted to the other.

To Phillip's horror, both men charged Stephen Conway, one with a saber and the other with a wide-bladed knife large enough to be reckoned with seriously. As he ran his horse at full speed between the man with the saber and his victim, Phillip lashed out at him with his own weapon. Out of the corner of his eye, he saw Conway fend off the slashing knife with his cape.

Deftly, he turned his mount and went at his chosen opponent again. This time, their blades clashed and locked, nearly unseating them both in the process, as their horses began to move in a tight circle. The scent of sweating horseflesh and leather, mingled with desperation, in the bizarre dance of death. Suddenly, Phillip shifted sideways and brought round his free hand, landing a fist solidly against the right temple of his opponent. The man's grip faltered, his blade slipping past Phillip. With his sword hilt, Phillip cuffed the brigand under the chin, knocking him squarely off his horse.

The man struck the ground with a pained grunt and rolled out of the way of his panicked steed's hoofs. Phillip slapped the horse's hindquarters to get it out of the way and turned toward the thief in time to see him reaching inside his cloak. Whether the man was drawing a pistol or a knife, there was no time to hesitate. Phillip grasped the hilt of his dagger and, seemingly in one motion, let it fly.

A pistol dropped to the ground and discharged wildly, just before its owner fell, a startled look on his face. His heart pounding with the frantic pump of adrenaline, Phillip swung about to see the third man riding off, as though the hounds of hell were on his heels. To his dismay, Stephen Conway lay on the ground at his horse's feet.

A sick knot rose in his throat. Damnation, he couldn't be too late, again! He should have left with Conway. They could have explained to his old maid sister that they'd met on the road and Conway had hired him, rather than have Phillip arrive and apply for temporary employment, as they'd planned. How difficult could the woman be?

As Phillip dropped to the ground and knelt by his new-found friend, the man started trying to rise. Relief flooded him. At least the lad was alive.

"Where are you hurt?"

"The bloody beggar slashed open my ribs!" Conway swore, breathlessly. "If my horse hadn't reared, I'd have been stuck like a pig. *Dieu*, but the size of that knife!"

It was too dark to see how bad the wound was, but Phillip could certainly feel the ghastly separation of flesh and the blood soaking Conway's clothing. He threw off the cloak and hurriedly stripped off his linen shirt. With the sleeves to secure it, it would apply some pressure and perhaps stifle the bleeding, until he could get the man to a physician.

"I don't know what brought you after me, but . . . I'm bloody glad you came. Those blokes were set on doing me in."

"They'd been watching us all evening," Phillip informed him, as he tied the makeshift bandage tightly. "I saw them follow you from my room upstairs." He glanced up, as a few large drops of rain splashed on his face. That was just what they needed, he grumbled silently.

"At least you have the damp cloak, *mon ami*," Conway jested, in a strained voice.

Phillip awarded the young man's attempt at courage with a forced smile. "You need a doctor," he said, donning the beer-scented cloak again. When it got wet, it would be rank as hell. He grabbed Stephen's arm and helped him to his feet. "Point me in the right direction. This is your country."

"To the Chateau Royale, monsieur. My sister, she is able to see to this little scratch. She is a licensed midwife and a passable physician."

Thunder burst ahead of them, and Phillip groaned inwardly. They'd be going right into the storm. "You think you're up to riding through this?"

Stephen Conway managed a grin. "Do I have a choice, *mon ami?*"

Phillip smiled back, genuinely this time. Here was a man who could make the best of any situation, he thought, somewhat in envy. Mayhaps some of his zest for life might rub off. If one were condemned to live after a tragedy, one might at least find some bit of personal relish to it. To date, he had not.

The dark clouds, which had crept along the eastern horizon and engulfed the city, finally clashed outside the Chateau Royale, but its guests were snug and safe from the torrential rain and lightning that ensued. Exhausted from a long night in the taproom of the inn, Arissa Conway hardly noticed the storm or the sudden wind that swept clean the heaviness in the air. Lost in a sweet dream, she burrowed farther into her pillow, her lips curled in a wistful pose, which gave the man, who stood over her bed, cause to hesitate before clamping his hand over them.

Suddenly, her sleep was interrupted by the warm fingers of a faceless intruder. At first, she thought her sweet dreams had turned into a nightmare, but no amount of mental shaking would make him disappear. She stared, wide-eyed and confused, at his hulking figure, which exuded the strong scent of cheap beer. A flash of lightning illuminated the room, and he seemed larger than ever and twice as sinister. A scream burst from somewhere within her frozen chest, but emerged as no more than a frightened whimper through her nostrils, as she struggled to collect her wits.

"Quiet, mademoiselle! I mean you no harm." There was a sense of urgency in the stranger's voice, despite his assurance. "Your brother sent me. He needs you. If I let you go, you will not scream?"

Arissa nodded, her gaze wary, as he eased his hand away

from her mouth with equal caution. "Stephen," she managed, her voice strangled by her anxiety. "Where is he?"

"In what, I presume, is his room."

In his room? A different brand of alarm bolted through her, as she sat up. Dear God, he's stirred one too many fires of rebel passion. Only that afternoon, Adrien Rueil, the newly appointed colonel of the local militia, was asking about him, and his inquiry was not about recruitment. He was investigating those who were in favor of the *bastonnois*, or the colonial rebels.

"He's hurt?"

"A gash on his ribs. I would have taken him to a physician, but . . ."

No longer intimidated by the cloaked individual, Arissa shoved off the bed and rushed to shut the half-raised window, where rain was pelting in. "I am a doctor of sorts, monsieur. Please fetch my bag on the desk in the downstairs parlor. I'll see to my brother."

She eyed the stranger once more, warily, but yielded to her instinct to trust him not to help himself to any of the valuables in the family part of the inn. After all, he had obviously brought Stephen home, despite the amount of liquor he'd evidently consumed.

"Take the lamp in the corner stairwell," she advised, crisply.

Arissa knew her way without light to the large room her brothers shared across the hall, although the lightning outside the gable casement provided an ample supply. Opening the door, she told herself that she must be calm, and swore silently at herself for allowing Adrien Rueil and his rebel hunt to disconcert her so. Her neighbor's speech to the habitants earlier that evening had been filled with malicious contempt for the Americans, who had already advanced into Canadian territory.

While he'd not been able to alarm her patrons sufficiently to enlist in his cause, he'd certainly spooked her, especially when he informed her that Governor Carleton was considering seizing the properties of rebel sympathizers. How could Stephen be so foolish as to take up such a cause and risk not only the Chateau Royale but himself! Had he been attacked by a Loyalist? A gash on the ribs could only be so bad, unless it was a puncture . . .

" 'Rissa!"

Her brother lay sprawled across his bed atop a wet cloak, his muddied boots extending over the edge, so that she had to step around them to approach him. It wasn't even his cloak, but the scent of good brandy on his breath, that distracted her, explaining his jovial tone in the midst of his indisposal. No doubt he and the stranger had been tipping cups all night long. Her mouth thinned in disapproval.

"What have you done this time, Stephen! I did not think drunken brawls were your sort of entertainment."

"I do not think the fellows were drunk, *ma petite soeur.*"

Color drained from her face, as she began to unwrap a bloodied bandage tied about Stephen's slender waist—a shirt bound by the sleeves. "You were attacked?"

The same deep voice, which had summoned her to her brother's bedside, preceded the appearance of the medical satchel at her side. "Set upon by thieves along the road."

"But for Monsieur Monroe, I might have been found in the city ditch in the morning."

Thieves! Consumed with relief that the violence was not politically inspired, the stranger's name passed Arissa by. However, as she peeled away the blood-soaked shirt, she was stricken once again by the sight of the ghastly wound. *"Mon dieu!"*

It was a gash, a deep one. To the bone, she thought, in dismay, as she probed gently with her fingers, and a bit too long, even to have been inflicted by a dagger. It was more like sword wound, as though it had struck from the side and been drawn along the rib cage.

"Mademoiselle, are you all right?"

Arissa flinched at the inquiring touch of the stranger's hand on her shoulder, but nodded abruptly. "Move the lamp closer, if you will, monsieur. I need to see to cleanse the wound and then suture it, although it appears from the amount of blood loss that it should have bled sufficiently free of foreign debris."

Upon rising from the edge of the mattress, Arissa poured water from the pitcher on the washstand between the two single beds in the room, grateful that Chiah had the foresight to see that it was filled, in case her brother came in after everyone had retired. Stephen was inclined to do that, more often than not. Using one of the fresh linens neatly folded beside the washbowl, she returned to her perch and began to sponge away the dried blood and bits of linen from his shirt that clung to the wound.

"I washed the wound out with brandy before wrapping it," her companion offered, from the foot of the other bed, where he'd divested himself of his cloak.

"Good. Stephen was lucky to have you, in more than one respect," Arissa acknowledged, too absorbed in her task to notice the way in which he'd made himself at home, much less that it was her brother's cloak he tossed aside. "I will need your help in a moment again, if you will be so good as to wash your hands."

When satisfied that the wound was free of any additional foreign matter, she opened her father's case and withdrew the curved needle and length of thread for the ligatures. These she placed on a clean, folded towel, along with the surgical scissors and adhesive plaster.

"Would you like a towel to chew on?" she asked, glancing at her brother's pale face, as she rose once more and moved the bag out of her way. "The other side, monsieur," she added bruskly, directing the man who'd stepped up to the bed to assist to assume a position opposite her.

"Ah, I have been remiss. Since you have taken to ordering my friend about like a servant, it seems the least I can do is to introduce you. Arissa, this is Phillip Monroe. Monsieur, this is the sister I was telling you about."

More reminder than reprimand, the introduction made Arissa flush with embarrassment, as she looked up at the stranger who had roused her from her bed. As he straightened and extended his hand, she realized he was as tall as her brothers, with broad shoulders which tapered down to a narrow, belted waist. Yet, it was her shock that he wore no shirt—only a soft leather vest—that robbed her momentarily of her senses.

She stared at the golden brown swirl of the lightly furred and muscled plane where the glistening gold of a pendant lay nestled, strung by a leather thong. "But of course, that was your shirt!" she stammered, referring to the wadded garment she'd discarded at her feet. "I . . ."

Both men were watching her now, the stranger with polite detachment and Stephen with a raised brow which managed to restore some semblance of her wit. Her brother may have lost a good deal of blood, but he was still in possession of his oft times goading sense of humor. She brushed the dark auburn braid that had fallen over her shoulder behind her back, primly.

"I shall have to apologize for my lack of manners later, Monsieur Monroe. For the moment, we have a more serious matter at hand." As if to wipe away the hint of a smile haunting her brother's lips, she shoved the twisted towel into his mouth. "This will not be pleasant, Stephen, but I shall be as quick as I can."

The wound required ten sutures. Her mind once again focused on her work, rather than the distracting stranger. Arissa ran the needle through Stephen's inflamed flesh quickly and knotted each thread, as she'd seen her father do many times, while Phillip Monroe pressed it together with surprisingly steady hands. Although the storm, which was now diminishing in fierceness, had cleared the thick air with a cooling effect, Stephen had grown more ashen and perspiration filmed his brow.

"I shall apply these strips of adhesive plaster between each stitch, bandage the wound, and, voilà! You can get the sleep you need," she announced, with forced brightness, for his sake. "And if you are not up to it tomorrow, I shall go to the provost myself and report this assault."

"There is no need, 'Rissa. I'm certain the blackguards are well away from here, by now."

Suspicion once again clouded Arissa's expression, heightened, as she noticed for the first time the pouch hanging at Stephen's waist. "But not with your purse."

"I told you, Monsieur Monroe came to my rescue and stopped the robbery before it was successful! Now are you going to bandage this bloody thing and let me sleep, or interrogate me?"

Tight-lipped, Arissa returned to her ministrations. Stephen did need his rest and she was agitating him. After washing the wound once again, she applied lint to it, using gauze to secure it, with the stranger's help, for her brother, regardless of his bravado, had weakened to the point that it was difficult for him to raise himself, so that she might wrap the bandage about his rib cage.

"I'll be back with some tea to help you sleep," Arissa announced, when the task was completed. The opiate would also prevent inflammation, if luck were with them, although the wound had been a clean one, for the most part. "Would you care for something from the kitchen, monsieur?" she said to the stranger. "Some bread and cheese, perhaps, and . . ."

"A glass of our finest brandy," Stephen put in amiably, from the bed. "It's the least we owe him for saving my life," he added, upon noting the brief flash of disapproval on Arissa's face.

"But of course," she agreed dubiously. After all, from the reek of him, he was already well preserved. The man might smell like an alehouse, but he had saved her brother's life. That surely deserved a sampling of their imported stock, and nothing less.

"I'll accompany you, if you don't mind. There's no sense in hauling the food upstairs."

Arissa glanced Monroe's way in speculation. He looked tired and travel-weary, not a jot as threatening or intoxicated as she'd first perceived. "This way then, monsieur." Perhaps their guest would be more informative than her brother, and she might discover the truth about Stephen's brush with danger, rather than the concoction he'd conveyed. He always was a bad liar.

" 'Rissa . . ."

Arissa turned at the door at her brother's call. "Yes, Stephen?"

"If you are going to entertain our guest, put on your robe, *ma petite,*" he advised her, gently.

Her robe? Arissa glanced blankly down at her thin nightshirt, where the bodice clung to her youthful breasts, now taut with the cooler change of temperature brought on by the squall. Her robe!

Embarrassment rose a hundredfold to her cheeks, as she belatedly pressed her shift to her chest with her arms, as if to cover that which nature had generously endowed her with. Mumbling, "I shall join you momentarily, monsieur," she darted into the dim lit haven of her room to fetch the garment she'd forgotten, in her haste and concern for her brother.

Two

Once she had regained as much of her composure as was possible, under the circumstances, Arissa found her way down the narrow back staircase, through the parlor, and to the kitchen below it, where the stranger had once again made himself at home. This time he was rummaging through her corner cupboard, where she kept her good china dishes—not the pewter or wooden trenchers reserved for the taproom.

"I'll fetch the cups, monsieur! It is you who are the guest," Arissa reminded him with an authoritative hint of reprimand in her voice. After all, who was this man to be going through their things as if he owned them, she thought, regaining her customary air of composure.

"Found them!" he announced, turning, unaffected by the command in her voice, with a cup nestled neatly in its saucer in each hand. Lifting one precariously, he brushed a shock of light brown hair off his forehead, where it had been plastered by the ride in the rain. "When I didn't see any on the shelf over the fireplace, I figured they'd be in here."

He flashed a guileless smile, as he approached the table and placed them there, making it difficult for her rise of disapproval to take serious root. Having apparently taken stock of his own attire and finding it lacking, he'd discarded his vest and pulled a fresh shirt on for a degree of presentability. It hung loose over his trousers and was unlaced carelessly at the neck.

Still, Arissa felt the need to be wary. "Will you have tea or brandy?"

"A toddy of both would be a pleasant end to an otherwise harrowing night. I recommend one to you, as well." His tone was matter-of-fact, neither accusing nor patronizing.

"What . . . me?" Arissa found herself stammering, unable to hide her astonishment that he'd seen past her calm manner and steady hand, as she'd tended Stephen's wound. She was still shaking inside, and her speculation as to what had brought about the attack had not given her one comforting moment's reprieve. Once again she damned Adrien Rueil for setting her nerves on edge, with his subtle threats about seizing property. After all, her eldest brother, Martin, was serving with General Howe in Halifax. That should certainly speak for the family's loyalty, and she was not in favor of this revolution spreading to Canada. Even Stephen's obsession with the cause was something she felt would pass quickly, like most of his infatuations for such things.

"Although I have never had someone literally pull me from sleep," she stipulated, "I have been awakened in the night on other occasions to tend to a wound from some silly fight, or to help with the birthing of a baby." Why she felt the need to defend herself to this man, she had no idea, except that it was the middle of the night, she had had a shock, and wasn't in the clearest state of mind, at the moment.

"Then it will help you go back to sleep, now that your duty is done, mademoiselle."

Instead of answering, Arissa approached the large stone hearth. It wasn't as huge as the one in the adjoining kitchen, but it was of an impressive proportion, designed for cooking. Taking up a thick pad, she lifted the kettle of water, which was always kept over the coals of the fire, off its trammel and set about preparing the tea on the small stretcher-based table that served as a work station and informal dining table, when she ate alone.

Once the brew was prepared, she put out a third cup for Stephen. Then, leaving the tea to steep, she fetched a decanter of brandy from the closet on the opposite side of the hearth from the corner steps. It was where the family's finer liquors were stored, so she took care to keep from her guest the location of the hidden key. How successful she was, she couldn't tell, for even though she was at the opposite side of the room, she sensed he watched her every move.

"Will you have some bread, monsieur? I have some loaves from supper and some plum jam."

"The toddy will be fine, mademoiselle. I, too, am tired and in need of a good night's rest."

Arissa arched a brow at the man, as she removed the cap on the decanter. "You are leaving tomorrow, then?"

"That all depends on you."

"Me?" Once again unable to hide her astonishment, she held the bottle suspended over the rim of the teacup, waiting.

Instead of answering, the stranger put his finger under the brandy bottle and tipped it until the cup was filled to the rim. "Sit down, mademoiselle, and I'll explain all to you that I can."

Taken further back by his direct manner, Arissa did as she was told. Here was a man who was obviously accustomed to giving rather than receiving orders, a capable man, judging by the sinew that moved subtly on his forearm, which was bared by the rolled sleeve of his shirt.

"Then you will have a lot to tell, monsieur, for I have many questions, particularly about my brother's whereabouts and the nature of this attack upon his person."

"Stephen said you would."

A wary prick at the nape of her neck brought her gaze up sharply, her brother's earlier introduction of her to Monroe coming to mind. *The sister I told you about. Dieu!* Surely Stephen was not trying to play matchmaker! Only last year, Martin had tried to arrange a marriage to Adrien Rueil. Arissa knew the effort was born of her brothers' promise to honor their father's deathbed wish to see their adopted sister taken care of, but it was nonetheless annoying. Ironically, if anyone was doing the caring for anyone, it was she for them, or at least that was so where Stephen was concerned.

"So Stephen has discussed me with you," she stated flatly. "I can only hope he was completely candid."

She oversaw the running of the Chateau Royale and, to a small degree, carried on her foster father's medical practice, while Stephen decided to try his hand at fur trading in the wilderness for a season, with the voyageurs. And when she needed him most, now that Gaspar was laid up with a broken hip, he was off giving speeches about revolution, which forced her to work the bar in the taproom. She loved Stephen dearly, but he was so idealistic and reckless.

A thoughtful smile from her guest flashed over his cup, as he brought it to his lips, the result of some sudden and private amusement, which drew Arissa from her irritated tangent of thought. The stranger looked even less intimidating now, so natural and genuine was he. His look wasn't contrived to charm, yet it had that affect. Perhaps it was because it was reflected in his gaze.

"Not quite, I think."

Arissa's aloof demeanor wavered, undermined by a strange flutter somewhere in her chest. Indigestion, no doubt. A man as practiced with a smile as that surely must know its effect.

"You're much prettier than I imagined. He told me you were an old maid and a midwife."

"Did he?"

Uncertain as to exactly how to react to the compliment, she focused on cooling her tea, unaware of the fetching purse of her mouth, as she did so. Perhaps his charm was a means to an end, after all.

"Well, I am a midwife. I trained under my father. As for old, I am twenty-six and have already turned down a wealthy and influential suitor. Stephen should have warned you that I am not interested in marriage." She met his encompassing gaze in challenge.

"A committed old maid, I believe were his exact words," her companion informed her. "It's the old part that's was misleading. Twenty-six isn't old."

Unaware, Arissa breathed a sigh of relief. "Then he didn't bring you home to marry me," she murmured, to no one in particular.

The man across from her laughed aloud. "No, mademoiselle, we discussed employment, nothing more."

It felt as if the steaming tea before her was scalding her cheeks, as she digested the stranger's words with a healthy dose of being put in her place. What a dolt he must think her! It was just that every time her brothers brought home an eligible bachelor . . . She broke off, realizing she had no idea what this man's marital status was. Good heavens, where was her mind tonight?

"Employment," she managed, grateful for the dim light of the oil lamp over the hearth. So Stephen had had her problems at the inn in mind, after all. She laughed in order to release some of her embarrassment, as well as a twinge of guilt for her silent condemnation of her brother. "Well that is good, because I do need a man to help with the inn. My brothers, however, they sometimes act as matchmakers, and I had thought . . . well, we can both be relieved, *non?* It was silly of me to even think . . . but then, I must admit, I was shaken by this night's events." As if to demonstrate how rattled she was, she added a dash of the brandy to her tea.

"I doubt you'll need your brothers to find you a suitable husband, when you decide you are ready to wed, Mademoiselle Conway, but that's your business. Me, I just want some work and a place to stay for a while."

Your business. Arissa liked that. Yes, there was respect in those . . . what color were his eyes? That, too, in the dim light was hard to make out. All she could see, could sense, was their intensity. He wasn't flirtatious, after all. He was . . . sincere, she decided, with a degree of caution.

Before she made a further fool of herself and was captured by his intuitive gaze, she diverted her attention from the well-placed features of his face to his clothing. His shirt, like the one that had serviced Stephen's wound, was of good linen, finely woven, not coarse like that of cheaper cloth. And that was gold, she thought, noticing again the rich glint of the medallion all but hidden behind the open laces of the garment.

His boots were in good repair, she noted, glancing sideways in order to examine them. His long, outstretched legs, strong, sturdy ones straining the material of his trousers in a way that suggested manly strength and sinew beneath, permitted an easy view.

"Do I pass inspection?"

Refusing to let the heat that seemed to radiate from her face lessen her contrived air of detachment, Arissa answered with a question. After all, as a prospective employer, one had the right to inspect the applicant to be certain he was suited the position available. "You are well dressed, monsieur, which makes me wonder why you need a job?"

"To remain that way."

"You said you would answer my questions," she reminded him firmly. Quick-witted, daring, direct, obviously a man of some means, she reasoned sharply. Why would such a man want menial employment at an inn? He was too good, over qualified.

"Bon, you want to know who I am, where I am from, and where I am going."

"You are American!" The revelation came out of the blue, with sobering dismay. But his French was perfect, part of her argued, in the man's defense. Still, if the man was a rebel, that would explain Stephen's wound and the stranger's presence. Americans were everywhere these days, stirring up trouble. As Adrien had said, their army was not so far away. Disappointment mingled with alarm as she went on. "I am sorry, Monsieur Monroe, but I cannot . . ."

Arissa broke off, as he covered her hand with his plaintive one. "Just hear me out. You owe me that much for saving Stephen's life."

For a fraction of a second, their gazes locked and Arissa found herself holding her breath. Yes, she would listen to him, she owed him that much, but not with her hand captive beneath his stronger one. It was too disconcerting. Even as his fingertips, soft against her wrist, told her he was not accustomed to the labor required of him, they also suggested his willingness to become hardened to such tasks. She nodded permission for him to make his case and purposely withdrew her hand, so that she could restore some semblance of order to her thoughts.

"My name is Phillip Monroe. I am a clerk by profession and am originally from New York. There is too much turmoil in the colonies for me, and I've come to Canada to start over."

That was it? Arissa wondered in surprise, after a long pause of silence. "You have no family?"

"Not anymore . . . none which would keep me there."

She waited a moment for him to explain, but when it became apparent that no further elaboration was coming, she pressed on. "Why would you stoop to such menial work as this?"

"A man has to start somewhere, make new acquaintances. As I stated, it is only temporary, to earn my room and board, until I can secure a position in the city or move on to Quebec. I am weary of all this talk of war. I just want peace."

"Then you have come to the wrong place, monsieur," Arissa told him, laconically. "For that, you may have to leave the continent."

"Even that requires money, mademoiselle." He leaned forward on his elbows. "If I had not been so low on funds, I would not have changed my mind about staying at the tavern where I met your brother, and then tried to catch up with him. You might have had more than a knife slash to sew up."

"Knife?" she echoed in surprise. "*Sacre bleu,* how big was such a thing."

"It was a hunting knife, a long one, like the trappers use."

"I see." Arissa mulled over his words carefully. "This attack on my brother . . . was he spreading this independence nonsense about at the tavern? Could that be the real reason he was attacked?"

"Your brother makes no secret of sympathizing with the Continentals."

He was evading her questioning again. "And you, monsieur, where do your sympathies lie on this matter?"

"I've learned to avoid expressing my opinion on politics and religion. They make enemies out of friends and turn brother against brother. This dissension is spreading like a plague."

"That is a good tactic to practice, if a difficult one." Arissa could relate well to the exasperation now infecting her companion's voice. "My eldest brother is a captain in the militia, serving under General Howe in Halifax.

He's engaged to marry Colonel Dawson's daughter and will return with his bride to England when his enlistment is up to run her family holdings for her father, a devoted professional soldier. Meanwhile Stephen . . ."

"Is leaning toward the other side?"

"Where was Stephen, and what was he doing tonight?"

"Playing cards at the Chop House. He'd done well, I might add."

Hardly a night different from that of any other blooded Loyalist, Arissa thought, in relief. She looked up sharply. "And were you in the game, monsieur?" Perhaps he had a weakness for gambling, as well as drink. She would have to discuss with Stephen in the morning the good judgment of hiring a man so fond of liquor to tend the bar.

The man shook his head. "What little coin I have is too dear to risk at cards. I was an observer."

Conservative, neutral, Arissa mused, all the things which would entice her to accept him. His act was so perfect, he had to be sober, despite the stench of him when he first came in. No, she wouldn't let the fact that Gaspar was bedridden push her into a hasty decision. She and Chiah, Gaspar's Pawnee wife, were managing fairly well with her in the taproom, and Chiah at her regular post overseeing the kitchen and room staff.

"At any rate, that was why I changed my mind about staying over and decided to accompany your brother home. He was a tad in his cups, traveling with a fat purse . . . beside, he'd offered me free lodgings and work."

"It's not easy work," Arissa warned him, a little miffed that Stephen had charged into this headlong, without consulting her.

"With your permission, I'll manage."

Again, Arissa was jolted. "With my permission?"

"It doesn't take a genius to realize who bears the most responsibility here."

Phillip Monroe had all the right answers, not to mention being one of the finest specimens of manhood she had ever seen. At least he looked perfect at night, in the dim light of the lamp on the mantel. She blushed at the scandalous direction of her runaway thoughts. She was tired.

"The responsibility is shared, monsieur," she answered, modestly, hoping she did not appear overly pleased at his insight and apparent respect.

The stranger rose from the table and reached for the third cup Arissa had prepared earlier. "I'll take this up for you, if you wish, mademoiselle. Since I suspect the work here begins early, I'm going to take my leave, with your permission, of course."

It was late, Arissa realized, a glance at the clock on the shelf by the staircase confirming the hour at half past three. "By all means, monsieur. But I will administer the tea myself. I want to check the bandage."

Stephen was sleeping when they arrived in the upstairs chamber, but he awakened instantly when Arissa checked the layered gauze to be certain the bleeding had been arrested. While she coaxed him to take opiate-laced tea, Phillip Monroe watched in silence, seated on the other bed, where he'd taken the single liberty of removing his boots, which he placed at the foot.

That was something else she would speak to her brother about. They couldn't have one of the servants living in the family quarters. It wasn't done. Even Gaspar and his wife, who were like family, had their own cottage behind the inn.

"Can you believe our luck in finding Phillip, *ma petite?*" Stephen asked her, as she rose from the bed with the empty cup in hand. "He is heaven-sent, *non?*"

Arissa cut a sideways glance across the room at the man now stretched out, fully clothed, on her eldest brother's bed. His feet hung past the footboard. "That remains to be seen, monsieur."

Whether Phillip Monroe heard her or not was hard to tell. He lay perfectly still, aside from the gentle rise and fall of his chest, his eyes closed and hands folded behind his head. He remained that way until Arissa left, after bussing her brother on the cheek.

"Well, you are still here, *mon ami*. That is a good sign," Stephen Conway volunteered, lowly, from the other bed. "Your sister is no fool, and she's not an old maid."

Conway laughed and then caught his breath at the pained price, giving Phillip some degree of satisfaction. He didn't like surprises, and Arissa Conway was one he particularly disliked.

"She is also not neutral," Phillip went on, grimly. "You can charm her."

"I came here to gauge the mood of the people and map the layout of the city—not to charm your sister."

"Leave her to me, then," Stephen sighed, wearily.

"Believe me, I shall." Phillip lay silent for a moment. "You don't think she'll report those bastards to the provost, do you?"

"*Non.* Not as long as she suspects the attack had something to do with my politics."

With a sigh of relief, Phillip turned over and punched the pillow to make a dent for his head. The last thing he needed was the officials investigating the incident and, hence, questioning him. He wanted to keep as low a profile as possible and observe as much as he could to prepare the way for the American army to take Montreal.

When the sun peaked over the eastern skyline of the city, Arissa intended to be up. After all, she didn't want Chiah finding a stranger making himself at home in the kitchen—not that the Indian woman couldn't run him out. Arissa merely hoped to avoid confusion.

However, it was well past daybreak when the creak and

groan of wagons outside, combined with the heavy thudding of crates being unloaded, dragged her from her bed. Blaming the window she'd closed the night before to muffle the morning alarm of the cock's crow, she hastily washed, dressed, and combed her hair, before descending to the main floor.

To her amazement, Phillip Monroe and five other men were unpacking a large crate, while Gaspar Le Boeuf supervised from a bench near the stone hearth in the gable end of the room.

"What on earth? . . ." Arissa exclaimed, loud enough for Gaspar to overhear.

"The new man, he carries this Gaspar into the taproom himself!" the ex-trader explained merrily, but upon seeing that she was staring at the large crate, he went on. "A billiard table, mam'selle! It looks to be a magnificent one, *non?*"

A billiard table! Dumbfounded, Arissa stood frozen at the foot of the steps and simply stared, unaware of the way the sunlight from the window behind her caught the reddish cast to the long hair she'd tied back with a ribbon. She and Stephen often wished they'd had such a luxury in order to compete with some of the bigger taverns, but it was too expensive for their purse.

It wasn't until Phillip Monroe backed away and gave her a prideful grin that she realized how engulfed she was in the project, or, more specifically, in watching the man who had taken charge of it. Hastily, she focused on the item itself.

"There we go, *messieurs!*" Phillip announced, removing a canvas tarp littered with straw packing to reveal the baize cloth of its top in pristine condition. "I thank you for your assistance and extend Monsieur Conway's gratitude as well. Were he not so indisposed from the punch of Chop House brandy, he would offer it himself."

"What do you think, mademoiselle? Is this not beautiful? Your brother has outdone himself this time!" Gaspar called to Arissa, from his comfortable perch.

Arissa hardly heard him, for she was taken aback by the concerted effort on her new employee's part to cover Stephen's real reason for being abed. It certainly didn't bode well. There should be no shame in admitting one was attacked by highwaymen in the middle of the night.

She glanced back at Gaspar, seeing the man for the first time in her confusion. "And what takes you out of bed? You will never walk right if you don't lie still until the bones mend!"

Propped up against the wall and cushioned by pillows, Gaspar motioned at the bench, which had been covered with blankets. "This is like a bed, *non?* And it permits me to have so much more company. It gets lonely in the cottage with all the pretty women working in the inn."

"He seems comfortable enough."

Arissa turned to address Phillip Monroe, but was interrupted before she could protest.

"Bonjour, Mademoiselle Conway!" One of gentlemen who had helped with the table approached her with an outstretched hand.

Arissa recognized him as one of the landowner's from Sorrel, who always sought lodgings at the Chateau Royale, when in Montreal on business. "Bonjour, monsieur. What have you to do with all of this?" she asked, motioning toward the large table.

"The stakes were too high, and I was too unlucky, it seems," he admitted, sheepishly. "Your brother's clever playing has won you a billiard table fresh from its crate."

"Stephen won it?" She glanced, incredulous, at Phillip Monroe to see a confirming nod.

"And being a man of honor, I have delivered it as promised. It is just arrived from England, so perhaps I will not miss what I have not yet enjoyed," the man went on, wistfully. "Such is the whim of Lady Luck, *non?*"

Arissa shook herself from the quandary of whether to be thrilled with the prize or disapprove of the means by which it was won. Of a more practical nature, she didn't approve of gambling. She'd seen many a good man ruined right there in the taproom. "But surely, monsieur, you will stay and have breakfast, our compliments, of course."

"I heartily accept. This morning's travel has worked up a grand appetite for me and my companions, what with finding two bodies on the way here. The provost held us nearly an hour."

"Bodies?" Arissa hoped her alarm did not show to the degree she felt it.

"Oui, two men—scoundrels, by the look of them, and no great loss."

She dared not glance at Phillip Monroe, lest she give away whatever secret he and her brother were keeping from her. She longed to ask if one of the dead men possessed a large hunting knife.

"I recognized them as two of a trio of men who were drinking cheap beer at the Chop House last night and watching us at the game table. I told the provost that, most likely, the third one is the culprit."

"It would seem so, his leaving his companions like that," she agreed, numbly. She cleared her throat. "Well, in that case, you must eat an extra large meal to pay you for all your trouble and your civic duty. It is good that we have such fine citizens as yourself to help the authorities."

Her guest brushed aside her compliment with a wave of his hand. "Bah, it was nothing. A bit of excitement, eh?"

Arissa smiled weakly. "Regardless, enjoy yourselves, with our compliments, *messieurs.*"

Once her guests were seated, she summoned Phillip Monroe from the assembly of the billiard table into the private kitchen adjacent to the inn's large one on the ground floor of the establishment. Two bodies and Stephen's injuries were too much to be coincidence. If there were something amiss about the attack, she certainly had a right to know why it should be kept secret, and this time she would not be sidetracked by compliments or talk of employment.

Not one to mince words, she addressed the subject directly. The peeve at having overslept, now compounded by this startling revelation, surely connected to her brother's injury, infected her tone. "And what, sir, was the meaning of your implication that Stephen was indisposed from too much drink, rather than by a vicious attack by brigands? What has he to hide?"

Undaunted, Monroe shrugged and met her agitated gaze head on. "I merely repeated what your brother asked me to."

Brown, she thought, distracted by the rich color of the eyes she'd not been able to distinguish the night before. Except that brown hardly described the amber flecks which lightened their hue to a jewel-like quality. Nor their full intensity, which, Arissa realized, was warming her cheeks to a flaming color.

"There's not much meat in *that* stew," she countered, stiffly, willing away her discomfiture to hold out for the truth, not to mention control of the conversation. After all, she was the employer. "I expect my employees to be completely honest, sir, or I will not have them!"

"Mademoiselle Conway," her companion began, in a patronizing tone, "I regret I'm not at liberty to say anything more. I gave my word to your brother and am attempting to keep it, as any man of honor would do. If you would know anything else, you'd best ask him, rather than press me to violate that trust."

He must have been a clerk in a lawyer's office, the way he managed to turn the burden of guilt on her! Arissa lifted a defiant chin in response to the hint of challenge sparkling in his gaze. "Very well, sir, I will do just that."

"But you should eat something first, don't you think? It will improve your humor."

Her humor? How dare the man! "My humor, monsieur, does not need improving! What needs improving is my company. Now see that that mess from the billiard table is cleared away. I am expecting a shipment from the docks presently and will need you free then to unload them."

"It's already here, mademoiselle."

"Where?" Arissa asked, once again tossed off guard.

"It arrived at daybreak and your people showed me where to put it."

"Oh." Arissa stumbled mentally. "Then I suggest you check with Gaspar and Chiah for further instructions, once the crate for that thing is broken up and removed to the kindling pile."

"They seem to be good people," Phillip commented, as he turned to go up the winding back steps to the main floor. Instead of proceeding, however, he hesitated, his foot on the first tread.

Instinctively Arissa knew the character of the Le Boeufs was not the subject most on Phillip Monroe's mind. "Is there something else, monsieur?"

"Yes, there is. With all due respect, I left the colonies to avoid dissension. I will not be caught up in your family quarrels either. I merely wish to earn my keep, is that clear, mademoiselle?"

Arissa had never had an employee redress her, and she was once again rendered dumb. There was an element of reason to his request, she realized, with a pang of guilt. But this wasn't a family quarrel. She was only concerned for Stephen.

"I apologize for demanding you betray your word, monsieur. My curiosity, however, is not born of a meddlesome nature, but out of concern for my brother," she explained. Her sincerity deepened the cerulean hue of her eyes, as she spoke. "Stephen has a reckless nature which makes him act before he thinks, sometimes. I fear that he may jeopardize the Chateau Royale with his new Yankee politics, but more importantly, that he will jeopardize himself. Perhaps you have not loved anyone so much that you want to protect them."

"Excuse me, mam'selle." One of the serving girls stood in the doorway separating the two kitchens, carrying a tray with steaming tea, fresh biscuits, and jam. "Madame Le Boeuf sent this for you. The bread is just out of the oven."

"Put it on the table, please, Jeanne."

Arissa observed Phillip in silence, as the girl followed her directions and then exited the room. He'd focused his attention on something of interest outside the window, waiting for her to continue or finish the confrontation she'd begun. Then, as if sensing Jeanne's departure, he turned a somber face back to her. The change from his earlier rebellious demeanor was so striking that Arissa felt a pang of sympathy, although she could not pinpoint the reason for it. Was that pain behind his veiled gaze?

All she knew was that the air between them needed lightening. He did not seem a bad man, and he had saved Stephen's life. Of that she was more certain than ever. Perhaps, once she talked to her brother, her doubts about Phillip Monroe might be assuaged.

"I think I will have some tea and biscuits, before I speak to Stephen," she said brightly, taking her companion's earlier suggestion to heart. "After all, it is the honey that catches more bees than vinegar, *non?*"

The man glanced over at the table they shared the night before, a hint of a smile returning to his face by the subtle apology for her earlier sharpness. "I doubt it'll take much to sweeten your disposition." With a nod, he started up the corner stairwell to the taproom and disappeared, leaving Arissa, before she was obliged to reply to his unexpected compliment or to show just how much at a loss she was to summon an adequate reply.

Three

If anyone were to disprove the age-old adage, it would be Stephen, Arissa thought later, as she changed the bandage on her brother's side. The good night's sleep had done wonders to restore his strength and stubbornness. Neither honey, nor vinegar, however, would extract a word, aside from his original account of his mishap. She'd never seen him so close-mouthed.

"I tell you, Arissa, I was riding back to the Chateau Royale after a grand night at the tables. Monsieur Monroe was good enough to loan me his cloak, since it was beginning to rain and mine got accidentally soaked when I bumped into a barmaid carrying a tray of filled pitchers. We were to exchange them again, when he arrived at the Chateau Royale today to report for work."

So that was why the stranger smelled like a brewery. "But why did he come after you in a wet cloak, then?" Arissa asked, skeptically. "It was a horrible night for a ride."

"You will soon see that Phillip is a very cautious type. He started thinking about my purse and my . . . well, my state of . . ."

"Drunkenness?" she provided, evoking a slight flush on her brother's pale face.

"*Oui*, that too," Stephen admitted, sheepishly. "I was celebrating my good fortune, *ma petit soeur.* Did you not see the billiard table? Is it not what we dreamed of getting?"

Arissa was torn between hugging him and smacking him. Instead, she squeezed his hand. "What am I to do with you, Stephen? You are incorrigible!"

"At any rate, Phillip happened to see three men, who had been in the inn earlier, ride out after me, and he became suspicious," Stephen went on, guilelessly. "To my good fortune, he caught up with me in time to chase away the brigands."

"Chase away or kill?" It was unnerving to think Phillip Monroe capable of murder. Yet, when she'd first seen him leaning over her bed, that's what she thought he was about . . . that or worse.

" 'Rissa, he either had to kill them or let them kill me. Thankfully, he chose the first. For such a quiet man, he fights like a demon! On a horse, no one would even know of his disability."

Arissa started. "Disability? I noticed no disability."

Stephen lay back on his pillow and eased his arms behind his head, lest he pull too hard on her handiwork. "So you are noticing him, are you?"

Pain creased his forehead, but he'd not lost his penchant for teasing her. No sister—adopted or blood born—could want for more loving brothers than she. That was why it was so hard to remain miffed at them, despite their often ornery natures.

"I have considered him as I would any prospective hireling," she retorted, primly. "Which is why I wonder that neither of you will tell the provost what really happened."

" 'Rissa," Stephen cajoled, taking her hand between his. "Phillip's an American. Do you think he would be treated fairly? You know how the authorities are frowning on anyone who even does business with the colonies now. My silence is the least I owe him for saving my life, *non*?"

Reluctantly, Arissa nodded. Stephen seemed to make

sense. She picked up the conversation again. "So what is this disability you speak of?"

"It is a limp, a very slight one. He says it only shows when he is tired, or if the weather is very damp and cold." Stephen chuckled to himself. "Although the rain did not seem to impair him last night. The bloody devils would have done me in, but for his riding at them and shouting like a banshee from hell."

With his cloak flared out from those wide shoulders, Arissa could well imagine such an intimidating sight. "This limp, then, is it a birth defect?" she asked, her professional interest piqued by the ailment.

Stephen shook his head. *"Non,* an accident. There was a fire last year. A wall collapsed on his leg, while he was trying to rescue his wife and child from a burning building. I think he runs from that more than the political upheaval."

"He's widowed." She echoed her thoughts with a combination of empathy and horror. Her own words resounded accusingly in the back of her mind, making her feel all the worse. *Perhaps you have not loved anyone so much that you wanted to protect them.* No wonder he'd turned so wooden! "His wife and child were killed?" she queried, in a brokenhearted tone.

"His wife at least, I believe. I am not certain about the baby. I did not wish to pry, and he stopped talking about it."

"That poor man! No wonder he wants to start over here!" That is, if he still did, after her behavior this morning, she thought dourly. She owed him an apology. Another one! Heavens, what had gotten into her? She was as quarrelsome as a drunken Adrien Rueil!

Stephen raised himself up on an elbow, as Arissa hurriedly gathered up the soiled bandages and tossed them in the basin. He'd won one battle and could rest easier, now that his sister had stopped asking questions. "Now don't go mothering him. It's his business. Just treat him like you would anyone else."

"I know men better than that," she countered, defensively.

Arissa picked up the basin, reining in her impulse to do just that. If she apologized or treated the man any differently, Phillip Monroe would know she'd been asking about him. If he wanted her to know about his tragedy, he'd tell her. All she could do now was to act her normal, cheerful self and hope he wouldn't hold a grudge.

When the stage arrived that afternoon from the ferry at St. Paul, it came with the news that Governor Carleton had actually threatened a group of English businessmen who supported the American cause with closing them down and imprisonment. The furor among the patrons stimulated their thirst, and the taproom became so busy that, after seeing to her brother's supper and changing the dressing on his wound, Arissa had to help Phillip behind the bar, so that Chiah could continue to keep the meals arriving from the kitchen.

Arissa wondered if the governor was wise in making so many enemies within his province. How could he expect the people to rally behind him, if he continually threatened them, rather than supported them per the example set by England's good king. Already, he'd put off the populace—at least the habitants—by demanding they enlist in a militia headed by officers to be appointed by the government, not elected from among the troops, as before. No one would volunteer—especially the common people—with a pampered member of the noblesse at their lead, rather than one they had faith in to elect to command.

It was only worsening matters, she thought, glancing over to where Phillip Monroe was preparing a pitcher of flip for one of the tables. Other than a tendency to cut too much sugar for the drinks, he did rather well behind the bar. She was surprised at his knowledge of the different types of concoctions required, although, had she not discovered the reason he reeked of alcohol the night before, she would have guessed his expertise the result of having spent a lot of time at taverns sampling various mixtures. To her knowledge, he'd not sampled a taste since the ale he had with his supper.

Approaching his task in keeping with his quiet nature, he spent more time serving drinks than generating conversation at the bar, as was Gaspar's talent. Speaking only when spoken to, Phillip tactfully remained neutral on the political debate going on, heightened by the arrival of Adrien Rueil. As for the flirtations of the serving girls, he was either oblivious to them or aware that he was being supervised.

Which was exactly what Arissa was doing. After all, she was his employer, she thought, watching, as he put the coin in the money box and gave change, counting it out loud for the benefit of the patron. At least things had slowed to the point where she was no longer needed, she thought in relief, from her perch on a stool near the door to the bar. The kitchen was slowing the demand down for drink with food.

"Your new man, where does he come from?"

Arissa started at the sound of Adrien Rueil's voice at her side. A moment ago, he was at the new billiard table with a group of his friends. "New York. He came north to get away from all the squabbling . . . that and the grief of losing his family," she added, convincingly. "He is going to work for us, until Gaspar is back on his feet, then move on, I suppose, start over in the city or Quebec."

"Doing what?"

"He is a clerk."

"He's a bit athletic for desk work, don't you think?"

"You will have to ask him about that, Adrien. I have told you all I know," Arissa averred, impatiently.

Stroking a golden lock off his forehead into a flawless wave, Adrien straightened to his full height and motioned for Phillip to join them. His appointment as militia captain had certainly gone to her neighbor's head and addled his brain, Arissa fumed, stepping away to take over for her employee at the bar. She'd overhead more than one insinuation that Adrien's zeal for the job might just get him shot in battle by his own men. To think, Martin had tried to make a match for her with such a man!

While her eldest brother had forgiven her for refusing Adrien's proposal, Adrien had not. The pompous young man still could not believe that she, the adopted daughter of a lowly English physician, had chosen life at the tavern, rather than that as the wife of old French nobility at the seigneury granted his great-grandfather. Even though he'd promptly married a school friend of Arissa's afterward, he still had a way of undressing her with his mercury-gray gaze.

Arissa made it a point never to be completely alone with the man, his visual and verbal insinuations made her absolutely furious. She dared not let on to Stephen about them, lest her brother plunge headlong into a duel, which would be as good as Adrien Rueil would like, crack shot that he was. That was Adrien's way. Bang! Arissa slammed a tankard of beer on the serving girl's tray, earning a wide-eyed look, and forced herself to take a calming breath.

The truth was, it wasn't just his flirtations, she admitted, with a grudging glance in Adrien's direction. She had learned to handle the advances of men during the first year the Chateau Royale had been converted into an inn from the mansion her father had built. It was the way he looked down on her and her brothers, since they'd been forced, by circumstances, to make the conversion. Doctor

Robert Conway could have left them wealthy beyond measure, were it not for his good heart and poor ability to collect his debts.

At his demise, the large mansion he'd built, to accommodate patients who'd traveled a good distance for treatment, had yet to be paid for. It was Stephen's idea to convert the place into an inn and, with Martin's investment and her and Stephen's work, it had paid for itself the first year and made them a comfortable living, beside. Still, it hadn't stopped Adrien Rueil from acting as though he'd done the family a favor in asking for her hand in marriage, much less assuage his wounded pride, when she refused.

Arissa stole another look at the two men, as she tapped a pitcher of beer for a group of peasants, or habitants, who'd wandered in after their day in the fields. Adrien was flawlessly attired in brocade, his linen cuffs ruffled and pulled so that just the right amount showed at the end of his sleeve. His flaxen hair was fashionably powdered and waved on the top and tied in the back. Although the shorter of the two, he assumed a superior stance with his thumb locked in the lapel of his coat, his thinly lined brow arched imperiously, as he listened to Phillip Monroe's soft spoken account of himself.

In his bar apron, with shirtsleeves rolled to the elbow, the newcomer held his own. Though his light brown hair was disheveled and his attire mean in comparison, Phillip appeared to be repressing a smile. It was almost as though he were tolerating Adrien, rather than answering to him. Moving closer on the pretense of tidying the bar, Arissa tried to overhear what she could of their conversation.

It didn't take long for her to realize that, once again, Phillip Monroe was putting to use his gift of speaking without really revealing a lot. If this was a sample of the words being exchanged, Adrien had learned little more than she'd already told him. At the moment, it was her neighbor who was talking about his favorite subject, no less—himself. With a good deal of admiration of Phillip's sharp maneuver in reversing the conversation, Arissa pretended to concentrate on crushing sugar in the bottom of a pewter mug with a toddy stick. However, when the new man made a suggestion to boost the flailing enlistment of volunteers that Adrien, as recruiting officer and colonel of the local militia, lamented over, Arissa thought him a genius and stared at Phillip as though he were just that.

"A muster with a turkey shoot! *Sacre bleu,* but that is wonderful!" Adrien exclaimed, slapping his hand on the bar. "Better yet, we will give away a beef, too! Why, every marksman within miles of Montreal will come for such prizes!" Pleased with the idea, Adrien ordered another drink from Arissa. "If I wish to appeal to the peasants, I must think like one, *non?* Forget trying to reach their sense of honor, tug at their greed, instead!"

"I'd best be getting back to work," Phillip spoke up, ignoring the thoughtless insinuation.

"And what about you, *mon ami?* Can you shoot a rifle or musket?"

"All day long," Phillip told him, as he walked away, his limp, Arissa noticed, more exaggerated than usual. Suddenly he broke into a lopsided grin and looked back over his shoulder. "Of course, I'm not saying that I can hit anything. I'm more accurate with the pen." Reaching for the refreshment Arissa had already prepared, he gave her sly wink.

She couldn't help but smile, despite Stephen's describing Phillip Monroe as a fighting demon. Nothing pleased her more than to see Adrien stymied so masterfully. Remembering the extra lump of sugar Rueil required, at the last moment, Arissa grabbed her companion's arm. "Wait. I have to add a second sugar."

"Here's the tongs."

As she reached for the instrument, her eye caught sight of the large, raw place on Phillip's hand, obviously a broken blister. He'd been splitting wood before the stage arrived.

"You should use gloves . . . at least until your hands become accustomed to real work."

Her companion didn't say anything. He didn't have to. Arissa realized what she'd said, even as she did so, but the words tumbled out anyway, as inconsiderate and insulting as though Adrien had mouthed them. Flushed with the heat of embarrassment, she groped for a saving comment. Not even Adrien's impatient clearing of his throat at the end of the bar distracted her from Phillip's inquiring appraisal.

"I meant physical work, of course." No, that wasn't it either.

"The word is menial, Arissa, and I am withering of thirst, while you fawn over a hired man. Never did I think I should see such a day!"

This time Adrien did fetch her attention. "I'm not fawning over anyone, Adrien Rueil! I was merely noting that Monsieur Monroe's hands were in need of ointment. I'd make the same observation of you or any man, considering my calling in medicine."

"Mademoiselle, whether you intended to act flirtatious or not, that is exactly what you were doing and, since your brother is not here to protect you, I feel that obligation, his being my best . . ."

"Your drink, monsieur," Phillip interrupted, having taken the noggin from Arissa and finished preparing it. "And with it, my assurance that you need not fear for the lady's honor, where I am concerned. Lovely as she is, I have other interests which preclude at present the pursuit of female companionship."

Of all the! . . . Arissa marched to the end of the bar and opened the small half door enclosing the taproom.

She hated it when Adrien spoke of other people in their presence, as though they were not there, and she hated it even more when she was the subject. Left with an inexplicable sting from Phillip's denouncement, she found herself annoyed at both men, now.

"I wish I, just one time, could understand why a man, who is supposed to be an intelligent creature, cannot fathom the fact that some women not only can succeed in life without them, but wish to do so!" She sharply switched her gaze from Adrien to Phillip. "I will be in the kitchen helping with the glasses! Perhaps, if the two of you try, you might be able to spend the rest of the evening without feeling the need to protect me or explain why I am not of interest to you!" With an angry tilt of her chin, she stormed around the bar, skirts rustling, and down the winding staircase to the lower level of the inn.

After venting her frustrations in washing dishes and closing the kitchen, Arissa maneuvered the winding steps again, back to the main floor, carrying a tray of washed noggins and pewter cups for the taproom. Aside from Gaspar and the stage driver, who were engaged in a game of droughts, and a pair of travelers making use of the new billiard table, everyone else had either gone home or to their rooms. Behind the bar, Phillip was stacking a tray of goblets and tankards in need of washing.

"I'll get these ready for tomorrow," he volunteered, as Arissa set her tray down.

"Not with those hands, you won't! Just leave the cups and the girls will wash them in the morning," Arissa assured him. "If you'll close the grate, I'll put these away and then see to those hands. That is, if you're not afraid I'll seduce you with my fawning and ointments," she added, wryly.

Phillip glanced at her, as he reached overhead and untied the rope holding the grate at ceiling height. "Seems to me he doth protest too much. Is Rueil one of your jilted admirers?"

"One." There was no point in telling that Adrien was the only one. No one else ever had the nerve to approach her for more than a dance. She didn't consciously discourage men, they just seemed to keep a respectful distance. Her friends always said she was too serious. "He still can't get over the fact that I preferred my small medical practice and running this inn to being his wife."

"So wealth and influence have no influence, eh?"

Arissa noticed the bulge of her companion's biceps, as he lowered the grate until it fell gently against the rails at either side of the bar. She usually let it bang closed. Although she consciously ignored the masculine display, a very feminine reaction registered within. "Not enough money in the king's treasury or power on the throne could make me put up with Adrien's obnoxious manner, day in and day out."

"He is rather impressed with himself, I take it."

Phillip waited in the doorway, arms folded over his apron. Some of his chestnut brown hair had fallen from the neat queue at his neck and hung about his face, mischievously. As Arissa rose from putting the last of the noggins on its respective shelf, his gaze followed her.

A self-conscious hand went to her apron, as if to clear it of unseen debris and smooth it over her skirts, beneath the full impact of his attention. How long it took before she could summon an answer, she had no idea. "It was his father's fault, really," she explained. "Seigneur Rueil spoiled his only son. He gave Adrien everything he wanted and made the boy think the world revolved around his wishes. All the other children laughed at Adrien behind his back, including my brothers."

"But not you," Phillip suggested, with uncanny perception, maintaining his stance against the jamb of the opening to the bar. "Let me guess. You felt sorry for him."

He went on, when Arissa's gaze widened. "You told him what you really thought of him, in hopes of saving him, while the others worshiped his position and ridiculed him secretly."

"How did you know that?" she asked, frozen, waiting for him to move aside.

"Because, mademoiselle, I am an observer, and I have observed that you are a serious young woman who speaks her mind. Because you are something he can never have, Monsieur Rueil wants you all the more."

Arissa shook her head, modestly. "I would not say . . ."

"That he does not make suggestive comments to that effect whenever he gets the chance?"

"He is nothing I cannot take care of myself, monsieur!" she declared, drawing up to a height that placed her gaze on a level with Phillip's chin. It had been clean shaven earlier, but now boasted a shadow of a darker shade than the chestnut of his hair. She raised her face to his in silent challenge. "Do you wish me to see to your hands or not? I am tired and ready . . ." She swallowed the *for bed* that was on the tip of her tongue, along with all the luscious suggestions it seemed to imply. "To retire for the evening," she finished, awkwardly.

Adrien was not here and she was still making a fool of herself, she lamented, silently. Why could she not just act herself? She'd never had such a problem before, she thought, stepping past Phillip Monroe, as he moved aside. Candle lamp in hand, she led the way through the front hall and into the private parlor.

It was a large, but cozy, all-purpose room with windows at both ends, adorned in brightly patterned curtains. Although there was a bit of a chill to the night air now, the centrally located hearth still blazed with the colors of early fall flowers, like those arranged in a nearby Oriental vase. Two wing back chairs in peacock-blue damask graced either side of the fireplace, while a settee closed the intimate grouping opposite it. This separated the room from its dining function, marked by a large gateleg table which folded out when Arissa formally entertained, and the office, marked by bookshelves with cabinets beneath them, all of which surrounded a magnificent rosewood desk. A bed hidden behind a wooden panel to the right of the fireplace sometimes served to accommodate special guests, when the need arose.

Upon setting the lamp on her father's desk, Arissa turned to peruse the contents of the cupboard to its left, until she found exactly what she sought. She put the lard-based ointment out and found a clean linen cloth and bottle of rose water for cleansing the raw skin. "Now, monsieur, your hands, *si'l vous plaît.*"

She had seen last night that these were not the hands of a common laborer, and the ax handle had only proven her case. Yet the cartload of wood delivered that morning had been split and brought inside, as if hands accustomed to the ax handle had disposed of it. Perhaps his heart was much like his hands, she thought, as she gently cleansed the raw places with the rose water—raw from loss, yet still capable of love.

"If I had not seen this, there might have been infection, monsieur," she scolded gently, shocked at her probing thoughts. It was a bad habit her brothers constantly warned her about—becoming personally involved with the many troubled souls who drifted through the inn. *Don't mother him.* Stephen's words came back to her.

"Guess I'm not used to being taken care of."

His awkward silence seemed to finish, *"At least since the death of my wife."* Arissa wondered how long he'd been widowed, and then shook herself to concentrate on her work. To keep from irritating already inflamed skin, she ever so cautiously blotted first one palm and then the other. That done, she dabbed a small about of ointment on her finger and began to rub it into a small circle in the palm of his hand, which was nearly half again the size of her own.

"Eventually you'll get calluses, that is, if you stay on very long. I am surprised at Gaspar's resilience and mobility with that crutch of his." She worked the creme between his fingers where the flesh had split, continuing to those unaffected. "At any rate, I was very pleased with your performance . . ."

"That's enough, thanks."

Phillip snatched his hand away so suddenly that Arissa was startled. As if realizing how odd his reaction was, he reached across and scooped up a dab of the ointment with the hand she'd just treated. "Now that I see how you go about, I can do the rest. No sense in my keeping you up any later. I've got to help Chiah get Gaspar to bed anyway." He slid off the edge of the desk, where he'd perched to facilitate her ministrations.

Bewildered, Arissa put the lid on the ointment. "Fine. I . . . I'll leave this out on the desk, so that you can put more on in the morning." She got up. "And do wear gloves, until you build up calluses! You do have gloves, don't you?"

"Some riding gloves. I'll be sure to wear them next time."

What on earth was the matter with him, she wondered, catching her breath, as he nearly tripped over the sill of the door separating the main hall from the private quarters of the house. He looked as if she'd bitten him, she thought, as he made his sudden and bemusing exit. And he does have a slight limp. She could hear it as he crossed the empty hall into the taproom. What a strange man—an interesting one, she admitted, but strange.

Later, after a quick bath in scented water, Arissa blew out her lamp and was just about to slip into bed when she realized that she'd not checked on Stephen. She pulled on her dressing robe, lest she meet Phillip Monroe again, and made her way across the hall in the darkness. Hesitating at the door, she tried to look for any light through the cracks in the jamb that would reveal their new man might be readying for bed himself.

Seeing none, she walked barefoot to her brother's bed-side and eased one hip on the edge of the mattress, lean-ing forward to test his forehead for fever. It was cool, she realized, in relief. He stirred only slightly, as she rose and stood in the window glow. Drifting into a spontaneous prayer, she clasped her hands to her chest and sought out the round, ethereal source of the light bathing her. *Heaven protect Stephen from himself and heaven protect them all from the American army.*

"I love you, *mon precieux frère,*" she whispered to the sleeping figure, before turning noiselessly and quitting the room.

Even after the latch clicked, Phillip Monroe remained motionless in the shadows. Wearing only a nightshirt, he'd heard her knock and had been about to reply, when the girl opened the door and came inside. A shocking stab of envy struck him, as he pressed into the recesses of the shadows and watched Arissa's tender display of af-fection.

It had only been ten months since Deborah's death and, while his leg had healed, his soul had not. His body might respond to the presence of a lovely woman, but his heart was not ready for love again. Only by substitut-ing his passion for freedom's cause for the passion he reserved for Deborah had he survived this long. He was on a mission where it didn't matter if he died or not. He volunteered because of the danger and risk of death—a risk proven all too real, considering the attack on Conway. Had the men thought Conway was himself? Was there a security leak in the army intelligence?

Phillip wondered which had shocked him more: the unexpected attack or the fact that Conway's sister was not the plain spinster he'd expected, but a beauty swathed in a night shift all too revealing, despite its modest design. If Arissa hadn't been so worried about her brother, she'd have surely seen how dumbfounded he'd been. And damn the man, Phillip swore, with a grudging glance toward the sleeping figure. Conway had not only seen his shock, but enjoyed it.

The wretch deserved every twitch of pain he suffered! Phillip decided, stripping off the last of his clothing to slip into the turned-back covers. As he burrowed into the comfortable pillow, not the least weary of the image of the night dress clinging to ripe femininity, a familiar scent, one he'd been too exhausted to pay heed to the night before, assaulted his nostrils.

Rose water! The bloody sheets had been rinsed in rose water! Once again the tightening in his loins began to intensify, and Phillip swore into the pillow with vehemence enough to wither the hardiest summer blossom.

Four

"Captain McBain to see you, mam'selle."

Arissa glanced up from her mending, a measurable pile, considering her procrastination, and another tribute to her aversion to the typical homemaker's role. After the morning rush of getting travelers off and on the stage or the ferry, things had slowed down a bit. She'd taken advantage of the lull to catch up on her sewing chores, her practicality winning out over her heart. The regular splitting sound of Phillip Monroe's ax swing outside and the sunshine warming her through the window, however, had nearly lulled her to sleep.

"McBain?" she echoed, blankly at first. "Oh, of course, Captain McBain! Serve him whatever he wishes from the taproom and tell him I'll be with him momentarily."

Captain McBain of Halifax! At long last, the medical inventory she'd ordered from London had arrived. Arissa put aside her stitchery and hurriedly brushed the wrinkles out of her periwinkle day dress. Having adapted her organizational skills from her father, she knew exactly where to find the copy of the order she'd given the man in early spring. Though painstakingly made, she'd still gone over it again and again, even after the good captain had set sail for England.

Another female might have pinched her cheeks and bitten her lips to color them, or at least stopped to be certain each curl to the mass of golden tresses was caught in the feminine blue bow, securing it at her neck, before rushing into the taproom to meet the handsome sea captain. Arissa, far from ordinary, refreshed her memory instead of the list and checked the weight of the leather purse she'd taken from the bottom of the locked desk drawer. It was her savings—spoons casted from melted silver whenever she collected enough scarce coin to do so. This she'd learned from her mother, who had seen too much worthless printed currency during the days of the old regime.

Her cheeks were flushed the shade of the petite roses on her dress, when she entered the taproom. This was her day, the first day of her prospective financial independence. Martin would not have to worry about her, nor would Stephen. The first could marry the daughter of the English colonel he was engaged to and move to England, after his enlistment was up. As for the latter, if and when Stephen was ever ready to settle down, he could marry and take over the inn without the worry of two hens in the roost. And neither of them need care for their little sister, because she would be doing quite nicely for herself—she hoped.

Stephen, who was up and about now with little discomfort at all, was sitting at a small round table near the hearth with the swarthy captain. Both men rose upon seeing her enter the room. The captain's silver-grazed gaze mirrored his appreciation, as he took in Arissa's appearance, but she was too consumed with the matter at hand to pay him heed.

"Bonjour, *capitaine*. How glad I am to see you!" Arissa said, earnestly. "My things, they are here?"

"Aye, that they are, lass. I wouldn't dare disappoint one of Montreal's fairest flowers!"

This time Arissa did blush. Much as it appealed to her feminine character, she was always discomfited by flattery.

So many of her friends simply took it as their due, and with such grace!

"Now that alone was worth bravin' the worst 'o gales!" the seaman teased, delighted by her reaction.

"You had bad weather?" She was not only concerned for the captain and his crew, but for her medicines. Some would be ruined, if water penetrated their packages.

The captain tossed his dark head back and laughed. "No worse than the usual. If the old Atlantic can't toss ye about a little bit, she'd don't consider ye've had a complete voyage."

"The captain was saying you've ordered medicinal supplies, Arissa. I thought we'd stocked thoroughly this spring." Stephen leaned back so that Phillip Monroe could place a tankard of grog and noggin of ale on the table. Stephen was still drinking on the light side, since his injury.

"Can I fetch you anything, mademoiselle?"

Distracted, Arissa shook her head at the man, who'd given up his wood chopping to serve the visitor. "Thank you, but *non*, monsieur." She shouldn't have put off telling Stephen, but he'd made himself so scarce since spring. And she couldn't have told Martin, his being stationed in Halifax. Beside, if she hadn't ordered right away, it would be next May before she could put her idea to work, and then a summer's sailing time lost to boot.

"Actually, Stephen, I placed an additional order," she admitted, stalwartly. "And I have my own money to pay for it!" With a flourish, she shook out her store of coin silver. She'd been collecting it since she was a little girl, selling buttons on the side to her father's friends and associates. "I intend to distribute it to the apothecaries and physicians from Montreal to Quebec. I already have a few orders," she added, proudly.

"But why?" Her brother clearly thought she'd lost her

mind, which reminded her why she hadn't broached the subject before.

"Because I wish to operate an enterprise of my own, *mon cher.*" She put her hand on Stephen's. "I do not wish to be forever under your and Martin's care. Someday you will find a wife and this inn, grand as it is, is hardly big enough for two mistresses."

"Then I will help you!" her brother blurted out, magnanimously.

"Stephen, I have the money right here!" Arissa argued. "It is enough, *non, mon capitaine?*"

"Just the agreed upon amount, by my judgment," Captain McBain put in, balancing one of the spoons on his finger. He'd obviously been paid in such a manner before.

"But I cannot allow you to go into such a venture by yourself. Who will look out for you? You have entirely too kind a heart to be in business." Of Martin, Arissa would have expected such stubborn resistance, but not from Stephen. "How do you know these orders are legitimate? What if you put all your money into supplies enough for two winters and no one needs them?"

"Begging your pardon, monsieur, but considering all the political conflict about to erupt, stocking up on medical supplies might just be a stroke of genius."

Arissa glanced in surprise over at the bar where Phillip Monroe stacked the last of the glasses the girls had washed and brought back from the kitchen. He held Stephen's incredulous gaze stubbornly, until the logic of his words sunk in. Much as she hoped that Phillip was wrong about the possible need of her goods as a consequence of war, she was grateful for his unexpected support.

"You already said she was skillful as a Scot with coin. Why don't you give her a little rope. Having an independently wealthy sister surely would be no embarrassment."

Skillful as a Scot. That pleased Arissa, not only her brother's compliment, but that Phillip had remembered it. "Wouldn't that be a lovely thought, Stephen? Then you'd not have to worry about seeing me married off. I could take care of myself." Her face beamed at the prospect.

"I don't care if you never marry, if that's what makes you happy, 'Rissa," Stephen confessed, solemnly. "I just hate to see you give up your spoons. Why, you've collected them since you were little enough to ride piggyback to town and back!"

Which was exactly what she'd done—taken turns on Martin's, Stephen's, and her father's backs, the day she had the first spoon cast. She'd never forget it. "If my estimates are right, *cher,* I have more spoons than I could ever use. You heard monsieur Monroe. I am a genius!"

She didn't need Stephen's approval, but it would have made things much more pleasant. She watched her older brother's face, wondering at the emotions that battled on his boyish features. Had she insulted his manhood, she wondered, by indicating that he might not be able to take care of her? Although still determined, Arissa felt a pang of remorse.

"C'est bien!" he agreed at last, offering her reprieve. He held up one finger in stipulation. "But you will not run off with your riches and leave me to deal with Gaspar and Chiah!"

"Not until you take a wife," she quipped, saucily. "Even then, I might remain nearby to be certain that you are treated right." Unable to stand the suspense any longer, she turned back to the captain. *"Capitaine,* where is my shipment? I have already cleared a cool, dry place in the closet at the top of the stairs."

"Outside with my men on a cart."

"Then you sit here and entertain my brother, while Phillip and I see to it! The grog is complimentary!"

With a chuckle, the captain drained his cup and set it down. "Stephen, you will see to the *capitaine's* thirst, *s'il vous plaît.* I need Phillip with me."

Thankfully the supplies were not bulky, once unpacked. Nonetheless, they filled the closet shelves, now cleared of the inn's linens, each jar and package in its own place. Anodynes of opium and laudanum, Epsom salts, quinine, ipecac, camphor, benzoic acid—there were enough medicines that, combined with wines and other solutions to make them palatable, would keep an apothecary well-supplied for a long time. To have them close at hand for treating patients on the spot, was all that more convenient, Arissa thought, as she surveyed her new stores. And she still had not infringed upon the shelf set aside for the local herbs and plants brought to her by the Indians, some of which, even now, were hanging to dry in the overhead enclosure of the barn.

"Some people could get lost in here and not give a hoot whether they came out or not," Phillip Monroe remarked, laconically, glancing at her orderly rows, which had already been labeled in anticipation of the shipment.

Arissa came out of her joyful reverie, aware of a sudden of the closeness in the small enclosure. The scent from the lamp mingled with the manly one of her companion in an overwhelming capacity. She met his gaze sharply, uncertain of his meaning, yet decidedly unsettled, not necessarily unpleasantly, by the idea of being confined in the isolated closet with a man such as he.

"There's enough fixings in here to make a man merry for many a day."

"Oh . . . yes," she agreed, breathing easier at the explanation, and yet dismayed that he felt compelled to add it. Had she been so transparent? What was it about this man that made her such a bumbling idiot? He was still grieving for his wife, not flirting with her. "That's why I'll keep it locked," she recovered, smoothly.

Leaving Phillip to fetch the lamp, she turned to exit the small walk-in space, when her feet became tangled in some of the packing that had yet to be cleared away. She felt his free hand graze her waist, but it was not in time. To her chagrin, she landed in a heap of skirts in the doorway, her head ringing from where it struck the jamb. In an instant, Phillip had put aside the lamp and knelt beside her.

"I'm sorry, I was reaching for the lamp when you stumbled . . ."

"I'm all right," she assured her penitent companion. *Just further humiliated,* she finished silently. Upon seeing an indecent portion of stockinged leg exposed, she hurriedly tossed her skirt over it. The effort spoke in her head, making the room shift unnaturally.

"I'll see this mess cleaned up as soon I get you to your room."

Arissa shook her head. Another mistake. "No, really, just give me a hand and, if I can untangle my feet from all this packing and straw . . ." She laughed spontaneously, as Phillip obliged her. "It looks like a bloody stable." The contents of the upended crate they'd used to gather all the straw in was now strewn everywhere.

Her skirts were littered with it, as if she been tarred and strawed, rather than feathered. As she brushed the front, Phillip did the back, before thinking better of it and devoting his efforts to plucking the stuff from her hair, instead.

"I think I'm good enough," she announced, misstepping into him. Her hand went to what was beginning to be a nasty swelling, just below her hairline.

Phillip steadied her, his eyes drawn irresistibly to the obstinate straw that clung to the ruffle adorning the ripe swell of her bosom. It would have to stay there until she noticed it, he chastised himself sternly. She didn't, however, have any business stumbling to her room, especially since she had to navigate around the main stairwell, he reasoned against the warnings that flashed throughout his body at his decision.

"Wh . . . what are you doing?" Arissa gasped, as Phillip Monroe suddenly gathered her up in his arms.

"Taking you to your room. You've a nasty crack there."

Arissa put her hand to it again and settled against him in resignation. It was easier than arguing, even if she were inclined to. Of course, the man was only being gallant, but there had been little honest gallantry in her experience, and it was pleasing.

However, she did stop him before he deposited her on her bed. "Not yet, monsieur. I do not wish to fill my bed with this straw. I would undress first . . . after you leave, of course," she added, looking up in time to catch his disconcerted expression.

It gave way to a smile. "I'll send one of the girls up to check on you, in case you stumble again."

"Oh, that's not necessary . . ."

"Sometimes a doctor needs a doctor, doctor." Phillip deposited her beside the bed and held her until he was certain of her footing. "It's either that, or I stay." The very idea affected him even more, as he watched her reaction with interest. To his relief, she chose to take him lightly, which was just how he'd meant his threat to be, despite the inner stirrings it provoked.

"Send the girl, Monsieur Bad Boy! And thank you for your help and your gallantry."

Phillip bowed slightly, as he backed through the plank door. His brown hair fell over his face with boyish mischief. "My pleasure, mademoiselle."

For a moment, Arissa's attention remained on the closed door, as she listened to his slightly off-cadence footsteps retreat down the hall. She had yet to bring up to

Stephen her disapproval of Phillip Monroe living in the family quarters, although her objection amounted to more than a hired man quartered beyond his station. Yet she could not exactly pinpoint the reason.

He was a quiet gentleman, with an occasional outburst of a grand sense of humor. He respected her equally to her brother, and his coming to her defense over her new endeavor certainly was in his favor. The reticence was all on her part, she supposed, or due to his effect upon her. Every sense in her being came alive when he was around, and seemingly unfounded warnings rang loudly in her head. Although what they forewarned, she also was at a loss to know.

Besides, he and Stephen had become close friends. They called each other by their given names in the privacy of the family quarters. If she were to remove him from them, she would have to quarrel with Stephen first. The worst of it was, she wasn't sure whether she really objected to Phillip's presence now, as she had at first.

So what was the point? she argued with herself in disdain, as she slipped out of her dress. Here was just another end to yet another pointless debate concerning Phillip Monroe, which was the man's most irritating effect, and it wasn't even his fault!

In the days that followed, the temperature began to make its dramatic drop, swiftly heralding the last of summer's short, warm weather. Just as cool was the manner in which Phillip Monroe acted, whenever Arissa was around. For the life of her, she could not recall having said anything to offend him, especially after his support of her new endeavor. But something definitely had changed between them.

It was almost as if he were afraid of being left alone with her, for she'd seen him walk to the front of the inn to use another stairwell, sooner than be caught on the same one with her. Even when they were cloistered behind the bar during the evening rush—which was becoming habitual with the news about the shocking capitulation of St. John and Chambly to the Americans—Phillip concentrated on his task of serving drinks, with little to say beyond that which politeness dictated.

When Stephen asked him to accompany her into the city to make her first pharmaceutical deliveries and take orders for her next ones, Arissa fully expected him to object, politely of course. Phillip was always polite. Instead, he agreed, although with a degree of terseness, and made himself available for the packing and loading of her precious supplies.

"Monsieur Monroe," Arissa began, as the small calèche lurched forward at the whistle of the whip in the air. "I hope you will pardon me for being so bold, but I am one to speak my mind." This brought a twitch of a smile to her companion's lips, encouraging her. "Have I, perhaps, offended you? It seems of late that you are, how should I say, very distant, not at all as when you first arrived."

Instead of looking at her, Phillip concentrated on the carriage horse ahead. "There is a lot of work to be done for one man at the inn . . . and I have been preoccupied with my own thoughts, thoughts which have nothing to do with you or your brother," he added, resisting the urge to cross his fingers to annul the lie. The fact was, Arissa Conway would not leave his thoughts, no matter how he tried to banish her from them.

She invaded them day and night. She was in the taproom laughing gaily at some funny story one of the habitants passed on to her. Her voice managed to transcend the general roar of the camaraderie. Or she was hastily clearing her dining table in the parlor of its centerpiece without thought to the linens she'd just pressed, to lay down a wounded child, who'd split his leg open with a corn knife. She used a tone for frightened children that was surely as anesthetic as any potion in her closet.

What a wonderful mother she'd make his Jonathan. Phillip had been so stricken by the unbidden thought—especially combined with the more primal responses she evoked in him—that he'd been days getting over it. It was too soon. His mother was doing a fine job with her grandson. Beside, there was an independent streak in Arissa that warned him she'd be no contented housewife, like Deborah.

"Things have been really busy with the fall of those two Richelieu forts to the Americans," he evaded, smoothly. "Who'd have believed they'd come this far?"

He glanced over at her face, angelic and framed by the ribbon ties of her bonnet. For a moment he dwelt on the all but invisible sprinkling of freckles on either side of a doll-proportioned nose. She wasn't beautiful in the classical sense that Deborah had been. She was . . . wholesome and fresh, like spring morning. No, fall morning, he amended silently, admiring the way the sun seemed to play on the burnished curls peeking out from under her hat.

"I may have to move to Quebec yet, or take your advice and leave the continent," he quipped, thinking the escape not an altogether bad idea, were it not for his assignment.

"If Montreal is overrun by Americans, I may go with you!" Arissa had no concept of the impact her innocent jest made on the man beside her. She frowned, her full lips thinning in displeasure. "Why can they not simply be content to free their own country and leave us be?"

"I think the rebels are so in love with their ideas that they simply want to share them with their neighbors and make everyone on the continent their friend."

"By forcibly taking our forts?" Arissa asked, skeptically.

"British forts on Canadian soil. They are not against the Canadians at all."

"You sound as though you are for them!"

Phillip chuckled, once again chiding himself to be cautious. Unlike Deborah, Arissa delved deeply into the political issues discussed in the taproom. Her opinion was a strong one, even if, in his opinion, wrong. "I am simply looking at both sides objectively. My one opinion will not make a whit of difference in what will or will not happen."

"Well, the muster next week, will certainly raise a defense enough to keep the Americans from crossing to Montreal! There would already be a large force for them to contend with, if the Governor had not appointed the likes of Adrien Rueil as their leaders, rather than letting the habitants appoint their own, as the Old Regime did. Not even I would wish to fight under his leadership."

"The Americans do that. A man will follow a friend—and one he respects—a lot quicker than a pompous, power-hungry fool," Phillip agreed.

Their gazes locked suddenly and both Phillip and Arissa erupted into laughter.

"It does not take you long to assess a person, monsieur," Arissa observed, ignoring her pang of guilt for finding such humor at Adrien's expense. For all his pomposity, he still meant to defend his country to the death. His motives were not completely selfish.

"Some are easier to read than others."

On that, too, she had to agree. And Phillip Monroe was one of those who was difficult to read. His sudden bursts of congeniality were often smothered willfully into submission, his more reserved nature taking over. Like now, she thought, somewhat disappointed. He was once again concentrating on the horse, the road, and anything else that would keep him from having to converse with her.

She cursed her insatiable curiosity, which desired to know more about her companion. She wanted to know about his wife, what she was like, and was life so unbearable without her? There were times when Arissa had watched Phillip unawares, times when he seemed so lost in a private world of desolation. She wanted to take him by those wide shoulders and shake him, force him to talk about it. Talking was healing. That ever so slight limp the fire left him with was the least of his afflictions.

She knew it intuitively. She hadn't worked with the ill and afflicted for ten-plus years without developing such a keen insight. After her mother's death, when Arissa was fourteen, her father permitted her to go along on his visits as his "nurse." She'd seen a lot for her twenty-six years, and regretted not a moment of it.

Ahead, the walls of the city loomed large and imposing. As a child, it had appeared to her a great walled monster with many gates for its mouths and blockhouses perched at intervals along the tops of the wall, to serve as eyes in every direction. It no longer frightened her, but now gave her a sense of security.

"Those walls are in pitiful shape."

"What do you mean?" Arissa demanded, annoyed at the unexpected contradiction of her notion.

"I mean, they were built to hold up against Indians with bows and arrows, not soldiers with artillery."

Of course the Governor would know such a thing, she told herself, as they passed through the Côte Des Neiges gate and drove to Nôtre Dame Street. As if in answer to her query, she noted work being done on the walls and breathed a sigh of relief. Carleton had not rushed back from Quebec for nothing. The British soldiers were shoring up the fortifications.

"Governor Carleton apparently agrees with you, monsieur," she remarked, smugly.

Phillip could see the man had ordered patches put on

a lost cause, but kept the matter to himself. It was upsetting Arissa, and he didn't want to do that until he had to. Although she was frequently exposed to the merchant and working classes, there was still enough of her mother's noble background to impair her thinking toward freedom. The idea of government by a king was simply too ingrained in the minds of the noblesse to comprehend independence.

Were Quebec predominantly English, rather than French, his mission would be needless. The Continental Congress could not rest assured of the Canadian support and alliance. As it was, the Canadians appeared greatly divided on the idea. As to which side was predominant, well, that was up to him to report. Meanwhile, the particulars about the city's defenses, added to his information, couldn't hurt.

Before they went to the Market Place, Arissa made her deliveries. With an appreciation of good records and professional demeanor, Phillip was once again impressed by the way the young lady went about her business. The small ledger she carried with her accounted for every item delivered and ordered, while another notebook recorded items her new customers requested she carry. Visits to three apothecaries, two private physicians, and the two hospitals took up the major part of the morning. While the institutions had already stocked their winter supplies, they were relieved to know there was an alternative, this side of the ocean, should they run low, what with all the talk of hostilities in the air.

To humor him, and show off Montreal's ability to defend itself, Arissa took him past the Citadel and the Governor's Palace on the Parade. There, a statue of King George had been restored to dignity, after having been painted black by rebellious fools, as Arissa had referred to the perpetrators, and adorned with a necklace of potatoes and other denigrating trappings.

"I cannot see how they could do such a thing, when the English king has been so good to us as a conquered people!" she fumed, with the most fetching purse of her lips. It was enough to divert Phillip from his own convictions—at least momentarily. "When the city was nearly burned down, it was the king who sent moneys to rebuild. We did not come up with the moneys ourselves. We did not have it!" She said this with a flourish of her arm toward the neatly rowed houses with their tiled and lead roofs, each separated by a mandatory firebreak.

Phillip longed to argue that the habitants could have raised it, or at least, the government they chose could have. Arissa was intelligent and would surely understand, once that fiery passion of patriotism was directed toward freedom. It was ironic how fiercely protective she was of those who protected her, from her king to her brothers. When the Americans finally came, something told Phillip it would take both Stephen and him to protect the vivacious and opinionated young woman from herself.

He owed at least that much to her for his deceit, he thought later, after the stock was delivered, although he refused to entertain the idea of the reward of such gallantry, as he accompanied her on the rounds with one of the physicians at the Nunnery. He was repaying a debt, not granting a favor. He mentally shook the subject off and tried to pay attention to his companions.

To his astonishment, the two discussed some of the hospitalized cases with mutual respect, while more than one patient greeted Arissa as no stranger to the building. She either knew them from the taproom, from church, or from the time she frequently donated to the hospital wards within and without the city. As Phillip watched her exchange words with them, he realized that that special soothing tone was not restricted to children alone. Rich with compassion, he felt an uncommon urge to reach out and tap it, to assuage the raw pain still eating at his insides, giving him little real rest.

"Although they have not ordered anything, we can cross to St. Peters, after we pick up the things Chiah asked for at the Market Place," Arissa announced, as they left the Nunnery. The clock at the Parish Church on Nôtre Dame rang the hour of two, and she grimaced. "I should have gone to the market first. I only hope there will be enough vendors still on hand to do my shopping."

As mature as she acted, her childlike expression of dismay was perfectly heart melting, Phillip thought, climbing into the wagon beside her, without daring to dwell upon it too long.

"And you, you have not eaten since breakfast!"

He snapped the reins over the animal's hindquarters without touching it. It was a well-trained carriage horse and needed no such physical prodding. "It was a hearty breakfast," he assured her. "You know how Chiah is."

Arissa grinned in relief. Indeed, she did. If you didn't take thirds, Chiah considered you underfed, which, in Arissa's case, was all the time. "We will eat a tidbit in the Market, and then I will treat you to a fine supper before we leave the city."

"No need for that. A tidbit is fine."

The clip in Phillip's voice told Arissa she'd once again blundered. Perhaps she'd stepped on his manly image by offering to pay for his supper, she mused, although she could see no difference in supplying it at the Chateau Royale, or supplying it at one of the finer inns within the city.

"Room and board are the wages we agreed upon, monsieur, and therefore I will see you paid, whether we are at the Chateau Royale or gallivanting about the city." She softened the challenge in her voice. "Besides, you are a stranger, and it is the least I can do to show you our fair city. I think that perhaps you will become one of its finest citizens someday, *non?*"

The mademoiselle did have a point, Phillip conceded, over the demanding prick of his pride. Food and lodgings were his pay . . . which was why he had no coin to speak of in his pocket, a situation he rarely found himself in, at home in New York. If there were any jingle between the two of them, it came from the purse prudently tied to Arissa's tiny waist.

His attention fell there, as it had with embarrassing frequency all morning. The cropped jacket she wore showed it off to perfection, dropping from the swell of her bosom to just above it, pronouncing the sheer femininity of both. Then there was the provocative show of boot-laced ankles revealed by her skirt, a scandalously short version, by English standards, which he'd heard the French women had adapted from the practicality of those worn by the Indian squaws. He had to admit that, of the two fashions, he favored the one Arissa wore now, rather than the longer, more concealing versions.

"I promise that, when you have accumulated funds of your own, you may return the favor," the young woman by his side cajoled, with keen intuition. "That is," she faltered with a becoming blush, "if you so wish. You are certainly under no obligation . . ."

"At your command, mademoiselle," Phillip agreed, with a surrendering inclination of his head, saving her further awkwardness.

He had such a way of making her feel as though she had to explain herself, Arissa lamented, as her companion pulled the carriage alongside several others lining the block surrounding Place Royale. A commonly dressed boy rushed up eagerly from a group of youngsters gathered at the corner near the Nunnery grounds and offered to stay with the carriage. Having used the lad's services many times before—for this was an upright way for the street urchins to earn coin—Arissa felt no compunction about abandoning the calèche, as she led the way to the Market with Phillip Monroe at her side.

She had no more than placed an order to one of the livestock vendors for the Muster, which Adrien Rueil was promoting most enthusiastically, when a commotion broke out at the end of the square. Soldiers clad in scarlet were charging through the rows of booths and stalls toward the gate, shouting to the people to clear the way. In amazement, Arissa glanced up at the fortifications to see the ladders, which accessed them for their repairs, being pulled in, with a sense of urgency.

"*Mon Dieu,* what is happening?" she gasped, as Phillip Monroe drew her out of the path of yet another flurry of soldiers coming through one of the alleys and pressed her up against the wall of one of the warehouses. Instinctively she drew against him. There was something about his silent strength that was overwhelmingly inviting, under the bizarre circumstances.

Before Phillip could answer or speculate, one of the officers above the gate fired his weapon to silence the rise of alarm generating in the square. "Messieurs, médames, let the soldiers pass. The city is under attack by the *bastonnois!* We must close the gate!"

Five

"The *bastonnois!*" The way Arissa said the word, one would have thought it meant three-headed beasts breathing fire. She glanced around frantically, her fingers tightening on Phillip's arm. "Phillipe, we must get home!"

Phillipe. It was the first time she'd addressed him by his given name, or, at least, its French pronunciation. It took Phillip a moment to rebound from its effect, in the midst of all the turmoil surrounding them. Damnation, he was losing his ability to concentrate on anything! He stole another glance at the wide blue gaze turned up at him. Almost anything, he swore at himself sternly.

"Something tells me that's going to be more than a notion, mademoiselle."

Despite his willfully detached observation, the look Arissa gave him tore at him. He longed to pull her even closer and assuage her fears that the Americans were no threat to her or any of the Canadians, that they came as liberators, not conquerors.

Instead, he stepped away from her alarmed grip on the pretense of looking for a way to oblige her. "But we'll give it a try."

As they made their way toward the side street, where they'd left the calèche, Phillip took note of the activity along the walls. The pandemonium had settled down, and training was taking over. Nonetheless, the fact remained that the city was undermanned and poorly fortified. What confused him was that there had been no official word sent to him of an upcoming attack.

He'd only sent his first report back a week ago, indicating the unpredictability of the general population. It was clear that the noblesse was for the Crown. The English merchants spoke loudly enough in favor of the rebellion, but their actions remained to be judged. As for the habitants, they wanted to go on with their lives and ignore the entire conflict.

The sound of drums drew his attention up the street where troops had been assembled on the Parade—that is, if one could call them troops. They were mostly citizens, French volunteers, and English Canadians, interspersed with a smattering of Indians. The cohesive force that held them together was departmental officers and a handful of regulars—hardly the reaction of people waiting to be liberated, Phillip assessed grimly, recalling the favorable information passed on to the American forces by the more zealous of Canadian allies.

"Perhaps if we can get to the Côte des Neiges Road ahead of them, we'll be allowed to pass," he suggested, helping Arissa onto the seat of the calèche, after she paid the boy for his short-term service. In a flash, the child was gone, eager to be a part of the excitement, rather than stuck on a side street where he could only be tantalized by the commotion.

The moment they emerged from the alley, it became clear that they were not the only ones with the same idea. Oxcarts and wagons were lined up at the landward gate, but none were moving. Instead, soldiers were directing them onto side streets to keep the gate clear. Already anticipating his answer, Phillip climbed down from the calèche and walked ahead to speak to the officer in charge.

"Governor's orders, sir. No one is allowed in or out of the city!" the man informed him, with no hint of apology.

"But, monsieur! I have an inn just outside the city. The Chateau Royale." Phillip turned in surprise to see Arissa standing behind him.

"And a fine one it is, madame."

"Surely you understand why I must return there! There is only my brother and . . ."

"The Governor says nobody leaves until the emergency is over," the officer reiterated, with the manner of one impressed with his position. "It's a shame your place isn't inside the city. There won't be a floorboard free in any of the public houses tonight, I'll wager."

"The man's right, mademoiselle," Phillip chimed in. He'd been so busy noting the city's reaction that he'd not thought beyond that. "I think our time had best be spent finding you accommodations."

After all, he could sleep in the calèche and keep warm with the lap robe folded under the seat, but he certainly couldn't expect Arissa Conway to rough it in a like manner—even if there were room, Phillip mused, as he escorted his troubled companion back to the vehicle. Beside, with her safely tucked in somewhere, he'd be free to scout about.

"The Nunnery!" she said suddenly.

"What?"

Arissa pointed back toward the beautiful gardens of the hospital they'd visited earlier. "There is no point in wringing our hands over that which we can do nothing about," she advised, assuming a resolute posture. "They will have extra beds, or at least floor space."

Bemused by her resilience to command, Phillip frowned. "Don't you have any friends in the city who might offer more comfortable accommodations."

"Oui, I have friends, but we are not so close now . . . not since my father died and we became innkeepers," she added, matter-of-factly, leaving Phillip to piece the rest of it together.

No doubt the noblesse had turned away from her, much to their loss, he thought. If only he could turn that independent nature toward his cause, things would be much more . . . Phillip broke away from the train of his thoughts and focused on Arissa's proposal, hoping he'd not missed so much as to appear idiotic.

"Beside, my services may be needed at the hospital, if those damnable Americans are really out there." Realizing what she'd said, Arissa placed an apologetic hand on Phillip's arm. "You are the exception, monsieur. I do not find you damnable at all, but quite charming."

Color burst in full force on her face, the moment the words were out and, once again, Phillip felt as tongue-tied as his distracting companion. He watched as she teetered between retracting the compliment, which had so innocently slipped out, and struggling to change the subject. She managed the latter with an awkward sigh of relief. "There," she pointed out a break in the line of carts and wagons. "We can cut through there."

The sisters at the Nunnery not only offered to accommodate them, but welcomed Arissa, wholeheartedly. With the horse and calèche taken into the stables on the grounds, Phillip was soon caught up in the process of setting up beds for those, who, like he and Arissa, were trapped in the city. He chafed to be free to circulate through the streets, now silent with apprehension, and ferret out the meaning of the gunfire which echoed in the distance. But he could think of no good reason to leave his duties and walk out, aside from the natural curiosity which brewed within and without the hospital corridors.

Late in the afternoon, the gunshots ceased and an even greater hush than before fell over the city, until the news arrived that Major Campbell's troops had been victorious. The enemy had been captured, including their leader, the same Ethan Allen who had taken Ticonderoga! A wave of relief followed the news throughout the city, and spontaneous victory celebrations erupted in every tavern. These, however, were curbed by a curfew and the order remaining in effect that no one be allowed in or out of the gates, until it was certain that the American attempt on Montreal had been aborted.

"I tell you, mademoiselle, he is a giant, this Allen fellow. Two of the Indians, they pulled their muskets on him, after he turned over his sword, and he does nothing but seize monsieur Johnson as a shield, like shaking a rag doll in front of him."

Arissa checked the bandage on the cobbler's arm. It was still incredible to her that for so much gunfire, there had only been one dead and five wounded of Campbell's troops. Even this was no bullet wound, but an accidental cut received from a broken pitcher in the celebration afterward. Word had it that Allen had lost ten men and five were in the fort infirmary.

"And when General Prescott confronts him as the man who captured Ticonderoga, he has the nerve to threaten the general with his fist! It was the size of a ham! 'Ye shall grace a halter at Tybum, God damn ye!' the general hollers back. Never have I seen such a sight!"

"So you think the fighting is over now?" Arissa asked, shuddering inwardly at the description she'd heard of the rough-mannered Americans. How could Stephen wish to associate with such belligerent men as these? Why couldn't they be like Phillip?

The man on the bed swelled with pride. "But of course! If only a handful of citizens could capture their great Ethan Allen, who is to say what we can do if the rest of our men join the militia?" He snapped his fingers. *"Voilà,* there would go the threat of the Americans!"

An echo of enthusiastic agreement rumbled around the room, which was mostly filled with those who were stranded in the city and could not afford and/or find lodgings elsewhere. From the shadows of a thick support post in the dimly lit room, Phillip Monroe took it all in—the support, the enthusiasm—none of which weighed favorably for the American cause. Just where was all the rebel sanction reported by Brown, Livingston, and Walker, to name a few?

And what little did exist, that damned fool Allen had all but wiped out, he thought, angrily. He made the Americans look like swaggering, bragging, glory-seeking militants. The hold of an English brigantine was likely the best place he could serve the cause, at the moment.

"Such a face, monsieur! I have seen it on those of little ones who are in need of a nap."

Phillip shook himself from his troubled reverie and managed a tired smile at Arissa's good-natured jibe. "I am a bit ragged," he admitted. "And you must be exhausted." She had been making beds and assigning people to them, as though she owned the facility. It was in her nature, she laughed, when one of the sisters insisted on giving her a rest.

"I wasn't exhausted until I just stopped."

"Then I recommend the doctor find a bed, if there is one left, and put it to use. I have a feeling we'll be out of here early tomorrow. We do have a bed, don't we?" Phillip mentally stumbled. The idea was too awakening to lend attention to, so he let the faux pas go unnoticed.

"I am an innkeeper, *non?*" Arissa shot back, missing his blunder entirely. "I have two set aside, unless someone has claimed them without my knowing."

She noticed Phillip's limp was more pronounced, as they approached the two vacant pallets stuffed with straw against the wall near the door. He had worked as hard as she in anticipation of filling the ward with weary travelers or the wounded, and it was telling. "There, did I not tell you?" she announced softly.

Next to the empty makeshift beds a man, his wife, and

two children were spread out. He was snoring, not so softly, his arm stretched across his wife's shoulders, despite the small gap of floor between them.

Arissa stared at the sleeping figures and then glanced at Phillip. "Would . . . would you mind terribly if I slept against the wall?" Somehow, she didn't object to Phillip Monroe being next to her, but a total stranger . . .

Her thought process came to a shocking halt. Weeks ago, Phillip Monroe had been a total stranger, but she no longer thought of him as that. He was a good employee, she conceded, in an attempt to ascertain exactly how she viewed him now.

"I don't mind at all." As if to demonstrate, Phillip climbed on the pallet from its foot and stretched out. His feet hung over the end, as they did on Martin's bed. He tugged his blanket over his hips, where it could be easily reached, once the night temperature grew colder.

He was a friend, she decided, still hesitating, as though the decision had to be made before she took the place next to him. He looked up at her, taking in her expression, and Arissa could feel the blood stinging her face. So why was her body suddenly making more of this than it was? Determined not to give her gentlemanly companion one reason to suspect the unladylike reactions warming her from head to toe, she hurriedly set her bonnet aside and settled on the pallet, her back to him.

"What a story we'll have to tell Stephen tomorrow!" she managed lightly, tossing her hair over her shoulder, as she cradled her head on her arm. There hadn't been enough pillows to go around. "I'm so glad the Americans have gone . . . except for you," she added, mindfully. "You really have been a blessing for us, monsieur."

Phillip gently blew a strand of the wild silken hair, now freed from its ribbon-adorned bonnet, away from his face. Within him, an emotional battle engaged, fired by guilt and the shameless, unadulterated desire of a more physical one. Thank God, she hadn't called him *Phillipe*.

The following day, when Phillip turned off the Côte des Neiges Road to access the inviting tree-lined lane to her home, Arissa roused from an inadvertent nap and pulled away from her companion's shoulder, flushing deeply. Whatever must the man think of her?

They'd had no choice but to make beds on the floor of the hospital hall next to a family of four. Then, that morning, when Phillip had retrieved her hair ribbon out from under his arm, where she'd nestled in the curve of his body sometime during the night, she'd been flustered beyond speech. Gentleman that he was, however, he hadn't said a word to add to her embarrassment, although his smile . . .

Well, she'd never known such a wonderful companion as Phillip Monroe. He'd insisted she looked wonderful for having slept in her clothes, and then went on to see that she had a decent breakfast before leaving the city. It only seemed natural to lean into his shoulder again, as yesterday's fatigue caught up with her.

Absorbed in the warmth of her reverie, Arissa hardly noticed, as Phillip stiffened next to her, staring ahead at the inn yard where several men on horseback were gathered.

"What the devil is that all about?"

Surprised, Arissa tried to make out the identity of the visitors, Phillip's initial alarm infecting her as well. "Are they Americans?" After all, if they'd made one raid on Montreal, who was to say another was not in the making?

Phillip didn't answer. Instead, he slowed the pace of the carriage horse in approach.

"*Non*, that is Adrien Rueil's bay stallion!" she announced, in relief. "And there are Messieurs Rigaud and Aubert . . . they are neighbors." A puzzled look replaced that of concern. "But why are they here? Adrien!" Arissa called out, as Phillip brought the calèche to a halt. "Are you recruiting again?"

Standing at entrance to the Chateau Royale, Adrien turned, the brass buttons glistening on his splendid coat, and smiled, except that it wasn't a genuine one. Arissa knew his expressions too well to take it as such. Something was amiss.

"We are recruiting, mademoiselle, but not patriots. It is traitors we seek."

Stephen! Her brother's name had no more than echoed in her thoughts, when she saw Stephen emerge, his hands tied behind his back, a guard on either side.

"How dare you!"

Arissa fairly leapt from the seat of the calèche to the ground and stomped up to her fair-haired neighbor, skirts swirling with the same anger firing the summer storm of her gaze.

" 'Rissa!" Stephen warned, lowly.

"You were here running the inn. I'd wager there were many witnesses!" she argued back.

Adrien put his hand on Arissa's arm to calm her. "We are just taking him for questioning, *ma cherie.*"

She jerked away. "Questioning? Then ask here! Do not drag Stephen off like some criminal!"

"We're just doing our duty, mademoiselle," Adrien told her, tersely.

"Well then, if my family is suspect, then take me too!" Arissa shoved her hands behind her back and turned it to Adrien Rueil. "If taking one innocent to prison makes you the big man, monsieur, then two shall enhance your grand image even more!"

"Phillip . . ."

Phillip Monroe answered Stephen's desperate plea quickly, saving Adrien Rueil of having to make a decision about the rebellious young lady challenging him. With a determined sweep of his arm, he caught Arissa up and hauled her inside the inn.

"What do you think . . ."

"Enough, mademoiselle. You're only making it worse for him!" Phillip whispered through his teeth. "They are going to question him and see that he has had nothing to do with the attack. He has not left the Chateau Royale since he came home from the Chop House with the billiard table," he reminded her, avoiding the mention of the untoward attack, before adding with a certainty, "Then he will come home."

"If he's innocent," Adrien Rueil put in from the doorway.

"The only battle he's fought, monsieur, has been here in the taproom," Phillip shot back, with a cynical chuckle. "The only plans he has made have been to accommodate your muster for the Crown." Arissa squirmed in his hold, but he kept her restrained, his arm hooked about her waist.

"And what about you, monsieur American?" Adrien ran a suspicious gaze over the two of them, one golden brow arched higher than its mate. "Where were you yesterday?"

"Phillipe and I were in the city placing orders for your affair!" Arissa challenged, ceasing her struggle. "The Chateau Royale wishes it to be successful, so that an end may be put to this bullish invasion."

"Phillipe is it? Really, Arissa, I had thought you above becoming familiar with a hired man."

Arissa flushed an even deeper shade. "Phillipe is more than a hired man, he is a friend," she declared defiantly. "Which is what you evidently pretend to be."

"A *friend?*" Adrien's gaze took on a new light, as he probed Arissa's flashing one.

"The mademoiselle and I stayed at the Nunnery last evening, along with the others who could not leave the city," Phillip cut in, making his declaration in such a way as to forbid the least scandalous thought. "We were helping the sisters prepare for an onslaught of wounded, which fortunately did not come. Instead, the rooms were overrun by farmers and their families caught within the city walls during the panic."

"How noble of you, monsieur, considering the fact that you are an American and a man."

"Adrien!" Arissa gasped, incredulous at her neighbor's insinuation. At that moment, were she a man, she'd call him out herself over the insult to both herself and Phillip. Instead, she swallowed her outrage enough to speak. "Phillipe is a gentleman, which is more than I can say for you, at the moment. I am ashamed of you!" Her eyes ached to release her emotion, but she would not give Adrien Rueil the satisfaction.

"Monsieur, if you wish to take me for questioning, then do so. If not, it would be more seemly for you to go on about your business, rather than upset Mademoiselle Conway further, with your unfounded and thinly veiled insults."

Arissa felt Phillip's hold on her waist fall away, as he stiffened behind her. Glancing over her shoulder, she saw the steel set of his jaw and the inflamed whiskey-burn of his gaze. So caught up in Phillip's startling reaction was she that she failed to note the slight flicker of satisfaction on her neighbor's face.

"You said once, monsieur, that you were not so good with a pistol. Therefore, I would watch my words carefully."

Adrien's warning chilled Arissa, drawing her attention to the cold calculation glittering frostlike in his eyes.

"I always do," Phillip answered, guilelessly.

"So you would defend Mademoiselle Conway's honor on the dueling field?" Adrien sneered. "With what, monsieur, your pen?"

"Phillip, just let him be off," Arissa heard herself saying. "He is an expert shot."

To her surprise, one corner of Phillip's mouth tugged with some secret amusement. "I've no intention of dueling, mademoiselle. It's a foolish notion, to my way of thinking. Beside, why defend something that doesn't need defending? Your honor is exempt from all slander."

Arissa felt as if she were basking in a warm summer sun, rather than the frank appraisal that settled on her. Her senses reeled from the outrage of Adrien's insult to the overwhelming delight of Phillip's response. Here was a man in possession of himself, not a hothead like Adrien. Here was a man worthy of her admiration.

"A coward's philosophy, if ever there was one."

Adrien's barbed remark cut through the electric warmth that charged between her and her companion. But everything was going to be alright, Arissa thought. Something in the way Phillip assuaged her—not touching her physically, yet embracing her with his gaze—told her so. She turned back to Adrien.

"You are such a hothead, monsieur. Why do you not go about your duty, so that Stephen will be home in time for supper? There are real traitors and enemies walking about free, even as we speak, while you choose to pursue the innocent."

"The men in your family have given you entirely too much rein for your own good, Arissa. Someday you'll meet a man who will tame that indominatable spirit of yours."

Arissa laughed, despite the uneasiness that pricked at her spine. Her neighbor had made it clear, on more than one occasion when he was in his cups, that he was just the man to do so. But Adrien was a married man now . . . and Phillip Monroe was here. That, perhaps, emboldened her the most. With the graciousness of sending off one of her customers, she stepped forward and took Adrien's arm.

"Perhaps, monsieur, but until then, I am afraid you will have to accept me as I have always been." She sobered suddenly, upon seeing her brother outside. "And please bring Stephen back. I know he is innocent."

Her plea more in keeping with the woman he preferred, Adrien Rueil took her hand from his arm and raised it to his lips. "I shall do my duty, mademoiselle, but I will do what I can for your irresponsible sibling. *Au revoir.*"

Six

Phillip Monroe watched Arissa's back, as she stood in the doorway following the departing men with her gaze, until they'd disappeared over a rise. With that, her stiff posture gave way, compelling him beyond reason to put his hands on her shoulders. To his surprise, instead of drawing away, she leaned against him in silence, continuing to stare out at nothing in particular.

For the longest time, neither moved nor spoke. Finally, Arissa raised her arm and wiped her eyes on her sleeve, then straightened and stepped away. Phillip could see from the wet streaks left on her cheeks that she'd been crying. Burying the innate impulse to kiss away those trails of despair, he remained still, his willpower reinforced by a wild thrust of guilt. He was recently widowed, for God's sake! Here he was lusting after another woman—a remarkable young woman, admittedly, but nonetheless, he hadn't had time to mourn Deborah properly. Yet, was it so wrong to wish to comfort the innocent?

"Thank you for coming to my defense," Arissa said softly. There was but a faint tremor in her voice, yet it shook Phillip to the core with its need, disrupting his inner struggle and adding to it in great proportion.

"I was no Sir Galahad." Not in gallantry or purity, least of all, thought, he rued silently.

"No, you were wiser. You didn't let Adrien bait you into

a duel. He thrives on them, you know," she went on, oblivious to his inner turmoil. "I think he feels more a man each time he bests someone on the field. Think how awful that must be, to have to kill or inflict injury on another in order to feel worthy of oneself."

"You're feeling sorry for him again." Phillip found that fact disturbing, yet he managed to keep his annoyance out of his voice.

Arissa sank on a nearby chair, suddenly exhausted. *"Sacre bleu,* you're right!" she swore under her breath. "I'm so mad at him I could chew him up and spit him out, yet I try to find excuses for him." She looked up at Phillip. "There are no excuses for Adrien Rueil. He's just thoughtless and mean." Arissa hesitated, as she studied the tall man before her. "And you, monsieur, are the opposite. I must tell you that I was leery of having you about in the beginning, but now I can see that your chance meeting with Stephen has been a blessing."

She pushed up from the chair and suddenly rose on tiptoe to plant a grateful peck on Phillip's cheek. "Thank you, monsieur, for coming to the Chateau Royale."

Phillip remained motionless, as a scalding heat swept like wildfire over him at the innocent gesture, settling in the most volatile of places. Thankfully, she turned and started for the steps to the upper chambers, before temptation got the best of him.

"Merci, mademoiselle, for hiring me," he managed at last.

His husky answer was too late, for Arissa had already disappeared in the stairwell. Dropping into the chair she'd vacated, Phillip swore vehemently, in an effort to release the building tensions coiling in his body. Strike him blue, this was the last thing he expected to run into, and certainly was the last distraction he needed!

The preparations for the muster and shooting match, however, offered balm to his confused state of mind,

keeping him almost as busy as the women in the kitchen.
More kegs and cases of liquor arrived, so that the back
wall behind the bar was stacked to the ceiling. Locals
came by every day to hear the latest about the event,
lingering until closing, their conversation shifting from
speculation on Adrien Rueil's recruiting success to the
dramatic arrests of Thomas Walker and his likes.

His house surrounded and put to the flame by vindictive
Loyalists, Walker had lowered his wife out of an upper
story window in her nightgown, before following her. He
now graced a hold in a prison ship anchored in the harbor,
along with other suspected rebels. With homes burned and
businesses confiscated—not to mention the Church's refusal to grant sacraments or Christian burial to any citizens
with rebellious sentiments—the whole atmosphere was
anxious.

If there were so many pro-American Canadians, who
would come to the muster to turn the enemy from the
south away? That was the question Phillip had most on
his mind. His next missive to General Montgomery at
Ticonderoga was a critical one that could possibly mean
the difference between Quebec becoming the fourteenth
colony, or nay. Since Ethan Allen's capture, it was anyone's guess what the resistance would be. The Canadians
of Montreal had certainly rallied in sufficient time and
number to thwart Allen's unauthorized attack, despite the
welcome the American troops had received in the
Richelieu Valley to its south.

With a grimace, Phillip rubbed the smooth planking
on the bar with a cloth to remove the sticky remnants of
last night's business, when Stephen Conway appeared in
the doorway, his slender figure silhouetted in the morning light.

"I'll have a tankard of the finest brandy we've got!
Damn me, but it's been a night!"

As Stephen made his way to the bar, Arissa entered the

room far more quietly, but nonetheless bedraggled. In her hand was the worn black leather medical case Phillip had fetched for her the night Stephen had been attacked.

"Boy or girl?" Phillip inquired, noting, in concern, the weary circles under her eyes.

He'd been closing the taproom the night before, when one of the neighboring farmers sent word that his young wife had gone into labor and needed the midwife. With all the recent activity, Arissa had been working both in the kitchen and the taproom, but she seemed to take a fresh wind and rushed, rosy checked, out the door with Stephen as her driver.

"Neither. 'Twas a false alarm."

"It looks like the mademoiselle needs a tankard more than you do," Phillip teased, good-naturedly.

Arissa stopped at the foot of the winding steps. "It is a snifter he needs and then some sleep, not a tankard. As for me . . ." She smiled, tiredly. "Sleep will do nicely."

"The next time, you drive and I'll tend the tavern," Stephen announced, leaning forward on his elbows, as Arissa climbed the stairs. "I was as nervous as the damned father! Why can't my sister enjoy sewing and soirees, like her former schoolmates?"

"She is a woman with her own mind, *mon ami*. You should be proud of her."

"That's easy for you to say. She's not your responsibility. I don't want her gadding about at night alone. Doctoring is a man's job and requires that risk. It's not safe for a woman, especially not now." Stephen took a healthy drink from the snifter Phillip gave him and savored the burning golden nectar in his mouth, before swallowing.

Phillip repressed a smile at the recollection that Arissa had said basically the same thing about her brother, feeling responsible for him. If Stephen hadn't been released with no evidence to prove his involvement in the Allen attack before nightfall of the day he'd been arrested, Phillip had no doubt Arissa would have stormed the city and created quite a stir. The way she'd paced from the tap-room to the kitchen and back, each time stopping to look down the road toward Montreal, there'd surely been something brewing on her mind.

She was so different from Deborah—full of fire and will, rather than the perfectly groomed wife and mother. It was all his first wife had been brought up to be and exactly what he'd sought as a companion to an aspiring attorney. Deborah had been the perfect hostess to his friends and was preparing Monroe Manor for all the an-ticipated entertainment that went hand in hand with his growing political prominence.

Not that he thought Arissa Conway incapable of enter-taining, Phillip thought, taking in the durable, but taste-ful furnishings of the tavern. It wasn't elegant. It was quaint and warm. She was such an enigma, a . . .

"Are you listening to me, or have you gone simple, like that grin on your face?"

Stephen's intrusion jarred Phillip back to the matter at hand, bringing an uncharacteristic flush to his face. "No, I'm just glad she's not my problem," he answered, a little too emphatically.

The truth was, he wouldn't want Arissa Conway out in the countryside alone either, if she were his responsibility. Not that that would ever be a question, he assured him-self. He turned away from Stephen's curious appraisal and began wiping the taps on the kegs. He doubted there was a tavern run anywhere as meticulously, but then Arissa Conway was a meticulous individual as well, when it came to cleanliness. He supposed it went with her being a particular woman and having medical training.

Deborah had been particular about such things. That was why she was spending the night in his old bachelor apartment over his law office, instead of at the Monroe mansion. She was redecorating and was supposed to have spent the night with her parents in Queens, but the baby had taken ill at the last moment and, good mother that she was, she didn't want to make the journey. A replay of his brown-haired wife tossing little Jonathan out the window flashed in his mind, unbidden, and he felt his heart seize, just as it had that horrible night.

With a mental shudder, Phillip forced the raw memory into submission and blinked his stinging eyes. He had to put the past behind him. He had to.

The tavern was filled before sundown with men from the outlying districts, including Indians from St. Regis and Lac des Deux Montagnes. One small contingent from St. Ours arrived, declaring they'd come, despite the enemy's threat to burn their farms. Here was not a gathering of rebels, but a boisterous union of Loyalists. No longer reluctant to express their support for the King, in lieu of the great Ethan Allen's capture, they toasted the Crown, the royal family, and all the generals, whose names they could conjure, some of whom Phillip had never heard of. Adrien Rueil who, in order to make peace with Arissa, had solicited Stephen's assistance in signing on the enthusiastic volunteers, had hardly had time to consume more than one drink the entire evening. At least there would be a more accurate, if disheartening, number to send to Montgomery. It seemed Montreal was suddenly being inundated with people ready to fight for their king.

But for the closing of the bar, the ensuing party might have proceeded all night long. However, once the liquor was cut off, everyone retired to their rooms. Those who had no rooms made beds on the tavern floor, with the exception of an affluent couple from Chambly on their way to visit relatives in Longueuil, until the American occupation of the fort was over. They were accommodated with a pull down bed in the family parlor, reserved for the wealthiest patrons. Phillip had been incredulous when what he'd assumed to be a closet on the opposite side of the hearth from the corner family stairwell opened up to produce it. What hadn't come as a surprise was that the idea that to convert the room into a suite and hide the bed in the closet had been Arissa Conway's. There was little doubt in his mind that the young lady would become successful at whatever she put her sharp mind to. She was likely to multiply her investment in medicinal supplies, regardless of whether the Americans invaded or not.

By the time he and Gaspar had checked behind the staff to be sure all the fires had extra wood for the deep fall night chill, the inn was quiet. Stephen, a bit in his cups from his day at the billiard table with some formidable Canadian Rangers, had gone to bed as soon as the taproom closed. His resilient sister, who had risen after a morning nap to brightly greet guests and see that both cups and bellies were full, had given into her fatigue from the previous night's medical call, after seeing the parlor guests situated.

The only stirrings now were those made by the Indians, who had come in after Chiah closed the kitchen and sought floorspace near its fire. For that, they would pay nothing, Gaspar explained. It was the custom. If the white man were the guest of the Indian, food and lodgings would be furnished without thought to payment, and they expected the same. According to the ex-trapper, it was not out of the ordinary to come into the inn in the morning and find some braves, or an entire Indian family, for that matter, sleeping near the hearth, having arrived after the inn had closed for the night.

Considering the tales he'd heard about the French Canadian Indians, Phillip wasn't certain he could get used to that custom, for fear of being scalped while he slept. His smooth brow creased at the thought, as he took to the winding back steps leading up to the family quarters. Not that any Indian, aside from the French-influenced tribes, wasn't capable of such atrocity, he reasoned on in a rambling manner that suggested his own weariness. Regardless, he was glad he kept his brace of pistols loaded and within reach of . . .

His foot struck something soft and yielding in the darkness of the stairwell, snatching him from his thoughts. Freezing in midstep, he reached out and discovered something of more substance further up the steps than the long skirts he'd stepped on. Blinking his eyes in the dim light of the lamp burning at the top of the stair, he made out Arissa Conway's sleeping figure. With her head resting on folded arms against an upper step, she'd apparently stopped to rest and had given into exhaustion.

Smiling to himself at the childlike picture of such an ambitious and mature woman, he slipped his arms beneath her and lifted her from the steps. At first she stiffened, her gaze overwide, as she attempted to separate the fog of sleep from the reality of the moment. But upon hearing his, "It's only Phillip, sleepyhead. I've got you," she relaxed against him.

"I can walk." The protest was only halfhearted, diluted by a yawn. "I was on my way upstairs, and I thought I would rest for just a moment and . . . *voila!*" She looked up at him. "You must think me a silly goose."

Phillip pushed the door to her room open with his foot. "No, just a tired young lady." At the threshold, he set her on her feet reluctantly and steadied her. He could still feel the heat of her body cradled against him, which made it more difficult to back away. "I'd suggest you do whatever it is you ladies do to prepare for bed, and get to sleep. Tomorrow will be worse than today."

"You were a married man. Don't you know such things?" Once again, her eyes grew wide, this time with dismay. "Oh, I am sorry, Phillip! I didn't mean to remind you of your wife."

Phillip managed to turn the corners of the grimace

that claimed his mouth into a semblance of a smile. She'd actually done him a favor, considering the bent of his instincts at the moment. "Deborah was a modest creature," he explained, not really knowing why he felt so inclined. "She was always in bed when I came to our room."

Arissa leaned against the open door, intrigued and now wide awake. Something about the man managed to waken every nerve in her body in a most unsettling, yet pleasant, way. So he didn't mind speaking about his wife. "Was she beautiful?"

"Very."

The greenish part of her nature cringed at the conviction in his answer, but she chose to ignore it. "Stephen told me of your loss. I . . . I am very sorry for you. Perhaps your new life will offer you a brighter future."

"That's why I'm here."

His terse answer told her that was the end of the conversation concerning Deborah Monroe. "Well, we had better get our rest. Tomorrow is a big day," Arissa reminded him, changing the subject smoothly. "I hope we will have such an army enlist, that the Americans will chase their high tails back to the colonies and leave us be."

"That's *high-tail it,* mademoiselle," Phillip informed her, his mild amusement failing to counter the discomfiture her remark evoked in him.

"As long as they go, I do not care how they do it . . . everyone, but you, of course. You are one of us now, Phillipe Monroe." The smile she gave him ran through him like a thousand tiny fingers teasing treachery from his body, while his mind staggered with a pang of guilt over his intentional deceit.

"Bon soir, mademoiselle." It was a pitiful reply, but it was the best Phillip could summon. At that moment, he hated himself. As a spy, he could afford no conscience.

As a widower, it seemed he needed much more of one. As a man, he was not in control of himself, which was something foreign to the disciplined character he'd prided himself on. There was only one alternative in this encounter with his beautiful and innocent enemy—retreat.

The grounds surrounding the inn the next morning were crowded, as men from the surrounding areas of Montreal reported in for the shooting matches. To handle the excess, Arissa ordered kegs set up on tables outside with hot cider and rum to take the chill off from the fall air for the participants. Gaspar, seated on a stool, was able to handle those and speak with his former trapper friends at the same time. By noon, a cow, a pig, and several fowl had been won as prizes, and Adrien Rueil's list of volunteers amounted to over two hundred, not including Indians, whom the Governor, recalling the bloody disasters of the last war, had specified to use only as scouts.

That afternoon, the assembly gathered to begin drilling under the direction of a delegation of junior officers from the city. Phillip watched what he could through the window, for he'd not left the taproom since rising that morning, except to fetch more kegs. He'd send no written message as to what he saw transpiring. Instead, it would be verbal, accompanied by the medallion about his neck to verify it was indeed from him.

"Give my best to your family," he said, in a friendly tone, as he later shoved a customer's change toward him, change that included the medallion. "I'll wager that turkey'll come in handy."

His contact, a short wiry Frenchman with land both in the colonies and in Quebec, pocketed the coins. Dressed in the short canvas trousers, long shirt, and colorful sash of the habitants, a small cap perched cockily on the side of his head, he laughed. "That it will, *mon ami!*"

"Now you didn't forget to enlist in the volunteers did you, monsieur?"

The Frenchman's smile remained frozen, as he turned to look at the man who'd placed a hand on his shoulder. Phillip purposefully kept a nonchalant manner, despite the fact that Adrien Rueil's attention was fixed upon his contact, rather than him. Once again, he was glad there was no written message to discover, should suspicion be aroused.

"Twice, I think! Once last night and again today! It must be the good liquor they serve here, *non?*"

"Then why are you not drilling, like the rest of the recruits?"

"Even a soldier becomes thirsty, *mon ami.* Come, join me!"

Adrien took the cup from the man's hand and placed it back on the counter. "I think not, monsieur. I would rather you join me and learn the meaning of discipline."

Phillip's contact looked back over his shoulder, as Adrien ushered him toward the door. "Save my drink, monsieur. I shall return for it later!"

Through the window, Phillip could see his man fall in beside a line of new recruits, mostly habitants from surrounding villages and towns. No doubt he would drill until dark and then slip away toward the river, where his canoe waited. In Phillip's estimation, a further advance against Montreal would require caution. The Americans' warm reception in the Richelieu Valley, where only the British-held forts offered resistance, was somewhat misleading. The Canadians were not as eager to welcome them, as some of their pro-revolutionaries had reported. From all he'd heard and observed, the resistance would grow stronger the further north the Americans advanced toward Quebec.

His superiors had wanted an unbiased opinion, and he had sent it. They needed more men and more supplies to take Quebec, which was exactly what he thought the American army would have to do—take it. Arnold and Montgomery would not arrive as liberators, but as aggressors. He sighed heavily and dropped a large number of pitchers into a shallow tub for one of the girls to take to the kitchen for washing. Congress and Washington had counted on—no, hoped for—the first, based on initial reports from Canadian allies. The latter meant the liberation was going to be a lot harder than they'd planned.

"Phillipe, you are looking so grim!" Phillip looked up to see Arissa settling on a stool on the opposite side of the plank bar. "Have you had bad news, too?"

"Too?" he questioned, noting the dismay on his charming companion's face. He glanced at the letter she held in her hand.

"From Martin," she explained. "He has been sent to New York with the marines." A glaze came over her eyes, but she blinked it away, resolutely. "Damn those rebels! I hate them! I heard Adrien and the officers talking. General Gage was supposed to send Montreal more troops, Martin's included, but now they are off to New York." She looked at him, disconcerted. "Have the Americans a big army in New York?"

Phillip ignored his first inclination to lie and ease the fear gnawing at the brave front Arissa tried to show. He didn't want to tell her any more lies than were absolutely imperative for his mission. "It's pretty well fortified, although I would think the main army is with Washington. There are many Loyalists in New York, though, who will reinforce the king's men." It had almost had the atmosphere of a civil war when he'd left it this summer, with opposing forces gathering and squaring off in the various districts.

That there were Loyalists in New York seemed to offer some peace of mind to Arissa. At least Martin and his men would have allies. She tucked the missive in her starched apron pocket. Once again, Phillip Monroe had lifted her spirit. Ordinarily, she would have gone to Stephen to express her concerns about Martin, she realized, watching the rippling movement of his shoulders beneath his shirt, as he lifted the tub of dirty tankards and pitchers up onto the bar for washing.

There were others to go down, but in his consideration for the staff, he never filled the tubs to capacity. Both male and female employees liked him and his quiet, teasing manner. He was so thoughtful of everyone, from the lowest scullery maid to Gaspar and Chiah. And even herself, she thought, warming at the memory of his carrying her to her room the night before. It had made her feel both ridiculous and wonderful at the same time. He was an exceptional man and she really liked him . . . a lot.

"Mademoiselle, Chiah wishes to see you in the kitchen. She's says the pig is ready to come off the hearth."

Arissa shook herself, glad that Phillip had been occupied with tapping a new keg of rum, instead of catching her staring at him so brazenly. She slid off the stool and started toward the stairwell. "Then, by all means, let's take a look!"

Roast pig, pit-cooked beef, succulent venison, oysters, smoked salmon, breads of all variety, squashes and puddings, and yams and sausages later served to satisfy the appetites of men gathered in the taproom. Pitchers of beer, flip, grog, and other concoctions flowed from behind the bar, where Phillip worked, with Gaspar helping as best he could, considering his crutch. His hip was healing well, but it still pained him to be on it for any length of time. Arissa had put a stool behind the bar for him to rest upon.

Later, one of the men broke out his fiddle and the boisterous crew made the best of the opportunity to dance with anyone who would agree to be a partner, from a passing kitchen wench to each other. Even Arissa joined them from time to time, laughing as she was swung about with such enthusiasm that her feet often left the floor. From a table near the billiard game, Adrien Rueil and the officers watched the festivities in a detached manner, as if their command dictated they remain aloof from their new recruits. Nonetheless, the group drank and ate as heartily as their charges, keeping one girl constantly busy running pitchers back and forth to their table.

After the taproom bar had been open an extra final hour, Phillip Monroe finally lowered the grid-like portcullis over it and the kitchen and taproom girls left the dancing to begin the cleanup. Tub after tub of pitchers and tankards moved back and forth between the kitchens and the bar, while Phillip replaced his keg stock. Gaspar had retired to the hearth to spin a few yarns to the few remaining guests, who were to sleep on the floor, before he hobbled back to his cottage for the night, while Arissa inventoried the bottles.

Although Gaspar's stories were fascinating to all, her favorite was one he didn't tell at the bar. It was too romantic. Like the others, he swore it was true that his partner had kidnaped a beautiful New York debutante in retribution for the British exile of his Acadian family. The man, Beaujeu, intended to use this leverage to convince the girl's influential father to help him find his mother and sisters. However, by the time he decided to return the girl, the two had fallen in love. In the end, the Acadian abandoned his wealth and place in Montreal to return the woman he loved to her home, and risked death to remain with her.

Arissa sighed wistfully, and sobered to reality, inventorying the shelf reserved for their imported brandy. Someone at Adrien's table had had an expensive taste for the French liquor, which meant she'd have to fetch replacement bottles from her private stock in the family kitchen.

"I'll go get the brandy from downstairs," she informed Phillip, holding up the empty bottles in explanation.

"Stephen will be heartbroken, dipping into the private stock!"

Arissa chuckled, well aware of her brother's fondness for good brandy. "He will have plenty of money to replace it. The government in Montreal will pay for most of this."

"If the Colonies recruited this lavishly, they'd have the biggest army in the world," Phillip observed, wryly. The fact was, the Congress could barely raise money to outfit the troops, much less entertain them.

"Then let us count our blessings, *non?*"

"Right."

Arissa's spirits were too high to notice the lack of feeling in Phillip's reply. The excitement of the day, the profits she saw mounting, and the general fun, despite the hard work it involved, had yet to wear off. She was still running on adrenaline, which was twice as strong as the cider she'd been sipping, off and on, throughout the day. In truth, she should have been exhausted, but she wasn't.

The clatter of dishes from the adjoining large kitchen filled the smaller private one, in spite of the closed door between them. Perhaps she would help Chiah and the girls, once the taproom was in order. She took the key to the private closet from its place behind the large pine sideboard and slipped it into the lock. With a click, the door swung open, revealing the musty darkness of the family wine cellar.

With one of the lamps from the sideboard in hand, Arissa stepped into the large walk-in closet. On either side of her, racks of imported Madeiras, Canaries, brandies, and other liquors of distinction were stacked from the packed dirt floor to the thick beams of the low ceiling. Beyond them were a few kegs of better spirits of a stronger nature. Arissa put the lamp on a shelf and drew a small towel from her apron to dust off her selections, when she sensed—more than saw—that she was not alone.

With a startled gasp, she pivoted to see Adrien Rueil standing in the small doorway, his arms folded across his chest. Exhaling in relief the damp, musty air she'd inadvertently gulped, she dropped her hand from her chest, where it had flown in her panic.

"Adrien, you've scared me witless! What are you doing down here?"

He stepped toward her and, as he unfolded his arms, she saw a piece of paper in his hand. "A bank note from His Majesty for your exemplary service. You've made it a perfect day, Arissa."

"Well," she began modestly, "I would not say it was I alone, but . . ." Arissa took the note, her eyes brightening at its generous amount. The governor was surely desperate for recruits! "Adrien! How wonderful!"

"I told you I'd take care of you," the man informed her, with a smug tilt at the corner of his mouth.

"You certainly have!"

"I can be just as lavish in other ways, Arissa."

Arissa grew still, as he closed off the last step between them, so that her back was to a rack of dusty bottles. "Don't ruin the day, Adrien." Her fingers tightened on a corked bottle beside her. She would hit him, if she had to. "Go home to your wife and daughter."

Seven

"My wife!" Adrien snorted in disgust. "She is cold as a fish. It is a wonder I even have a child!"

"You have had too much to drink, *mon ami*. I don't think you would be talking about such things, if you had not." With her free hand, Arissa patted Rueil's shoulder. "Come, let me fix you some coffee or strong tea."

"Damn the tea, it's you I want!"

Before he could embrace her in his clumsy attempt, Arissa pulled the bottle from its rack and shoved it between them. Adrien was so thrown off guard that he stumbled a step backward, to stare at the cold, dusty object that appeared where only a moment ago, her tempting mouth had been. Testing his bottom lip, lacerated by a tooth in his ardor, he swore.

"Damn you, woman, you are an exasperation!"

"So are you, Adrien, but, still I am your friend," Arissa countered evenly, taking note of the blood that seeped onto his fingers. "Now you need to rinse that in salt water."

How she ever managed to keep the tremors of fear sweeping through her out of her voice and manner, Arissa did not know. With Adrien, she had always been able to back him down, even as children. Her father had told her it was because he was really a coward at heart. However, when Adrien snatched the bottle from her and slung it on the dirt floor, where, to his further chagrin, it bounced, Arissa could not help but jump.

"Damn you and your salt water, you clinical bitch!" he ranted, stalking toward the door. "You possess a poor measure of gratitude, and blood that would freeze . . ."

The venomous tirade halted abruptly with a startled gasp. As if he'd struck a stone wall, Adrien bounced backward in front of the door, only to be steadied by a familiar pair of forearms. Arissa had admired the way the sandy brown crisps of hair swirled about the veined sinew revealed by a rolled up sleeve too often not to recognize them as belonging to Phillip Monroe.

"Excuse me, monsieur. Have you seen Mademoiselle Conway?"

Instead of answering the seemingly innocent question, Adrien stepped around the yet unseen obstacle in his path. "Out of my way! She can be in hell, for all I care."

The stillness that followed was broken only by Adrien's angry retreat up the stairs. It seemed to Arissa like an eternity before Phillip Monroe peeked around the door, a roguish grin on his face.

"Is it safe?" He tried valiantly to smother it with an attempt at sobriety. "You were gone so long, I thought perhaps you'd locked yourself in."

"Your timing was perfect." Laughing to relieve her tension, Arissa knelt to pick up the bottle which had survived Adrien's sling. Mechanically, she put it back in its place. "Adrien has had too much to drink."

She met Phillip's inquiring gaze and knew instantly that his appearance had not been accidental. Something about that knowledge pleased her immensely. As cool as it was in the small chamber, it was suddenly warm. Her American had that effect on her.

Her American? part of her queried in surprise. Was he as aware of her as she was of him? Did he feel this magnetism drawing them together, as if they had no will of their own.

"Are you all right?"

She was fine, more than fine, now that Phillip was here. Adrien's advance had unnerved her, but not enough to drive her shivering into the arms of any man who came to her rescue—only those of Phillip Monroe. His weren't exactly extended to her in invitation, but when she nodded and stepped up to him, they came around her as though she'd somehow known they would.

Arissa hugged him about his lean waist, her face pressed against the open laces of his shirt. The virile scent of the liquor he served and that of the man himself mingled faintly with a spicy talc that had likely been applied after his morning toilette. It was more intoxicating than the entire contents of the wine cellar and made her giddy with a desire to be even closer than they were. When instinct gave way to the reality, however, of what she was doing, she pulled away sharply.

"I . . . I was a bit shaken, but . . ." Her voice was pitched higher than she would have had it, as though her wildly beating heart had pounded it out of her vocal chords. "I have always managed to handle Adrien Rueil. It is like my father once said: It is not hard to back down a coward. His drink was talking tonight. He does not really think me a . . . what did he say . . . bitch?"

She waited for Phillip to reply, searching the swirling emotions which surfaced in the hot whiskey gaze meeting hers. *Dieu*, but what was it saying? She could well guess. The burning imprint left from their brief embrace fired her conscience with guilt. Never one to flirt, she'd done worse. She'd brazenly walked up to the man and hugged him! His reaction had been no more than polite. His coming to look for her was nothing Gaspar would not have done.

Confusion welled in her eyes, as she let loose an unladylike oath. "I am always one to speak my mind, monsieur, but at the moment, I am at a loss as to what to say, except to apologize for my impulsive behavior."

"You're not yourself . . ."

"Non, but then I find that when I am around you, Phillipe Monroe, I am never myself. I act the silly goose, and that makes me angry!" she grated out, her fists clenched at her sides. Her palms were as moist as her mouth was dry. "Here you come, a man recently widowed and still in love with his late wife, eager to start a new life, and I am throwing myself at you! I do not know what to think of myself, much less know what you surely must be thinking of me! I am not looking for a husband, monsieur . . ."

"So you said . . ."

"But if I were," she went on, poking him in the chest in a righteous fashion, "I would choose a man like you." Arissa stepped back and swallowed, her declaration done. "There! I have made a complete fool of myself, but I will not play those games of the heart. I hope that we are still friends."

"Of course, mademoiselle. I admire frankness in a woman." Phillip moved forward, reaching for her shoulders, but Arissa would stand no patronizing. She dodged around him and darted out of the chamber like a wild bird spooked by gunshot.

"I have work to do. Bring up three bottles of the good brandy, *s'il vous plaît."* She fished the key from her apron pocket and tossed it to him. "Lock the door and hang the key behind the sideboard." Then, with a rustle of skirts, she was gone.

Fool! Idiot! Arissa had called herself those names, and more, so many times that she'd lost count during the following week. How could she have said such a thing to a total stranger! Except that Phillip Monroe was no longer a stranger, he was a part of the Chateau Royale and a part of her life, even if a temporary one. Thankfully, he acted as though nothing had happened. It was she who was most affected by her bold admission.

Embarrassment and humiliation played the heaviest part in her emotional turmoil. But how could she help it if she had attended a girl's school in the city and then spent her time away from it as assistant to her father? There hadn't been time for the parties and soirees where she might have narrowed the use of her feminine wiles down to a fine art. In truth, she wondered if she had any wiles with which to work.

Besides, the few affairs she had attended had been boring, and the men had been possessed more of gallantry and etiquette than brains. She'd learned to deal with fact and reality out of a medical bag, not dreams or fits of giggles veiled behind a fluttering fan. She was uncomfortable with frivolous talk and flirtation. Her only expertise was in discouraging men, not in encouraging them. Unless they were bold ones like Adrien, she hardly noticed them as a woman might a man . . . at least she hadn't, until Phillip Monroe had come along.

Arissa muttered an oath under her breath, as she scattered ink over the ledgers spread on her father's desk. They needed to be updated, but somehow she could not keep her mind on the task. Beside, it was getting on toward dark and the light was fading.

She preferred to be in the taproom mingling with the customers, except that was where Phillip was, and she made herself scarce there since her catastrophic admission of attraction to him; at least as scarce as possible, considering the increasing threat of the American army and the business it brought in.

The tavern was buzzing with talk of the rebels' defeat of the governor's troops at Longueuil, and Preston's surrender of the British fort at St. Jean. Adrien Rueil ranted during his off-duty hours from the top of the billiard table about Carleton's choking reluctance to risk landing the troops to disperse the enemy. A number of his men swore in agreement with him. The entire noblesse from which Carleton had chosen most of his officers was enraged.

It was the only thing that managed to distract Arissa from her humiliation—that and the fear that it was only a matter of time before the enemy was in Montreal. As if Providence were on the city's side, a snow-laden northeaster had blown in, stopping almost everything and stranding several of the Loyalist volunteers at the inn. Their presence, as far as Arissa was concerned, was heaven-sent, not for the business it provided and the handsome pay received by the government for the soldiers' keep, but for the protection it offered.

A light knock on the foyer door drew Arissa from her fretful reverie. "Come in!"

One of the serving girls bedecked in a white apron and cap entered the room timidly. "Excuse me, mademoiselle."

"What is it, Jeanne?"

"There is a boy outside who says that Madame Louvigny is having her baby again." Jeanne was almost apologetic, as she glanced out the window at the snow-covered ground. "They need you at once."

Although grateful for the distraction, Arissa frowned, as she closed the books and rose from the table. It was still a bit early, according to the date the young woman gave her, although the patient appeared big enough to be at full term. Perhaps it was another false labor. She followed Jeanne's gaze to the window. *Non,* this was exactly the type of situation in which a baby might come into the world. Inconvenience seemed synonymous with being a midwife.

"Have the carriole hitched up right away, and tell Stephen. Remind him to dress warmly. Oh, and have foot warmers prepared in the kitchen," she added, as an afterthought.

It only took her a few minutes to fetch her cloak and cap, but, to her dismay, the extra petticoats and jacket that she wore beneath them delayed her considerably. She should have been ready for this event, but there had been so much going on that she'd all but forgotten her expectant patient. Thank heaven the farm was only a few miles away.

With her father's medical bag in hand, Arissa made her way down the private stairwell to the ground floor kitchen, the door of which opened beneath an outside staircase exiting from the taproom to the back barnyard. It was there that she discovered that her brother had left for Montreal earlier on some overnight errand, without bothering to tell her.

"He say you be in bad mood if he tell you, so he go," Chiah explained, stoically.

"Then I'll drive myself," Arissa declared in annoyance. It had been too good to be true, Stephen Conway remaining for more than a month at home. She doubted even that would have happened, if it hadn't been for Phillip's presence. It seemed to have a settling effect on her brother, something she could not say for herself.

"No, I will drive you," a familiar voice informed her, firmly.

Arissa turned to see Phillip Monroe duck under the short doorway and into the bustling kitchen, buttoning the dark cloak she'd managed to remove Stephen's bloodstains from. "With all the military activity of late, Stephen would have both our hides if I let you go out alone." He raised his voice to silence the protest which formed on her lips, and went on. "Gaspar can take care of the taproom, between his crutch and stool. He's going to get one of the girls to fetch things for him."

"Did Stephen say why he was going into the city?"

"I think he was just restless since the snow came and cut us off from up-to-date news."

"The bloody rebels are at our doorstep and Stephen picks now to leave!" Arissa folded her arms across her chest and stepped aside to let the boys with the foot warmers pass to the sleigh.

"Babies not know about wars and such," Chiah remarked, a smile lighting her eyes, despite the expressionless fix of her lips. "Mademoiselle better be gone."

Phillip pulled on the second of his gloves and put his hand on the latch of the door. "Ready?" he asked, reluctant to let out any more heat than necessary.

Pulling her hood over her woolen cap, Arissa stepped forward and through the door Phillip opened for her. A cold gust of air swept around the corner of the house, as she trudged through the snow and stopped to allow her self-appointed driver to help her into the carriole. At least the night was clear, the first in several, she thought, seeking out the warmth of the hot bricks in the floor of the vehicle with her booted feet. Once Phillip was seated beside her, she pulled the heavy woolen lap robe over them and sunk her hands into the fur muff Stephen had given her for Christmas the year previous.

With the squeaking of leather and rope, and the jingle of the harness bells, the sleigh lurched forward at Phillip's gentle command, gliding feather-like over the snow-covered ground. The setting sun behind them cast a golden-red glow over the sparkling landscape ahead, giving it a blazing fairy-like appearance that would become even more ethereal when the moon ahead of them gained possession of the sky. A perfect night for a sleigh ride, Arissa decided, glancing sideways at her companion.

To her surprise, their gazes met. "Warm enough?"

"Yes, quite," she managed, without stammering. "We Canadians are used to this kind of weather."

"Well, this New Yorker isn't, quite," Phillip answered, with a shiver. "I hope the farm's not too far away."

"Didn't you put on extra clothes?"

"Double shirt and trousers, just like Gaspar said."

Arissa grinned. "He has taken quite a liking to you. You never seem to tire of listening to his stories."

"I don't."

Unable to think of anything else to talk about, Arissa occupied herself by studying a small cottage with its stone fence and sharply pitched lead roof, now blanketed white. It stood stalwartly against the winter backdrop, its windows glowing faint and warm with light. Smoke curled from its chimney, dispersed by occasional gusts of wind, which carried with it the tempting aroma of supper cooking on the hearth inside. No doubt the family was gathered about the single table in its one room at that moment, she thought wistfully.

"You know, you ran away a little too quickly the other night."

Arissa gave Phillip a blank look. "What?"

He smiled, patiently. "You didn't give me time to tell you what I thought about you."

"What?" she echoed again, this time much fainter. Perhaps it was because her heart had suddenly lurched against her throat.

"Well, I'm not looking for a wife, at the moment, but if I were," he stipulated, "I'd want her to be just like you. You're a very special and unusual lady, Arissa Conway. I could have knocked Adrien Rueil's bloody head off, when he came charging out of the wine cellar, if I hadn't understood what he felt as a man."

"But he is not half the gentleman you are," Arissa managed, through the well of delight that warmed her far better than the heated bricks at her feet. As a man . . . Could it have been longing she saw in his eyes that night, instead of anger and disgust. A practiced female would have known the difference, she thought, laconically.

Phillip turned away, his handsome profile chiseled against the glow of the winter landscape. "So maybe now you needn't feel so wretched about your utterly charming compliment to me, and you can stop avoiding me." Suddenly he glanced sideways and stuck out his hand. "Friends?"

Shocked at his insight concerning her, Arissa shook it firmly, feeling as enveloped by his presence as her small hand was by his. "Friends!" she agreed readily.

His words seemed to lift a heavy weight from her shoulders, lightening her heart in the process, so that the rest of the journey to the Louvigny's farmstead passed quickly, with the usual conversation concerning the recent military events and their implications. It struck her as ironic that Phillip had traveled all the way to Montreal, only to have the war follow him. She found herself wistfully thinking how wonderful it would be if the two of them could get away from the wretched conflict together, an idea she condemned as frivolous even as it took shape.

When they arrived at the small, two-room cottage, they were met at the door by monsieur Louvigny. The poor man was as pale as a ghost and quite frantic. He practically ripped Arissa's cloak from her shoulders in his eagerness to show her to the back bedroom, a shed-like extension from the main cottage. Leaving Phillip to do his best to calm the distraught first-time father, she went inside to the mother-to-be.

Upon pulling back the covers to examine her patient, Arissa discovered the sheets were wet and stained, where the water had broken. After examining the woman, she shoved a dry towel from the stack on the dresser beneath her to make her more comfortable.

"Your husband is right. This time I think you are going to have a baby," she assured the wild-eyed woman on the bed. She placed her hand on the patient's abdomen. "How often have you been having contractions . . . pains," she added, when confusion grazed her companion's face.

"All afternoon. Sometimes they come and . . ." The young woman gasped. "One is coming now!"

"Don't hold your breath, *ma petite*. We should learn from the animals. Have you not seen a dog whelp? She pants like so." Arissa demonstrated. "It seems to distract one from one's pain, *non?*" she asked, as the girl imitated her. A quirking attempt at a smile was all the answer she got. It was a strong contraction, yet the young woman had not dilated accordingly.

"H . . . how long do you think it will be?"

"The baby will come when it is ready." Arissa smiled. "I do not mean to be evasive, but no one can tell with this sort of thing. First babies usually take longer."

"It's gotten worse since Andre sent the boy for you." The pain had passed and the woman's voice had steadied a bit.

Arissa patted her hand, warmly. "Well, we shall be ready when the baby is, *non?*" As her patient nodded, she started toward the curtained doorway. "I'm going to fix some tea. Shall I get you some? It might make the time pass quicker."

"Well, I haven't eaten anything since morning."

"Two teas it is!"

Phillip and André Louvigny were seated at a small planked table on stools in front of the hearth, when she entered the room. Two horn cups sat in front of them, along with a bottle of homemade spirits she discovered to be made from apples.

"Your wife is going to be fine, and so are you, from the look of things," Arissa teased, good-naturedly. "First babies take time. It will be a while, yet." She glanced at the hearth, where two kettles of water were simmering gently. "I am proud of you, André. You remembered exactly what I would need. The water, the extra linens . . ."

"Because I have done this once, already," the young man reminded her. "The baby's things Linette made are in the trunk against the wall."

Arissa nodded and quickly made the tea, which she poured into two mismatched cups. After adding a dash of honey from the jar kept on the table, she carried them back to the bedroom.

Linette Louvigny had another contraction before Arissa was able to prop her up with pillows sufficiently to drink her beverage. The young woman's hands shook, as she lifted the steaming brew to her lips and sipped it.

Her stomach growling, almost as though in protest that a simple cup of tea would suffice for the supper she was missing, Arissa tried to make her own tea stretch as long as it would, all the while mentally going over what she would need from her bag. She'd put out the instruments on a towel on the trunk, as soon as she finished.

"Oh!"

Linette Louvigny's pained exclamation startled Arissa from her thoughts, in time to see the teacup sliding from the saucer the patient held limply in her hand, spilling its scant contents onto the quilts. Arissa hurriedly put her own down and recovered the other cup and saucer.

"What is it, *ma petite*, another pain?" If so, that would make them about five minutes apart, Arissa noted, silently. Too close, when she'd only dilated the width of three fingers.

"I'm sick!"

Reacting instantly, Arissa grabbed the metal washbowl from the shelf beneath the bedside table and held it in front of the girl. With her free hand supporting Linette's back, she held the retching woman, speaking soothingly to keep her as calm as possible. The spell lasted only a moment, producing little progress. At least, so Arissa thought, until Linette came up again from the pillows, this time doubled in pain.

"*Dieu,* but I think it's coming!"

Arissa shoved the basin on the shelf and eased the woman back to her pillows. "You keep panting like mama dog, and I will check."

"I can't! It's hur . . . rts!"

"Linette?" André Louvigny's alarmed voice echoed from the other room.

"It's the baby!"

Arissa tossed back the covers from the foot of the bed. Incredibly, her patient was right. She was almost fully dilated, apparently from the retching.

"André, I need you in here with your wife!" she called out, hoping he might be able to calm the young woman down and distract her. "Now slide down further, *cherie.* Come along," she coaxed the thrashing female on the bed. "It should not last much longer."

Not with the baby's head now visible. Arissa threw open her medical bag and removed a few simple instruments. It did not appear that she would have much to do except let Mother Nature take her course. Linette was young and healthy, with a wide hip span made for delivering children.

With a darting prayer for a healthy newborn, Arissa took her position. The miracle of childbirth never failed to excite her, despite the twenty babies she'd delivered on her own, not to mention those she'd assisted her father with.

"Linette, you must keep your feet out of the way! Do not kick so!" Arissa glanced anxiously toward the doorway. "André, where are you?" She could not calm the hysterical woman and deliver the baby at the same time.

"He's fainted." Phillip Monroe strode into the room, his handsome features set like stone, as if he'd braced himself for an execution.

"Calm her! If she keeps thrashing so, she will harm the baby!"

With a short nod, Phillip perched on the side of the bed and seized the woman's hands. "Linette, Linette! You heard the doctor. You're going to hurt your baby. You must try to be still."

A tempest would have calmed at the low, compassionate rumble of Phillip's voice, Arissa thought, as her patient made a decided effort to heed his advice.

"Think about that beautiful baby you're going to have in a few more minutes."

"And pant, Linette, like the mama dog."

In spite of the quizzical look Phillip gave her, he chimed in, demonstrating, until the woman was following his lead.

"That's the girl. I'll bet that baby's going to be as pretty as its mother, and just as brave."

"I . . . want a boy for André," the woman gasped between pants.

"A boy! That's what I have, a bald toothless bundle of giggles and smiles."

The loving description struck a chord in both women, but only Linette replied. "You . . . you have . . . a son?"

"A handsome one . . . good too."

Linette panted and moaned through another contraction, and the baby's head cleared. "Ah!" she gasped in relief when the pain subsided in intensity. "You . . . your wife must be relieved."

Phillip smiled and wiped Linette's wet brow with one of the towels on the table, but his voice wavered with his own pain. Arissa felt it, despite her preoccupation with the delivery.

"She was," he answered stiffly. "My mother keeps Jonathan now."

"I am so . . . so sorry."

"It's a boy!" The birth of the newborn shoved the past

aside, bringing with it all the excitement any of them could handle.

"Merci à Dieu!" Linette exclaimed in a tearful rush, as a small cry erupted from the squirming newborn in Arissa's hands.

Once she was certain the baby was breathing normally, Arissa wrapped it in clean toweling and handed it to its mother. "See if you can fetch André and take the water off the fire, so that it will be cooling. I must tend to the mother."

Her latter ministrations were as easy as the first. It had been a surprisingly smooth birth, although Arissa doubted she would convince Linette Louvigny of that. The pain, however, had passed and would soon be forgotten. If not, left to the women, second babies would become extinct.

"The father's alert and ecstatic, but I have a feeling we need to straighten things up a bit, before he comes in." Weak stomach, Phillip mouthed, as he reentered the room with a kettle of water for the bathing. "He's a little weak in the knees," he explained, when Linette gave him a questioning look.

"Poor André!"

Arissa glanced at the baby, torn between bathing it or its mother. The baby should be done in the other room by the hearth, where it was warmer. She picked up the tiny gown and diaper and turned to Phillip, only to see him already holding the little one.

"I was right. He's a handsome one all right." The glaze in his eyes cut at Arissa's throat like a sharp blade. He missed his son. He surely was planning to send for the child later, when he was settled. For if such love for a stranger's newborn could shine so in his gaze, she could well imagine how he must have felt the first time he held his own son.

"You seem to have had practice with babies, monsieur.

Perhaps you would not mind bathing the little one near the kitchen hearth, while I help his mother freshen up?"

Phillip looked startled at first, but quickly mastered his insecurity. "I've done it once before, at least enough to know they don't break too easily," he added, with a mischievous grin. "Maybe I can teach that husband of yours a thing or two."

Linette laughed. "I hope so, monsieur. André is afraid of babies."

"Don't be too hard on him. He's so worried about the tot's mother that he hasn't had time to deal with the new arrival. This is natural to you women. We men have to get use to it." Clucking gently over the baby's face, Phillip made his exit, carrying Linette and Arissa's gazes with him.

"I cannot believe I have let a stranger take my son to bathe."

Realizing that she had not had the time to introduce Phillip properly, Arissa apologized. "I'm sorry. His name is Phillipe Monroe. He works for us at the Chateau Royale and escorted me here."

"He is a fine man. Such love and compassion he shows on his face! He looked so natural holding the baby."

"Yes."

If she had admired Phillip Monroe before, she did so even more now, Arissa thought, turning to the task of bathing her patient and changing the bed. How many more intriguing and wonderful sides did he have, that she'd yet to see? He was too good to be true, and when a woman could find no fault in a man, there was only one explanation Arissa could think of—she'd fallen in love.

Eight

Phillip and Arissa left the Louvigny house in high spirits. Once the mother and babe were bathed and reunited in a freshly changed bed, André Louvigny insisted they share some bread, cheese, and applejack. He'd recovered from his shock and, although he did his best to be a good host, he could not keep his eyes from the sight of his wife and child nestled together on the bed.

"I will bring you three of our fattest chickens!" he promised, as Phillip snapped the whip in the air over the sleigh horse to begin the thankfully short journey home.

The night air was at least still, which made the journey more tolerable. With the foot warmers reheated, and their blood warmed from the homemade apple brew, it was comfortable under the folds of the woolen lap robe. That Arissa's leg was pressed against her companion's, in an effort to omit room for any draft, made it even warmer.

Still high with the rush of excitement over Jonathan Louvigny's entrance into the world—for Linette was especially indebted to Phillip for talking her through her ordeal and distracting her with tales of his own son that she'd decided on the name Jonathan for her newborn—Arissa hummed one of the gay melodies she'd learned in the taproom over the years.

"You seem mighty bright for someone who ought to be dragging, by now," Phillip remarked, good-naturedly.

She turned toward him, her smile as bright as the moon glazing the snow-covered landscape about them. "I am. I cannot help it. They were so happy, and I was privileged to be a part of it." She grabbed Phillip's arm playfully. "Can you not feel it, too? God, let us be part of his marvelous plan!"

"How can you talk about the Almighty's plan, no more than a breath after humming that little sailor's ditty?"

Arissa giggled impishly. "I suppose I come from a confused background, which makes me a confounding woman. At least that is what my brother thinks, not to mention Adrien."

"Confounding," Phillip agreed, adding, "bemusing, intriguing, and perfectly lovable! I wonder that your brothers haven't had to keep you locked in some tower to keep the eager swains away."

Sobering, Arissa sighed. "Now you make fun of me, monsieur. I know that I am not the proper model for a good wife, at least according to a man's standard. I am too willful! There, I admit it!"

"Ah, but you have just the right degree of lovableness to make it tolerable. It's a rather exciting combination."

Lovableness? Exciting? Arissa hardly knew where she got the breath to speak so boldly. "So you think me exciting, Phillipe Monroe?"

Instead of answering, he looped the reins about the handrail in front of them. "I think the horse knows his way from here, don't you?"

Her throat suddenly dry, Arissa nodded. She didn't even try to draw away when he took her in his arms, the sweet-cider scent of his breath tantalizing her nostrils, as he put his forehead to hers. "I think," he rumbled lowly, the timbre of his voice acting like talented fingers tripping up her spine to graze the back of her neck, "that you are one of the most fascinating creatures I have ever met, Arissa Conway." He pecked at the rosy tip of her nose. "In your own innocent way, you tempt me more than the devil himself. You almost make me forget the past . . ." He stopped, as if suddenly struck a terrible blow. "But I can't!"

Phillip swung away and swallowed the sob that had nearly escaped. Although she longed to take him into her arms and tell him that it was all right, Arissa remained still, already missing that brief, heady closeness they'd shared, soul to soul.

"You will put it aside someday, Phillipe," she advised, sagely. "You must do so, if not for yourself, then for your son. Your bitterness and self-blame are like a boil that must be lanced and drained before you can be yourself again and the father your little Jonathan needs. That is your problem, *mon ami,* not your memory of Deborah. That should always remain sweet and untarnished, like childhood memories that can not be relived, but can be treasured forever."

Phillip did not reply, although Arissa did catch a hint of acknowledgment in a nod when he reached for the reins, once again in possession of his torment. She'd never seen him in such pain, yet she could easily see how his compassionate involvement in assisting her had ripped open barely healed wounds. She ached with frustration that here was an illness she could not treat with bandages and salves. Wounds of the spirit were far beyond her capacity to heal. All she might do is offer comfort.

The inn yard was still. They drove into it noiselessly, aside from the anxious snorting of their horse. Although a feedbag had been brought along, the unexpected evening's exercise had worked up the appetite of the plump and spoiled beast, and it made it clear that another treat was certainly expected. Leaving a brooding Phillip to see to the animal and sleigh, rather than awaken a stable hand, Arissa made her way to the downstairs kitchen entrance.

The big room immediately enveloped her with warmth. She paused by the door until her eyes grew accustomed to the dim light from the hearth, where three Indians were rolled up in blankets on straw pallets she and Chiah had made up for such visitors. Although neither stirred, Arissa felt quite sure they were aware of her, as she slipped through the connecting door to the family kitchen area.

A smile lit upon her face instantly at the sight of a black kettle of water hanging over a gently lapping fire and extra wood on the hearth. Dear Chiah had put bath water on, in anticipation of her arrival. Touched by the woman's thoughtfulness—for she knew how Arissa craved a bath after attending a childbirth—Arissa grabbed two pot pads and removed the lightly simmering water from the fire. A full bath was out of the question at this hour, but a standing one was not, she thought, pouring the hot water carefully into the large washbowl on the stretcher-base table, conveniently moved next to the hearth for that purpose.

In addition to having brought down her dressing robe, gown, and slippers, Chiah had even put out a blanket to hang for privacy over one of the strings stretched from two nails driven into the thick exposed beams. Although usually used for drying herbs, it served perfectly to provide for a room divider. Once it was in place, Arissa started to peel off her layers of clothing, until she was down to her innermost shift. Only then did she liberally rub her washcloth in rose-scented soap and attack her skin as fiercely as she did hurriedly. Even the nearness to the hearth could not deter the night's chill to a damp, near-naked body.

"Arissa?"

She froze at the sound of Phillip's voice on the other side of the blanket. "I'm bathing. Maybe it will relax me so I can get some sleep." Silence ensued for a moment, before she spoke again. "I'm just about through, if you'd like to do the same. There's plenty of hot water and . . ."

"No!"

She apologized at the sharpness in Phillip's answer. "I'm sorry. That was thoughtless. You must be exhausted."

"No, damn it, I'm sorry!" She heard his frustrated shuffle back and forth, as she pulled her nightdress on over her head. "I'm not tired. I'm wound up tight as toy top."

Arissa's lips thinned in bemusement. "Then fix us one of those hot toddies, like the one you had the first night, and I will be out in a moment. Here is the teapot," she offered, handing it out of the small enclosure. "Tea is on the sideboard, and you know where everything else is."

Once she'd donned her robe and slippers, she combed out her hair about her shoulders with her fingers, as best she could, and then took down the makeshift dressing screen. Phillip was busy preparing their toddies, as she gathered up her layers of discarded clothing and put them in a pile near the steps to carry up. He made no attempt at conversation and, if anything, avoided even looking at her.

"If you would like, I could fetch something to put in your tea to help you sleep," she offered, sensing his coiled frustration.

How terrible it must be to have lost a loved one in such a violent, helpless situation. It wasn't like the death of her adopted mother and father, where illness had taken its toll and the end came as a relief. His wife had been healthy and young, a mother in her prime and very much loved. Life was so unjust.

Phillip shook his head. "No, I'm befuddled enough, as it is."

"Would you like to talk about Deborah?"

"No!"

"Phillipe . . ." She leaned forward and put her hand

on his, unaware of the way her pronunciation of his name sent shivers of something far from cold through him. "I may be, what did you say . . . bemusing, intriguing, willful, and lovable . . ." She'd never forget those words, or the little smile that had tipped his lips wistfully as he spoke. "But I am also your friend, first and foremost."

He avoided her gaze, instead concentrating on filling his teacup to the brim with the golden brandy.

"I get the feeling you blame yourself. How can that be?"

"I wasn't home!" The answer was shot like a bullet at her, as if to impede the advance of her painful questioning. He sipped long and thoughtfully from his cup, as if that were all he had to say.

Despite the fact that he did not wish to address the issue, Arissa felt it was imperative that he did. He needed to purge this anguish that had driven him from his family and son.

"Where were you?" she prodded, gently. "Working late?"

No, at a damned Sons of Liberty meeting, my other passion! Phillip wanted to shout back, but he dared not. "I was at a meeting." Because he wanted to be, not because he was required, he swore, in recriminating silence.

"So you were working to make a better life for Deborah and Jonathan. How can you see shame in that?"

The sharp look Phillip gave her told her that she'd struck a chord that he had not considered before. She gave him time to dwell on it, to finish his toddy. When he set down the empty cup, she filled it half-full of straight brandy. He needed it to relax, to exorcise his torment.

"A better life . . ." he sneered, after a while. His fist curled, fingers biting into his flesh. "I should have been home with her. Then she would have a life today."

"You did no more than any man would do. It is a manly thing to leave the home to work, to make things better for their families. You were doing no more. You had no idea such an accident was going to happen. It was God's will, and nothing you could have done would change it."

"God's will?" Phillip laughed, humorlessly. "I don't think so. The fire had been set . . . at least it appeared that way."

"Mon Dieu!" Arissa whispered, stricken. "But why?"

"I told you, there was too much dissension, neighbors against neighbors."

Arissa shook her head. "If that is the case, I wonder that more Loyalists than yourself have not come north, where it is safer . . . or where it used to be safer," she added solemnly. "This is such a frightening time for us all."

She got up and walked over to the hearth, basking in its golden glow, which seemed to set sparks of light dancing on her dark auburn tresses. Crossing her arms, she shivered, despite its warmth. Unaware of Phillip's undivided attention, she knelt and tossed a few smaller pieces of wood on the fire, her robe drawn tightly about the round feminine curves of her hips and buttocks.

"So we have to look to the future, Phillip Monroe," she went on, brushing off her hands as she straightened. "We can not stay in the past. I am venturing out in my own business enterprise, and you must venture out for a new life for your son. He is what is important now."

"Maybe you are an old maid."

Startled by her companion's comment, Arissa looked at him with such bewilderment that he almost laughed.

"I mean, for someone so young, you have an old head on your shoulders," he explained.

"Oh." Arissa shifted under his intent appraisal and feigned a yawn. "Goodness, but that brandy works fast. I am ready for bed. How about you?"

Instead of answering, Phillip rose from the table, shoving the chair out of the way, as he did so. As he closed

the distance between them, Arissa felt as though her feet
were glued to the floor. There was no escape from the
sudden deepening of his gaze. It was like a whirlpool of
emotion, beckoning her to become lost in its intoxicating
autumn swirl.

"Arissa." His voice was strangled with huskiness.

Suddenly it came to her what she'd said. Embarrassment only compounded a strange heat, already seeping
through her limbs from her very middle, where it was
first kindled.

"I . . . I hadn't meant . . ."

"I know," he answered, running his palm along the
side of her face to cup her chin. "It's part of your irre-
sistible charm."

Her heart stopped at the compliment and then burst
forth with an unruly rhythm that echoed in her neck and
ears. Although his hand only cradled her chin, it felt as
if a thousand more were turned loose upon her body.
She was alive, every part of her, every nerve, aroused with
an unparalleled anticipation. She moistened her lips, unable to summon word, only reaction.

Suddenly, as if she'd set off some unseen release, Phillip drew her to him. "God forgive me!" His mouth swept
down to claim her own.

Startled as she was, at the same time, she was ready for
him, as if her body knew that which her mind did not.
Her lips parted, inviting his tongue to explore her mouth,
to taste even as she tasted him. Strong, masterful, and
masculine, his fervent seduction rendered her soft and
yielding, all that was feminine in her begging for more
of this man-to-woman union.

A kiss was not enough. It was like crumbs thrown to
one starving, serving only to whet the appetite for more.
Who hungered the most was difficult to tell, for even as
Phillip sought out the satin flesh of her neck with his
lips, his hands tugging at the silk ribbons which held her

robe in place, Arissa was tearing at the hem of his shirts, eager to seek his manly flesh with her trembling fingers. As her robe came off her shoulders, forcing her arms to her side, Phillip backed away.

Held captive by his ravenous gaze, Arissa never noticed the cool rush of air between them, but stood motionless, as her robe slipped to the floor. Phillip ripped off his two shirts and slung them aside, the ribbon which had held his queue in place going with them. With his hair loose and heaving chest exposed in a blood-warming fashion, he looked more the savage than the man. At least, it was a savage gaze that raked over her, from head to toe, stripping her of her nightshirt in such a manner that she felt driven to obey its brazen command.

As she slowly tugged at its drawstring neckline, she couldn't help but turn toward the fire in a poor attempt at modesty. It was insane, but then insanity ruled the moment. She could still taste him, as she ran her tongue over her lips and along the inside of her mouth, where he'd plundered so headily. Her neck burned, as if his kisses—if one could call the kneading, nuzzling, suckling enticement that had seared a permanent trail on her tender skin, kisses.

She managed to open the neckline of her shift, so that it hung just on the edge of her white shoulders, yet once again modesty intervened. She knew what she was doing. She'd almost dared to think of it, although never carrying her scandalous thoughts where Phillip was concerned quite this far. Maybe she should stop now, bolt for the stairs, before it was too late. For that one single alternative, a myriad of objections raged from every part of her.

Phillip stepped up behind her, and now her back was warmed by him, as the hearth warmed her face. "I want you, 'Rissa. God forgive me, but I do."

He nuzzled through her thick hair to kiss her neck, giving rise to gooseflesh all over. She shivered and leaned into him. The unmistakable steel of his arousal, pressed against her thinly clad buttocks, betrayed the removal of his trousers. She stiffened in shock, but he caught her about the waist as she started to pull away, and pressed her back.

"Don't be frightened, love. I've no intention of forcing you to do anything you don't want to, but you've got to know what you do to me." He kissed her neck again and shuddered. "You're the first breath of air I've tasted since leaving New York. You make me want to live again, 'Rissa." He turned her slowly in his arms and met her limpid gaze. "To love again," he finished, huskily.

He lowered his mouth to hers, caressing it gently, at first. He was trembling and taut with the restraint of the passion that riddled his body, eager to be unleashed. Yet, as the affection deepened, he ran possessive, hungry hands over the curves of her back and buttocks, as if he wanted to touch all of her at the same time, to brand her as his.

Arissa reeled in reaction. She loved him. She'd known that before she knew the searing magic of his kiss, his touch. It was a conclusion that had been reached apart from the heat of passion, which was threatening to consume her at any moment. It was only natural, this gnawing need that burst into fiery blossom in her innermost being. Their need was mutual, his for healing, hers for fulfillment of the love that had been growing ever since they'd met. The man and woman in them had known it right away. It simply took Phillip and Arissa a while to catch up.

When Phillip ceased the ravaging of her lips, her face, and the pulsing hollow of her throat, he hesitated once more, searching the simmering sapphire pools of her gaze. Then the hands that had cupped her shoulders slipped the one remaining barrier of thin cotton between them over her arms and waist, where it dropped to the floor. He made a strangled sound, as he savored every inch of her naked body with raw craving, and Arissa flushed wet and warm in pagan response.

Like a gentleman bedecked in the finest garb, Phillip fell to one knee and took her hands, urging her down on the pile of discarded clothing and towels. "You look like . . ." he broke off, blinking away the glaze in his eyes. "Like an angel."

"I do not feel so angelic, monsieur," Arissa ventured, of a sudden, unaccountably timid. Nervous, she reached for the blanket she'd taken down and folded, and spread that over their clothing.

"I should at least have the decency to carry you to a bed, but I fear I haven't the endurance." Phillip laid down on the makeshift bed, watching her keenly. "Do you understand that, love?"

Arissa didn't answer. For the first time she noticed Phillip's legs. They were long and well formed, but mottled with scars—scars from the burning timber that pinned him down, as he tried to save Deborah's life. A rush of compassion urged her to run her hand over them ever so gently, as though what she felt in her heart, the tears that spilled down her cheeks, could at that moment erase them and all his pain.

" 'Rissa!" Bolting upright, Phillip seized her once again, dragging her away from her maddening ministrations to the blanket, with a plea in his voice.

"Don't be embarrassed, Phillipe," she chided him. "I have never seen such a beautiful sign of unselfish love." She wiped away the tears that slipped from his eyes, as he covered her with his body. "It is you who are the angel," she whispered, her voice shaky with emotion. Without the slightest thought to appearances, she embraced him with her arms and legs, hugging him tightly. "You must love me, Phillipe, or I shall go mad." It was only natural to grind her hips upward, pressing the softness of her femininity against the probing length of his arousal.

"I'm far from an angel, love, but I am mad. You make me that way." He slipped his hand between them, his fingers moving unerringly to a highly sensitive area.

Arissa gasped with mingled shock and delight, as his fingers delved even more deeply into the moist, eager haven of her innocence. *"Dieu,* but I can not bear much of this pleasure!" She writhed beneath his ministrations. "Stop . . . I think," she added, hesitantly, in ardent confusion.

"If you keep wriggling, I . . ."

"Enough!"

Arissa pulled away the tantalizing hand with a desperate sling and raised her hips against him, with a hard and grinding motion. She knew what she wanted . . . needed, but the exact protocol for getting Phillip, or that part of him, which she so desperately craved, where it belonged, was foreign. Was it the man or the woman . . .

"Sweet Jesus!"

Arissa was driven against the hard floor, impaled by Phillip's wild, breath-depriving thrust. *The man,* she registered, lost somewhere in a daze between the slight discomfort of his invasion and dizzying fulfillment. Having squeezed her eyes shut, when Phillip made his startling attack, she now opened them and stared in wonder at his unshaven face and rumpled hair, until she made out the burning desire in the eyes peering through at her.

There was more to come, she could tell. This was just a single course in what promised to be a banquet of passion. She reached up and stroked his chest, moving her hands up and around his shoulders and down the bulging sinew of the arms supporting him. "Ah, Phillip!"

The mere mention of his name sent a shudder through him and, before she could return her hands to his shoulders to coax him down, he drew back and impaled her once more with his fierce possession. No longer did he hold back. He loved her with his entire being. Abdomen to abdomen, he rocked her rhythmically, while feasting on the jarring temptation of her pale, upthrust breasts.

The sensual assault came from so many fronts that Arissa could do no more than react and enjoy. When she would make the slightest attempt to return his fevered attentions, they would become more intense, driving her into a wanton frenzy of desperation for more and more, until she seemed to explode from within; shuddering, gasping, and clinging to Phillip as she clung to consciousness. She wanted to miss none of this ecstasy to which she'd been introduced.

Suddenly, she was snatched into reality again by Phillip's convulsing body, filling her, shaking her more deeply than she could imagine. He groaned her name, as if with his last breath, and continued to move in and out, as though savoring their union, until he could move no more, and lay semi-conscious upon her. Then, as if suddenly aware of his heavy weight, he rolled away, but not before pulling her and the blanket under her against him.

Still feeling as though floating on clouds, rather than lying on a hard, cold floor, Arissa nuzzled his neck and made a purring sound of contentment.

"I need to get you in a bed before you catch a chill," Phillip murmured weakly against the top of her head.

"You sound like you need a doctor."

A chuckle rumbled in his throat, causing his Adam's apple to quiver. "I just had one, thank you."

Arissa joined in his uncharacteristically bawdy humor, idly toying with the leather thong he wore about his neck, when she noticed the coin was gone. "Where's your medallion?"

As if confused, Phillip checked the leather himself. "Lost it, I guess."

Arissa tried to ignore the pang of disappointment that reared its head. After all, it wasn't likely he'd have taken it off for her sake. This hadn't exactly been planned. She was shaken from her reverie, when Phillip suddenly forced himself to his feet. Bending over, he wrapped the loose ends of the blanket around her and scooped her up in his arms.

"It's bedtime for you, love. I could get a little too comfortable snuggling with you before this fire, and things might get embarrassing in the morning."

Arissa sighed. The same thought had crossed her mind, but she'd been too content to bring it up. "I can walk upstairs."

Phillip shook his head. "Wouldn't think of it! I've thought about getting my hands on you for so long, I don't want to let go, until I have to."

Smiling, Arissa laid her head against his shoulder. It sounded good to her. Keeping her knees and arms tucked in as tightly as she could, she continued to toy with the leather thong, until Phillip stopped at her bed and braced her on his knee in order to turn back the covers.

"Guess this is good night."

There was a naked man standing over her bed, a scene she'd never envisioned before, but he was too magnificent in his male glory to complain about, scars or nay. If anything, they gave him a more rugged, virile look. He bent over and gave her a chaste peck on the forehead. "See you in the morning."

Arissa hated for their interlude to end, yet she reluctantly saw the practicality. To spend the rest of the night in his arms would be yet another taste of heaven. *"Bon soir, mon cher.* Sleep well."

When the door closed behind Phillip, Arissa tugged her blankets up over her shoulder and closed her eyes. The lazy lethargy that claimed her made thinking impossible. All she could do at the moment was feel, and what she felt was a giddy happiness she never dreamed possible. This was love.

Love. The word echoed over and over in her mind, each time sounding more beautiful than before, until the silent lullaby was interrupted by a jarring of the bed. She snapped awake in time to see Phillip slip beneath the covers, and then he was against her, cradling her in his arms.

"I thought you were going to bed."

"Your brother is spending the night out, so why shouldn't I?"

"I hope he is in no trouble."

Phillip wasn't exactly certain why Stephen had decided to stay over at Chambly, for that was where he'd really gone. However, trouble was doubtful. Gambling with the Americans there was the more likely reason for his not coming home. Beside, Arissa's brother was the furthest thing from his mind at the moment. This soft, feminine creature snuggled against him had just taught him a much needed lesson in life. There was life after death, a wonderful, vibrant life.

Strike him blue, he could not believe that even now, he wanted her again, if anything, more fiercely than before. But she was surely exhausted and needed rest, after her long day, not to mention after their lovemaking. What she needed was to be held. That much he could do, at least for a while, he thought, driving aside the sharp pangs of guilt that reared their ugly heads for a few more precious moments.

Nine

The inn was still sleeping later in the dark morning hour, as Phillip Monroe ever so carefully disengaged his arm from around the satiny shoulders of the young woman sleeping soundly beside him. She stirred only briefly, her lips assuming that inviting purse that could drive a man mad enough to want to devour it. The thought crossed his mind, thrusting life into that part of him which could not think. Resolutely he exercised restraint, made much easier with the second thoughts of the irresponsible behavior that followed their lovemaking. While she'd been warm and willing, he still had owed Stephen Conway the respect of not seducing his sister.

It may have been time to put Deborah and the past behind as a precious memory, not a painful reminder of what was lost. It may have been time to discover life again, but not in a torrid, breathless rush on the kitchen hearth. Arissa deserved more than that for her compassion and guileless acceptance of him. She was too much a lady, he thought, recalling the small attempts at modesty she'd made, despite that new and consuming arousal burning like blue fire in her eyes. It had been like making love to an angel and she-devil at the same time. The change from one to the other was as fascinating as it was exciting.

His mind filling with both tender and fiery memories of Arissa Conway, Phillip eased out of the bed, before his control gave way. Despite the harsh November cold of the bedchamber and the frost that formed with his every breath, he hardly needed the blanket in which he'd brought her in upstairs earlier, which he now had wrapped about his naked torso.

As he tiptoed to the door, he glanced back once more to see Arissa bundled up to the neck in quilts, clinging to the pillow he'd left in his place. Her thick silken tresses were spread in a tumble about her face. She was beautiful, both without and within, something that could not be said for all women. Much as he had fought it, he was lost the first night he'd seen her, flustered and embarrassed one moment, then composed and all concern for her brother the next. As she treated Stephen, she had already started healing him as well, forcing Phillip to recognize that he was still a man, a living man, and that his wife, much as he'd loved her, was lost forever. Deborah . . .

"You common bastard! *Dieu,* but what have you done?"

Phillip blinked in the darkness of the hallway and cleared his vision, but not in time to avoid the fist that smashed into his jaw. Had the anger in Stephen Conway's voice instinctively made him brace, he'd have gone sprawling back into Arissa's door. As it was, he staggered and caught himself on a bench in the hallway. Conway wasn't expected until late tomorrow morning. Groaning inwardly, he started to speak.

"For the love of God, Stephen, keep quiet. You'll wake your sister."

In answer, Stephen thrust a bundle of clothing at him. From the faint scent of roses and the mingled feel of soft linen and coarse canvas, Phillip did not have to guess that these were the garments he and Arissa had discarded in the kitchen in their feverish ardor. How could he have been so careless? He'd acted like a young boy with his first woman, not a husband and father who'd been just months widowed. But then, since meeting Arissa, he hadn't exactly been his normal, conservative self.

"Your bed is not disturbed, your clothes and those of my sister are spread all over the kitchen below," he hissed, lowly, "and now I find you coming naked out of her room!"

"Stephen, I don't blame you for being angry. God knows I regret these circumstances, but I want you to know that I fully intend to marry Arissa." Phillip seized his bottom lip too late to stop the unbidden solution that flashed through his mind. Marriage? Was he ready for that? Had Arissa's sweet fire exorcised the guilt and lingering grief over Deborah's death?

"I will see that you do, monsieur," Stephen growled, in wounded indignation. "Damn your miserable hide, I trusted you!"

"I am a man of honor and will do the honorable thing. I don't know what else to say!"

"I'd like to hear a lot more, but, for now, I regret we must speak of other things. I have orders for you."

Realizing this was what they'd been waiting for, Phillip was instantly alert. He took the folded parchment from Conway's hand. "Montgomery is moving?"

Stephen motioned him into the room and closed the door behind them. "*Oui*, he and his men are at Île de Soeurs with the Second and Fourth New York. Colonel Haskill expects you to join the Fourth New York immediately."

In the minute it took to don clothing and read his orders by the light of the lamp Stephen had brought up from the kitchen, Phillip's regrets concerning the girl sleeping peacefully in the other room mounted. They needed to talk before he left, but there was no time.

"I've had your horse saddled. Your unit rides at daybreak with our Canadian recruits. We are to arrest the officers of the noblesse appointed by Carleton and any

Loyalist troops lingering outside the city. You and I are to help identify them."

Phillip pulled on his boots over his second pair of trousers he'd pulled on, his mind torn between duty and Arissa. He caught the cloak Stephen tossed him and, standing up, swirled it over his shoulders.

"This is more important than romance, *mon ami*, although we will surely address the subject of my sister more thoroughly when time permits."

Stephen's perceptive reminder was hardly sympathetic, though Phillip didn't really expect it to be. He'd betrayed their friendship and trust.

"I will make it right, Stephen. You have my word, as an officer and a gentleman on that."

As he started out the door and down the hall to the back stairway, he heard Stephen's laconic reply. "That may be so, monsieur, but I do not think proving your merit as such will be so easy, where my sister is concerned."

The taproom wasn't particularly busy when Arissa descended the steps during the serving of breakfast. She'd blushed a thousand times since rising and going through the motions of dressing, often looking at the pillow next to her own that Phillip had used. There was still a faint scent of him, or was everything about Phillip Monroe so ingrained in her memory that she imagined it? Several times, she'd sniffed the indented spot where he'd laid his head, before making up her bed. Then, in a half-dreamy state, she'd crossed to her brothers' room to make the bed in there, where he'd no doubt spent the remainder of the wee morning hours to preserve her reputation.

"Bonjour, mam'selle. Will you have some coffee and croissants?" Jeanne asked, as she met Arissa in the narrow winding passage with a tray of dirty dishes bound for the kitchen.

"That sounds delightful. I'll be right down."

Arissa wanted to find Phillip and personally thank him for having the presence of mind to clean up the private kitchen after their lovemaking, before anyone discovered their clothes scattered. She'd found them tossed on his bed and quickly put them away before one of the staff came up to tend to the family quarters. A warm flush swept through her, even as she contemplated their fiery union, bringing color to her cheeks, as she stepped up to the bar and leaned forward on her elbows. Perhaps with Phillip Monroe, her complexion was destined to remain within the range of blushing pink to hot red.

"Why, Gaspar!" she exclaimed in surprise, as she came face to face with the ex-voyageur, instead of the man she loved.

"Was it a boy or a girl?" Gaspar inquired, a certain glint in his eye that betrayed more than casual interest rested on her answer.

"What did you bet on?" Arissa countered knowingly.

"A boy."

She chuckled. "Then you are a winner. It is a beautiful boy, whom Linette named after Phillip's son, Jonathan. If it hadn't been for Phillip's talking her through the delivery and telling her about his own baby, I don't know what I would have done." She glanced about the taproom. "Speaking of Phillipe, where is he?"

Gaspar's grin faltered. "Alas, I can not say. His horse was gone this morning when the stableboy went out to feed and tend the animals."

"He left no message?"

"None that I or Chiah know of. Though Chiah said he rode off with your brother. You know how she is—hears every little leaf that hits the ground. It's her Pawnee blood."

Arissa frowned. "Well, if he was with Stephen, no doubt it's for Stephen's best interest. I wonder what sort of trouble my brother's into this time, now that his wounds are healing so well?"

Gaspar gave an expressive shrug. "We will hear about it, of that you can be sure."

When the noon hour approached and the stage from Longueuil had not arrived, Arissa began to feel uneasy. Of course it was likely that the intermittent snow flurries which had ensued in the early morning hours had slowed them down, she reasoned, as she reconciled the account the governor had paid on a weekly basis for volunteers. Fortunately, there was plenty of livestock for sale and hunting had been good, as well, for the men's appetites were considerable.

She glanced at the clock, not for the first time since beginning her paperwork, and grimaced. She was tempted to drive into Montreal to find Stephen and Phillip, for that was where her brother had gone the day before. She hated waiting and worrying over Stephen's need to fetch Phillip at such an outlandish hour. Yet, she could not imagine the reason.

Maybe her brother had won another billiard table, or something else as bizarre, and, being in his cups, dragged poor Phillip out of bed to help him haul it home, she consoled herself. After all, if it were serious trouble, Stephen couldn't have come himself to get Phillip, he'd have sent for him.

The sound of horses approaching made the breath she'd inadvertently held give way to a sigh of relief. At least the stage from Longueuil was more predictable than Stephen. She started to put her ledger away, when a series of surprised shouts and the scramble of men and scraping of benches made her freeze in alarm.

"Les Bastonnois!"

The name echoed over and over again, until her blood

began to thaw with the realization of what was happening. Wincing at the sound of breaking glass, she hurried to the window overlooking the front of the inn in time to see a sizable troop of mounted men. They were a tatterdemalion mob, some in blue uniforms, some in brown, and others in common dress, pitifully inadequate for the weather they were having. Some were armed with swords and pistols, and all were armed with rifles. A few among the uniformed lot wore cockades in their tricorn hats, leaving Arissa to believe them to be officers.

"Dieu!" she whispered, staring at her worst fear, incarnate. The Americans were taking the Chateau Royale, and no doubt others were demanding the surrender of Montreal at the same time. The stage from Longueuil had most likely been intercepted by them, to keep the element of surprise on their side! Thank God for the volunteers occupying the inn!

She turned away from the window and reached for the rifle her father had always kept over the parlor door. It was loaded and, thankfully, she had been tutored in its use to the point of being a fair shot—if she remained calm and had time to take aim. Perhaps they might stand them off, considering the lack of cover afforded the invaders, although the thought of what that would do to the inn made her shrivel inside.

"Hold your fire, *mes amis*. It is I, Stephen Conway!"

Arissa's hand froze on the latch to the door adjoining the taproom. *Stephen?*

"The citizens of Montreal are at this moment negotiating the terms of surrender with General Montgomery of the Continental Army. Your commanders have been arrested. Will you force the Americans, who wish to come here as friends, to fight you, or will you accept their terms."

"What terms?" someone in the room boldly demanded.

"They invite you to join them as brethren in their fight for liberty . . ."

A round of dubious snorts erupted, showing the habitants regard for that option.

"Or you may take your weapons and return to your homes with the promise not to raise arms against them. They are men of honor and intend to treat you as such, if your actions merit it. They will give you five minutes to make up your mind, *messieurs*. Then they shall enter, in whatever way they must. For the women's sake, I pray you will use your God-given sense."

The women! Arissa leaned against the door, rifle in hand. The poor servant girls must be hysterical, although she was certain Chiah was doing all she could to keep them calm. Oh, Stephen, what have you done? And where is Phillip?

A sickening feeling twisted in her abdomen, as she contemplated the most plausible answer. She closed her eyes. *Dieu*, but he could not be one of them! Perhaps Stephen hoped to spirit him away, before one of the men at the inn might take his hostility out on Phillip, his being an American. After all, Phillip had saved Stephen's life.

She moved back to the window. The troops had spread out now and surrounded the house. Half were dismounted, rifles and sabers ready. If Montreal were already surrendering, she mused, echoing the words being bantered about in the taproom, what was the point in a bloody confrontation? Her heart seemed to sink in her chest at the signs of surrender that wafted her way. What else could they do, but turn the Chateau Royale over to the Americans?

What would become of it? Would the motley troops plunder and burn it to the ground? No, Arissa told herself sternly. Now she was becoming hysterical. Stephen was obviously their ally. Somehow, they would weather this invasion, like their fellow countrymen in the Richelieu. They did not have to support them. Just coexist with them until the Governor drove them out.

"We wish to return to our homes!"

Arissa almost smiled, but for the seriousness of the situation. The men hadn't really wanted to volunteer, anyway. It was the lure of the shooting match and prizes and the free drink that signed most of them on Adrien's command. Adrien! she thought in alarm. Had he been arrested? Once again she scanned the invaders surrounding the inn for Adrien's expensive cloak and prancing racehorse. Perhaps he'd been taken by another troop.

She stared in disbelief, as the *bastonnois* began to enter the inn, rifles still ready. The quiet occupation had a hypnotic effect, holding her spellbound with apprehension, when the door opened from the taproom. With a small squeal of fright, Arissa raised the rifle to her shoulder instinctively, but upon seeing that it was Stephen, lowered it to rest the brass-adorned butt on the floor.

"Mon Dieu, but what have you done, Stephen?"

"For the love of God, 'Rissa, give me that, before you hurt someone, or yourself, for that matter."

Stephen strode up to her and snatched the rifle from her hands. "What were you going to do? Take them on alone? You are the only one who has offered resistance!"

"How dare you speak to me in that tone, when you have just turned our inn over to the enemy!" she snapped back. "What will they do, quarter here?"

"That's the idea." Stephen backed away from the doorway, where he'd returned the gun to its rack overhead.

"And how are we to be paid?"

Reaching into his pocket, he withdrew a heavy pouch and tossed it on the desk. "With this, *ma cherie.*"

Arissa made no comment, for at that moment, Phillip Monroe stepped into the doorway. Tailored to his broad shoulders was a short blue uniform coat with crimson facing. In his gloved hands, a tricorn hat, complete with cockade, indicated an officer of rank. Buff trousers skimmed the sturdy legs, which she'd so tenderly caressed the night before, as if trying to absorb his pain, yet today they appeared as fit as any she'd seen. Her speechless study ended at the pair of polished black boots, worthy of an officer in the enemy's army.

"So the wolf has finally shed its sheep's cloth, *non?*" She nearly choked on the bitterness infecting her voice.

"That's *clothing,* love." Phillip braced himself, with a breath. "Regardless, I suppose I deserve those words."

Incredulity lit upon the fire in Arissa's gaze. *"Suppose?"* She swore. "There is no suppose to it, monsieur! You are a liar, a deceiver, a thief of . . ." She broke off before she admitted her final humiliation. He'd taken her heart and innocence in a charade. "You deserve much worse, monsieur, and never, never presume to call me your love. I feel nothing but the bitterest contempt for you and your lies. Now get out of my sight!"

"Arissa, I think the two of you should discuss this calmly," Stephen suggested.

She turned to her brother, with a dismissing wave of her arm. "Discuss what? I would believe nothing he has to say, not now or ever again!"

Her voice trembled, only serving to inflame her more that she should appear so weak, when she needed strength. God help her, it felt as though her legs were turning to water, as it was. She wanted them out, both of them!

"Your marriage, of course. You can not simply dismiss last night."

He told Stephen? Arissa impaled Phillip Monroe with blue daggers of unforgiving accusation.

"Get out, both of you!"

"Arissa . . ." Phillip stepped forward, his hand extended. "It isn't what you think. We were both a bit careless and . . ." He ducked, as a heavy medical book flew past his head, narrowly missing him.

"Get out!"

"Arissa, I have every intention of doing the right thing . . ."

Unable to intimidate him with hurling books, Arissa seized the fireplace poker and raised it over her head. *"Mon Dieu,* you will leave me this instant or I will . . . oh!" She winced in pain, as Stephen, having sneaked up behind her, wrenched the weapon from her hand.

" 'Rissa, I've never seen you so angry!" He nodded toward the set of decanters on the brandy table. "Perhaps a strong drink will . . ."

Before Stephen could finish, Arissa grabbed the expensive French crystal decanter and slung it at him. It struck his leg, exacting a yelp, before shattering on the brick hearth. "Liars! Both of you! Damn you to hell!"

If they would not leave her, then she had no alternative but to quit them. Grabbing her skirts in her hands, she dashed toward the small corner stairwell, ignoring Phillip's "Arissa, please wait!" and blindly raced to her room. With the door bolted behind her, she flung herself on the bed. The raw hurt and rage that boiled inside her choked off her sobs, cutting mercilessly at her throat, while unseen hands wrung her heart and lungs until it hurt to breathe. How could they have done this to her, two men whom she'd given her heart to, in complete trust?

Upon hearing someone seize the latch to her bedroom door, she buried her tearful face in the pillow.

"Arissa, this is Phillip. Please let me in . . . talk to me."

"To hear more lies? *N . . . non!"*

"To hear the truth, damn it!" The veneer of patience with which he'd first begun started to crack. Arissa flinched, as he shook the door.

"I was the fool once, but not twice, monsieur. Now go plunder with your men and leave me alone. You've taken all you can from me."

"Damn it, girl, I could take this door down, if I choose, but I'd prefer . . ."

"To have your way easily, like you did last night? That I do not doubt!"

"Arissa! . . ." The threat literally thundered from the other side of the door. "I am trying to be a gentleman!"

"A gentleman would go away and leave me be, monsieur. He would not scream like an angry bull and threaten to tear down my door. If you speak the truth, which I doubt, then be a gentleman and leave me in peace."

The loud silence beyond the planked door was almost unbearable. Arissa sat up on her bed and looked at the latch, still taut with Phillip's unseen hand on the other side. She moved back against the headboard, drawing her pillows in front of her, as though they could keep him away. Her breath was still in her chest, moving no more than the latch. When the mechanism finally relaxed in its catch, she let out a sigh of relief.

Nonetheless she waited, listening for the slightest indication that he'd abandoned her door. Another eternity seemed to pass before she heard his footsteps moving down the hall, stiff, as if his bad leg was bothering him. At least he had not lied about his handicap, minor as it was. Such things were hard to feign, although she wondered if he'd really been injured in the manner he said, the manner which had softened her heart even more toward him. Numb with shock and its resulting distress, she let the pillows drop from her, as the retreat faded. Phillip a spy. It was a torturing thought.

He'd lied about wanting to start over in Canada, away from the political turmoil. Perhaps he'd even lied about his precious Deborah and their son. He'd had all the perfect answers, all the exact qualities she sought in a hired man—and more. He'd demonstrated respect and offered encouragement to her to follow her dreams. His character was so perfectly conjured that even she, who mistrusted most men, had been charmed and taken in most heartily—so heartily that she'd shamelessly thrown herself into his arms and admitted her attraction to him. She'd given him her body and her heart to salvage a soul lost to grief, just as Stephen had warned her not to do.

Maybe that was because her brother had known the real Phillip Monroe suffered no such traumatic past. His greatest trauma was becoming accepted at the Chateau Royale. If anything, Stephen was as much to blame for thrusting Phillip upon her as the man himself. How could her brother have been so blinded by this cause that he'd undermine their love for each other. She would die for Stephen, if need be, and yet he'd let this stranger in their midst to drive them apart.

The noise of horses and voices outside drew Arissa from the bed to the window, where the volunteers from St. Our were mounting up to head home. They'd preferred to have been there in the first place. At the same time, the soldiers were taking over the barn for their animals. To Arissa's surprise, there were actually amiable exchanges taking place between the two opposite forces. Meanwhile, the scraping of chairs and benches below indicated the Americans were losing no time in making themselves comfortable. Once again the Chateau Royale would be filled for the night.

She closed the curtain and pulled the shutters to. As bedraggled as some of the troops had appeared, Chiah and her girls would be kept busy, not to mention Gaspar at the bar. He would need help, but that was Stephen's problem. These were his guests. She washed her hands of them. She had no intention of leaving the family quarters for any task that could be construed as supporting the enemy. It was a matter of principle . . . and pride.

Ten

By evening, Arissa had spent all the tears and frustration she intended. She'd thought her worst nightmare had come true when she saw the American troops taking over her inn, but when she'd seen Phillip wearing their uniform, fear turned to hurt, and hurt to rage. The one man to whom she might have turned to for comfort was one of *them*. She lamented that the enemy had not come a day sooner. At least that would have lessened her humiliation, to some degree. Instead, she'd allowed herself to be victim of the ultimate betrayal, not of politics, but of love.

The crying and ranting over Phillip's treachery had done no more than exhausted her, so that she'd slept most of the afternoon. The rest, however, had at least managed to clear her mind to assess the situation. What was between her and Phillip was no longer an issue. She would have nothing more to do with him and his lies. The Chateau Royale, however, was another story.

She had not worked so diligently to see it desecrated by a ruffian occupation. Their officers seemed of a civilized nature, but the rest left her with serious doubts, at least on appearances. She would watch these bullish indigents like a hawk and keep an account of their food and lodgings, to be certain they paid. They were customers, unsolicited, but customers, nonetheless. Stephen had shown their money in coin. That being the case, she would treat them as such. She had no choice. Her only real option was not to like it.

Thank heaven they had not invaded the family quarters. There she would have her peace—at least physically. It had taken her twenty-six years to let her heart go and to have it so callously taken and abused by deceit. It would surely take as long for the pain to go away. She stared at the wrinkled garment she'd slept in, thinking her heart as crushed as its once pristine, ironed chintz.

After changing into a fresh rose-colored dress with a pin-striped underskirt, Arissa arranged her hair in a simple fashion, with a bow at her neck, and braced herself to descend from her private haven. She had to write up the invoices for the additional supplies ordered during her dramatic trip to the city with Phillip, for she'd promised delivery before the end of the month. With the door bolted between the taproom and the parlor, she could tend to her business and have her evening meal.

Afterward, she'd summon Gaspar and Chiah to warn them to be especially conscious of counting the dinner and serving ware and to pass the word on to the staff. She also wanted to reassure all of them that because they were lodging and feeding the enemy, it was not by choice and, therefore, surely no harm should come to them from Governor Carleton, when the Americans left. This was war.

As she started down the back winding staircase, cautiously lifting the ruffled rose hem adorning her printed underskirt, voices rose to meet her. They were men's voices, engaged in formal conversation, rather than the general disjointed discussions that often drifted her way from the taproom. She slowed warily, as she took the last few steps and then froze at the sight of a group of uniformed officers gathered at her mother's cherry banquet table, which had been set up before the parlor hearth.

Indeed this was too much! She stepped into the room

with a regal sweep of skirts, unnoticed until she spoke. *"Messieurs, pardonez moi . . .* pardon me," she said, switching to fluent English, "but this is my private parlor. Could you not find seating in the taproom?"

Chairs scrapped the polished wide pine flooring, as the men made an effort to rise in deference to her unexpected presence. At the head of the table was a bearded officer who appeared to be senior to those seated around him. Tall and thin, with a narrow face, he approached her in a gracious manner and extended his hand.

"Mademoiselle Conway, I am Lieutenant Colonel Benjamin Haskill at your service. I have rented this room from your brother for my own use as office and lodgings, but I would be delighted to have you join me and my men, now that you are no longer indisposed."

Indisposed? Arissa's blank look was drawn to Stephen Conway, who followed in the officer's footsteps.

"You are looking much better now, *ma cherie*. Do join us." Stephen's expression was anxious, as well it should be, Arissa thought to herself, considering what he brought upon their home. "Chiah says you haven't eaten since breakfast."

"I'd lost my appetite in all the excitement." She allowed her brother to escort her across the room, her assessing gaze sweeping about the table until it came to two empty chairs—the one vacated by Stephen and a second, obviously reserved for her. Next to it, to her utter dismay, Phillip Monroe waited, obviously her other dinner partner. He'd looked so much like the others in his uniform, but now there was no denying that unsettling amber brown gaze of his. Her stomach took a queasy turn, making her wonder if she'd even be able to swallow a single mouthful of the sumptuous spread. Which was the least digestible—her anger or her hurt—she couldn't guess.

"I'm glad to see you're improved, mademoiselle," Phillip commented, politely, holding her chair until she was seated.

She managed a weak smile, her strength diverted to quelling the emotional swell from the raw wound in her chest. Damn them all, she would not cry. She busied herself arranging her large dinner napkin, taking care not to brush the solid thigh less than a hand's breadth from her full skirts. To do so would be her undoing. Nonetheless, she knew it was there. She could almost feel its manly warmth, which she'd savored only hours before.

"We were just enjoying some of the Chateau Royale's fine wines before dinner, mademoiselle," Lieutenant Colonel Haskill informed her. "Will you have a Madeira?"

Madeira. She and Phillip had had some the morning after their night together in the Nunnery. She'd become drowsy from its strong effects, not to mention fatigued, and slept on his shoulder. She glanced inadvertently at that shoulder, now adorned with braid and brass. Heaven knew she needed fortification of some sort, although she hadn't much tolerance for strong liquor.

"Thank you, yes, monsieur," she answered, avoiding Phillip's searching gaze.

Stephen had spared their guests nothing in welcoming them to the Chateau Royale. Aside from a delicious, steaming chowder, fish, fowl, beef, and pork had been prepared in a number of elegant ways, some smothered in rich sauces and others ensconced in Chiah's famous pastry. Puddings and custards, winter greens and squashes added color to the table. Meanwhile, the sideboard boasted an immense trifle, flanked on either side by small cakes and apple tartlets.

Ordinarily, she would have swelled with pride at the tempting, tasty display. Instead, she thought, at this rate, the purse her brother had tossed on the table would not feed them for a week. She glanced around, noticing the way the men ate. Despite their attempt at manners, they were obviously ravenous, as though they had not eaten like this in a long while. They looked it, as well. Like their colonel, they were gaunt in face, even the heavier-set of them. Only Phillip, Stephen, and she ate with any degree of temperance.

"This is a celebration, mademoiselle," Phillip Monroe explained, after catching the widening look of incredulity on her face, when his fellow officers not only finished what was put before them, but asked for more. "These men have been on army rations for weeks, on the march."

"I guess it does make us look like a bunch of hungry animals, Mademoiselle Conway," the colonel picked up, "but these men have done without for so long. Add that to the exceptional spread of the Chateau Royale, and even I have overindulged, for this once." Lifting his napkin politely, he unsuccessfully smothered a rolling belch. Arissa pretended not to notice, as she had been doing throughout the meal for a number of the members at the table.

"I hear some of Arnold's men were actually boiling candles to make gruel," one of the younger men offered. "They've had more of a hellish time of it than we."

"There is another American army?" Arissa could feel her face draining of painfully mustered spirit. Not even a fresh dress and a glass of strong Madeira were sufficient to bear up to this news. Quebec was being overrun, and the King could not send aid until the spring thaw!

"Our scouts report that Arnold's men are closin' in on Quebec from the east."

"Oh!"

Arissa's mind whirled, furiously. Two large armies and Governor Carleton only had skeletal British forces, at least according to Adrien Rueil, before Montreal was abandoned. Quebec, however, was better fortified, with a concentration of trained forces there, as well as eager volunteers. That was what she'd heard, here and there.

There must be sufficient numbers to hold out, for she'd also heard Carleton had turned down the offer of many of the Indian tribes to reinforce them. Perhaps it was not so bad, after all, she reasoned, uncertainly.

"Our reason for being here is to patrol the Côte de Neiges area, in case of Loyalist activity," Colonel Haskill told her. "Although, from what we've seen so far, there'll be little resistance. Most of your habitants don't seem to care one way or the other whether the British are here or not."

"And the noblesse want to keep them in power, so's they can enjoy all that royal favoritism. But don't you worry your pretty little head about anything. Once the lobsterbacks are gone, your menfolk, both rich and poor, will have a say in how things are run."

"Lieutenant Lewis is our Thomas Paine," the colonel informed her. "He keeps reminding us of what we have to gain, when we're cold and hungry and miss our families."

Arissa leaned forward, addressing the pale, red-haired officer in genuine curiosity. "So, lieutenant, you consider the fact that if you were to go to trial, that your fate might be decided by men who have no education or knowledge of the law?"

Lieutenant Colonel Haskill laughed. "No doubt, there are some details to be worked out, Mademoiselle Conway, but men smarter than the lot of us put together are taking care of that. Our task is to clear the way for them."

"What if all the Canadians do not want to have this sort of government you speak of?"

"The majority rules, mademoiselle," Lewis put in, enthusiastically. "Not one king or a group of his appointed nobles, but the people."

Arissa put her fork aside. "It is a curious theory, but it goes against all the French-Canadians have known. They do not subscribe to the English law, let alone this people-law of which you speak. And do not think that they are fooled by all this talk of brotherhood, when some of the very leaders you mention call them bloodthirsty Papists and worse."

"The freedom we fight for, Arissa, is freedom of religion as well, to be able to worship as one is led, without fear of persecution."

Arissa afforded a slight nod at Phillip's explanation, but avoided his gaze. The velvet strength of his voice undermined her defenses in a devastating way. If it had that same effect on the population, the province would be as lost as she had been. She took another sip of the Madeira to regroup.

"Your brother states that your family is not Catholic."

"He is correct, Colonel Haskill, but that does not diminish my concern for those that are, those who are our friends and neighbors. My father was English, and I was raised in his faith, but my mother was French-Canadian and I am also sympathetic to her people and their faith."

Haskill lifted his glass to her, a smug smile stretching his brown beard to its full width. "An admirable trait in a woman, that compassion for others. Unfortunately, it hampers the female's ability to fully understand politics and war. Nonetheless, we worship you lovely creatures, for where would man be without them? Here, here!"

Arissa colored at the implication of the toast, the heat from her neck bursting on her cheeks.

Before she could reply, Lieutenant Lewis followed with another. "And to General Montgomery, who, as he put it, will sup on the New Year in Quebec or in hell."

The general round of enthusiasm increased with the clinking of her mother's crystal glasses and the hearty support of the General and his intent.

Instead of lifting her glass, Arissa held it in her hand, twirling the dark red liquor, so that it almost breached the brim. "No doubt he will welcome the warmer climate," she murmured, in a soft but bold, tone.

" 'Rissa!" Stephen chastised in horror.

Smiling sweetly, she put down her glass. "I deal with practicality, not some dream of glory. If this Arnold's men are half-starved and sick, and even those men here are not equipped for the Quebec winter, how do you expect to take a town that is defended by hardened and well supplied British troops? They have but to stay safe within their walls and wait until reinforcements come in spring, *non?*" She assumed a guileless innocence, as she glanced around at her attentive audience, expectantly.

"My dear young lady," Colonel Haskill spoke up, "These men have fought God's own elements, abandoned their warm hearths and families, and lived on sheer willpower. Do you think the fat and comfortable British troops are a match for them? Ours are driven by the call for freedom, to fight for their own land. What drives the British? Wages and perhaps a promotion to fight a battle that is no threat to their homeland? We are offering free land to any British soldier who decides to join the cause for freedom! There is room for all here in the colonies and in your Quebec!" By now, it seemed as if the flames from the candelabra had leapt into the officer's fervent gaze. "We are winter soldiers, not pampered summer soldiers! We eat hardship and spit it out. Those bloody-backs have seen no army like this. We are the first. The first American army of the Continental Congress!"

Applause burst from every chair at the table, ending with each man standing. Conspicuously seated, despite the pressure Stephen placed on her arm to join the others, Arissa maintained a gracious countenance. As the commotion died, the colonel turned to her and lifted his glass. "And here is to showing the lovely mademoiselle the promise that awaits all who believe in our fight for freedom."

"Here, here!" Again, there was a round of enthusiasm, the most exhorted at her side, as Phillip Monroe drained his glass. Arissa had only meant to glance his way, but his intense gaze captured her attention and would not give it leave. *Promise?* she thought, allowing her carefully restrained bitterness to rise sufficiently to reinforce her feeble defenses against that intoxicating way he had of delving into her eyes and beyond to her soul. *Non,* lies!

Coolly, she turned to the colonel. "It is the weight of your coin, monsieur, which will convince me, more than your gallant speeches, of your ability to carry out your mission. Then, perhaps, I will believe that these ideals and dreams are worth more than the paper on which you print your Continental bills."

"*Mon* colonel, you have my deepest apologies. My sister, she does not mean insult."

"By no means," Arissa chimed in, with an innocuous look. "I was merely debating your politics and . . ." The pressure of Phillip's thigh against her own caused her to falter. ". . . and exercising good judgment in business."

"My dear, you just worry your pretty little head about keeping us lodged and well-fed, which seems to be your forte, and let us men deal with the politics. Women should not concern themselves with such things. They're minds are more family- and hearth-oriented."

Arissa stiffened in her chair, only to feel the harsh stomp of Stephen's boot on her foot. She couldn't help the little yelp that escaped her. "Well, if you gentlemen will excuse me, I have some *home* and *hearth* work to be seen to." She rose from her chair without the help Stephen and Phillip hastened to offer. "I leave you superior male minds to your politics and dessert."

As the officers jumped to their feet, Lieutenant Colonel Haskill walked around and took her hand. "I meant no insult, Mademoiselle Conway. You are a gracious hostess and a credit to your brother."

"Nor I, monsieur. But apparently, I haven't the stomach or the mind for such manly discussions. It distresses my head terribly, so that I must retire to my room."

"I'll escort you there!" Phillip Monroe was at her side instantly.

"I'd rather you not, monsieur." Arissa swung abruptly away toward his superior. "Colonel, since I value my home and hearth, I would be indebted if you were to order at least my private quarters upstairs off-limits to your men."

"I regret, mademoiselle, that my officers are sharing your brother's room."

"Then my door, at least, monsieur. I need time to adjust to this occupation, and I give my word that I shall endeavor in return to be as congenial as I can—or at least impartial, considering you are not here by my invitation."

"Arissa . . ."

"Mademoiselle Conway to you, *Capitaine* Monroe," Arissa snapped at Phillip. Catching herself, she returned her attention to the colonel. "I can find my way to my room on my own, monsieur. Beside, I am sure you have much to discuss with your spy *capitaine*, and far be it from me to keep him from his duty. It has always been first and foremost on his mind, I can assure you."

With a cordial *"Bon soir, messieurs,"* Arissa moved, with a graceful sway of skirts, to the stairwell, carrying the gazes of all those present with her, until she retreated upward, with light, hasty steps that echoed softly.

When Jeanne brought up hot tea later, Arissa sent her messages to Chiah and Gaspar, via the girl, to be watchful of their inventory. Then, grateful that she didn't have to expose herself to the company of the intruders again, she prepared for bed, mentally planning her work for the next day, so that, if at all possible, she could avoid Phillip Monroe completely. Both physically and in thought.

She'd have Jeanne help her move her ledgers and records to her room. Although the ladies' writing desk there did not compare in convenience to that of her father's, she could make do. No doubt, she could have the new invoices written and still have time to take the calèche into the city before noon to make the deliveries. There were only a few, this being the beginning of her new career. Besides, with the enemy encamped in her home, she felt the need to escape, at least for a while, and see how the city was faring.

Eventually, she fell asleep, going over every item on each order, having memorized them and mentally placing their exact location in the hall closet for easy retrieval. The moment the dream world claimed her, however, her conscious efforts to avoid thinking about Phillip Monroe were overridden by memories which demanded to be acknowledged. There she could go into his arms and seek his strength and reassurance that all was going to be well, both with the war and with the two of them.

His kisses made her forget his charade—everything except that ageless attraction that drew their bodies ever closer, until not even their clothes separated them. His caresses drove her insane with pleasure, igniting a hunger only the two of them united could satiate. There were no secrets, no lies, only passion and breathlessly whispered endearments, meant for each other only. She was riddled with a wild ecstasy that ultimately she saw mirrored on his face. His angular, well placed features were contorted with rapture, his hair damp and tousled from the heat of their passion. It rocked them both, body and soul, shaking and shaking . . .

" 'Rissa!"

Arissa gasped, as she was suddenly pulled out of the throes of Phillip's lovemaking into the cold reality of the room. The blankets fell away from her, as she tried to shake the dream from her head. Instead of the man she loved, Stephen sat on the edge of her bed, holding her by the shoulders. Still damp and breathless, she placed her hand to her chest. It had been so real! *Dieu*, but how could this be?

"You were having a nightmare, *ma cherie.*"

Arissa overrode the private impulse to debate that. "What is it? What is wrong?" There had to be some reason for Stephen to be here in her room at this hour.

"It is Lieutenant Colonel Haskill. He is debilitated with pain in his chest. It could be his heart."

"Or indigestion," she remarked, dourly, recalling the many times he'd burped behind his napkin. "Besides, I am not so sure he would like to have this feeble-minded female tend to him. I'm only fit to tend the home and hearth."

"I have told him you are a doctor, or the closest we have to one . . . that you trained under Father since you were fourteen."

Arissa slid off the bed and shivered in the cold, chilling her damp body. Thousands of goose bumps assaulted her flesh in protest. Was it only last night that she had been so warm with Phillip's lovemaking that the evening air did not bother her? She shook herself mentally and pulled on her robe. This had to stop. To invade her dreams was unfair. She was helpless against him, there.

As she followed Stephen into the hall, she saw Phillip, now divested of his jacket and leatherstock. His ruffled shirt was open, as if he'd been preparing to retire, himself, when his superior summoned him. Backing away, he held up both hands in surrender to the narrowed look Arissa gave him.

"I'm on our side of the hall, mademoiselle!"

His mockery setting no better with her than the fact that he'd imposed himself upon her dreams, Arissa hurried down the steps after Stephen, all too aware that Phillip followed.

"I've assured the colonel that you are an accomplished physician," he informed her, from behind.

"I wonder you don't suspect me of poisoning him," she came back, dryly, nearly crashing into Stephen, who had stopped abruptly in front of her. He glanced back at Phillip Monroe in a most disconcerted manner.

Arissa shook her head in disbelief. "Surely you jest!" she challenged her brother, reading his expression clearly.

"It was only mentioned in passing. Arissa, the man is in pain."

Lips thinning in disgust, Arissa nudged her brother on. She knew full well that Haskill suffered from a drastic change of diet, overeating, and the resulting gastric distress. It was a wonder that some of the other officers were not complaining, the way they had gorged themselves.

Haskell lay on the pull-down bed next to the hearth, his dark beard making his face look all the paler in the lamplight. Lieutenant Lewis and three other men were present. In a similar state of dishabille like Phillip, they rose to their feet from their place at the now-banquet table, which had been moved to the far end of the room, where it was kept, leaves down, when not in use. The lieutenant colonel followed her with his eyes, as she passed the bed and fetched her medical bag from beneath her father's desk.

"I asked your brother not to bother you, mademoiselle, but he insisted," the man informed her, crisply, despite the perspiration on his brow betraying his distress. "I am certain this malady will pass."

Arissa could not help but smile. "So am I, monsieur, but I have some elixir in this bag that will help it pass faster and offer some comfort until it does." She glanced at the men seated at the opposite side of the room. "There is enough for any of you who think you need it."

She took out a bottle of the elixir, flavored with blackberry wine to disguise the citrus of bismuth, ammonia, gentian, and laudanum. It was enough to relax the aggravated digestive system and purge the source of its distress. She handed the bottle to the colonel.

. "You may take one to three teaspoons tonight and another such dose in the morning, that is, if you are still in discomfort."

"What if it's my heart?"

"The laudanum in the elixir would help that, monsieur, but I do not think, from your obvious symptoms," she said, gently pressing against his bloated stomach, "that it is anything more than severe gastric indigestion. As you said, you have been on army rations for so long, and then to eat such an amount of rich foods as you did . . ."

Arissa shrugged and reached for the man's wrist to take his pulse. Again, there was nothing to indicate anything except what she suspected, nor was his brow feverish. It was merely damp from the gripping gastric distention. "A little additional blackberry wine could be considered medicinal and . . ." She took out a jar of camphor and placed it on the desk. "If your distress is very intense, you may wish to rub this on your abdomen . . . unless you would prefer I do it."

"No, no," Haskill denied hastily. "I didn't want a lady doctor to start with."

Smiling smugly, Arissa closed up her bag and put it back under the desk. "I will fetch some of my things in the morning, *mon* colonel. I am certain that you will feel much better, although I do not recommend a heavy breakfast. You must give your stomach some time to adjust to our rich cooking."

It was a sixth sense that brought her to the table of officers, arms folded across her chest, as she spoke. "So you are not feeling so well, too?"

"Mademoiselle, you could rub that . . ."

"Myers!" Phillip Monroe's outburst cut the man off, forcing him to look down, sheepishly. "Aris . . . Mademoiselle Conway, I don't think your services are needed here any longer."

Sheer obstinacy made Arissa linger in front of Lieutenant Lewis, the young, red-haired officer with such a zeal for his cause. Well aware that Phillip was watching her, she placed her hand on the young man's forehead, as she'd intended to do in the first place. He hadn't looked well at the supper table, and he looked even worse now.

"You have a fever, monsieur," she observed, flatly. "Stephen, bring the lamp over, *s'il vous plaît.*"

"Oh, I'm alright. I just ate too much trifle."

"And lost it," one of his comrades teased. "Some people will do anything to have a pretty doctor look at them."

"I wasn't complainin'!"

"That's enough!" Phillip warned, ominously. He moved next to Arissa. "What do you think is wrong?"

Arissa examined the young man's eyes and then held the lamp even closer to examine his skin. He was freckled, making it difficult to determine if a rash accompanied the fever. His coated tongue confirmed what his friend had insinuated—that his stomach was upset.

"Perhaps he drank some bad water. Perhaps the fever comes from something else," Arissa thought aloud. "For tonight, I suggest that you take a quinine solution every three hours." She cupped the patient's chin. "Do you think you can do that?"

Lewis wiped his brow and nodded. "I don't think I'm gonna be gettin' a lot of sleep, the way my stomach is feudin'."

"Then wait here."

She kept the quinine solution in the medical cabinet next to her father's desk, along with a number of clean spoons. As she carried the large, green bottle across the room, she stopped long enough to take a decanter of the blackberry cordial from the oriental painted liquor cabinet.

"This will help chase down the taste. I have made no elixir to disguise the flavor of this, I am afraid."

"Thank you, mam . . . I mean mademoiselle."

"You are very welcome, Lieutenant Lewis. And if you get worse in the night, you will send for me, *non?*"

This time, the young man actually looked away in embarrassment at the poorly suppressed snorts made by his colleagues.

Arissa ignored them. It didn't matter what the ruffians thought. This young man was ill, although the seriousness of it remained to be seen. A fever was an indication that something was wrong somewhere. "Meanwhile, you put a wet linen towel on your forehead and on the back of your neck. You can see to that, *non*, Phillipe? You know where the spare linens are kept."

Arissa bit her bottom lip instantly, but it was too late. She'd not only called him by his familiar name, despite her resolve to remain as aloof as possible, but made it evident that he was quite at home here. No doubt, like many of the men she'd heard boasting of their conquests, he'd already made his comrades aware of his. She shrank inwardly, but refused to act as if anything were amiss.

"I'll take care of him. Now you get yourself upstairs and get some rest. You need it."

He said the words with such certainty that Arissa could not help but know what he was referring to—their long night together. Why was he acting as if he cared about her health? Or was it perhaps because she had given herself to him, that he was establishing a certain claim to her before the others—a license to order her life, given her surrender to him.

Arissa would have argued, except that she was tired. There had certainly been no rest in the sleep that had claimed her earlier. She pulled away from Phillip's scrutiny and pointed a challenging finger at the lieutenant.

"You take care of yourself. You too, *mon* colonel. *Bon soir, messieurs.*"

As she started up the steps, Phillip fell in behind her, this time without asking. Her back ramrod straight, Arissa continued to the top of the steps and consciously measured her step to her door. The last thing she wanted was to make him think he affected her, one way or the other. Her hand upon the latch, she turned, her nose nearly brushing the open ruffles on his shirt in the process.

"Is there something else, monsieur?"

"I need to talk to you, Arissa." His voice dropped at the sound of footfalls on the steps at the end of the hall.

"But there is nothing to say between us, monsieur."

"I want to marry you, damn it!"

Arissa pushed open the door, as some of the officers entered the hall. "Which one of you, monsieur . . . the lover or the liar?" she quipped, lowly, before slipping into her room. "I, for one, cannot separate them." She started to close the door, but not before she saw the anger flash on his face. Her mouth went dry, yet somehow she managed to raise her voice sufficiently for all present to hear, before putting the cold, lifeless door between them. "I remind you, this door is off limits, so, *bon soir, Capitaine.*"

Eleven

Perhaps it was the Madeira, but Arissa slept what was left of the night soundly, without the interference of dream or of man. With conjured enthusiasm, she rose and dressed for the day, eager to be about her planned business. Because she intended to travel into town, she donned a vermilion skirt and matching short jacket, both of which were openly admired when she entered the taproom to see about having the calèche brought about at noon.

"You look as if you have accepted things rather well," Gaspar remarked, from behind the bar, where he sat perched on a stool leisurely sipping hot coffee. It being morning, there was more demand from the kitchen.

"Did I have a choice?"

The older man shrugged. "Such is life. There are times, especially in war, when choices are made for us by fate . . . even choices of the heart."

His narrowed appraisal made Arissa shift uncomfortably. Did everyone know about her and Phillip? "I feel betrayed by Capitaine Monroe's friendship and have every reason to be angry at him . . . and Stephen! *Dieu,* my own brother had a hand in this!"

"I believe the man is in love with you," Gaspar went on, ignoring her defiant outburst. "Old Gaspar, he sees many things in here. When you come into the room, that somber face of his lights up like the summer sky. Oh, he pretends not to notice, but I do not miss much. It was that way with your father and his bride."

Arissa looked at the man in surprise. "You knew my parents before they were married?"

This time, it was Gaspar who shifted in discomfort. For twenty-three years he'd kept this secret, and today he almost let it out. Perhaps Chiah was right, that his mind was not as sharp as it used to be. But then, what else about him was as good as it had been when he was young?

"After they were married," he proceeded smoothly. "You know how stuffy your father could be." Gaspar puffed his chest out and pursed his lips in a way Arissa had seen her father do on hundreds of occasions. "Your *maman* would come into the room, and he would act as if he were deep in thought on some matter of great import, the no-nonsense English gentleman, all the while following her with eyes that twinkled with love."

"Well, what you saw twinkling in Phillip's eyes was lust, if anything . . . or perhaps apprehension that he might get caught," she added, with a unrelenting smirk.

Gaspar chuckled. "Apprehension that he might get caught, yes, but not in the way you mean. Imagine his predicament. He was sent here on duty and found love in the last place he expected it. Worse, he couldn't confess his charade, because he'd fallen in love with an independent-minded female firmly planted in the enemy camp. *Voila!* What was he to do?"

"Go home . . . or go to someone else's tavern."

Arissa turned away from the bar. She didn't want to hear this. If Phillip had truly loved her, he'd have confessed and thrown himself at the mercy of her heart. She'd have forgiven him. . . . Perhaps, she thought, frowning. *Sacre bleu,* who was to know? It didn't matter now, anyway. The cards had already been played by the bloody war.

"Stop playing Cupid and just have my carriage ready

at noon," she called over her shoulder to Gaspar. "And would you send Jeanne to the parlor to help me move my things up to my room?"

"Perhaps you should speak with the Colonel Haskill before you make too many more plans for today."

Arissa paused at the door leading across the hall which separated the taproom from the parlor. "Why is that?"

Upon seeing Gaspar's discreet glance at the men seated at the various tables and that typical maddening shrug, which meant he had nothing more to offer, she resolved to do just that. Instead of barging into the room, as was her custom, she hesitated at the door, since it was rented as a guest room, and knocked. At the Lieutenant Colonel's booming, "Come in!" Arissa entered.

Once again, the dining table had been set up formally for the officers, and the colonel's bed was hidden behind the paneled wall. Stephen and Phillip among them, they were in the midst of their breakfast. There were sausages and ham on a platter, as well as scones with an assortment of jellies and jams to tempt their gullets, but most seemed to have preferred the large tureen on the table filled with a bland porridge.

"Please, remain seated," Arissa insisted, as they started to get up from their chairs.

"Will you join us, 'Rissa?" Stephen inquired, hopeful at the smile gracing his sister's lips.

"Thank you, but *non*. Colonel, if you do not object, I would like to start moving some of my personal papers and books to my room, since your occupation of this room at this time seems indefinite."

"Not indefinite, mademoiselle," Haskill corrected her. "We're just here for a few weeks, until Montreal is secured and the offensive against Quebec is readied."

"Oh, I see." Arissa hoped she did not appear overly pleased. She glanced about the table, avoiding Phillip Monroe's quiet appraisal. "So, is everyone feeling better this morning?" Her attention came to rest on an empty chair, one that had been occupied by Lieutenant Lewis on the previous night. "The lieutenant is not better?" she asked the colonel.

"I was going to ask to you have a look at him when you came downstairs. The men say he's thrashed with the fever all night, but I've seen men get fireburnt before."

"Fireburnt?"

The colonel shook with a patronizing chuckle. "Too comfortable in a place to want to leave. He has patrol duty along the Côte des Neiges, and the wind's been whipping up most of the night. After that wonderful elixir you gave us, not to mention the blackberry cordial, he's fit enough for duty. He just doesn't want to go, as he has such a fine looking physician to dote over him."

"His fever was quite real, monsieur," Arissa argued in the young man's defense. "And you said last night that he was your source of enthusiasm. It does not seem in character for him to feign illness."

"Mademoiselle, a warm hearth and a pretty woman is enough to make any man act out of character, after what this army's been through. You haven't had the experience with men that I have. Why I've seen soldiers swallow to-bacco to induce a fever, or drink scalding chocolate to inflame their throats, so they could shirk their duty and spend the day in the infirmary, where it was warm and cozy."

The condescension in the officer's tone ignited sparks of indignation in Arissa's lofty gaze, as she looked down at him. "And you, monsieur, have not had the experience with the ill that I have." She pulled her bag from under the desk. "I will have a look at him."

Colonel Haskill moved to block her way, his brow creased as he obviously tried to censor his reply for a lady's ears. "Mademoiselle, you may own this inn, but I own the men in it. I want to make that clear. You have no say in army matters."

"I shouldn't think so, colonel. My say, as you call it, concerns the welfare of humanity. Apparently, in your opinion, the two arenas do not cross." She looked him straight in the eye. "And that, monsieur, gives me great cause for concern."

Without further *adieu*, she turned and headed up the steps to her brothers' room, now the officer's quarters. After a tentative knock, she went inside.

Straw pallets had been put on the floor for the men and were lined up on both sides of the two single beds, which had been, as Arissa supposed, still occupied by Stephen and Phillip. On one, near the shallow hearth, which was in need of fresh wood, Lieutenant Lewis lay, fully clothed and wrapped in blankets. Even as she approached, Arissa could see that he was shivering and unaware of her presence. As she knelt down beside the young man, two of the girls assigned to clean the rooms came in, one carrying linens and the other wood for the fire.

"See if you can get this fire going nicely, Lisa, and you, Celia, fetch me a pitcher of fresh water and a basin. You can leave those towels right here."

"Is he very ill, mademoiselle?" one of the girls ventured.

"I'm d . . . damned dyin'," the lieutenant chattered, searching Arissa's face for confirmation. "I knew I'd get it! I h . . . had the burial detail."

"Burial detail?" Upon noticing both girls standing and staring, she waved at them to go about their business.

"The pox."

Lisa gasped behind them, as if she'd been burned by the kindling she'd dropped on the hot coals.

"Lisa, he is only guessing," Arissa reassured her. The last thing they needed was a panic. "You will keep this to yourself, until I can confirm exactly what is wrong, *non?* You know I would not endanger you or any of the staff."

"But of course, mademoiselle."

"A chill and fever could mean anything, so off with you, Celia."

"Of course, mademoiselle," both girls echoed, Celia hastily taking her leave.

They were not convincing, but then, Arissa didn't feel she was either. Instead, she began to unwrap the blankets from round the young man. The fourth and innermost was not from the inn. It was ragged and in a wretched state of filth. And this was an example of an officer's equipment, she thought, wryly.

"Now I am going to unfasten your shirt and examine your chest and neck, although this is most likely an influenza," she cajoled, amiably. "You have been cold and wet and hungry . . ."

"The sick are over at the big place next to h . . . here," Lewis interrupted. "That's where Haskill'll likely s . . . send me. He's been keepin' 'em sep'rate from the rest of us."

"Do you mean the Chateau Rueil?" It had to be Adrien's home! That was the only large estate nearby.

The young man shook his head in confusion. "I dunno. It's where they took one of them n . . . noble officers, what thinks their higher than most f . . . folks. He . . . he's got a pretty wife and baby."

Dear heaven, Arissa fretted, as she searched her patient's burning skin for any sign of rash. If this was smallpox, he was in the early stages, for there was none.

"Jesus, mam, have you got anything in th . . . that bag for my head. It's fit to bust."

"But of course," Arissa assured him, her mind assembling the facts, as she knew them. Headache and fever could be anything.

Above his head—for he had no pillow—was the bottle of quinine she'd given him the night before. It was half-full now. At least, he'd been taking it, although it hadn't seemed to help. She reached in her bag and took out a vial of laudanum, mixed in an elixir with potassium bromide to make it more palatable.

"A spoon every hour or so." She took a clean spoon from her bag and gave him a dose. "And your quinine, when was the last time you took it."

"It was dark. Jesus, that stuffs tastes like . . ." he hesitated, his manners catching up with him. "It's pretty bad."

"Where is the blackberry cordial I gave you?"

"Colonel Haskill needed it."

Something very unladylike crossed Arissa's mind about the lieutenant colonel. "Lisa, fetch me a bottle of blackberry cordial from the taproom, please. Meanwhile, I am going to bathe the monsieur in cool water to try to get that fever down. I only wish someone had called me earlier," she fussed, clearing away the basin of used water and towels. It was cloudy with dirt, making her wonder just how long it had been since her patient had bathed. She took stock of the ragged blanket he pulled up over his naked chest, and made a face.

"Give me that thing and I will fetch you another to use, while we wash it."

"If . . . if it's all the same, mam, I'd just as soon keep it."

"It's alright, Lewis. I'll take responsibility for it." Arissa started at the sound of Phillip Monroe's voice behind her. He leaned over his bed and drew off one of his own army issues, a blanket in much better condition. "Matter of fact, I'll trade you."

"I ain't complainin', sir, but I'm just too whipped. I just want to stay like I am, if'n it's okay with the lady. Every time I move, it feels like either my brain is gonna bust right through my skull, or I'm gonna heave out my guts . . . no offense, mam."

Arissa climbed to her feet with Phillip's help, her face mirroring her concern. "He's really sick, Phi . . . *Capitaine*. I can guarantee your Colonel Haskill that."

Taking her arm, Phillip walked her to the door, leaving the patient to wrap himself up again in his coverings. "Any idea what it is?" he asked lowly.

Arissa glanced back at the youth. "He thinks it's smallpox. He was on a burial detail for some who died of it, I think."

"Is it?"

The extreme gravity of her companion's expression and tone gave Arissa cause for alarm. Did Phillip know something she did not? "It's too early to tell," she hesitated. "These sick men at the Rueil's home, do any of them have the smallpox?" She knew the answer before Phillip even spoke. Her anxiety settled in her stomach in a squeamish fashion. Dear Heaven, what next?

"Most of them. It's been dogging them since they left Ticonderoga. They've been kept isolated, so I understand."

"And what about inoculations? Haven't the healthy men been given inoculations?

"Have you had one?"

Arissa brushed aside his concern. "Since I was a child, as did both my brothers. And you?" She swore at herself for showing the same for him. But a life was a life, even if it was a liar's life.

"I had a mild case as a child, when my father was a emissary in France."

So that is where Phillip learned to speak French so fluently. Arissa moved out of the way of some of the other officers returning from their meal, forced closer to Phillip in the process. Although they were not staring, she sensed their undivided interest.

"And the others," she asked, resuming the conversation. "They have been inoculated since the outbreak?"

Phillip edged her further through the door and away from curious ears and traffic. "Is there somewhere we can talk?"

"Here is fine," she said, moving past her room to the corner of the hall opposite the private stairwell. "Now, tell me about the inoculations."

"There've been none, at least none authorized."

"What?" Phillip's words were too incredible for Arissa to conceive!

He placed a finger over her lips, making her aware of her raised voice. Leaning against the wall on one hand, he bent over so that his words were for her only. "There's been no time, so I understand it. The outbreak's been recent on the march. I think Montgomery is hoping it will die out."

"But how many lives is he willing to risk, Phillip? This is smallpox! It is deadly and contagious. *Mon Dieu*," Arissa swore, her thoughts going to Celeste Rueil and her baby girl. "Adrien's wife and child, they must be evacuated! They should not be exposed to your sick army." She shook her head in confusion, unable to comprehend such a dangerous situation. "Where are your army doctors? Are they inoculating the men, now that this march is over?"

"Come on. We can't talk here."

Before she realized what was happening, Phillip ushered her through her bedroom door and closed it behind him. For a moment, Arissa stood frozen, unable to think at all. She stared at him as though he'd lost his mind.

"Damnation, Arissa, I'm risking court martial for this, but if you don't keep your voice down, it . . . it's not going to go well for you! You can't keep verbally assaulting Lieutenant Colonel Haskill and the American Army."

"What will they do to me, a simple woman fit only for

the hearth and home? Shoot me?" she rallied, indignation thawing her stupor.

Phillip ran frustrated fingers through his hair and shook his head. "I don't know, maybe lock you up somewhere. Damn it, this is war. It's an enemy occupation."

Arissa lifted her chin haughtily. "It certainly is!"

"We'll get to you and me in a moment."

Not if she could help it, she thought, slapping away his warning finger. "I want to know why you are not inoculating your men?"

"Because we can't afford the time it will take for them to recover from the inoculation. That's the official word. It's not my decision to make!" he argued back at her accusing look. Phillip swore beneath his breath and looked away, as Arissa eased down on the trunk at the foot of her bed.

"This cannot be!"

"Montgomery and Arnold intend to take Quebec City by the New Year, you heard that," he explained, impatiently. "They can't do it with an army recuperating from inoculations."

"Can they do it with a dying one?"

"They're keeping it isolated!" he reiterated. "I've got orders to move Lewis to the Chateau Rueil immediately. Word is, Montgomery is marching into Montreal today. Once the city is secured, the sick will be moved to the Nunnery's hospital and contained there. That's why you can't go to the city, as Gaspar said you'd planned. There won't be much going, in or out, until it's firmly under American jurisdiction and all the dissidents are contained."

Arissa listened, numbly. What manner of commanders were these to take such risks with their own men? What manner of government would rule, without regard for their own people? The colonel was right. It was beyond her ability to understand, especially as someone devoted to preserving life.

"You are disgusting!" she declared, spitting out the words as if they were bilious and vile. "You and your officers and your army!" She pointed to the door. "Get out of my room! At least leave me this!"

"Arissa, you don't understand . . ."

She jumped to her feet, her fingers biting into the flesh of her palms. "Oh, I do!" she shouted, furiously. "Such unfeeling, contemptuous . . ." The rest of her oath was smothered under Phillip's hand. In a moment, she was pinned against him by the strong arm at her waist.

"For the love of God, Arissa, Stephen and I are making this as easy for you as we can, but you've got to cooperate! I'm warning you as best I can." He held her, relentless, until she stopped squirming. "Now I am trying to be a gentleman and will continue to do so, but you must act a lady, not like some outraged child."

She would have screamed, but for the hand that still silenced her. How dare he accuse her of being childish for her concern over the welfare of his own men! Instead, she nodded, as though agreeing to the terms. Warily, he set her free, but not warily enough.

Turning within the circle of the arm he gradually withdrew from her waist, she slapped him soundly. "Don't ever touch me again!" She didn't shout this time, but her whisper was filled with vehemence. "I can't believe I ever felt sorry for you!"

"Felt sorry for me?" Her slap had not phased him, but her unexpected declaration forced him back with a much fiercer blow.

As his astonishment gave way to a darkening countenance, Arissa crossed her arms across her breasts. "Of course!" she averred, ignoring the pinpricks of apprehension on her spine at the reckless course she'd impulsively embarked upon. "You were the poor soul with a game leg, grieving for your lost wife . . . or was that a lie, too? Were you ever married?"

"Damn you!"

Arissa moved farther away at the warning rumble in her companion's voice. "I believed it. I didn't want a man, but you were so pitiful that I . . . that I . . ."

"Bedded me in a merciful attempt to offer me comfort?" It wasn't a question. It was too sardonic and mocking for that. "I hadn't realized how devoted you were to your healing profession."

Stung into action by his biting words, Arissa bolted forward, her hand raised. "How dare you!"

With no sign of any impairment, Phillip quickly seized her wrist and wrestled it behind her, backing her bodily in retreat, until there was no place to go. With the plaster wall cold against her back, and Phillip pressed hot to her breast, Arissa wanted to scream, but somehow, he'd covered her mouth again with those damned smothering fingers. Her nostrils flared with short, rapid breaths, infected half with fear and half with outrage. Despite her efforts to free herself, she inwardly shrank from the singeing anger on Phillip's face.

"By God, if it weren't for my friendship with your brother, I'd take you to that bed right now, my little angel of mercy, and show you who the real liar between us is."

. Arissa's protest roared in her ears, unable to escape Phillips silencing hold.

"You're the one who's tossed the gauntlet, 'Rissa. You're the one who's drawn the line between us."

Again, she shrieked her denial, her unbidden tears of frustration blurring the dark expression clouding her captor's face. She twisted her head, trying to escape the steely fingers, her teeth cutting into her lip in the process. The salty taste of her blood registered somewhere in her mind, but it made such a small impact compared to that of Phillip, pressed full against her, one leg thrust between her own.

She hated him. She hated him for lying to her. She hated him for being one of the heartless soldiers taking over her home, and, more than anything, she hated him for making her face the fact that all her hate could not stop the woman in her from caring about—no—wanting him.

She stopped struggling, for the more she fought, the more aware she became of the powerful male body holding hers hostage. The female within her shivered at its overwhelming domination, remembering more how it pleasured, than how it deceived.

"Please . . . go!"

Her plea was no more than a mumble, yet it was more effective than all her defiance. Phillip relaxed his hold on her wrist, so that her flesh no longer grated against the rough-finished plaster of the wall. Arissa closed her eyes, forcing wet humiliation down her cheeks. To her amazement, the reluctant tears seemed to melt away the strength of the fingers enforcing her silence. Afraid to move, lest she again provoke that heretofore unknown, angry beast in him, Arissa kept her eyes closed and breathed more deeply, unaware of the involuntary trembling of her body.

"Promise me you'll curb your tongue . . . at least around the others."

Arissa nodded, her throat too taut to speak. A strange weakness seeped through her, lightening her head, so that, but for the wall behind her, she might have slipped to the floor when Phillip stepped away. How easy it would be to escape into a swoon, or, at least, so she thought. Never having been one to do so, this was as close to fainting as she'd ever come.

She pressed her hands against the wall and stiffened her knees. *No, I mustn't!* she told herself, sternly. She'd surrendered enough, as it was. Beside, he was still close. Though her eyes were closed, her other senses were alert and very much aware of his nearness.

"Think about what I've said, Arissa."

His voice had softened, but when he touched the side of her face with his hand in a caress, Arissa started, her eyes flying open. Now she could see that the volcanic temper which had consumed his face was gone and, in its place, apprehension, as if he fully expected her to fly into hysterics again.

Hysterics, she reflected. How unlike her! Not only did she no longer know Phillip, but she hardly knew herself. She didn't answer. In spite of herself, she kept staring into his gaze, as if looking for something, anything, to believe in. Her lips quivered, as he gently traced them.

"Meanwhile, have it your way, love, if that makes things easier for you to accept," he finished, renewing his earlier mockery. He drew his hand away, seemingly lost in thought. "There may be an element of truth in what you said, after all, *ma cherie.* Maybe it was the loneliness and grief you say you pitied that led me into this hellish tangle."

Arissa flinched at the sound of her accusation from Phillip's lips. It was so cold, so heartless, so devoid of the love she'd thought was there.

"Regardless, I have my duty to do," he announced, as if reminding himself. "I'll be using the carriole to take Lewis to the Chateau Rueil. I think he'll be more comfortable in it than on the back of a flatbed wagon."

She nodded in agreement.

"And I'll see what can be done about moving Mrs. Rueil and the baby to the city."

"That would be good." Her voice was dry and hollow.

"Truce?" He extended his hand expectantly.

Arissa accepted it, mechanically. "Truce."

Phillip slowly backed away, then turned and walked to

the door. Arissa clung to the wall behind her, until he exited and disappeared into the hall. As the latch fell back into place, her legs seemed to dissolve beneath her and she slid to the floor in a heap of skirts and petticoats. God, what had she said? What had he said? she wondered in confusion. And what, in the midst of this hellish tangle, as he'd phrased it, did a truce entail?

Twelve

Truce. A truce meant keeping a polite distance, no matter how much it hurt or angered. It meant holding a storehouse of emotions inside, which was just as well. It was impossible to sort them clearly, especially when Phillip was in the room. It meant acting out the role of hostess and physician on the enemy's terms, a distasteful charade forced upon her by the damnable war. It was all a game. However, now that she knew the rules, Arissa could play it.

Phillip was holding up his part of the truce, just as well. Indeed, he'd made good his word to see Celeste Rueil and her baby girl safely delivered to her parent's home in the city, immediately. The rest of the time, he was devoted, as were all the men, to preparing for the march to Quebec. To Arissa's surprise, a great number of habitants came forward, offering extra blankets and clothes to outfit the poorly supplied troops. Even more volunteered to help as guides and soldiers. Now that the Americans were in power, their support had become more obvious.

Meanwhile, the sick had been moved to the city hospital, under the care of the sisters of the Church and the Army physicians. Since Stephen was the more gracious of the Chateau Royale's hosts, Arissa managed to obtain permission to leave the inn in his hands in order to go into the city as often as she wanted to offer her help at the hospital. However, because she was a transient care provider, she was not allowed to treat those in isolation with smallpox.

The sisters who tended those with the dread disease remained isolated with them, but there were plenty of other patients filling the wards who required and welcomed Arissa's services. Dysentery, pleurisy, pneumonitis, and influenza abounded among the malnourished, fatigued, and homesick soldiers. Exactly as Phillip had predicted, her private store of medicinal supplies was selling beyond her expectations throughout the city, at the hospital as well as at the apothecaries and private practices.

She almost felt guilty over the increasingly heavy box of coins she kept in the trunk at the foot of her bed to show for her earnings. Yet it seemed she was to profit from the war, whether she wanted to or not. Consequently, Arissa felt obliged to try to do more for those suffering in the wards. She took time to read letters to them and write responses, as well as to talk to the homesick about their families, as she bathed their fevered bodies, soothing both body and mind.

They were farmers and clerks, merchants and aristocrats, all willing to fight and die for this wondrous freedom they touted. Their faith lay in their God and their chosen leaders, not in an official appointed by a king who had never truly understood their country, much less been there. They'd raised their army among themselves, with no help from a monarch, and were determined to throw off England's yoke, or die trying.

There had to be more to this quest for freedom than she understood. Of that, Arissa was convinced. The convictions of these men were too strong to ignore. She'd read the flyers and booklets put out by their fellow patriots—blood stirring literature. Yet, when she looked about her, the same self-sacrificing attitude that they believed would guarantee triumph she saw as their own enemy, as well.

They were willing to march against a well-fortified, well-supplied town with short supplies, half of their troops in poor health, some dying, and put all their faith in God, their leaders, and sheer willpower? It was more than Arissa's practical nature could fathom. Nonetheless, she couldn't help but admire their spirit and determination, if she could not see the plausibility of their cause.

Which was why she'd decided to join her fellow Canadians in helping the Americans, for humanitarian reasons, if for no other. Her father's clothes were still packed in a trunk in the attic, as were the clothes Martin had left behind, upon joining the military. Even if Martin's still fit him, they would be outlandishly out of style, by the time he thought to ask for them—if he ever did—which absolved her of any guilt on that part.

With a finger lamp in hand, Arissa started up the attic stairwell, after an upsetting day at the hospital. The sisters told her that Lieutenant Lewis had passed away the night before. They'd given her his few belongings—his pistol and kit, canteen, and haversack—to return to his commanding officer. Another soldier would be better outfitted, she supposed, as the result. That was how desperate this ragtag army was.

A scraping noise near the top of the steps washed her mind of all thought and put her senses on the alert. Surely it could not be a snake, this time of the year! Even as she shuddered at the idea, there was another sound, something of a gasp, decidedly human.

Now why would anyone be in her attic? "Hello? Who is there?"

Gooseflesh rose on her arm at the answering silence.

"You can either show yourself, or I will call for one of the officers," she challenged, boldly, glad that she'd heard the voices of some of the colonel's staff down the hall, when she'd come up the stairs.

Indecision pervaded the silence. Then slowly one of the men she'd seen in the taproom showed his face. "It's me, mam'selle, and my buddy, here. We wuz just lookin' for a quiet place to nap, where Sergeant Coles won't find us, and this here big chimney's made it right comfortable. We worked in the cold yesterday, taking the roof off that big house till our feet n' hands was nearly froze."

"Roof off a big house?" she queried, curiously.

"The sick house. It bein' empty now, and that roof bein' lead . . . well, we kin use all the lead we kin git, you understand."

Arissa blanched. *Sacre bleu,* they'd removed the roof from Adrien's mansion! How terrible! "But everything will be ruined!"

"The lady's father sent some men for their belongins. Whatever is left I guess'll burn."

"Burn!" Arissa thought that was Indian warfare, not that of civilized men!

"Well, the colonel wants to show what happens to Loyalists who don't know their place."

Much as Adrien disgusted her at times, Arissa felt miserable for him and his family. His grandfather had built the estate. It was his heritage. She mentally shook herself. If she dwelled overmuch on all the horrible news, she would be in tears. How she hated this war, and this was only beginning!

"Well, *messieurs,* since you are here, perhaps you might help me take a couple of trunks downstairs. They contain men's clothing that might be of use to some of your troops."

"Glad to oblige, mam!"

Both men stood stooped under the slanted rough-beamed roof, as she joined them and pointed at two trunks jammed against the eave. "Now watch your heads," she cautioned, as the two men crouched down to fetch them.

When the stored clothes had been dragged out to a place where all could stand up, Arissa tried the catch on the first trunk, hoping she hadn't locked it. If so, she'd have to hunt for the key. To her dismay it was stiff and wouldn't give, when she pulled it.

"Here, mam'selle, let me help."

One of the men pulled out a long hunting knife and worked its tip behind the hasp. With a pop, it came open.

"Guess the dampness rusted it a bit. T'warn't locked at all," he declared, proudly. He wiped the blade, out of habit, on his leg and returned it to its sheath.

It wasn't the knife, however, that attracted her attention. It was his finger. It was bleeding profusely.

"My goodness, you have cut yourself! Let me have a look at that."

The man drew his hand back, defensively. "Naw, I just banged the nail a little." At that moment, his foot struck something and sent it skittering across the floor. Arissa picked it up and started to examine it, when the man reached for it.

"That ain't none of your concern, mam'selle." He snatched it from her and dropped it into a knapsack, which was slung over his shoulder.

Instinct made her press the man. The container was the sort used in the medical profession. "That vial, what was in it?"

"Ain't none o' your business, no disrespect meant, mam'selle."

"Ah, then it must be the colonel's business, *non?*" Arissa turned and started down the steps, when her gamble paid off.

"No, wait!"

"Jay, she's a doctor, she'd understand."

Arissa waited at the bottom of the steps, until the two

came to an agreement and motioned her back up. The one called Jay put the vial in her hand. She held up the lamp and studied it with an increasing alarm. *"Mon Dieu, is this what I think it is?"*

"It's the drainin's from a poc blister," Jay confirmed, grimly. "Hell, mam'selle, we's got to protect ourselfs. Me n' Oren don't wanna ketch smallpox and die. If old Haskill won't let the docs' inoculate us, then, by damned, we'll do it ourselves. Ole Seth Warner's done told his boys it's okay by him. Better to be sick a few days then to die."

"But you don't know what you're doing! You could inject too much and die anyway." Arissa held out her hand. "Let me see that fingernail. That is where you put the vaccine, *non?*"

Sheepishly, the burly frontiersman held out his bleeding hand. "I ain't put it in yet. You come up n' stopped us. Word is, it don't show under the fingernail, though Warner told his boys to take it in the thigh."

"Where did you get this serum?"

"Stole it from the doc's bags when we moved the sick. Took another, in case we lost it or . . . or whatever," Oren piped up, producing another vial.

"When was that?"

"Today, when we took some New England boys over."

Arissa stared at the clear variola. If it came from a physician's bag, then its integrity could not be questioned. A man of medicine would know to draw it from a healthy pustule, rather than from a contaminated one. He would use a clean quill. She glanced at the two expectant faces and knew she had only one choice that she could live with.

"You two take the trunks downstairs and then meet me back here. I'll fetch what I need and do the inoculation myself. You'll need a mercurial purgative, as well."

"God bless ye, mam'selle. You're as saintly as ye are fair to look at."

It took the riflemen from New York state more time to move the trunks than it did Arissa to fetch her bag from her room and mix the purgative elixir in the supply closet. With Colonel Haskill in the parlor, she didn't dare take it from her father's medicine cabinet, lest he question her. When the two returned to the attic, she was ready for them, a small quantity of the serum in a fresh quill.

Since Jay's finger was still open and bleeding, she placed a small drop in the wound. Oren, however, preferred the thigh for his puncture and, because Arissa had made the cut, suffered less bleeding than his companion. She wrapped a length of gauze around his leg, keeping her eyes averted from the nakedness exposed by his dropped trousers, even though she was accustomed to it, of late, at the hospital.

"It need's be just a little more than a scratch, and no more serum than a drop. In three days, the pustules will break out and your sickness will get worse. Blisters, fever, headaches, swelling . . . the purgative should help this distress some. Also drink warm beer . . . but by then, you will be under the good care of the sisters." She carefully closed the vial when she was through. "You have enough here to do all your men with that other bottle."

"You'd do it for 'em?"

Arissa hesitated, thrown off guard. She hadn't meant that. "I cannot!"

"You're a doctor, ain't ya? Ain't ya promised to save lives?"

"I am not a licensed physician. My practice is limited to what I learned under my father's tutelage."

"Well they's a lotta scared fellas down there would rest a lot easier, knowin' they was gonna git a lick of the pox, rather than a bite. They got homes and families they want to go back to. Even if ye're just practicin', ye got some obligation."

"They will be sick for about two weeks, some maybe less," she answered, her reluctance faltering.

"But they won't be dead."

"*Non*, they won't be dead." Heaven help her, how could she turn her back on those who wanted to be inoculated, those who asked for nothing more than life, rather than the risk of death? Tiredly, she nodded her head. "All right, I will do it, but we must be discreet. I will inoculate those of you who wish it, until the serum runs out."

Oren gave her an all but toothless grin. "Ye're a real angel of mercy, mam'selle."

"A real angel," Jay chimed in.

"Well, you had best be getting back to whatever it was you are supposed to be doing and . . . oh!" Arissa took up the small bottle of purgative. "Take this for as long as you need it, and eat lightly."

Oren chuckled. "We're mighty used to that."

Arissa waited until they were gone, before coming down herself and buttoning the attic door behind her. It wasn't a matter of making the right choice. It was the only choice. She knew that. These men deserved to be protected, from the dread disease. If the general had to postpone his plans a few weeks for them to recover, there was time. Quebec had a long winter, and the Governor and his troops were not going anywhere.

"What are you up to, *ma cherie*?"

Arissa nearly dropped her medical bag at the sight of her brother standing before her bedroom door. "I had papa's and Martin's clothes brought down from the attic. They are doing no one any good up there."

"And you needed your bag for that?"

Arissa laughed, hopefully in a convincing manner. "I haven't been to my room yet to dispose of it. Were you looking for me?"

"As a matter of fact, I was. Colonel Haskill was thinking of having a party to show our appreciation for all the help coming in from our Canadian allies. Naturally, where better to have it, but here at the Chateau Royale?"

Arissa went inside her room, leaving Stephen to follow her. "Does he have the money to pay for such an affair?"

"Let me take care of that. I've rather enjoyed running things here, of late, although, I admit, I will be glad when General Montgomery gives the word to march."

"You are going with them?" But of course he was, she answered herself, before Stephen echoed her thoughts.

"But of course, *ma cherie*. This is what I have been waiting for. Only one thing more would make me happier."

"And what is that, Stephen?" She could well imagine. Knowing Stephen, he wanted to be at the lead of the attack.

"That you and Phillip will stop playing this silly game of detached civility and marry. He is perfect for you!" Stephen added in a rush, cutting off Arissa's exclamation of disdain. "You were in love with him, can you deny that?"

"Stephen," Arissa said, dropping on the edge of her bed. "I am tired. I have had a distressing day. Lieutenant Lewis died."

Her brother made a grimace. "I am sorry to hear that."

"Would you tell Jeanne to send up some tea and toast? I shall eat that and go to bed."

"I will be delighted to, *ma cherie,* but first, answer my question. Did you love Phillip Monroe on the morning I came home to find him sneaking out of your room."

Stephen could be so persistent, when he chose to be, Arissa thought, in annoyance. There was only one way to get rid of him.

"All right, Stephen, I loved the man he pretended to be. I loved a charade, a lie! Now that I know what he is, I detest him!"

Stephen propped his foot up on the trunk at the end of the bed and leaned forward in challenge. "How do you know he is not the same man. Clothes do not make the man. I have heard you say that many times about Adrien Rueil."

"Stephen, leave us alone!" Arissa punched a pillow and stacked it atop a second. "We both agreed we were attracted to each other for the wrong reasons. Just stay out of this." As she lay back, she placed her hands on her head, squeezing gently to ease the pounding that had been threatening all day.

"Dieu, are you sick, 'Rissa?" He rushed around to her bedside, all concern. *"Ma cherie,* I would not upset you for all the world. I only want you to be happy."

He had such a tender heart, Arissa thought. Of her two brothers, Stephen was decidedly the more sensitive. She took his hand and squeezed it with affection. "I will be happy, Stephen, when all the troops are gone and our lives return to normal. For now, I would be happy to have a light repast and sleep."

"You spend too much time at the hospital. Perhaps you should not go everyday."

"Those poor souls need me, if not for my medical skills, for someone to listen to them. If I had my way, I would quarantine the entire army for the winter and let them recover." She smiled. "I suppose I would make a poor general, *non?"*

"But you would make a wonderful doctor! It is a shame you did not pursue your studies."

"I would have had to be a boy, too, Stephen. But that does not worry me. I am content to be as I am. Now please, plague me no more about Phillip Monroe. We are both content now. Leave us that way." She formed her lips into a pout, which had won many battles between her and her older siblings. "Now let me rest, *s'il vous plaît.* I will be fine in the morning. Then I will help you plan your party."

* * *

Accustomed to planning for numerous guests on various budgets, the prospect of selecting a menu and making the arrangements for the supplies posed little problem for Arissa. She was able to do that and continue with her work at the hospital afterward. What was more difficult was making herself available for the men who had heard that she was willing to discreetly inoculate them with the smallpox vaccine.

Those who were stationed at the Chateau Royale were easy. There was always an excuse to slip in here or there, or to ask one of them to help her bring up supplies from the taproom. Those from other units, however, were more difficult to meet, although fewer in number. Hence, she started making a short shopping stop every other day on St. Peter, after the bells of Parish Church struck three. Her calèche driver got to the point where he anticipated her wanting to stop by the apothecary's and dressmaker's shops after her afternoon at the Nunnery, and accommodated her without question. After all, she always returned with a small package, and there were guards on the street corner with whom to chat, while she went about her errands.

Within a short time, her discreet work began to tell. The isolation wards of the hospital were becoming fuller. However, the number of recoveries from the dread disease seemed to be increasing. Among themselves, the sisters suspected the men were inoculating themselves, for the newer of the cases did not seem as severe as those they'd first tended.

Of greater concern to Arissa, however, as she left the hospital and cut through the cultivated gardens—where evergreen lent the only color against the snow-bedecked hedges and trees—were the unfamiliar names that appeared on the list kept in the main entrance of those who had not fared so well. The black-edged list of the dead, despite her efforts, was still alarming. Surely the general and his officers could wait a few weeks for their troops to recover from a mass inoculation! She simply did not understand.

"Mademoiselle, over here!"

Arissa was startled, not by the hail, but at the identity of the man who waved at her from across the street, where the calèche was waiting. What ever was Phillip Monroe doing picking her up.

Her puzzlement must have shown in her expression, for the moment she reached the vehicle, her companion explained.

"I had to go to General Montgomery's quarters at the Chateau de Ramezay to pick up the orders for my trip and told the corporal there was no sense in both of us going back into the city."

Phillip helped her up into the calèche and then climbed up beside her. She gave him as much room on the narrow leather seat as possible, fearing that even now, when he touched her, there was a part of her that would remember and react. Until now, their respective duties had enabled them to keep an easy distance. She knew Phillip's rank was captain, but his involvement with General Montgomery and the higher ranking officers led her to think his value was more than that usually afforded that rank.

"What trip are you taking?" It was a polite question, and one that would satisfy her curiosity as well.

"I'm going to meet Arnold's envoy at *Trois Rivières*. I think we'll be moving out soon." He waved amiably at one of the lads playing target practice with snowballs, as one of the wet missiles struck the hub of the two-wheeled vehicle. "That should make you happy."

Arissa cut her gaze sideways at the edge in her companion's voice.

"There will certainly be less work for the staff. How long will you be gone on this trip?" she asked, refusing to take the bait he'd given her. She was getting rather good at this game, for someone who had never played before.

"Overnight. I'm leaving first thing in the morning."

"You do not want to miss a party, eh?"

"I haven't danced with a pretty girl in a long time."

Her heart thudded against her chest. No, she wouldn't look at him. "Well, there are many pretty girls in these parts." She paused. "Your leg, it doesn't keep you from doing that, then?"

He was looking at her. She knew it, and yet Arissa found herself glancing in his direction. The moment their gazes touched, she realized her mistake. "As a doctor, I am curious."

He winked at her. "I'll show you at the party, mademoiselle."

Arissa thinned her lips. That was not fair. That went beyond being civil. "If I attend, monsieur."

They passed the little row of shops where she'd planned to stop, for word had reached her that two men from the New England troops were eager to be inoculated. They, however, would have to wait. The corporal was easy to fool, but Phillip had a way of seeing through her. It wasn't worth the risk.

Did their truce include dancing? Arissa pondered later, as she bathed and changed into a dark green, pleated caraco with a linen apron of printed flowers in vibrant autumn hues. After surviving the carriage ride with Phillip less than a hand's breadth away, she thought she was quite up to challenge. She'd managed small talk rather well, for someone not given to it.

The music had started already when Arissa descended the main staircase, the habitants' passion for it overriding the protocol of awaiting the arrival of General Montgomery and his staff. She'd left a quill and what little was left of the vaccine in the stairwell of the attic, in case the two soldiers from New England chose to attend the festivities. Upon entering the room, she saw the spread Chiah and the staff had put out for the informal affair.

There were cheeses and breads, meat pasties and small cakes, and a number of other assorted fingerfoods which did not require the eating utensils locked in their respective chests in the kitchen below. So far, her personal inventory at the end of each week had spoken well of her staffs diligence. Two large bowls of punch graced either end of the three tables that had been put together as one. One of the punches was surrounded by crystal decanters, indicating the spirits included in its recipe. The other was a lighter, fruitier selection with a cider base for the ladies and the fainter of heart.

"Get out of here!" Gaspar shouted, when she started into the small enclosure behind the bar. "I will not have such a pretty distraction beside me, while I am trying to serve our customers!"

Arissa backed out, laughing away the typical flamboyance of the barkeeper's compliment. "If you get too busy, at least send for one of the girls."

"Gaspar, he is almost like new. Look!" Leaving his crutch resting against the corner kegs, where it always seemed to be when Arissa saw it, Gaspar skipped the length of the small enclosure to her, grabbed her hands, and danced around her in a circle. "See!" he declared proudly. "It is because I have the best doctor in the world."

"And a belly full of flip, I'd wager," Arissa countered, good-naturedly.

The fact was, Gaspar was much improved. He'd started getting better the day Phillip Monroe carried him into the taproom, where he could socialize with his friends and the travelers. It hadn't crossed Arissa's mind to do such a thing. She had thought complete quiet and rest in his cabin was best.

Still lingering near the bar, she scanned the crowd of habitants, interspersed with blue uniforms and the fringed buckskinned garb or homespun of some of the other soldiers. They were mingling, as though they'd been friends for years. Why, the blushes on the farm girls' faces were enough to light up the room, without that of the chandeliers burning from the rafters overhead.

Arissa's wandering gaze came to halt upon recognizing Linette and André Louvigny. Standing next to them was Phillip Monroe, all soldier in appearance, but for the little bundle he held in his arms. He was laughing at something one of the parents said, but his eyes were solely for the infant. The warmth in them was enough to heat the room, she mused, somewhat envious, as he gently poked at the baby with his finger and made a ridiculous face.

She should never have accused him of not being married, she thought, with an unanticipated pang of guilt. She'd seen the medallion with his and his wife's names on it, as well as their wedding date. And now she was seeing again that special glow the Louvigny's baby boy brought out in him, surely that of a father who adored his own son and was reminded of him.

"Bonjour, *ma cherie.*"

When Arissa turned to see who had claimed her hand, she met her brother's mischievous gaze. He raised it to his lips and brushed her knuckles gently.

"My, but you are looking especially beautiful tonight. Too beautiful to hide back here. Those plain gray dresses you wear to the hospital, they make you look drab, like an old woman."

Stephen had a way with words, Arissa thought wryly, enough to earn a healthy slap for such compliments from anyone but his sister. His talent, however, lay in being able to talk his way out of a faux pas, so that one hardly noticed. And the dear had checked with her each night to inquire of her health and fret over her long days at the hospital.

"Come with your older brother and dance, before the General arrives and I must be the gracious host to him." He linked his arm in her own. "Beside, I must tell you what wonderful choices you made for the party."

"Better you host the monster than I, *mon cher,*" Arissa shot back, with a stiff laugh. Somehow, she didn't think she possessed Stephen's charm and quick wit, at least in sufficient quantity to hide her disdain for the army's ir-regular health regulations.

The dance was a simple country one formed with two lines done in a repetitive fashion to fiddle music. Arissa danced with friends and neighbors, as well as with some of the familiar soldiers she'd come to recognize by face, if not by name. However, when she chasséd down the outside of the line and came about to meet her next partner, none other than Phillip Monroe awaited.

She'd known he would ask her—he'd said as much. If she were honest with herself, perhaps that was why she'd taken such pains to dress and put her hair up in golden ringlets, adorned with green laced bows to match her dress. She'd even pinched her cheeks, until she feared they'd be blue rather than pink and added an extra dash of rose water to her bath.

But then, she always took pride in her appearance when she attended a social affair. That bit of vanity was ingrained by her mother, she rationalized, as Phillip took her hand and bowed gallantly. Then the two of them were chasséing down the center of the line to its end.

"My son's namesake is here. It's his first party," her partner told her, stepping forward and swinging her around in time to the music. "I do have one, you know . . . a son."

Arissa nodded, her pasted smiled fading. "I know. I'm sorry about . . ."

At that moment, her neighboring dancer took his turn to swing her, cutting her off before she could complete her apology.

"I'm sorry about some of the things I said. I was upset," she managed, when they were reunited.

"You seem to be warming to us a bit more, like your friends and neighbors." Phillip took his turn with his lady neighbor to his left and then stepped back to Arissa.

"The men more than their officers, I think. Present company excluded, of course," she added, hastily, not wishing to ruin the moment with a stupid faux pas.

"They adore you . . . the men, of course."

At that moment, the ladies formed a circle, sweeping Arissa away from the knee-weakening look in Phillip's eyes. She caught her breath and realized it was for the best. A moment longer, under that whiskey-eyed spell of his and . . . Well, she wasn't sure just what she'd do. When Phillip switched from detached to charming, it played havoc with all her resolve and defenses.

The circle came to a stop, and she was about to curtsy to her new partner, when the man in her thoughts drew her firmly from the line and inserted a giggling farm girl in her place for her startled partner.

"What are you doing?"

"I need to tell you something."

His tone was so conspiratorial that Arissa followed, as he stepped into the hallway and drew her under the shadow of the wide main stairwell, where a long wooden bench stood braced against the wall. As Phillip sat, he pulled her down beside him. Arissa felt like fleeing in panic, yet she sat, poised as proper, as her mother had taught her. Did he know? Could he know how vulnerable she was at that moment? Had he sensed it in the other room and, like a seasoned hunter, seized at his prey when the opportunity presented itself?

"What is it, Phillip?" Arissa uttered a silent oath for having used his familiar name.

"You're beautiful, Arissa Conway."

The compliment set Arissa back. "Well I . . . that is . . . that's very kind of you, monsieur," she managed, at last.

"Arissa . . ." Phillip seized both her hands and pressed them to his lips.

"Phillip, what are you doing?"

"Making a damned fool of myself," he declared, irritably. "Damn it, Arissa, I wish I could just throw you over a horse and take you away from all this."

"I would prefer a calèche."

"Damnation, woman, I'm serious."

She knew Phillip Monroe in his quiet, humorous manner. She knew him a bit, when he was at the edge of his patience, and yet remained cool and in charge of a situation, as he'd been the day Adrien Rueil tried to goad him into a duel. Here, however, he was clearly at the edge of his patience and not the least in control.

"I do not think that this lies within the boundaries of our truce, monsieur," she said, astonished at the calm in her own voice.

"I think it's time we start being honest with each other."

Arissa chuckled, being far from amused. "*Mon cher*, I am not convinced that you are capable of that, judging by your past performance." Yes, she congratulated herself. She was playing the game marvelously. For once, it was he that was thrown off guard, groping for words.

"Your problem is, you can't separate truth from reality."

Flinching inwardly at the poorly repressed anger in his accusation, Arissa agreed succinctly. "That is correct, monsieur. Your mastery of deceit and cunning made it impossible. Otherwise, nothing . . ." She grimaced, as she faltered and quickly regrouped. "Nothing would have

ever happened between us. That is that, *non?*" She lifted
her chin in challenge, just in time to see the flash that
severed his last shred of reserve. It burst golden in the
amber haze of his eyes, almost hypnotizing in their ferocity, so that when he seized her shoulders, crushing the
crisply ironed ruffles resting on them, and dragged her
to him, she was taken unawares. As her lips parted in
protest, he claimed them, hard enough to silence them,
yet tender enough to kindle a series of like responses
throughout her body.

There were no explosions of wild passion, which drove
her to return his sensual assault. They might have frightened her, shocked her into realizing how vulnerable she
was. Instead, his assault was coaxing, cajoling, teasing,
promising heady sweetness and security within the strong
confines of the arms now encompassing her. Not hot
enough to make her burn with passion, it was just warm
enough to soften her resistance, so that she melted gently
against him. Her body thrilled at the contact, dismissing
any objection her dazed mind could muster.

All she could feel was his gentleness, his strength. All
she could hear was the warm rush of their breath, mingled in soft moans of surrender. And something else . . .
something that did not belong in this intimate rhapsody.

"*Atten . . . tion!*"

Phillip pulled away so hastily that Arissa nearly tumbled forward. Where soft sighs still rang in her ears, the
hiss of a fierce oath took over. Leaving her seated on
the bench, Phillip leapt to his feet, straightening out
the jacket that had somehow come off his shoulder during their brief interlude. Finding her own strength
again, Arissa started to rise too, surprised at the amount
of rearranging of her own clothing that was necessary,
but suddenly, Phillip eased her back down with a firm
hand.

"That, *ma cherie,* was the truth," he whispered hoarsely,

his eyes fixed not on her, but on the front hall, where a rush of cold air announced the arrival of new guests. "For now, duty calls. The General has arrived."

Thirteen

General Richard Montgomery was a genteel man in appearance, tall and slender, with a balding spot on the top of his head that revealed itself when he bowed and touched Arissa's hand to his lips in greeting. Somehow she'd been expecting a fancified version of the hoodlum, Ethan Allen, who, according to rumor spread by those who'd seen him marched through the streets of Montreal after his capture, had the backwoods colonials growing in stature and crudity by the day. Montgomery possessed an easy, affable condescension toward officers and men alike, yet it was clear that they not only respected him, but held him in high regard. He was, as Phillip and Stephen had told her previously, a gentleman and a soldier.

As a humanitarian, Arissa had her doubts, but kept them to herself under the warning threat lurking in Phillip's eyes. As hostess, she afforded the general one dance, accepted his praise for her hospitality and her brother's immense aid to the cause, and then retreated to the kitchen, lest the temptation to speak her mind grow too great to bear. Besides, the general and his officers were engaged in conversation centered on the impending march to Quebec City, rather than focusing on the lively entertainment their men enjoyed. The more Arissa heard of that subject, the more absurd it seemed, to her way of thinking.

Since the food had been set up in a buffet style, it freed many of the girls to dance, so that most of the staff left in the kitchen were married and enjoying the pink flushes and quick snatches of excitement their younger coworkers conveyed, when a platter needed replacing.

"Oh, how I would love for Private Meers to toss me over his horse and carry me away, like Gaspar's Acadian friend did to his woman! It would be so romantic!" Celia sighed, waiting for her empty tray of meat pasties to be refilled by those hot from the oven.

"If he carried you anywhere, it seems it would be to Quebec City," Arissa remarked, dryly.

She, too, was fond of Gaspar's romantic story of his Acadian friend and his captive bride. War had cost the young trapper his family in the ghastly British exile of the Acadian peoples, and, in desperation, he'd kidnaped the daughter of an influential New York merchant in hopes of forcing the man to use his power to find the lost mother and sisters. However, love knew no political bounds and, despite his resolve to return the miss to her father and her resolve to hate him, they fell in love. When it came time for her to go home, she would not leave him. They had learned that there was merit and blame on both sides of the terrible war.

Rumor had it that he and his wife were drowned, while being kidnaped by an escaping British spy, who'd come to rescue the lovely Tamson Stewart. Gaspar, however, told a different ending to the story. Alain Beaujeu not only found his mother and sisters living happily in the colonies, but took his captive bride home and settled there with her. He had lost the Beaujeu family land that his late father had worked hard for. He'd lost his Acadian heritage, as well as the inheritance of a noble title and estate in France, all for love.

Some English family now owned the little Acadian farm from which Alain's father had eked out a living. A cousin and his family lived in splendor in France's Chateau de la Galisonne. As for Alain Beaujeu, he owned a grand estate on the Hudson near Albany, where he raised a family of his own with his bride, Tamson, and kept close contact with his mother and sisters, the latter having married happily and settled throughout the colonies. Each had given up their past life, snatched from them by the war, and found love in a new land.

The story haunted Arissa that night, for it had been her favorite of all Gaspar's tales. Love winning triumphant over war and politics sounded so heavenly in the story. But what she faced made it sound more like a fairytale—a wild fantasy not likely to happen in her life. She warmly remembered Phillip's stolen kiss. Its tender seduction came alive, making her toss and turn in her bed, almost as much as his passion-infected words. *That, ma cherie, was the truth.*

But then, duty called and Phillip was gone. He was all soldier again, standing at General Montgomery's side and watching her, as if he dared her to so much as sneeze in front of his precious superior. Alain Beaujeu abandoned his duty, his office, and his title for love. Even if Phillip meant what he'd said, she could not see him doing such a thing. Beside, he'd mentioned nothing of love. He'd said their passion was the truth and, God help her, she could not deny that.

Such was the quandary that dominated her waking hours, interspersed with bits of sleep until morning. She'd thought she heard Phillip rise, long before the rest of the house stirred, and when she rushed to the window to look, she saw a man mount Phillip's sorrel and ride off toward the north, a leather satchel attached to his saddle. He would be gone three days. With a frustrating sense of melancholy, Arissa went back to bed and this time fell soundly asleep.

Breakfast was being served in the taproom, by the time she rose and dressed the following morning. In readiness to drive into Montreal to the hospital, she wore one of her two plain gray work dresses and a crisp white apron. But for her simple hairstyle—her tresses bound by a white ribbon at her neck, rather than under the religious head-dress worn by the sisters—and the fact that her dress was fitted, while theirs were loose robes, she could easily be mistaken for one of them. Regardless, the color resembled her mood—gray.

As she opened her door to go downstairs, she was startled to see one of the officers about to knock on it. *"Mon Dieu,* but you gave me a start, monsieur!" she chided, breathlessly. "What is it? Is something wrong?"

"The colonel wishes you to come to his office, mademoiselle. He seeks your medical opinion."

"I think he liked our private stock of brandy overmuch," Stephen Conway put in, stepping out of the room across from the hall. "At least he seemed to be enjoying a bottle to himself after the General left." He put his arm about Arissa's shoulders. "Come, let's see what beast the brandy has made of him."

Arissa halted at the steps. "Wait. I forgot my bag."

She hurried back to her room to fetch it and then joined the men at the main stairwell. No doubt the man had a head the size of a large pumpkin and a stomach that felt as if it were shriveling to the size of a pea. From what she'd seen of him, she wondered if he knew the meaning of the word "moderation."

When they entered the parlor, the colonel's bed had been made up and was stored behind the paneled doors beside the hearth. The man himself was standing—pacing actually—before two riflemen, while four guards stood to the side at attention. Upon seeing Arissa enter the room, Haskill stopped in mid-stride and motioned her forward.

"Mademoiselle Conway, I fear I need your medical advice, not for myself," he stipulated, "though I could use a headache powder, but for these men. They say they are sick. That they've run a fever for two days. Do you know what I say?"

Arissa could imagine, but she waited for him to go on.

"I say hogwash! Now damnation, something is amiss. The General informed me last night that I had the highest rate of smallpox among my men, and I want to get to the bottom of this."

"It is hard to say how many men were infected by Lieutenant Lewis, before he was removed to isolation, monsieur." Arissa tried not to look at the men she recognized from having inoculated them a few days earlier. They were in the initial stages of a mild case of the disease.

"I don't believe it's taken this long! No, something is amiss here. Besides, these shirkers were at the party last night. They weren't too sick for that."

"We was thirsty, mam'selle. We drank warm beer all night."

Exactly as she'd advised them, she thought. Instead of answering, Arissa walked up to the men and felt their foreheads. They were hot with fever.

"Colonel, I believe that with the epidemic spreading, it is in the best interest of these men to have them sent into the city to the hospital with me."

"The hell I will. Strip!"

Arissa wheeled about with a gasp, her incredulous "What?" chiming in with that of her brother.

Haskill almost smiled. "Not you, mademoiselle. The men."

"Colonel, I hardly think this is fitting for my sister . . ."

"She's a doctor, isn't she?" Haskill challenged Stephen.

"You've seen many a naked man in your work, haven't you, doctor."

"Of late, I have," Arissa admitted, reluctantly. "I am certified as a midwife, first," she reminded him.

The colonel looked at the frozen men. "You heard me. I said strip. You're going to be examined here in front of me, and if I don't see a poc mark, your reporting for duty."

Arissa tried to ignore the plaintive looks the two men directed her way. There would be at least one poc mark, they all knew—one on the thigh.

"Just your trousers, gentlemen."

Arissa caught her breath. Did the colonel suspect? Had someone told him? "The marks usually break out on the face, neck, and chest first, monsieur."

"Then we'll look there next, if we don't find anything here." Haskill moved to the seat behind her father's desk. A knowing smirk had settled on his lips, as he watched the men drop their trousers about their ankles.

"Doctor . . . er, mademoiselle?" he prompted, motioning for Arissa to examine the men.

Bracing herself, she knelt down and looked at the leg of the first man. There, for all to see—even the colonel from his distance at the desk—was the festering inoculation. She opened her bag and reached in it for some gauze and carbolic acid.

"It is the smallpox, colonel. I hope you and your men have been inoculated."

"Those in this room have."

"How fortunate for you." She poured a bit of the acid on the gauze and wiped the oozing wound. "Have you broken out on your chest yet?"

"A couple places, mam," the soldier answered.

"Then I should wipe them, too. Afterward, pack your things. You must go to the Nunnery with me, until this passes."

Haskill rose from the desk and stalked around it, his eyes glittering, as if he took some perverse delight in the discovery. "Oh, they'll go, all right, but not till I'm finished with them. You can put your medicine bag away till then, Mademoiselle Conway. They'll need you more later."

As Arissa turned her quizzical gaze on the colonel, the man pointed an accusing finger at the men. "Let it go on report that these men have inoculated themselves against the specific request of command, just like some of Warner's undisciplined bunch. This, however, is a disciplined unit. Take them outside and have them flogged before the others, as an example of what will happen to anyone else who happens to contract the disease. I won't have my men inoculating themselves to get out of duty."

Arissa jumped to her feet. "Get out of duty! Colonel, they are saving their lives!"

"I don't expect you to understand, mademoiselle."

Her anger rising to a higher degree, Arissa stomped forward, squaring off before the tall officer.

" 'Rissa, *non!*" Stephen protested, rushing forward to take her arm. "This does not concern you! It's an army matter."

Pulling away from Stephen's grasp, she held her ground. "You will not flog these men for something they did not do!"

"Mademoiselle, the proof is there before us."

"They did not inoculate themselves. I did it!" she declared, hotly. "And I will continue to do so, since their own officer does not seem to care if they live or die! If someone must be flogged, then let it be me!"

"Mon Dieu," Stephen swore at her side, in surprise and dismay. "I can not believe you are saying this!"

She put defiant hands on her hips. "I did it . . . to at least twenty-five men. They are going to live because of it, and I am not sorry. I did my duty as a physician dedicated to life, nothing more, nothing less."

"Of all the impudence!" Colonel Haskill exploded at her side. "You've done this right here under my nose, when you knew better!"

"I did it under your nose, *because* I knew better!" Arissa shot back.

"Guards, take her under custody!"

"What?" Stephen protested, barely over the first shock.

"Sir, I consider your sister no better than a spy. She had willfully undermined the strength of our army, impairing our preparations to march to Quebec City."

"But this is an outrage." Stephen turned to Arissa. " 'Rissa, tell them you are sorry, that you didn't know what you were doing."

"But I did, Stephen. And if they intend to victimize a woman for doing what is right and moral in God's eyes, then let them!" She turned to the colonel and lifted her head haughtily. "If you wish to set an example of American justice, sir, then do so! Let my people see what you are really like! Liberators," she scoffed. "I'd spit on you, were I not a lady!"

"Guards, seize her!" Haskill shouted, his face now a mottled purple hue. "Him too, if he gives you trouble!"

Arissa grabbed Stephen, as he stepped between her and the guards. *"Non, mon cher, s'il vous plaît!* Your arrest will serve no one any good!"

Stephen struggled momentarily with impulse, letting her words sink in. *"Bien, ma petite.* But I will fight this in every way I can. If I can find no satisfaction, then surely Phillip will know what to do."

Phillip! Heaven only knew what he would do. He had warned her, she thought, offering no resistance, as the guards bound her hands before her. He'd even intimated that she might be locked up somewhere as a dissident. She forced a smile, dismissing the mumbled apologies of the guards who took her in tow. Well, it appeared that Phillip had at least told the truth on that account.

* * *

Stephen visited Arissa at the city tavern, which had been converted into a prison by General Wooster, for citizens who persisted in agitating the new American order. The dungeon in the fort was already filled with arrested officers of the militia and afforded no more room, especially for female prisoners. Hers was a small room with a straw pallet for a bed and a small table for dining with a bench set in the dormer, the shutters of which had been nailed closed. There was no stove or hearth, so, to keep warm, she had to rely on the extra blankets Stephen brought her and the updraft from the room below, which boasted a large hearth in constant use.

Her brother had also brought her some books and candles for the lamp, to help her pass the time until Phillip Monroe returned from Trois Rivières. Stephen's attempts to see General Montgomery had been thwarted on a lower level by Wooster, who was to remain in command of Montreal when Montgomery moved on with the troops. The word that drifted up through the floorboards in regard to the fate of those incarcerated there was that Wooster intended to send them onto Halifax, where they could stir up no more trouble.

Although Stephen begged Arissa to recant her flagrant defiance of the order forbidding inoculation and plead that she did not know of any such issue, Arissa remained firm in her stand. She had known she was violating the command and was proud that she had put life ahead of military gain. By the third day of her incarceration, her brother was at his wit's end in dealing with her and had stormed out of the room in a fit of anger and frustration.

It was the following morning when Stephen returned, this time accompanied by Phillip Monroe. Although her dress was drab and wrinkled from having slept in it and her night shift in order to keep warm during the long evenings, her hair was brushed to a vibrant sheen and her face scrubbed pink, making her quite as presentable as possible. They might have put her in prison, but they had not stripped her of her pride.

"*Bonjour, Capitaine.* I take it your journey was a pleasant one?" She glanced about the room. "I would offer you both a seat, but as you can see, the furnishings are somewhat lacking."

"I will wait for you downstairs," Stephen offered, breaking the awkward silence that followed. He leaned forward and bussed Arissa on the cheek, before exiting the room. He was decidedly nervous about something.

"What is wrong with Stephen? Have I been sentenced to hang?"

Phillip tossed his cloak across the table. "You're bloody damned lucky you haven't been! I've been pleading your case to General Wooster all morning. You're being considered a spy for your covert little practice!"

Arissa took the bench, since her guest had refused it. "A spy!" she mimicked. "What a horrible thing to be, don't you think?"

"Damn it, Arissa, this is serious!"

"So was I." If the fury on his face and his clenched fists were any measure, she was only one word away from being strangled. Hence, she changed her tact. "So what is to be my fate? Am I being sent to Halifax as a dissident?"

"No."

Phillip's short answer brought her head up abruptly. A trickle of alarm invaded her senses.

"The General took into account that you have been devoted to the care of our men at the hospital, and I was able to convince him that your motives could be construed as pure. That your brother has helped the cause also went in your favor."

"So I am to go free?" she asked, somehow finding that hard to believe. Colonel Haskill had wanted her head.

"In a sense," Phillip answered, scratching his three-day growth of beard thoughtfully. "I've assumed full responsibility for you. You are released into my custody. Should you behave yourself in a fit manner until we march to Quebec, you will be allowed to remain at the Chateau Royale, under supervision."

Arissa breathed a sigh of relief. "Well, that is not so bad, *non?*"

Phillip picked up the small bag containing her belongings and put it on the table. "There's a bit more, but let's pack your things and get you out of this dark room. We've a stop to make before returning to the Chateau Royale."

"Oh, but I am a sight! Can't you take me home first and then run your errand?" she asked, shoving the book she'd been reading into the bag, along with her hairbrush and the linens Stephen had brought her.

"Not hardly." Phillip appeared to be groping for words, as she met his gaze with her curious one. "We're going to be married, Arissa."

"What?" She would have laughed, if his answer hadn't shocked the breath out of her.

"Arissa . . ." Phillip grasped her arms and turned her to him. "If I am to be responsible for you night and day, I intend to make it honorable."

"B . . . but that's an absurd reason to marry!"

"This isn't."

Phillip captured her lips before she could turn her head. With his arms wrapped about her in such a way that her own were pinned helpless at her sides, there was no retreat. It was absurd, she told herself, fighting to remain detached from the woman that leapt to life within her. When she married, it would be for love, not this dizzying reaction Phillip Monroe could invoke within her, at whim. This male-female chemistry was the ilk of what kept brothels in business, not a solid foundation for a life together.

Yet Phillip was relentless, not content until her limbs had weakened to the point where it was his strength that held her upright. Then, and only then, did he give her leave to speak with what little breath he'd left her.

"That is not fair, Phillip."

"All's fair in love and war, my little love."

Fourteen

The candles in the windows flickered against the frosted panes, dancing as gaily as the guests in the taproom. Across one wall was an assortment of hastily prepared foods from the kitchen of the Chateau Royale. Sliced roasts of beef, venison, and ham-filled platters interspersed with fresh-baked loaves of bread and baskets of rolls to supplement them, rather than the customary puddings made from the meat drippings or accompanying rich sauces. Even Chiah and Gaspar had joined the festivity, leaving the kitchen under Jeanne's watchful eye.

Apparently the wedding feast had been planned the day previous upon Phillip Monroe's return. The moment Arissa and Phillip entered the room after the short ceremony at the Presbyterian Church, she was smothered in hugs and kisses from her staff, as well as his men. Somehow she managed to smile, all the while wishing she could simply run somewhere and cry.

She hadn't thought it could get worse, but it had. On the way home, Stephen and Phillip informed her that her supply of medicinal goods, as well as her profits, had been seized by Wooster as fine for her act against the Continental Army. It was only because of Stephen's cooperation with them in allowing Phillip to carry on his charade at the Chateau Royale, that the inn itself was not confiscated. If Arissa were even suspected of further acts against the current occupying army and its government, it well might still be taken.

"I hope that that glaze in your eyes is one of happiness, *ma cherie*," Gaspar Le Boeuf said as he sat down beside her. Stephen had taken over at the bar to give him a break.

"I've lost everything, Gaspar," Arissa sniffed, in despondence.

"But you have found love, *non?*"

"Lust, *mon ami*, nothing more."

Her companion grinned, displaying what few teeth Mother Nature had left him with. "Ah, but what that can lead to! Do you not believe that most love begins as that? That such is what first attracts the male to the female and the reverse?" He pointed at Chiah, who was dancing with one of the soldiers. "True love, *ma cherie*, does not come until after the marriage. That is the love that is best of all and," he added, with a sigh, "the most forgiving."

Arissa didn't answer. Instead, she sought out Phillip's tall figure among the men gathered around the bar. She hadn't danced with him, or anyone else, for that matter. She may have had to marry, but she didn't have to dance. As though he knew she'd refuse him, he hadn't bothered to ask. Instead, he'd remained at the bar, drinking heartily to every toast that came his way.

"He is a good man and loves you, I think. I know he didn't want to wait until this morning to fetch you from town. He was going to wake General Wooster and get you out last night."

"It would have served the old pea wit right."

"Bah, look at that pout. You look like the little girl Arissa, who had to go back to the school instead of staying with her papa, *non?*"

"Look at me, Gaspar. I look like something he dragged in out of an alley, in this rumpled dress. The ceremony, it was so fast, I hardly remember what I said." Her chin trembled, threateningly. "This must be the worst wedding in history."

"*Non,* there was Alain Beaujeu's first wedding to Tamson. That was the worst," Gaspar disputed. "Poor little girl, she did not know she was even getting married to the heathen who had kidnaped her. She wasn't even sure he wasn't turning her over to the Indians to some ungodly fate. And instead of a wedding ring, he cut his hand and then hers, and pressed them together to marry their blood."

"He must not have been in love with her, yet."

"*Non,* I think that was the lusty love you referred to. But look where it led . . . happily ever after, I think."

Arissa rose, unable to stand another word that promised that dreams came true. This was a nightmare, not a dream. "I'm going to my room. You can tell my watchdog I have a headache, or whatever excuse you choose. I just can't stand this travesty any longer."

Although she tried not to look directly, from what she could tell in the periphery of her vision, Phillip never noticed her quiet exit to the corner stairwell leading to the private quarters. It was just as well. She needed some time alone, time to adjust to this sudden upheaval in her life. Everything had happened so swiftly—from the prison to the minister to the reception—that she'd not had a moment's time to think without distraction.

Upon opening the door to her room, Arissa was taken aback by the floral scent of bath salts. There before her, sitting next to the shallow hearth, was the small bathtub she usually used in the kitchen. A blazing fire kept the kettles of scented water beside it warm. All she had to do was empty the hot water into the tepid already in the bottom of the tub, and she could unwind in a heavenly bath! After her four days of imprisonment, washing out of the tin bowl with cold water, this was an answer to a prayer.

Caught up in her delight, she started to pull off her dress, when she noticed the open trunk which had held her coin at the foot of the big poster bed. The winter curtains, with their tree-of-life print, had been tossed up on the mattress. A hurtful pang struck her chest, for she was certain the little box in which she'd kept her coins was gone—confiscated. She fought back the sting in her eyes and neatly rearranged things, when she noticed yet another trunk had been placed in the room near the door.

It was compact, with brass corners and fittings, one of military design. She didn't have to guess to whom it belonged—her husband. Phillip Monroe had gotten himself a penniless criminal with no dowry for a bride. A little snicker erupted from her lips. It served the man right.

Arissa sobered instantly. Heavens, Gaspar must have put more rum in the punch than she had realized. Even though she'd eaten a few bites of this and that, she felt a little lightheaded. But then, she'd never had much tolerance for alcohol. Returning to the pleasing prospect of her bath, Arissa stepped out of her dress and shifts, standing naked in the room. The instant the cool air struck her, she realized her mistake of not having prepared the rest of the bath first and hurriedly set about doing so.

In moments, she found respite from the cold in the warm waters of the tub, her knees drawn up to her chest, within its restricted confines. To stretch out would be a luxury she'd never had, but this had served her well enough. It was deep enough to cover her shoulders and allow her to dip down sufficiently to wash her hair. She'd tried at the inn, but, without her special soap, it was hopeless. As she reached for the bar, imported from France, an outbreak of noise in the hall made her freeze.

If it were Phillip, he'd brought half his men with him, she thought, hastily pulling the linen towel she'd placed on a chair by the tub close, in case she needed it. The latch rattled on the door, and Arissa pulled the towel over her, sinking into the scented water as far as she could and soaking it in the process. She'd not thought Phillip would come up right away. Even in a real wedding, the groom always gave the bride time to prepare for the nuptial bed. A lump rose in her throat, as she glanced furtively at her bed, suddenly feeling faint.

"Oh no you don't, cap'n! You ain't gettin' away from us that easy!" she was able to distinguish from the general chatter of the celebrating group. The door rattled and then went still with the retreat of the rabble.

Only then did her heart begin to beat again. Arissa dropped the towel from her neck, shivering, despite the water's warmth. She'd gained a reprieve, but there was no telling how long it would last. With that annoying thought, she hurriedly went about her ministrations, cutting short the luxury she usually drew out until the water grew too cold for comfort.

Later, clad in her heaviest flannel shift, she climbed into the large poster bed and pulled the covers to her chin. She felt like the little girl who'd been sent upstairs to her bedroom in the townhouse that her parents had occupied before her mother's death—scared in the low firelight and certain that some savage Indian, or worse, a monster, was on its way to get her. That wasn't far from the truth, she thought sardonically. Except that Phillip Monroe was neither heathen nor monster.

Phillip's defense caught her by surprise. She'd paid far too much heed to old Gaspar, she told herself sternly. Whether Phillip loved her or not, he hadn't apologized for his charade. He'd relied on the attraction neither of them could honestly deny to smooth over everything. When she was in his arms, which was likely to happen soon, it almost did.

So how would she approach this, with her mind or her heart. Neither were that stable, where Phillip was concerned, she lamented, silently. Her heart would welcome him into her bed in a single beat, but it, like the rest of her body, had no worthwhile memory. It was her mind that would be tormented. The brain was supposed to control the body, not the reverse.

Damn the man, he'd not only lied, but brought his army down upon her like a plague. The independence she'd painstakingly groomed had been snatched from her unjustly, all in the name of duty. And now they were married . . . *till death do us part.* What if Gaspar was right? That they would reconcile their differences? That this lust could turn into love, as they came to know each other, just as it had in that charming story of his friend, Beaujeu.

With a cry of exasperation, Arissa turned and punched the pillow where Phillip's head would be when he'd finished his farewell party to the bachelors' world. Was that her head or her heart talking? Her fingers curled to caress her palm, as she pondered the quandary, determined to be rational. If there was a chance for a sweet ending to her and Phillip's story, it would have to begin tonight. And if she were honest with herself, she had to admit that she wanted a happily-ever-after story, like Alain and Tamson's. The fact of the matter was, she had nothing left to lose if she accepted Phillip into her bed, as a wife should. He'd already taken her innocence and her heart. All that hung in the balance at this point was a pride so battered and bruised that it could suffer little more harm.

As if these reflections might bite her, she reached for the covers still tucked beneath the pillow on Phillip's side of the bed and slowly turned them back. There, she thought, closing her eyes, in relief. He'd accused her of tossing down the gauntlet. Well now, she was putting out the white flag—not of truce, but of surrender.

When the clock struck midnight in the hall, there had been no sign that the celebration downstairs was winding down. Not one to endure idleness for long, especially with tortured thoughts to plague her, Arissa tossed and turned on the bed, more awake than ever. She'd studied every inch of the room she already knew so well, in the soft glow of the lamp she'd left lighted for her new husband.

There was a decanter of wine with two glasses placed on her dresser that she hadn't noticed before, which tempted her as a solution to her taut-spring nerves, but she wanted a clear head when Phillip came up—if he were ever coming up, she wondered, irritably. She couldn't imagine him being so inconsiderate, unless that part of his character had also vanished when he donned that handsome uniform.

When the clock struck one, the noise had died down some, or at least the fiddlers had given up their instruments for the night. Arissa threw the covers off and slid from the bed to pace back and forth in front of the hearth. What in God's name were they doing down there, planning the conquest of the bloody world? She tossed another log on the fire and watched the sparks fly up the chimney.

At that moment, she heard the approach of some men in the hallway and rushed to her bed with a sprightly jump. Tugging the covers up to her neck, she waited. But the men were evidently some of Phillip's fellow officers, retiring for the night, for their voices faded behind the closing of the door opposite her own. *Damn his bloody soul to hell!* Arissa swore under breath, as she once again left the bed.

This time she donned her slippers and dressing gown. Was this another game, one she'd not yet learned the rules to? Irritably, she snatched the top from the decanter of wine and poured herself a glass, which she downed quickly, in much the way the voyageurs like to take their brandy—straight and fast to the stomach. Well, she was done with playing games! She slammed the glass down on the silver tray. If she were a bride, then she'd bloody well have her groom and get it over with!

Without thought to the tumble of freshly washed auburn curls bouncing about her shoulders in wild disarray, Arissa stormed out of her room and spun down the winding staircase, her feet barely touching the steps. When she burst into the tap room, her robe was still billowing about her from her rapid descent, giving her the appearance of an avenging angel with snapping blue eyes.

"And just where is *Capitaine* Monroe?" she demanded of the speechless men gathered at the bar which should have been closed at nine, according to custom.

"Why 'Rissa, I thought you would be asleep by now!" Stephen exclaimed, stepping out from among them.

Phillip was not at the bar with the few stragglers who'd remained to celebrate with her brother. "This is my wedding night. How do you expect me to have a moment's rest?"

The men at the bar erupted in bawdy amusement, infusing Arissa with scarlet embarrassment upon realizing what she'd said.

"Come, *ma cherie*. I will take you to your husband, if that is what you wish," Stephen told her, taking her under his arm—the protective big brother with his little sister.

Eager to be away from the speculative eyes of his comrades, Arissa walked with Stephen across the room to the large stone hearth, where the fire was starting to die out. She followed his pointed finger to the large billiard table, upon which rested a body—a tall one with polished black boots befitting an officer and a gentleman. Lying over the man was his brass-adorned jacket, his leatherstock tied to one of the button holes. With one arm beneath his head and the other struck out recklessly, Phillip Monroe was sound asleep!

"Drunken fool!" Arissa muttered under her breath. "He thinks to mock me on my wedding night!"

Stephen caught her fist before she landed it squarely on his sleeping friend's stomach. "*Non,* that is not so, *ma cherie.* If you must blame someone for this, it is I."

Arissa looked at her brother, confused.

"I . . . we, Gaspar and I, we thought you were so miserable and upset that we devised a plan to give you a night to adjust to your new role as a married woman."

"What did you do?" Arissa asked, warily.

"We dissolved a few sleeping pills from papa's cabinet in his flip. He never knew . . ."

"You *what?*" Arissa leaned over the table and pulled up Phillip's eyelids. His pupils were wide and dilated. "*Mon Dieu,* you could have killed him!" She leaned over and listened to his breathing and heartbeat, both decidedly slower than normal.

"It was only a few."

"Which ones? Show me!"

"We only meant to be helpful, and Phillip was exhausted from his ride," Stephen explained, reaching into his pocket and withdrawing a bottle of medication.

"It says right here the dosage is one!" Arissa said, angrily. "How *few* did you give him?" They were made, if she recalled correctly, with an extract of opium and camphor.

"Two . . . maybe three."

"*Sacre bleu!* I cannot believe you did this! You, the son of a physician, should know better!"

"I've taken two before and had no problem, 'Rissa," Stephen argued, defensively.

"Maybe so, but you were not drinking on top of it!" She shook Phillip's head roughly in an attempt to stir him. He groaned a bit and tried to swipe her away with his arm. "Go to the kitchen and make a pot of strong coffee," she told her brother over her shoulder. "Very strong."

When Stephen was off, she hailed the men at the bar.

"You over there, get him up off this table and walk him about! *Vite!* Quickly!"

Phillip did not want to be walked. All he wanted was to be left alone. The only respite Arissa allowed him was time to sit and drink a cup of hot coffee. He spit the first at Stephen and one of the men, in rebellion, so that Arissa was forced to try her hand at it. She propped him up on a bench, his back to a pillow between him and the wall, and gently coaxed him into taking the strong brew, which she'd diluted a bit with cream to keep it from scalding him. Perhaps it was the gentleness of her voice, but he was far less defiant with her. With two more cups set aside to cool, she continued to talk to him and wipe his face with a towel Gaspar had brought over.

"For God's sake, woman, are you trying to drown me in coffee!" he mumbled, as she tipped the second cup for him to drain.

"I am trying to wake you up, *capitaine.*" Arissa took a napkin and wiped up that which had dribbled down his beard-stubbled chin.

"This bed is as hard as a slab of stone!"

Arissa laughed. He was coming around enough to move him. She motioned toward Stephen and his companions. "You heard the man. He wishes to be moved to a softer bed." As the men started forward, she cautioned, "But make him walk to it. I need to fetch some more water from the kitchen."

Stephen stopped her. "Should I take him to your room?" His awkward expression struck Arissa as sweet. Annoying as his antic had been, he'd done it with her best interest in mind.

"But of course. He is my husband, *non?*"

As she disappeared down the stairwell toward the kitchen, Gaspar caught Stephen's eye and winked. "What did I say? It will take more than a little war to stand in the way of love."

"Yes, but we damned near killed him!"

"Killed who?" Phillip muttered, his head lolling to the side, as Stephen hoisted the man's arm over his shoulder.

"You, you bloody bastard."

Gaspar chuckled. "I put only two of those pills in the flip. Your sister, she was overreacting."

"That's not like Arissa."

"Stephen, *mon ami,*" Gaspar tutted, patiently. "Our practical Arissa is in love, which is never logical or convenient."

"With who?"

Stephen grabbed Phillip's cheeks with one hand and squeezed them playfully. "With you, you brain-dazed fool." He glanced at the man on Phillip's other side. "Ready, *mon ami?*" At his nod, the men started up the main stairwell with Phillip hitting and missing the steps between them.

By the time Arissa arrived upstairs, carrying a kettle of hot water, Stephen waited outside the bedroom door. "He is in the bed. Franklin and I, we undressed him. I also gave him a dose of quinine in some blackberry cordial. For the headache that will surely come," he explained, upon seeing Arissa's startled look. "Perhaps it will undo some of my foolishness."

"Oh, well, that is good thinking. Thank you."

Stephen bussed her pinkening cheek. "You were a beautiful bride, and I think my brother-in-law is very lucky."

"And I am lucky to have you," Arissa admitted, returning the gesture. *"Bon soir,* Stephen."

"Arissa, I want you to have every happiness."

Smiling, she nodded. "I know, *mon cher* . . . and I will try."

Upon entering the room after Stephen made his way across the hall to his own, Arissa filled her painted porcelain washbowl with part of the warm water and set the kettle by the fire. After tossing on a few more pieces of wood, she walked to Phillip's side of the bed and drew back the covers to his waist. When Stephen said he'd undressed her husband, he'd meant it. Phillip Monroe wore naught but what he came into the world with.

Ignoring the distraction of his lightly furred chest or the crisp, narrowing trail leading down beneath the blanket, Arissa set about the bath he was in need of. His three days of travel had obviously not afforded him time for creature comforts, she thought, an amused tilt curling her lips. Nor had her four-day incarceration done much for her, in the same way. What a shabby pair they'd made as bride and groom! At least there was one bright side to their wedding. There'd been no church filled with guests to see them.

Phillip had drifted off to sleep again, but he was most cooperative in turning to afford her access to his back, as though he were thoroughly enjoying the pampering, even if he wouldn't remember it. Once it was dry, she turned him back over and, laying a towel over his chest, so that he didn't take a chill, she stripped the bottom covers from him to attend to his legs and feet. Immediately, she was struck by the very much alert male member, straining up, as if it wanted to be first.

A rash of heat flushed through her at the thought of washing it. Nervously, she rinsed the washcloth and soaped it thoroughly again. Instead of going to that which demanded, however, she worked on his long legs, tenderly skimming the scarred flesh with a surge of compassion. Here was a man willing to die for love. Perhaps some day, he would love her with the same intensity he had his first wife. But if that were to be, she had to earn it.

When his feet and legs had been toweled dry, Arissa braced herself to treat his eager manhood, as she had the rest of his body. It intrigued her that the rest of him slept so soundly, while the hard member she stroked with the warm, soapy cloth fairly throbbed with life. She'd heard the sisters mention such reactions while tending patients, but she'd not been witness to one. As she continued with the rest of his genitalia, she could not help but admire its proportion. Like the rest of his six-foot-plus torso, it was a magnificent specimen, at least to her limited clinical experience.

Magnificent. An unexpected tremor ran her through, tightening the moist feminine muscles below her abdomen in a hot, disconcerting way. Why, she was reacting like an animal, she thought, realizing how long she'd been running the soapy cloth up and down the length of his male member in mesmerized meditation. She dropped the cloth and withdrew her hand, as though it had burned her, when suddenly Phillip seized her wrist.

"God, woman, don't stop now!" he growled, his words slightly slurred, but nonetheless effective.

Arissa stared at him suspiciously. He wasn't exactly focused upon her, but the slow breathing that had alarmed her earlier was now short and rapid. She allowed him to guide her hand back to her task. Although his tutelage was clumsy, it was persistent. Of course, he was drunk, she thought, and drugged. Her fingers tightened with the urgency of those wrapped about them.

"Ahh . . . !" Phillip finished, with some unintelligible syllables. His eyes were closed tightly, as if in pain, but it was the reaction of his manhood that drew her attention, for it began to spill forth his seed, as though there were no end to it.

Half in panic and half in shock, Arissa grabbed a dry towel and covered it, holding the spouting beast down with one hand, while she shook his shoulder viciously with the other. "Phillip, have you lost your mind?"

"Ah, yes!" His voice trailed off, as his head lolled sideways, a sleepy smile gracing his lips.

"Phillip!" Arissa shook him again, irritably, but he only moaned and pulled away from her. "Damn you!"

She slung the towel aside and took up the washcloth with a vengeance. With quick, rough strokes, she wiped away the remnants of his private rapture, dried him, and tossed the quilts over his naked form, without a backward look. Her nose wrinkled in distaste, she discarded the dirty bath water, cloth and all, out the window, and then closed the sash and the shutters.

The bloody bastard had made love to somebody and, worse, made her party to it! she thought, availing herself of her now cool bath water to wash her hands and arms. She had heard men had such dreams, but found it hard to imagine. Who was it, she wondered enviously, that he'd found so stimulating? Could it have been her, or was it Deborah? Worse, was it some other woman?

She crossed her arms over her breasts and stomped by the fire to warm herself from the chill she'd taken at the open window. If this afternoon had been the worst wedding in history, this surely had been the worst wedding night. With a slight whimper of self pity, Arissa traipsed over to the bed and climbed in on her side, keeping as far from Phillip as possible. She wanted nothing to do with him or his dirty dreams. Nothing!

She lifted up to tuck the hem of her night shift down, when Phillip's long arm fell across her. As if he'd just discovered her, he hooked it about her waist and drew her up to him, burying his face in her hair, so that she could feel his breath upon her neck.

"You're driving me crazy, love," he mumbled, groggily.

She froze, as he found her left breast and cupped it in his hand, as though it were some sort of resting place especially designed for it. Turning abruptly, Arissa lay facedown on the bed to thwart his unconscious advance, only to have the renegade hand find solace on her buttocks. She held her breath, as he rubbed them in slow, circular motions, eventually coming to a contented halt.

She closed her eyes in frustration, her lower lip trembling. She wished she'd taken three sleeping pills.

Fifteen

The hard knock on the plank door of the bedroom made it rattle thunderously in its mortise and tenon frame. "Rise n' shine, cap'n! Haskill wants us in assembly in five minutes!'

Instinctively, Phillip Monroe rolled out of the bed, taking half the covers with him, and stood wavering in confusion. Of course he recognized Arissa Conway's room. That's right. He should be there. It had been his wedding night. With a bewildered look, he took in the round bathtub still scenting the room with flowers. Next to it on a table was a decanter of wine and two glasses. One had been used. He blinked, as though that might draw out his memory. If lightning were to strike him, he couldn't recall a thing!

Sheepishly, he shifted his attention to the girl sitting upright in the bed he'd just abandoned. Had he lost his fingers in that wild silken mass enshrouding her shoulders? A glimpse of the high-ribboned collar on her flannel night shift answered that in short order. He couldn't have, because if he'd succumbed to just the slightest of temptation where Arissa was concerned, she'd be as mother-naked as he was. Heaven strike him, what had happened?

There were no telling signs in the pristine blue gaze assessing him. She had neither the look of a woman satiated by a night of desire, nor that of one denied it. Damnation, he felt like one of her patients, instead of her husband, by the way she observed him.

"Your clothes, monsieur, are folded on the chair over there," she spoke at last. There was no display of her feelings in her voice, either. If anything, she didn't seem to know what to expect, which gave them both something in common.

Rather than seek answers that could well be humiliating on his part, Phillip turned his attention to dressing. At the moment, he'd rather have face that damned Haskill than this indifferent female he'd made his wife. He hurriedly donned his trousers and went to her dressing table to shave. He wasn't accustomed to his five days' growth, and it itched abominably. All the while he went about his ministrations, crouched over to take advantage of the low oval mirror set for a lady's use, he could see Arissa watching him coolly from the bed, where she'd propped herself up on the pillows. The resulting nicks from the distraction did little to improve his humor, which now was affected by a formidable headache.

"There is a quinine solution there on the table for your head," the girl on the bed informed him, as though reading his thoughts. The spoon beside it had been used, leaving him to believe this was not his first dose.

Had he had too much to drink? That was hard to believe, considering he'd been nursing a single pitcher of flip throughout the evening, being too distracted by congratulations to finish it. Every officer in their regiment was there, not to mention a few stationed in the city and, of course, everyone from New York's Fourth, except Haskill. He had wanted Arissa put away, and Phillip was certain this marriage, approved by Haskill's superiors, had not set well. The bastard probably intended to have his revenge this morning.

Phillip took the quinine and chased it with a bit of the

wine from the decanter—their wedding bottle. He'd
worked in the taproom enough to know it was French
and rare—a gift from Stephen, no doubt, considering
Arissa's lack of enthusiasm for the idea. He glanced at
her again. Obviously, he'd given her little reason to
change her mind about the wisdom of their marriage last
evening, despite his intentions.

"Thanks. Being married to a physician has its merits,"
he mumbled, still put off by her lack of reaction. Arissa
was a woman to speak her mind, yet she sat in the bed
like a stern angel, watching over the derelict sharing her
room, for that was exactly what he felt like, even after his
attempts to make himself presentable.

"I hope our night together was satisfactory, madame."
Phillip swore at himself, but he had to ask.

"It was . . . incredible," she finished, dryly. "I wonder
that you are able to perform any duty today, thanks to
your friends.

"My friends?"

"Stephen put sleeping pills in your flip to spare me a
night of ravishment. We spent most of the night trying
to get them out of your system with strong coffee and
walking, before I finally had you brought up to my
room."

Phillip scowled. Stephen! He thought her brother
wanted this union! Unless this was Stephen's idea of a
sense of humor . . . either way, he'd gone too far.

"So, I neglected my bride, and that's why you're so
distant?"

Arissa smiled without humor. "Oh, you managed to satisfy someone. *Who* remains to be seen."

"What do you mean by that?"

Shifting beneath his demanding gaze, Arissa shrugged.
"I am not sure, but I do intend to find out this evening,
when you return from duty. Have a pleasant day, monsieur."

224 Linda Windsor

Phillip fastened the leatherstock behind his neck and flipped out his soft brown queue, tied primly with a black ribbon. "I'll wager it'll be pleasant, the way Haskill pitched a fit upon finding I'd married you. He's going to make me pay."

Arissa came upright from her pillows. "It is I he hates, monsieur."

"You're bloody right about that!" He pointed a warning finger at Arissa. "Avoid him, 'Rissa. Say nothing more than you must, when you're around him. He'll still have you shipped off to Halifax, given half a chance."

"But why? Because I inoculated his men and saved their lives?"

"Because you made him look bad. We had the worst outbreak of the entire force from New York, when the General had asked his officers to try to keep the troops healthy until the New Year. That it was contrived right under his nose has not endeared you to him."

"Then I do not care. He is an insensitive, glory-hungry fool."

Phillip almost cracked a smile. "At least we agree on that much. It's a start. As for the rest of this, we'll hash it all out tonight, love. I'm sure there's an explanation for everything."

Although what it was, Phillip was at a loss to know, as he perused the room and his mysterious bride. What the devil was she talking about . . . he'd satisfied someone?

The wide steps were easier to descend than the winding ones to which he'd become accustomed. They were also easier on the ache that had gotten treated by the quinine his wife prescribed for him. Instead of joining the officers, who welcomed him into the taproom, he went straight for the bar and ordered a noggin of cider.

"Your mouth is as dry as cotton, eh," Gaspar observed, as Phillip tossed the beverage down and asked for more.

"And your head is as big as a whiskey barrel," Stephen

Conway joined in, coming up beside him and clapping him on the back.

Phillip chuckled, as if he were going along with the good-natured teasing, when suddenly he struck out at Stephen. His blow creased the young man's jaw and mouth, splitting his lip in the process. "I owe you that, Conway," he explained, as he helped the younger man up. "I honored my word to you about your sister, and neither she, nor I, needed your meddling. She's a practical woman who will listen to reason, not a hysterical type. Is that clear?"

Stephen rubbed his jaw, scowling. "We thought but to help you both—to give you both time to adjust to the wedding."

"I could do a lot of adjusting, unconscious."

Wincing at Phillip's biting words, Stephen persisted. "But it worked. You should have seen Arissa's face when she came down to fetch you. I tell you, we kept you so long that she came after you! That I never would have dreamed!"

"And she was livid at Stephen for what he'd done. You know those hysterics you say she is not prone to. Well, she tossed a few at us last night. She had all the men giving you coffee and walking you back and forth across the floor, until you sobered enough to get you to her room. It is a wonder you've decent soles on your boots." Gaspar grinned. "What went on after that, who is to tell."

"But I can assure you that your welfare was most on her mind. Most men would give their right arm for such a beautiful and attentive doctor."

Phillip's mind was tripping over thoughts. Had she revived him enough for him to make love to her? Had he been thoughtless and clumsy, without regard to her feelings? He picked up his second cup of cider. Well, that was something that could be easily explained away and remedied tonight. After all, he had been drugged. Feeling much better, he finished off the mild drink and walked over to one of the tables to join his fellow soldiers for breakfast.

According to Lieutenant Colonel Haskill, who enjoyed the noonday meal in the formal setting of Arissa's parlor, Phillip and his men had been sent to assist the loading of wagons and supplies for the impending journey to Quebec City. Although Jeanne had served him the main course, when it came time for dessert, he specifically asked if the madame of the house might join him.

Arissa, recalling Phillip's warning, put a smile on her face, as she entered the room with the steaming fruit cobbler and put it before the colonel. It was a difficult act, since he'd sent all his men out into the cold weather, while he remained behind to be coddled like a king. He motioned for her to take a seat next to him, while he sampled the dessert.

"As usual, the food is excellent."

"Chiah is a gifted cook."

A brief silence ensued. Arissa was not one for small talk, and the colonel seemed to be searching for a way to broach the subject he'd called her into discuss.

"I suppose congratulations are in order. Captain Monroe is a fine officer and gentleman."

Arissa was not yet wholly convinced of that, but she nodded in agreement. "I suppose I am lucky in that respect."

"Very much so, madame," Haskill informed her. "It's saved you from a wretched passage to Halifax."

"I only meant to save lives, not undermine the strength of either army. I'd have done the same to Carleton's troops, were such an unthinkable order issued."

Haskill put down his fork and leaned backward, arms crossed, his steel-gray gaze as cold as the sword hanging on a rack by his hat. "Those men will have to march through snowy winter weather tomorrow. We expect to meet Arnold at Quebec the first of December."

Arissa clearly showed her dismay. "Tomorrow!"

"And you shall be rid of us for a while, at any rate, until we take the city."

"Phillip, he will go, too?"

The colonel nodded. "Yes, he will, as will your brother. Mr. Conway has offered to accompany us as a scout. The General specifically requested them both."

It was crazy, insane, so much so that Arissa failed to notice the peeve in the colonel's voice. All she wanted to do was tell him what she thought of this outlandish campaign, but, recalling Phillip's warning, she held her tongue. "But I thought you would wait for the reinforcements I have heard about, those being sent by your Continental Congress."

Haskill chuckled to himself without amusement. "They will secure the city, once we've taken it." He leaned forward on his elbows. "You see, young lady, about one third of General Mongomery's troops are from New England. Their enlistments are up January first of next year. We have to strike while we can, while we have the numbers. That is why what you did to us was so devastating! A few weeks was all we'd hoped for."

Arissa pushed away from the table. "You are right, *mon* colonel. My mind is not capable of fathoming such decisions. If the New Englanders left, then the reinforcements would replace them, and you would be a few weeks more into the winter."

"It's the risk, madame. Our soldiers want to go home, from the General on down to the lowliest private. The sooner Quebec is taken, the sooner they can do just that—not to mention avoid your hellish winters. I understand the snowstorms we've had to date are but a taste, according to our guides."

Arissa pondered the statements, her answer ready. But dared she deliver it? Assuming a guileless expression, she took the plunge. "Then this entire campaign is futile. You are poorly equipped, undermanned, and those men you do have are either sick or want to go home . . . or both. I hope you will forgive me if I do not understand. I wish neither side ill. I only wish to survive, to run my inn, and to practice such medicine as I am trained to do." She dipped graciously at the stairwell and started to leave, when Haskill raised his hand.

"A moment, madame. I have your money to finish paying for our accommodations to date, since I am certain you are not inclined to donate such services to the cause."

"I cannot donate what my staff needs to live on, monsieur," Arissa answered, readily, taking the canvas back into hand. It was not as heavy as it should have been, giving her cause to open the drawstring. Down at the bottom was some manner of coins, but the majority of the money was printed on paper."

"Those bills are guaranteed legal tender by the Continental Congress."

"Which cannot afford to outfit their own men properly?" The challenge was out before she could censure it.

Haskill tossed down his napkin with impatience. "It is that or nothing, madame. You are a practical woman. Will you take a risk for some recovery or toss it all away on mistrust?"

Arissa tightened the string about the bag. "I take the risk, monsieur, because I am left no choice. But I do not have to like it."

When Phillip arrived that afternoon, he was cold and wet. Having left his boots and cloak in the private kitchen

downstairs, he tiptoed up the back stairwell to the room
he'd shared with Arissa, in order to avoid Colonel Haskill.
One of the junior officers could give the old man the
report that their supply train was loaded and ready to
move out. It hadn't been easy convincing the merchants—especially the English ones—to accept the approved Continental currency. For a group that hailed the
American invasion with open arms, the two-faced allies
had certainly posed a problem, not only refusing the army
credit, but insisting on dealing with the British, despite
the war.

Montgomery was at his wits' end in dealing with them,
and Wooster eagerly awaited the General's departure, so
that he could have his hand free with the greedy "allies."
Phillip shuddered to think of the Montrealers under General David Wooster, for the man was clearly a zealot and
could make more enemies than allies.

"Have a good night, sir," one of the officers, who had
come up the main stair at the opposite end of the hall,
encouraged, brightly when Phillip emerged.

Phillip nodded, taking no offense at the general chuck-
les afforded his comrades by the word that he'd spent
his wedding night drugged and sleeping peacefully, while
his bride had to come looking for him. He supposed the
humor had made the day more bearable, out in the bitter,
windy weather. As for him, he wondered if he'd ever thaw.

He started to knock on Arissa's door but, remembering
his new office as her husband, opened it slowly and entered. To his surprise, the room was aglow with candles
along the mantel and a hearty fire blazed in the hearth.
A small folding table had been laid before it with a setting
for two. The fine wine they'd but tasted the night before
had been poured into two glasses, while the meal itself
was hidden under domelike covers.

The tempting aroma of the roasted veal in some sort
of French sauce made his stomach growl with the same

ferocity that struck his loins, for perched gracefully in the window seat was Arissa Conway. She wore a dark gold peignoir with small brown silk ribbons, fastening it at its ecru-ruffled neck. As she lifted her head to acknowledge his presence, her pale, natural curls shook sprightly, like a cluster of giggling cherubs, from the single brown bow into which they'd been gathered.

"To what do I owe this . . . this honor, madame?" Phillip managed, finding his voice, at last.

"That part of me which finds favor in you has won out over that which thinks you to be a heartless deceiver." It had been a hard decision, one which had bedeviled her all day, her tone seemed to imply.

Arissa slipped off the windowseat and floated with billowing layers of the diaphanous robe and gown across the room to where he stood. She unfastened his coat and slid it off his shoulders, before tossing it on the trunk at the foot of the bed. "The fact that you are leaving tomorrow forces me to make my decision tonight as to whether I am to send my heart with you, or my hate."

The leatherstock followed the jacket. With nimble fingers, she loosed the laces on his shirt. "You never found your medallion, did you?"

"It's part of the past now." It had been returned, but Phillip was too distracted to explain what had happened to it. The messenger had returned it when Haskill's forces arrived at the Chateau Royale. His own surprise was nothing compared to this dreamspun scenario, yet he would reveal it before the night was out.

Arissa motioned for Phillip to be seated. "Is it, *mon cher?*" She handed him a glass of the wine and took one for herself. Her expectant gaze rested upon him, as she took the seat opposite him.

"Of course it is! You made me realize that I had to bury Deborah and get on with my life. You made me feel alive again, enough to do it."

"But how deeply is she buried, Phillip?"

Phillip was struck by the sudden glaze that sparkled in Arissa's eyes, picking up the candles' glow. Confused by her question, he continued to stare at her for some sort of hint as to what she was talking about.

"Do you still make love to her in your dreams?"

"What kind of question is that?" he demanded, losing patience with this bizarre nonsense. But upon seeing how deeply Arissa was affected, he calmed down. "Are you asking me if Deborah will ever cross my mind when I am with you?" She kept her silence, waiting. "Damnation, woman," Phillip swore, "How the hell should I know? Can you control your dreams?" He shook his head. "I can't make promises based on something I have no control over!"

"Then you might think of her from time to time."

"Yes . . . I guess." He finished the wine, finding its taste severely lacking in its ability to make their subject more palatable. "But the more I get to know you, the more my thoughts will be full of you, until there is little room left for that which is dead and gone. You have taught me to live for now, Arissa."

Arissa sipped her glass, her wet gaze averted to the fire.

"Would you mind giving me a hint as to what this is all about? Perhaps I can explain it, if I knew what the hell I was talking about?"

The eyes that came to his face were tortured and hurt. "Whom did you make love to last night?"

"You saw me make love to someone, and it *wasn't* you?" Phillip was clearly befuddled, now. Had she caught him out of his mind, rolling on the floor with one of the kitchen wenches? "You didn't recognize them?"

Arissa shook her head.

Phillip exhaled heavily. She was genuinely distressed. "Tell me more, Arissa, because this doesn't make one bit of sense to me."

"The men had carried you up to my bed and you stank like a pig!"

That didn't surprise Phillip. He'd done nothing but ride and sleep, since leaving Montreal at the beginning of the week. Time hadn't allowed him the luxury of a bath before the wedding.

"So, after they stripped you and put you in the bed, I gave you a bath and your . . ." She hesitated, groping for a word that was not so crude. "Penis," she decided, keeping the observation clinical, "became very . . ." Her face was a color deeper than the wine Phillip poured into their empty glasses. " . . . enlarged," she finished, lamely. "Well, you were asleep, and it was not, so I thought by the time I bathed the rest of you to get you fit for my clean sheets, that it too would relax."

"But it didn't," Phillip injected, hiding his amusement behind his glass.

With forced nonchalance, Arissa waved her hand. "Of course, this is a reaction that happens often at the hospital, when the men are simply incapable of . . . well of reaching their physical contentment," she finished artfully. "When the bath is done, it usually withers away."

"And this one didn't?" Phillip couldn't imagine why, since he had no recollection of this, whatsoever. Still, that manly part of him couldn't help but be impressed.

"No, it did not! When I attempted to wash it with the soap and water, it got even bigger. Why, it even had a pulse!" she said, giving away the nature of the hold she had exercised. "When I felt that, I let it go, but you grabbed my hand and forced me to keep scrubbing it, until it spit all over everything!"

At the distasteful wrinkle of his charming companion's nose, Phillip could hold his silence no more. He burst into laughter. "And . . . and what did you do?"

"I covered it up with a towel, until it had finished, and then washed you better than you deserved!"

"And you thought I was doing that in my dreams to my late wife?"

Arissa looked away, suffused with embarrassment. "The thought had crossed my mind."

" 'Rissa," Phillip cajoled, rising from his chair to approach her. He took her hand and brushed her knuckles with his lips. "Think, love. It was my wedding night. You were my bride. Who was most likely to be the woman on my mind at that moment? A wife who has been dead nine months and left me feeling as dead, or my new wife, who had brought me back to life again as a man."

"But did you come to me with your heart?"

"No, *ma petite*, you already have that." He drew her up from her chair, his body aching with desire at the scene she'd so innocently described. Slipping his hand behind her head, he bent down and kissed her tenderly, lingering until she struggled for breath. "And if you'll come to the bed, I'll show you that all I have is yours."

Arissa started to go with him, swaying in that direction with the relief from the torment that had plagued her through the night and into the day. But there were other problems that needed to be worked out before she could go to Phillip with a clear mind.

"*Non*, we mustn't yet!" She pointed to the meal on the table. "I prepared it myself, since there is little else I can do under Colonel Haskill's evil eye." She shrugged, suddenly endearingly shy. "It is simple, but filling."

Food was the last thing on Phillip's mind at the moment, but he gave in. When he took Arissa this time, he wanted the truth out and behind them, their differences settled. He wanted to be of one heart and one mind, if at all possible. He helped her back to her seat and reluctantly resumed his own opposite her.

"Well, I'm certainly anxious to sample my wife's cooking!" he managed, with a passable degree of enthusiasm.

Arissa set about serving the food, inadvertently providing a tantalizing display, as she leaned over and sliced the tender veal in mushroom sauce. Her breasts, firm and pliable as his memory reminded him, callously, moved in relation to her use of the knife with a gelatinous quiver that made him swallow an entire glass of the expensive liquor straight down. They peeped shyly, just at the edge of the lacy peignoir in a pure seduction of their own.

"Here is an extra large helping for you," the girl announced, dropping the meat on his plate, gently. "And let us not forget the sauce."

God no, not the sauce, Phillip mused, laconically, as hot as he'd been cold earlier out in the blasts of Canadian wind and snow.

The small potatoes and winter greens which accompanied the sumptuous meal were hardly noticed, for Phillip was too distracted by her nearness, her fragrance, not to mention the way she pronounced his name with her French accent. He had to consciously uncurl his toes when she finally took her seat and met his gaze.

"There is something else we must discuss, Phillip, before I wholly commit myself to this marriage."

He should have seen this coming. "My charade." His deflation was reflected in his voice.

Arissa shook her head. *"Non, non.* I have thought of that and reasoned it out. That you did out of duty, out of commitment to that which you believed in. It was like my inoculating the men. I did it for the same reasons, even though I knew I was betraying you, in a sense. I had to."

Phillip felt as if the weight of the world had been lifted from his shoulders, at her simple, but logical, analogy. Silently, he offered a prayer of thanks that he'd become attached to a practical female, one who could reason. He sliced a hearty chunk of the veal and popped it into his mouth.

"This is great. But then, so are you. I've never met

anyone like you, Arissa Conway . . . Monroe," he added, a bit embarrassed at the oversight.

Arissa smiled at the compliment. "And I would say the same for you, Mr. Monroe. I liked you very much before I loved you."

Phillip felt a rush of warmth flash through him, at the simple, but heartfelt admission. "What you liked about me, Arissa, is still there. I'm still the same man." And to hell with the food, he added silently. From the way she ended her admission on an upswing, there was an unspoken but still-hanging question between them. By God, he would hear it, if he wanted this night to end the way he dreamed.

"And because I love you so much, Phillip, I am so angry at you, I do not know what to do or say!"

Stunned, Phillip watched her bolt from her chair and cross to the window, arms folded and lips set in perfect pique. What a volatile creature she was. It was as stirring as it was annoying. "I spoke to Lieutenant Colonel Haskill today."

A small groan rumbled at the back of Phillip's throat.

"At his request," she explained, as if she'd overheard it. "He tells me that you and Stephen are leaving tomorrow for the march to Quebec. Then, as if the grand leader of a grander army, he tosses me a purse for the expense of feeding and lodging his men. And do you know what he gave me, Phillip Monroe of this rich, magnificent army?" Her voice had risen to a chalk on-the-board pitch, as she marched back to the table and tossed out a hand full of Continental bills. "Paper!"

Incredulous at the sudden change from confessions of love to anger over finances, Phillip grunted. "So all of this is over money?"

"*Non*, it is over worthless paper! I was told we would be paid in coin. Well then, where is it? I know of no one who will accept this from me when I go to pay the Chateau Royale's debts. Certainly not the herdsmen who provide my livestock . . . certainly not the dairymen or the egg women or . . ."

Phillip shoved his chair out and leapt to his feet. "Damn it, 'Rissa, I've heard your say. Now how about hearing mine? I can't believe all this is over money. Do you put that ahead of what you just confessed was love? Because if I've misinterpreted what you're saying, please correct me!"

Arissa turned away, her chin tilted in that defiant manner that evoked the urge to strangle, somewhere in the midst of Phillip's emotional quandary. "How can you say such a thing?"

The slight quiver in her accusation phased him briefly. "Because you said it."

"It is not the money, Phillip," Arissa swore, as she turned to face him. "It is what it represents to you and me. Tomorrow you march off with a poorly supplied army, half of it sick, and a pocketful of paper to replenish your supplies. Do you think that you will come back alive?" She shook her head violently, her curls emphasizing her emotion. "*Non*, you will be dead, and what of your wife? Beside missing the only man who has ever won her heart, she will have nothing but this paper to survive on. Your army has taken everything else from me, and now they are going to take you!"

Phillip glanced down at the Continental bills in his hand, all the while searching for an answer that would assuage her, when he spotted something unusual. "Great God Almighty, damn!" he swore, tossing the top bill aside to look at the next and then the next.

Arissa watched him sort through the bills as though obsessed, incredulous that he should pick a time such as now to count the money. They'd established their love. They were talking about their future, or lack of it, and suddenly he acts the bloody banker!

"Stop it!" she shrieked, slamming the remaining moneys out of his hand and scattering the bills on the floor.

"But you're right, 'Rissa. These are worthless . . . or at least part of them are. They're counterfeit!"

"*Dieu*, how can you tell?" she asked, suddenly intrigued.

"These two crosses don't meet the way they should." Phillip swore again. "The General needs to be notified at once. We don't want the Canadians to be paid in counterfeit bills. We want them as friends, not enemies."

Arissa looked at him solemnly. "Do you really think any of them will be good?"

Phillip put the money on the table and took her into his arms. "By all that is holy, and by my love for you, Arissa Conway, I do believe that money will be worth what it says. I admit, it's shaky now, but the day we win our independence, it will be as good as the English notes. A nation like ours, unfettered by Britain's trade restraints and taxes, can do nothing but grow. England feeds off all her colonies to make her fat and powerful. Now we want Quebec to join us in driving her off the continent. But if we fail, it won't stop the colonies from moving ahead, without our French and English Canadian cousins."

Phillip kissed a droplet of emotion which ventured down Arissa's upturned face. "And if anything happens to me, I promise you'll be taken care of. I'm fairly well fixed in New York, and you are my wife, legal and binding. I've already given Gaspar a letter to post to my office in New York to clear the way for you. If we fail in Canada, then you can go to the colonies and be taken care of by my family."

He stopped, as if reminded of something, and then reached into his pocket. To her surprise, it was a gold ring. He slipped it on her finger. "And if you've any doubts as to what happened to that gold medallion, well, it wasn't doing me any good hanging about my neck like

an albatross of memories. I thought it would better serve
me as your wedding ring and represent our future.''

Arissa held out her hand, looking at the polished gold
in astonishment. It was adorned with a garland of fleur-
de-lis and stars. When that began to wear off, a tearful
rush of emotion filled her. He'd destroyed his past and
reshaped his future, just for her. If he'd done that, couldn't
she just believe in him a little? But life was not like a clump
of gold. One did not have complete control over destiny.

"I don't know whether to take you to my bed and make
sure it is me that you love this time, or throw you out for
your insane insistence on marching off to your death."

Phillip embraced her, capturing her lips before she
could toss any more surprises at him. He'd had enough
of those, and now all he wanted was her. She gasped for
air, as he abandoned the wild plunder of her mouth to
rescue her uncorseted breasts from their ruffled lair,
where they'd taunted him all evening. As if starved for
their softness, he paid each one its respective due, until
he felt Arissa go limp in his arms, her slender hips
pressed imploringly against his own.

As he stopped his sensual pillage and picked her up
in his arms to carry to the poster bed, he gave answer to
the quandary posed by the breathless girl. There was no
other choice—not for him, nor for Arissa—now that the
barriers between them were clear for hurdling. They
could do it. Together he knew they could.

"I think you should take me to your bed, wife, and I
promise you will be made certain that it is you to whom I
make love this time."

Sixteen

The candles on the mantel had burned low. On the table, the food was cold. Beside the bed was a tangle of clothing, sheer silk, voile, and linen mingled with uniform wool and canvas. The bow that had held up Arissa's curls was wrapped about one of the posters, leaving her long tresses free for the silken pillage of Phillip's frantic fingers.

What had started as a slow discovery of each other, with one item of clothing falling after the other, progressed to touching those secret parts of the body, heretofore forbidden. Breathing became ragged with each new revelation, and shivers of sheer arousal riddled that which had yet to get its due, until their bodies were screaming for an end to this maddening torture which exacted sharp intakes of breath and groans of pure pleasure.

Arissa wondered that she could feel so alive, and yet burn and ache for more of Phillip's sweet torment. His lips, his tongue, his fingers were all devilish instruments that played a heavenly tune to which she could not help but dance. Yet she could stand no more music. Her body could endure no more on its own. It was Phillip that she craved, his hard arousal, moving deep within her, putting out the consuming fires which drove her insane.

Yet he was not through with his fiendish mischief, despite the way she trembled and called his name imploringly. She grasped his hair to pull him away from that place where he'd wedged his face, when suddenly she was invaded, not as she'd demanded, but in a way just as wildly devastating. His deep, plundering kiss flashed like white fire, blinding her to all but its searing possession. His hands clasped her buttocks to control their excited writhing, yet she could not fathom this sense-unraveling technique. All she knew was that she had to have her husband. She had to have him, there and now.

"Phillip!" Grasping his hair, she tugged at him, until he broke away from his bonding kiss. As he did, she bolted upright and clumsily reached for that which she hungered, pulling him with it.

"Careful, love!"

Her eyes widened, as if she'd hurt him, but the mischievous light in his gaze told her he was as eager as she to consummate this ageless passion consuming them. Humoring her, he permitted her to guide his sleek, hard member to the moist haven contracting convulsively in anticipation of receiving it. When she placed it exactly where she wanted it, Arissa lifted upward, seizing him with her quivering body and taking him down with her with the legs she'd swiftly locked about him.

"There!" she gasped, her voice ringing triumphantly over an intrusive ruckus that sounded like a thousand pots and pans struck by a whirlwind coming from the kitchen below.

She felt Phillip stiffen within and without her, and heard his muttered oath, despite the clamor. It was not them, she realized, feeling somewhat foolish. It wasn't even in the room. Yet from all the shouts and clanging, it sounded as though their kitchen had exploded.

Her eyes widened, as she stared up at her husband. *"Mon Dieu!* Are we under attack?" It couldn't be! Not now! she mused in desire-clouded confusion. Yet, if she were to die, what better way?

Phillip moved within her, apparently recovered from

his shock, and shook his head. She couldn't believe he was actually grinning. "No, it's the boys from New England."

He reached down and nipped at the rose-tipped peak of her left breast. "It's called a shivaree," he explained, giving the right its just due, as well. "They're just wishing us well. It's a custom, after weddings. Could go on all night."

Seeing the horror that struck Arissa's face, he bent down and kissed her. "It's just going to make it harder for me to make you happy." He thrust her against the mattress, gaining her undivided attention. "Think you can keep your mind on us, rather than on them?"

"As long as they stay on that side of the door, I suppose," she answered, uncertainly. "You Americans, you have strange . . ."

"All right break it up, boys. Colonel Haskill's orders. He wants everybody fresh and ready to ride in the morning!"

Arissa offered a little prayer of thanks for the troublesome lieutenant colonel when the noise died as abruptly as it had started. She reached up and circled Phillip's ears with her fingers, playfully.

"You heard the colonel, monsieur. You had better get your business done, so that you will be fresh and ready to leave in the morning."

"Another look like that one, and I may not be able to walk in the morning, Mrs. Monroe."

It was amazing to Arissa how many places Phillip found to torment her, without abandoning their union. To have him still within her was torture enough, for she longed to begin the pagan dance he'd once shared with her. All of her remembered it. All of her wanted it.

"*Sacre bleu*, monsieur, you are driving me mad!" she swore at last, tossing up one leg with which to turn him over. If he would not satisfy her, then she'd do the work.

Phillip rolled over easily, delighted to see his tawny-haired angel turn impatient temptress. He had pushed her to the point of frenzy, and it in turn affected him. He rose up to meet each of her downward thrusts and watched in fascination, as the firm globes of her breasts measured each impact in quivering delight. He could not believe his demure Arissa was this wild woman making love to him, digging her nails into his ribs, as she rode his ardor into body-shaking submission.

He grabbed her breasts, unable to resist anymore, and groaned, as his passion deserted his body into that which was tightly clinging to it, trembling to receive all he had to offer. Then, as if a final chord had snapped, Arissa fell against him, breathless and faint. He embraced her and rolled her to the side, before tucking the covers around her naked, perspiration-slick body.

He'd never known such passion in a woman. Who would have ever dreamed it? Not even Deborah had been so moved, though she tried to submit to her wifely duties with a smile and, at times, seemed to enjoy it. Phillip bussed Arissa on the top of the head, as she snuggled against him. This was enough to keep him warm through the entire bloody Canadian winter, and certainly through the night.

Everyone was up before daybreak, including Phillip. Although Arissa was still sleeping, he hadn't been able to resist the selfish urge to awaken her with sweet seduction and sample her passion one more time. Then, with a wide, slumber-infected smile, she'd gone back to sleep, so that his whispered, *"Au revoir,"* went unanswered.

He hadn't expected to see her again until his return, but as he and Stephen were mounting up, she came out, wrapped in a hooded cloak, handing them extra blankets and bread from the kitchen, along with the cartridge case Stephen had left hanging on the banister of the main stairwell. Her brother considered it a prize from his sea-

son as a voyageur, although Arissa wondered, by the way
he cherished it, if the young squaw who had made it for
him was not the source of his attachment to it. The Indian girl had even given up precious ribbons traded with
the trappers to adorn the strap—a true sacrifice, Stephen
had told Arissa, proudly.

But then, Stephen was not marching off on some folly,
hellbent on meeting his death. She could not be so self-
sacrificing, when Phillip leaned down to kiss her. She
turned away, tears streaming down her face.

"I will not say goodbye. It is only by this that I hope
to see you again . . . both of you!" she added, taking in
Stephen, as well, with her gaze. "I love you both with all
my heart, but I hate this foolishness that you are doing."

She sniffed, holding back a sob. Phillip wanted to dis-
mount and take her in his arms, but the lines were form-
ing to head to the wharf, where they were to board ships
for Quebec. As he turned his horse away, he looked over
his shoulder and called her name.

"Arissa! Until we meet again, love."

As he raised his hand, she slowly did the same. Then,
without warning, she spun about and ran into the house.
To Phillip, it felt as if part of his chest had been ripped
out and carried off by her. He would come back, he
promised himself. He'd never be whole again, until he
was reunited with Arissa.

The weeks that followed, including Christmas Week,
were tedious, after the troops left. There had been
enough coin in Haskill's payment to continue the operation of the inn, although there were few families traveling
about, because of the occupation. Most of the Chateau
Royale's business came from the regular habitants and
passing merchants, some of whom, even accepted those

Continental bills Arissa had learned to differentiate as genuine.

Although she decorated the inn with evergreens—one of her favorite tasks at Christmas—Arissa failed to get into the holiday spirit. The society of Montreal itself was no different, she heard from the few friends that visited. The Americans left in charge threw a few balls, but no one of any import accepted their invitation. What parties there were, were small, private family affairs. Even those were denied Arissa, whose adopted family was away fighting on opposite sides of the war.

She set about making Phillip and Stephen shirts, for work at the inn had been scant enough to permit her time to send a few of the staff home for the holidays. Since the news always came in the taproom, she set up a sewing table near the hearth to keep abreast of what was going on. Rumors were rampant, but most confirmed that Montgomery and Arnold were poised on the outskirts of Quebec, awaiting the right moment to attack.

Recalling Phillip's concern that they fight before the New Year, she sat by the window near the taproom hearth on New Year's Eve and stared out at the blinding snow, beating in furious silence against the side of the inn. If those poor men marched against the fort in this weather, they were surely doomed. The very idea left her sick and cold with worry.

There were drifts—some twenty feet in places—yet the American army marched in formation toward the great, walled city of Quebec in the distance. Although the freezing men took care to keep their lanterns turned to the rear, the wind occasionally had its way with them, twisting the lights toward the fort. Officers on horseback rode with their foot units behind General Montgomery, who had taken the lead with his Canadian guides.

Phillip Monroe had an uneasy sense of foreboding, as he watched the General squeeze through the first barri-

cade at Cape Diamond. Four posts had been felled to
create a narrow opening for the army to pass through.
Still no sound had been heard from the British guards
on the walls beyond. The advance unit had been quiet.
It had exercised all caution, leaving the horses further
back, out of the earshot of the fort. Yet the opening in
the barricade yawned like a gateway to hell, in the snow-
pelted darkness.

As Campbell's troops were hurried along, Montgomery
himself felled two posts of the second barrier and edged
through, undetected. Ahead was a two-story log building,
quiet, by all observation. The General drew his sword,
and his officers and guides followed. At the signal to advance, Phillip fell in with the others, but his cloak caught
in the narrow passage. Behind him, Stephen stopped to
assist, when all manner of hell broke loose from the
cabin. Canister and grapeshot spattered the wall, followed
by musket fire.

Phillip yelped, as a ball creased his arm, but a second
grazed his forehead, dazing him. Stephen pulled him behind the barricade, despite his insistence that he was all
right. He needed to see. Everything was blurred, made
worse by the snow.

"Dieu! Mongomery is dead!"

The words of the men chasing through the opening
set panic in those behind. Colonel Campbell tried to rally
the soldiers to shoot a round at the log house, but, to
their horror, the weapons misfired. The powder had gotten wet.

Stephen collared Phillip by the neck and started dragging him away from the debacle. Some were shouting
retreat all about them, while others were trying to regroup beyond the barricade. The misfire of the gunpow-
der, however, finalized the decision of immediate retreat
for the officers. Staggering in the hip-deep snow, Phillip
hardly knew which hurt him the most—his head, his arm

or his stiffening leg. The cold had been merciless, despite the blanket he'd tied about it.

"Stay here. I'll get you a horse."

Phillip shook his head. "No, I'll keep on with the rest."

"Then I will meet you with it."

Used to the deep snows of the Canadian winters, Stephen strapped on a pair of snowshoes and started out into the white, swirling cold.

"Form up, men, and cover the rear!"

Phillip looked over to where a junior officer was trying to restore order to the mayhem—Burr, he thought was his name, as he shoved himself upright on his rifle. "A line men, from me to Burr! At least you'll not be taking shot in the back!"

Gunfire still rang from the log house, but those inside seemed as confused by the outcome of the attack as the rebels. Phillip looked at the retreating army. If the powder could be counted on, chances were they could still rally and take structure. However, the order had been given by Colonel Campbell. At least a line had formed to cover the backs of the fleeing men—two actually. The first fired, at Burr's command, and fell back. The second then readied for fire.

"Captain Monroe!"

Phillip pivoted to see a blanketed man approaching him, looking more bear than human in the furs he wore. "Sir?" he answered.

At that moment the second line discharged and hot fire shot through Phillip's side. In disbelief, he stared at the smoking rifle his assailant was reloading, but then, like the rest of the snow-blasted landscape, they went out of focus. He dropped to his knees, grasping his side. Who was it? One of their own men? Why?

The questions bolted through Phillip's brain, as the bed of fallen snow welcomed him into it. Closer to the ground, he could hear above the footfalls of the retreating men and the more distinct sound of an approaching horse.

"Phillip! *Mon Dieu,* what happened! You, monsieur, help me get the *capitaine* on this horse!"

No, Stephen! Phillip flinched, as a second shot rang out, checking the warning which had never left his lips. A body fell, but Phillip could see nothing—only snow and the dark, gray-black sky. He waited for what seemed an eternity, before he heard the horse take off. Stephen? No, Stephen wouldn't abandon him. He'd saved the Canadian's life. They were family now.

The wound in his side was numb now from the freezing pack of snow he'd shoved against it. Gradually, he forced himself over on his knees, so that he might see above the snow-blanketed ground.

"Stephen!" he shouted hoarsely.

With no answer, Phillip began to crawl toward the place where he thought he'd heard the commotion. It couldn't have been too far from him. He felt sick to his stomach, and, despite the cold, he was perspiring. It was freezing on his face.

"Stephen!"

He had to stand up. He could see nothing from here. He lifted his rifle, which seemed frozen in his hand, and pushed himself the rest of the way to his feet. Some ten feet away, there was a large indentation in the snow. Driven by the fear of the unknown, Phillip staggered forward, until his feet struck those of the body lying sprawled there.

He leaned over to see the placid face of Arissa's brother staring blindly at the sky. A single hole in the middle of his forehead seeped dark scarlet against his ashen skin. His canteen, knapsack, gun kit, and blanket had been taken from him.

Who in God's name . . . Phillip swayed unsteadily and looked off in the snow-hazed distance. All he could see were shadows, retreating shadows. But why, he asked himself, sinking to his knees beside his companion. Yet, as his consciousness faded and he collapsed over Stephen Conway's corpse, the last vision that registered in Phillip's mind was Arissa. Sweet, loving Arissa.

Phillipe. Were she to die at that moment, his would be the last name on her lips. Yet Arissa was very much alive, unlike her husband and brother. Worse, she did not wish to be. She was tired of soldiers and false hopes, of sickness and death, of the purchase and outright seizure of Canadian goods by this liberating army. This Continental Congress had promised what it could not deliver. Its foolishness had cost her Phillip and Stephen, lost in action—which meant frozen to death during the New Year's Eve battle.

January and February, she'd gone about her task of running the inn in a state of numb disbelief. Through March and April, anger had begun to show itself against the invading army, but she'd survived. She'd made their occasional coin stretch as far as it would go and used their Continental notes, wherever anyone would accept them. Somehow, the Chateau Royale was still operating.

In a matter of time, they would all be gone, these *Bastonnois*. The British ships arrived in early May to rescue Quebec, and Governor Carleton was already pressing his way south to rid the province of the Americans for good. Meanwhile, there was something akin to panic in the air. Soldiers straggled in from all over the province with smallpox and died, others deserted, and the habitants, for the most part, had gone home. Such a disease-ridden, demoralized lot, she'd never seen before.

She did what she could for them. After all, they were human. But she gave nothing of herself. There was nothing left to give. It had all died with Phillip.

And now the ragamuffins were fleeing for their lives.

Word had it that many of the seigniors who had been officers in the American army had burned down their own homes in retreat, sooner than have the British seize them. For days, she'd watched wagonloads of Canadian women and children take the ferry to St. John, while the last of the American soldiers in the city were purchasing and seizing properties at will for their retreat. Even the lead roofs of the homes were being taken by the panicked mob, as if they still hoped to convert it to ammunition and rally back, at some point.

In the midst of all the chaos, Lieutenant Colonel Haskill found time from securing provisions about the countryside, to visit long enough to break the news to Arissa what she'd already found out months before. She'd been working in the kitchen, having had to let most of the staff go because she'd hadn't the coin to pay them. Much as she detested the man, she hurriedly made herself presentable, in hopes that he might shed some light on the circumstances of Stephen and Phillip's fate.

"They were with Montgomery's staff," Haskill informed her, abruptly. His tone indicated he hadn't approved of being shorted two men. "When I got the report of the missing, their names were among them. Since the General and most of his men were killed right there at Cape Diamond, I'd say that's where Captain Monroe and your brother got theirs." Although she had elected not to eat, the colonel was enjoying the chicken stew on his plate, not the least affected by the subject. "If they were wounded and unable to retreat with the rest, no doubt they've been found in the thaw."

"I searched the hospitals for weeks after the battle," Arissa said, at a loss to deal with the subject in as detached a manner as her companion. "It was there that I heard the news . . . from a soldier who had been with them."

Haskill chuckled and looked at her over a pitcher of beer. There was actually a twinkle in his gray eyes. "You don't have anything to fear now, mademoiselle. The captain marrying you put you in a nice, safe little niche. Being a widow doesn't change that."

Arissa was incredulous. "Is that what you think my concern is about, monsieur? My safety from the big American army?" She smirked in contempt. "My concern, my hope, is that there has been a mistake, that somehow they are alive."

"You don't strike me as much of a dreamer, mademoiselle. It doesn't become you. You're worried about your own hide. When the Brits come back, how do you think they're going to treat you, harboring the enemy and marrying one of them!"

"I am Canadian, monsieur. My brother, Martin, is fighting with General Howe at this moment. I expect to survive well enough, especially since I had no choice in furnishing your lodgings."

"And the marriage?"

"That too was forced . . . at first," she admitted.

Haskill nodded, as if digesting her words. "That's good, then, because I kind of thought you'd jump on the wagon with those other Canadian women, maybe looked Monroe's family up. He was right well off, from what I heard." He picked up his napkin and belched into it loudly. "I bet they'd welcome you like the plague, your kind having killed their son."

It had crossed Arissa's mind at one point to seek out Phillip's mother and offer to help raise the son he so adored. The prospect itself was overwhelming for a French-Canadian woman alone, searching out a family in the American colonies in the midst of a war. But to hear the colonel's idea of her reception finally buried it. Of course he was right. She was being foolish.

Despite Gaspar and Chiah's faithful support, she'd never felt so alone. She'd not even conceived Phillip's child. At least their baby would have given her more to live for.

"I will remain in my home and manage, monsieur," Arissa said, resolutely, as she got up from the table. "In the meantime, I must work to do so. Do have a pleasant retreat."

Seventeen

The return of British authority to Montreal brought everything Arissa expected. Those Canadian officers who had served in the American army and not fled were forced to set fire to their appointments, even if they burned their fingers in the process. A great number of them were ushered off to warships bound for the West Indies. The effects of all who followed the American army out of Canada were confiscated. Meanwhile, those citizens suspected of supporting the rebellion were arrested and tried. Some were executed. Penalties, however, were applied to the rest unevenly, and many remained without harassment.

Because Arissa had not fled, but remained, not only spoke in her favor, but saved the Chateau Royale from confiscation. Martin's name on the deed managed to offset Stephen's betrayal of his king. Her marriage to Phillip Monroe had been so short that it was overlooked. Adding to her plaguing guilt for having sent Phillip and Stephen off without her support, she reassumed her maiden name in hope that the wedding would remain undiscovered.

Beside the evacuated soldiers, only a few who worked for her knew of the ceremony, and their loyalty was such that she didn't question it. They knew the circumstances were not of her choosing, but they also knew of the love that had blossomed, roselike, in the snowy winter. It had been hard to hide, she discovered, upon hearing the girls in the kitchen, snickering about the romance of it all. The romance she questioned in her despondency, yet regardless, she had survived Phillip's loss. It hadn't been with the certainty she'd told Colonel Haskill she would, nor had it been without the tearing talons of guilt.

The inquiries had been terrifying for her, especially when each night she heard from the habitants about this acquaintance's or that one's misfortune. The invasion of the *bastonnois* was done. The war was over, as far as Canada was concerned. Her only worry now was for Martin's safety, for his last news had it that he was evacuating Boston with General Howe. God, he had to survive this war, she prayed fervently. Martin was all the family she had left, and she'd had such a loving family. She'd said as much in her last letter, fraught with pain hidden between the lines, telling of her bravado to salvage the Chateau Royale.

Lost in her thoughts, Arissa inventoried the dinner— and silverware, so that Chiah could retire earlier than usual. It had been an uncommonly busy day in the kitchen. The inn that had teemed with soldiers in blue and common attire, now was filled with red-coated soldiers, who were impeccable in dress and manner and paid with coin. Their love of drink was no less, and the celebration of the haphazard retreat of the Americans had made it a particularly loud and long night. Perhaps soldiers were not so different, after all, regardless of their colors.

It wasn't until she heard the scuff of a boot on the brick floor behind her that she realized she was no longer alone.

"Poor 'Rissa. It seems you're destined to be an innkeeper forever."

Arissa refrained from putting her hand to her heart and giving Adrien Rueil the satisfaction of knowing he startled her. He liked to keep people on the defensive.

It somehow boosted his insatiable ego, which had grown considerably since his release from prison to become a member of the board of inquiry, ferreting out traitors. She'd thought surely he'd have retired when the taproom closed, considering the long days he was spending trying to rebuild the Chateau Rueil, when hearings were not in session.

"There are worse lots in this life." She wrote the tally down before she forgot it and placed the ledger on the hook where it was kept. "So how is the new house coming along?"

The moment the American army abandoned Montreal, Adrien and the Loyalist militia officers were freed from prison. He looked frightful the first time she saw him, for he'd lost a good deal of weight. Now, however, working out under the spring sun and eating heartier meals, he was regaining his color and robust figure. Instead of returning to his wife's parents' home in the city every night, he often stayed at the Chateau Royale, especially during the week.

"The foundation has been cleared and the framing is ready to be erected."

"I know Celeste will be eager to get back into her new home."

"I know I will. Her father is the most arrogant of men."

Arissa nearly choked. This was clearly a choice between the pot calling the kettle black. "How is the baby?"

"Charisse? Very little hair, a few teeth, and she dribbles from both ends," he remarked, in distaste. "But she keeps Celeste occupied."

Recalling another night when Adrien had trapped her in the wine cellar, she locked the door to it quickly. Gathering up the bottles to replenish the stock in the bar upstairs, she led the way to the staircase. The poor man had been under a great deal of strain lately. Perhaps he only wanted to talk. "Get the lamp, will you, *mon ami?*"

Nonetheless, she hoped that Gaspar was still up there, but, upon emerging from the winding stairwell, she saw the portcullis pulled down over the bar. "Look, I'm glad that you are still awake, or I shall need another hand," she remarked, on reaching the locked door to the room with both arms full.

The truth was Adrien had not made the least of advances toward her since his release from prison. In fact, he'd been unusually genteel, where she was concerned. Perhaps the days of imprisonment had mellowed him.

"Here, take these," she said, handing over the bottles. After he obliged her, she fished the key from her apron pocket and opened the lock. "I think I will just set these in here and let Gaspar put them away in the morning! It has been a long day, *non?*"

"And an interesting one," Adrien added, backing away so that she might close up the bar again. "I was at the records house this morning to clarify the boundary between the Chateau Rueil and the Chateau Royale . . . I'm going to put up a fence to keep the pigs out of your garden," he informed her, lightly.

"Chiah will be eternally grateful."

"You can well imagine the turmoil down there, what with all the confiscations, etc."

"You didn't find the map?" Arissa asked, impatient for him to get to the point. She wanted to retire. Of late, sleep was the only respite from her state of chronic depression.

"I found a stack of marriage bans shoved in a binder of property maps; marriages which had taken place at the Protestant Church during the occupation." He gave her a patronizing look. "Arissa, I had heard that you and that English spy had married, but hadn't given it much credit, until I discovered this."

Arissa stared, as he produced a folded sheet torn from an official ledger. Although she knew what it was, she read over the document signed by both her and Phillip, as well as the minister—the public copy of the bans which, due to the hasty circumstances, had never been properly published.

"Perhaps I should call you Madame Monroe."

It was clear Adrien expected an explanation and Arissa felt compelled to give it. There was no telling what damage he could do with that evidence connecting her with an acknowledged spy and soldier of the enemy. Besides, she had no pangs of guilt about marrying Phillip as the enemy. She had suffered all the more for it ever since his death. If only she'd been more supportive . . .

"Come," she said, "let us sit down." *Dieu,* but she did not wish to dredge up her remorse over the way she'd sent Phillip and Stephen off. She lead the way to the table closest to the bar and sat down. "You see, *mon ami,* not all Loyalists were imprisoned. Some of us were forced to put up with the *bastonnois.*"

"I recall seeing you two together many times, when you didn't seem forced to enjoy his company."

"I believed he was who he said he was . . . and I did like him as a friend."

"A friend only?"

"That became of no importance. When the troops came, I hated him for his lies. I endured their presence here. But when I saw how sickly they were and discovered their leaders would not let them become inoculated for the smallpox, I could not help myself. I inoculated them secretly to save their lives, as I am devoted in doing for any man, enemy or no."

"How noble."

Arissa refused to take up the argument. She was tired. This was an argument like the war. No matter what one did, one was damned. "For that, I was arrested as a Loyalist enemy who sought to undermine the invasion of Quebec and was imprisoned for four days, with the threat of being sent to Halifax with other dissidents. But for Phillipe, I would have been."

"He proposed marriage to keep you out of trouble with his superiors?" Adrien exclaimed, with a dubious lift of his golden brow.

"*Non,* he assumed full responsibility for my actions and promised to keep me at the Chateau Royale and stop the inoculations," Arissa defended her late husband. "He married me because it was the honorable thing to do, since he would be watching me day and night." There was no point in Adrien knowing of the passion they'd shared prior to their wedding vows.

"And why did you marry him?"

"What?"

"Why did you marry Phillip Monroe?" Rueil reiterated, impatiently.

Arissa was taken aback by the question. "Why I . . . well, I had no choice." *Dieu,* it was like having her own private hearing. Adrien with power was an intimidating prospect, just when she thought she might be safe.

Adrien sat back in his chair and gave a sardonic laugh. "Brilliant!"

"I do not understand, monsieur, what it is that you are trying to say, but I am tired and . . ."

"You protected your precious inn both ways. If the Americans won, you were married to one. Now that the British have won, you were forced to marry the American for inoculating our enemy and making them unfit to fight. Such dedication to the king!"

It would have been simpler to let Adrien think what he would, but Arissa would take no insinuation that she used her medicinal skills for personal gain. "I made no such claims. My dedication is to life!"

"But no one has questioned you on the wedding, because it's been overlooked."

She nodded. "That is correct. If you are my friend, you will leave it that way and burn that paper."

"Naturally. I just wanted the story of this wedding," Adrien agreed.

Arissa waited uncertainly. It wasn't like him to be so agreeable.

"But secrecy has its price."

She knew it! Adrien did nothing without reward of some nature. "And what is that, Adrien?"

"I love you, Arissa."

If he'd shot her, she'd have been less shocked.

"I've always wanted you, but you were too headstrong."

"Adrien, you are married!"

"Only because you would not marry me."

"I didn't want marriage at all, not even with Phillipe!" She crossed her fingers in her lap. That was at least partially true.

Adrien leaned forward, a golden forelock falling from the carefully groomed waves of his hair. "Marriage is impossible for us now, *ma cherie,* but love is not. I will protect you and take care of you, now that Stephen is gone. You won't have work-reddened hands. You could live like a queen here!"

Arissa withdrew from the table, incredulous at the implication of his words. "You would have me as your mistress?"

"It's the only way. You could have been my wife, but that is your fault!" he accused.

Stepping back, as Adrien jumped to his feet, Arissa shook her head. "That is insane. Martin would kill you for such a proposal! Besides, I am doing fine without you. You are my friend and neighbor, nothing more."

"After tonight, *ma petite cherie,* that will change."

She should have moved toward the stairway but, in her shock, allowed herself to be trapped between the bar and the man approaching her. His face left her uncertain as

to the full extent of his intentions, for while lust certainly
fired his gaze, there was also a pitiful sense of pleading
in his gray eyes. It was that which gave her hope of rea-
soning with the man. How Phillip had disdained her pity
for him! Perhaps she should have listened more closely.

"I've always loved you, Arissa. You were the only one
who didn't mock me. Don't think I didn't know how the
others talked behind my back. But I overheard you defending me. I've loved you ever since."

Arissa felt the portcullis bite into her back and tried
to remain calm. "I have always been honest with you,
Adrien, as I am now. I want nothing more than to be
your friend."

The grate rattled, as Adrien grasped it on either side
of her, losing patience. "I can change your mind, Arissa!
Give me the chance! Don't force my hand!"

"Adrien, this is beneath you. It's blackmail! You say you
care for me, but subject me to this threat!" She lifted her
head, refusing to be intimidated by his overbearing presence.

"Better *I* discover the bans than someone else, someone who would think only of taking the Chateau Royale
for a pittance."

Arissa dodged the lips that moved toward her, but was
unable to escape the imprisonment of the arms that
closed about her. If she kept her head, if she didn't provoke his fiendish temper, she might divert him.

"Even if another discovered them, there is much in my
favor," she pointed out, wincing, as he brushed her ear
gently. "I told you, I was forced."

"You smell like wild roses." Adrien chuckled, softly, his
breath warm against the side of her face. It reeked of
rum, flavored only slightly with a stale citrus scent. "You
always were a wild rose: beautiful, but prickly and unman-
ageable. Your *bastonnois*, he could not handle you, and I
could see for myself that he wanted to!"

Arissa had been in the kitchen most of the night, so there was no telling how much Adrien had to drink. She'd seen him turn devil-mean over the course of an evening of imbibing. She had to think quickly.

"But I smell like dishwater and grease," she objected, turning sideways, within the confines of his arms. "Not fit for any man." If there was anything Adrien could understand, it was vanity. "At least give me a few moments to change and freshen up . . . just a little time to think. *S'il vous plaît, mon ami?*" she finished, pursing her lips in an imploring, yet beguiling pout.

It seemed an eternity before her companion ceased to ponder her suggestion, and he reluctantly backed away. *"Bon,* I will accompany you to your room."

The hopes of bolting her door until Adrien came to his senses died with Arissa's disappointed sigh. "If you would get the lamp, monsieur, I shall fetch a bottle of our best cognac from the bar to help you pass the time, until I can finish my toilette." While Adrien loved Madeira, cognac was his expensive favorite, used to toast at his wedding and upon his being appointed colonel of the local militia that never quite formed.

With a smile of satisfaction that things were falling so smoothly into place for him, Adrien picked up the lamp, while Arissa opened the bar once again. She took her time picking the bottle in order to assemble her wits. She could scream and awaken the soldiers, but that would lead to the exposure of the bans and Adrien, with his influence, would surely make an inquiry hellish. That is, if he didn't overcome her, first. He was a strong man and in the peak of shape.

"Forget the cognac, Arissa, any will do," Adrien spoke up, impatiently. His voice was fevered with his apparent success.

Arissa closed her hand around the wax-and-cork sealed bottle and locked the taproom, once again. "Of course, you will allow me the privacy of my dressing screen," she stipulated, modestly, while leading the way to the winding steps. "I had only two nights with my husband, Adrien. I . . ."

"But of course, *ma cherie*. I can imagine what the brute must have done, forcing you into marriage, as you say. I, on the other hand," he told her, slipping his free hand about her waist in order to buss the side of her face, before she took the first step, "have been known to pleasure a woman greatly, if she is a warm and willing mate."

And if not . . . Arissa controlled her shudder. When treating Adrien's wife as a patient, she'd seen bruises on Celeste Rueil's back and breasts that defied the woman's lame explanation of them. They'd been laid upon the poor girl by a riding crop, or worse.

"And if she is nervous?" Arissa demurred, sweetly.

"Then I will soothe all her fears."

He was completely the charming seducer, now that he was assured of getting his way. Despite the choking sensation of the velvet answer, Arissa drew away and started up the stairwell leading to the family quarters. She had one chance, and there was no room for error. Her heart seemed to thunder a dozen times for each step she took, making it hard for her to discern how close Adrien was behind her. If she missed . . .

Three steps from the top, at the most winding part of the stairwell, Arissa tightened her grip on the bottle and swung around quickly. It struck the side of Adrien's head, knocking him into the wall, as it shattered and soaked his brocade jacket. Amidst the play of their giant shadows against the curved plank walls, Arissa saw him reel backward. Recognizing new danger, she reached frantically for the lamp, before it fell and exploded into flame. Her fingers only brushed it, for Adrien let it go and seized her wrist with an agonized curse.

Down. They were going down. Shadows and fire, vile

oath and strangled scream, all filled the smothering enclosure. As if reaching for a lifeline, Arissa grabbed instinctively with her free hand and latched onto the rail, stopping not only her fall, but that of her assailant as well. Her arms felt as though they'd been yanked from their sockets. Why hadn't someone heard them?

To her horror, Adrien was pulling himself upright, using his grasp on her wrist as his support. Blood streaked across his fair complexion and stained his sun-gold hair, making his face as hideous as the murder that flamed in his eyes. The number of bottles she'd had to replace at the bar, in addition to the empty kegs stacked on the counter, answered her question. The soldiers surely slept the sleep of the dead drunk.

Adrien didn't swear at her anymore. His breathing was too rash and ragged, threatening to tear his bulging nostrils apart. Arissa knew death awaited her, if she didn't act quickly. Fear built up within her, until it shattered her frozen state. She kicked at his clutching arm with all her might, driving it against the wall with her booted heel in an unnatural manner. The sickening sound of bone cracking made her wretch inside, as she fell upward upon the steps to her back.

Even as a tread dug painfully into her spine, she kicked again, this time catching his ribs, as he gained his footing just below her. Holding his crippled arm, he glared at her with a malevolence that rendered her unable to scream, only to watch as he paused momentarily in midair, and then plunged straight backward. Kicking and reeling off step and wall, Adrien went straight to the bottom of the stairwell, where the globe of the lamp had shattered, its oil seeping freely. The fire took to his clothing ravenously, but neither moan nor scream emerged from his lips, as he fell limply to the floor.

Arissa couldn't move, although he rolled beyond her view. All she could see were his feet, kicking involuntarily in his fiery death. God help her, she wanted to go to him, to put out the fire, for she hadn't intended that. She'd only meant to knock him senseless, she'd . . .

"Mon Dieu!"

She heard a startled exclamation, followed by a heavy beating noise. Gaspar! Recognition of her friend's voice bringing untold relief. Perhaps he was beating out the fire with one of the rugs kept by the back door. She coughed in the smoke and tried to move again to help him, but her muscles would not obey her. A sob caught in her burning throat and forced the smoke from her lungs, wracking her shoulders unmercifully, until there was no air left. Holding her skirts over her face to filter the smoke, she breathed in again, when she noticed the silence. There was no more beating or thrashing.

"Ma fille, ma fille, mon Dieu, what has happened?"

When she showed her face, Gaspar was climbing up the stairs after her. In a moment, she was in his arms.

"I d . . . didn't mean to kill him! God help me, I didn't mean it! He . . . he was blackmailing me because I married Ph . . . Phillipe but I . . . could . . . couldn't . . ."

Gaspar let loose a curse Arissa had never heard from his lips. "The bastard deserved to die. I should have waited until he was in his room before I went out to the cabin. He just acted like he was the cat with the fish in his mouth, *non*? I heard him bragging of his prospects for the night, but he was flirting with Jeanne, and I paid it no mind. Jeanne, she takes care of herself."

He . . . he might have come to my room, anyway."

"And you would not have been able to fight him there."

Bewildered and dazed, Arissa pulled away, tearfully. "Gaspar, the fire!"

"It is out and the door is open to clear the air."

"And Adrien?" She shivered, uncontrollably. "I didn't

mean to burn him. I . . . I only meant to knock him silly with the bottle. I forgot the . . . the lamp and . . ."

"His neck, it was broken. The fire did not kill him."

Arissa took a deep, but shaky breath and closed her eyes. She'd only meant to knock him senseless and bolt herself in her room until he sobered. "I'm going to hang now, I know. I've killed a man!" she finished, her voice teetering on hysteria, as she buried her face in the thin man's shoulder.

"You are not going to hang! Gaspar will see to that." The older man rose to his feet, drawing Arissa with him. "Come, Chiah will take care of you in our cabin. Gaspar, he needs time to think. Whatever we do, it must be before sunrise."

Eighteen

Alain Beaujeu closed the ledger in which he'd logged the various accounts of counterfeit bills which drifted back from Canada. These particular ones with the bypassing crosses had all originated from New York, which was where most of the British attempt to undermine the currency of the new rebel government had been generated. But of this particular run of bills, he'd narrowed the point down to New York City itself. Hence, he thought, as he packed the ledger in his bag of clothing, he would be moving from this disastrous Canadian retreat at Ticonderoga to New York, by way of Albany, of course.

He ran his hand through his thick dark hair, only slightly salted with age about the temples. *Dieu*, he hadn't seen Tamson and the boys in three months. Running supplies to Ticonderoga procured from the islands by the ships of the Dutch-Acadie Company had been a demanding chore. Not only was he back at his old job as a government-appointed supply clerk, but this time he was purchasing the goods for his country from his own company. The profit was fair, but the chore of keeping it that way was a big one.

That was why he made the deliveries himself, and that was how he became involved in the counterfeiting investigation. Imagine his surprise when he'd delivered the guns and ammunition, only to be paid in counterfeit bills!

He believed in the Continental dollar—or at least in its future—but he would be damned if he'd allow the bloody British to cheat him!

He looked out the open window of the small cell afforded him in the fort. The grounds were filled with Canadian refugees seeking handouts. Every day their numbers grew. They'd come to the colonies in hope of establishing a new life of self-rule, not monarchy. Since the Congress was offering land grants for veterans of this bloody conflict, the prospects were good. It was such a shame that their fellow Canadians had not joined them in support of the American army, for together, with their pooled resources, Alain was certain Britain's flag could be banished from the continent.

Beyond, at one of the gates, he watched a death wagon pass. The duty-weary soldiers were dying so quickly of smallpox that the mass graves were opened in the morning and kept so for three days. But this was not his concern, he told himself, shaking off the overwhelming sense of loss. His was to supply the army by merchant, privateer, or both. And now he was to find the bastards printing counterfeit bills which he'd been paid for the much needed goods. He'd give all he had to the cause, but not to have it stolen from him by the blasted enemy!

As he started away from the window, his eye was caught by a curious trio. More refugees, no doubt, he thought, grimly. It consisted of a man, a tall Indian woman, and a young girl. While his appreciative eye might have remained on the lithesome creature with the honey blonde hair, it was drawn back to the man—a thin, gangly fellow with shoulders bent by age, and a long, hawklike nose.

Alain blinked, as if his eyes deceived him. There could be no other like him in the company of an Indian woman a full head taller than he. It had to be! Breaking into a run, Alain passed the single cot and table which crowded the room and rushed out into the fort yard.

"Gaspar! Gaspar Le Boeuf!"

"Alain, *mon ami!*" The older man broke away from his companions in delight and ran up to Alain, embracing him and then dancing about in a circle around him, before embracing him again. "But look at you! You who said you would not lift arms against the King of England!"

"I promised not to bear arms against my wife's king. As you can see, I wear no uniform." Alain pointed to his canvas trousers, brightly sashed in blue at the waist, and his red shirt. "Only the uniform of the voyageur. Except that I buy arms from whoever has them in the islands and sell them to the Continental army. It is they who bear those arms, not I." Alain laughed, a deep merry sound which drew the undivided attention of Gaspar's younger companion. "Besides, Tamson has fairly disclaimed the bastard. He's got the Scot riled in her."

Alain backed away from another of Gaspar's bearlike hugs and addressed Chiah. "You have kept your husband well, Chiah. I thought when he settled down that he would wither away, but I can see he is as ornery as ever."

Chiah returned Alain's hug with a genuine smile. "It eats him, so he is poor from it!"

"And who is this . . ."

Alain broke off, staring at the familiar features which studied him with the same intensity. The hair wasn't quite right, but the girl's thick, dark lashes and perfectly formed eyebrows could no more be denied than the way she chewed the fullness of her bottom lip. Her expression, her features, they all belonged to Jeanette de Montigny, but for those striking blue eyes and blonde tresses.

"Do not say a word!" Alain cautioned Gaspar. He bowed gallantly and took the girl's work-callused hands to his lips. "Mademoiselle, I had the pleasure of knowing your mother, but it is from your lips that I would hear her name."

"Estelle, monsieur," Arissa answered, lamely, for she

could not believe that she was actually standing before the heroic and romantic Alain Beaujeu of Gaspar's tales. "Estelle Conway."

Although he was older, he still cut a handsome figure in the mitasses and gay dress of the voyageur. Time had been good to him, leaving lines of laughter, white against his handsome tanned face, at the corners of his Beaujeu blue eyes. His whole family had them, Gaspar had said. The dark hair and cerulean combination had caught many an admiring gaze, and hers was no different.

With a disconcerted glance as Gaspar, Alain apologized. "You must pardon me for my boldness, mademoiselle. I had mistaken . . ."

"Alain, this is Madame Arissa Monroe," Gaspar intervened. "She was married to an American who was killed during the siege of Quebec and now seeks to find her . . . his family."

"You have my deepest sympathies, *ma cher.* If there is anything I can do . . ."

"You can find us a place to sleep, at least the women," Gaspar answered, quickly. "The journey has been hard on them."

Alain looked again at the bedraggled girl he'd have sworn was Jeanette's daughter. But that was impossible, for now that he'd had time to gather his wits, he recalled that Jeanette had no children by De Montigny and, the last he'd heard of her from his cousin in France, she was living a carefree life in Paris as widow of yet another French noble.

"They can have my quarters." He motioned toward the open door to the small room built into the wall of the fort. "It is not much, but it is dry and well-ventilated. I will see if I can get another cot."

"Chiah likes sleep on the ground," Chiah objected, taking the girl under her arm, protectively. "You and

Gaspar, you go find killdevil, while the madame and Chiah unpack things. My girl tired and need nap."

Alain slapped Gaspar on the back. *"Bien, mon ami,* but I will have a beer. I cannot drink the killdevil so easily, anymore. I become a wild man."

"You never could!" Gaspar retorted, smugly. "That is why you always had to wear the apron."

"The apron?" Arissa queried, as the two companions walked off together, most likely toward the trading post she'd seen on the way inside the giant fortress.

Chiah gave her that quiet smile, so characteristic of her. "When the boys play fiddle and dance, but got no girl, Alain have to wear apron."

"Oh." Somehow Arissa could hardly picture such a virile specimen of a man wearing any such thing, but then, nothing surprised her anymore.

She'd never dreamed she'd sleep on a blanket under the stars and walk along muddy roads with ruts deep enough to bury a wagon to the axle. They'd passed many a family in such a circumstance, unloading all their belongings to get the wagon and horse out of the mire. She'd never dreamed she'd be eating wild berries and game cooked over a campfire, or developing a tolerance for firecake, a meal and water mixture baked on the stones surrounding the fire.

When she'd heard Stephen describe them, she wrinkled her nose at the thought of eating them, ashes and all. However, the first time they'd resorted to the scant stores they'd brought along, rather than the land for their meal, she'd eaten the cake without complaint. She wouldn't dare insult Chiah and Gaspar, after what they'd done for her.

The night of Adrien's horrible death, Gaspar paid one of the kitchen boys to take Arissa across the river by canoe to Prairie to the house of a friend, where she was to wait for him to join her. She learned later that the husband

and wife had moved Adrien to her room and set fire to
the bed. Then, once it had gotten going well, they'd
sounded the alarm. The rug in the hall between Arissa's
room and that in which some of the British officers were
sleeping, had caught fire, demanding the men's immediate attention. This they dragged down the winding staircase and out the back door, covering the traces of
Adrien's earlier tumbling inferno with scorches of its own.

By the time the dawn broke, the family quarters of the
inn had been destroyed. Due to the diligence of the soldiers awakened by the alarm, the other half of her father's grand mansion had been saved. Chiah had shown
herself to be in such shock at the loss of her beloved
mistress that Gaspar had insisted on taking her to her
family in the Richelieu Valley, after he and his wife had
personally seen that Arissa's blanket-wrapped remains
were buried in the family lot on the hill between the
Chateaux Rueil and the Royale.

They then joined Arissa the following day with a few
of their belongings and a bag of her own, which Chiah
had packed before the fire. There they'd paid the boy
well with gold the couple had put away to keep his silence. Although it was doubtful such generosity was
needed, for the lad had always been fond of Arissa and
was against anything which might bring his mistress harm.
The following morning, they'd left on foot and, to Arissa's
dismay, traveled that way ever since, with the exception
of taking a canoe Gaspar had procured, where water afforded easier access.

She'd tried hard not to cry over the desperation of her
escape and the circumstances that led to it. Yet at night,
she was haunted by nightmares of Adrien falling down
the stairs, taking her into the burning flames with him.
During the day, she'd catch herself reliving the horrible
memory and twisting Phillip's wedding ring round and
round her finger, as though it were some talisman capable

of making her terror go away. She had rubbed the skin raw beneath it, requiring daily washing and the application of a salve from her medical bag, which Chiah so thoughtfully remembered. If only there had been a salve for her memory and one for her heart.

"I would have bet my right arm that your Arissa was Jeanette De Montigny's child!" Alain swore, after taking a healthy draft of beer. "After all, Jeanette's father had fair hair."

"And you would have kept it, *mon ami*," Gaspar informed him. Instead of drinking, he contemplated the pitcher in front of him, seeking and measuring the words he needed to say. "She was adopted at birth by the English physician who delivered her. The family had two boys, but his wife, a member of Montreal's noblesse, wanted a daughter. Since she could have no more children, Arissa was the answer to her prayers."

Alain studied Gaspar's face. "Are you saying that Jeanette had a child out of wedlock and gave it up?"

"Such a thing would have run her out of Montreal, if the secret were out, *mon ami*. You know that." Gaspar reached in his pocket and withdrew a yellowed letter, penned in a feminine hand. It had been given to him by the Widow de Montigny, before she departed for Paris, nearly thirteen years ago. Jeanette had kept in touch with the Conways and, thereby, her daughter, until her decision to leave Montreal. Ironically, Arissa's real mother left just three months before her adopted mother died.

Jeanette de Montigny had done one other thing for her daughter's welfare, before departing. She'd sent the letter in Alain's hands to Gaspar, leaving the matter to the voyageur as to what to do with it, for she was aware that the man knew of Alain Beaujeu's real whereabouts.

"This is for you, *mon ami*. For years, I have kept it because to deliver it, I thought, would do no good."

The letter was addressed to Alain in Jeanette's unmistakable handwriting. Even as he opened it, a strange foreboding overwhelmed him. He refused to give rein to the questions that assaulted him. Instead he took his time and read the missive from the past.

"My dearest Alain," it began. "I leave tomorrow for Paris and, in doing so, leave you with a great responsibility. It is one I have born alone these last thirteen years. In May of 1749, I visited friends in the Richelieu, and there I birthed your daughter. The physician who delivered her and his wife so wanted a little girl, and I knew that you and I had no future as anything more than lovers. So, my dearest, I gave her to them. We were like stars whose paths cross only once in a while in the heavens. Both of us were wild in our own way, you devoted to your wilderness ventures and I to my role in society. I wanted more than that for Arissa.

"You must know that these last thirteen years, she has lived happily with the Conways. She has two older brothers who adore her, and her mother, Estelle, loves her more than life itself. I fear you know that I have difficulty with such unselfishness. A good mother is something I was never meant to be. So, *voilà, mon cher.* You have a bright and beautiful daughter living happily in Montreal, now with her adopted family. Alain, I know how you are about family, but surely you can see she is better off with them than with either of us, especially now that you are married to Tamson. I shall love her as I love you, and always will."

The letter was signed simply, "Yours always, Jeanette."

Alain swallowed hard and raised his solemn gaze to his companion. "You knew about this and did not tell me?"

"Alain, you were married and having children with Tamson. You were happy. Jeanette was happy. Arissa was happy!" Gaspar explained, defensively. "Chiah and I, we worked for the doctor and his wife, and when they died, we continued to stay with Arissa and her brothers. They built a grand inn and she ran it. She'd just started a medicinal distributorship of her own. She has her father's business sense."

Alain grunted, still in shock. A daughter! Jeanette's daughter!

"And she is a doctor!" Gaspar announced, proudly. "My hip was broken and she made me good as new!"

"What?" Alain frowned. "Whoever heard of a woman doctor? Besides, she is too young! He counted mentally. Twenty-six. He had been so in love with Jeanette twenty-six years ago that he would have married her. But his first love had wanted to marry nobility. He chuckled to himself, better able to accept Jeanette's faults now than he had then. She had been a woman who knew what she wanted and had gotten it. The truth was, they'd have been miserable as a couple and, worse, he'd have never met Tamson.

"That girl has been studying medicine with her father since she was fourteen." Upon seeing that he had his friend's attention once again, Gaspar continued. "Oh, she went to the finest girl's academy in Montreal and was introduced to all the right people, but it seemed she had her real father's reaction to the noblesse. They bored her. She liked the business, helping her brothers, and caring for people. She is a certified midwife, but her doctoring is limited, because she's had no formal studies."

Gaspar spun the incredible tale, filling Alain in on the life of the daughter he'd never met, until now. She hadn't supported the war at all, thought it silly. Now *that* was a familiar stance, he thought, stepping back to another place and time. With one brother fighting for the British and another recruiting for the Americans, she'd remained as stubbornly neutral as possible, although she leaned toward the British. She mistrusted Americans. Then she met Phillip Monroe.

Alain perked up. "Phillip Monroe?" he queried in surprise. "From New York City?"

Gaspar nodded. "A widower."

"She married Phillip Monroe?"

"And lost her husband and brother at Quebec."

"Sacre bleu! But this is more incredible, yet!"

His turn to be bewildered, Gaspar asked, "And why is that?"

"Because he is . . . was my legal representative for Dutch-Acadie Company. I knew he'd lost his wife and gone to Quebec, but . . . *Mon Dieu!*" Alain finished, incredulous. "He was a brilliant attorney! He convinced us to expand from fur trade to commodities, as well. He has . . . had stock in the company."

Gaspar grinned. "He said he was a clerk . . . but that was part of his charade, I suppose. When Arissa finally came to trust this charming *bastonnois,* he showed up at the inn as a captain in the occupying forces. I can say there was more war there in the inn than outside Quebec City."

Again, Alain was intrigued, more so than ever. It was with a degree of pride that he heard how Arissa had inoculated the soldiers, risking incarceration, and with relief, that Phillip had come to her rescue. He'd married her, over her objections. Alain recognized that stubborn and reckless pride. It had caused most of his problems with Tamson, when they were fighting their attraction to each other.

And the marriage was like Monroe—honorable to a fault. It was one of the reasons Alain had chosen him over his partner, Jonathan Hale, to represent them. Now it appeared they'd deal with the less aggressive and ambitious Hale.

As Gaspar went on, Alain discovered there was little that passed his friend unobserved. It was also obvious that Gaspar was as attached to Arissa as Alain should be. He was a self-appointed guardian of the girl and had proved it in coming to her rescue, when there was no one left to turn to for help.

"*Bon,* I have heard enough," he said at last, shoving a handful of coin on the table to pay for the pitchers of beer they'd consumed. "There is just one more question."

"And what is that, *mon ami?*"

"Does Arissa know about her real mother and father?"

"She knows her mother was a member of the noblesse, who could not acknowledge an illegitimate child. I do not think she thinks hard of the woman, because she is of a practical sort and recognizes her mother left her better off. As for you, *mon ami,* she only thinks that you are a wonderful hero and in no way related to her."

"A *what?*" . . .

Gaspar became sheepish. "You know how I love to tell stories. I kept her brothers enthralled with those of our adventures, but for a little girl, romance adds a bit of charm, *non?*"

"Go on," Alain prompted, uncertain that he really wanted to hear what Gaspar had invented about him.

"I told her how you kidnaped Tamson to avenge your family's exile, but fell hopelessly in love with her, so much so, that you gave up your noble inheritance and country and risked your life to see her safely delivered back to her home." Gaspar shrugged. "It was something like that."

Alain made a growling sound and knocked at the back of his companion's head, good-naturedly. "I don't know whether to throttle you, or to be indebted, you old fur dog."

"Neither," Gaspar came back readily. "Go talk to your daughter."

* * *

There was no place for privacy in the fort. Soldiers and Canadian refugees, Indians and French traders, all milled both within and without the walls. Alain elected to take Arissa for an early evening walk, rather than remain in the confined cabin. He needed room for the expansion of the emotions he was feeling, the exercise to help vent them. There were twenty-six years to make up to the young woman walking leisurely at his side. Yet, he didn't know where to begin.

"Chiah and I walked around the refugee camp earlier today," she was saying, her limpid blue gaze taking in the same scene now.

She'd been confused, at first, that Alain had insisted on speaking to her alone, but accepted it in easy stride. Gaspar had apparently told her enough about him to allay any suspicion of him she might harbor.

"I was thinking that maybe, since I know Chiah and Gaspar will want to return to their home in Montreal, that it would be best if I remained here. Their house is legally theirs. My brothers deeded it over to them a few years ago," she explained. "But here, there is so much sickness . . . aside from the smallpox!" she pointed out in earnest. "Maybe I could make a difference with my medical skills, although my supplies are limited," she added, in chagrin. "Did Gaspar tell you I trained under my father? He was an English physician."

Well, he'd better start talking, Alain thought, or his new daughter would have her life laid out apart and aside from his intended plan for her. His friend had said she had an independent streak.

"Gaspar told me many things about you today, madame." Madame. That was not an address for one's blood. Alain cleared his throat nervously, as he'd been doing since they'd left Chiah and Gaspar to prepare some semblance of a meal for supper.

"I have an elixir that might help that irritation in your throat, monsieur. It's one of papa's formulas."

"You must have loved your father very much," Alain remarked, ignoring the offer. He felt oddly jealous of the flicker of affection in the eyes that were so like his own at the mention of the doctor. She had Jeanette's capacity for compassion, which was an odd trait for her mother, considering the woman's often selfish single-mindedness.

Arissa smiled. "With all my heart . . . and my mother too, of course. Although, if *maman* had lived, I would be married to some member of the noblesse, rather than following in papa's footsteps. And my brothers, why, if Martin knew of my desperate plight now, he would be doing his best to find me. I'm at my wits' end as to how to reach him, to tell him that I am alive and well. He won't know what to think."

"The brother fighting with General Howe?"

"*Oui*, that is the one."

There were ways of getting messages to the British, but that was not Alain's major concern now. Beside, all he needed was an enraged, adopted brother adding to the turmoil Arissa's discovery had already brought about. "So you have been basically happy, until now."

"Until the war. My entire life was undone by the war," the girl lamented, with a sigh fraught with emotion.

"So was mine," Alain told her, "but it was another war. That is the way of such things."

"Gaspar told me about you and your wife. I must say. It was most romantic."

Although Alain did not mind basking in the worship directed at him, he was anxious to have the truth out, all of it.

"Arissa, Gaspar did not tell you everything about me. There were some things he knew, that even I was not aware of until today."

"Oh?"

Dieu, but she looked like Jeanette when she cocked her pretty brow in that way and held her lips in that questioning purse. "Arissa, I am your father . . . your real father."

Alain stopped and breathed more easily. There, it was out, even if his companion looked as if she did not believe him. Nearby, a child stumbled amidst clotheslines and haphazardly erected shelters and started to cry. His mother, almost as much in need of a bath as her offspring, ran to fetch him up in her arms, cooing softly.

Needing no distraction, Alain led his stupefied offspring to a cluster of nearby trees on the outskirts of the encampment. Beyond was the stream from which they fetched water for consumption and did their laundry. Although the latrine ditches had been dug per military authority on the opposite side of the camp, Alain questioned the wisdom of the closeness of such things. Moving the refugees would do more to fight the dysentery and other maladies plaguing them than his daughter's medical skills.

Since Arissa had done nothing but stare at him, speechless, he went on. "Your mother was Jeanette de Montigny, a noblewoman of Montreal. I . . ." He broke off, wondering what had become of that silver tongue his wife accused him of having. Reaching into his pocket, he produced the letter Gaspar had given him earlier. "Here, it is all in here."

He waited, while Arissa read the missive, his arms crossed and fingers biting into his tanned flesh. Jeanette had said it best. They loved each other, but were not compatible for a lifetime. Perhaps one of the things he most admired about Jeanette was her ability to assess a situation and accept it for what it was, when it could not be changed. She was less driven by the heart than he, in that respect. For Alain, family and love were first and foremost.

Although there was a pleasant evening breeze, he was actually perspiring. It was like the day John was born, and James, and little Robert. Except that instead of looking for the first time on a tiny, squirming, whimpering bundle of love, he was watching a lovely, full-grown woman, clutching her breast with one hand and reading fervently through pools of sapphire. Whether the tears bode good or bad, he couldn't tell.

Alain had no idea what to expect, so he was certainly unprepared for the joyous sob that erupted from her quivering lips, or her rush to toss her arms about him and hug him, as though she were afraid he was going to go away. Even fainting had been a possibility, for one long, silent second. Heaven knew, he felt lightheaded, but he wasn't going to be moved from that spot. Arissa was his daughter, and he was going to be her father and take care of her, if he had to kidnap her to do it.

It was obvious, however, that kidnaping, for the present was not a necessity. He managed to untangle himself from her embrace in order to return it. Her hair tickled his nose, but he didn't care. Her nails bit into his back over and over, as if she couldn't get a firm enough hold on him to keep the torrent of emotion that was shaking her body from driving them apart. Alain wanted to whisper soothing words of comfort, as a father should, but the blade of emotion in his throat would not allow him to do more than return her embrace as heartily.

When her tears were finally spent, the girl backed away from him, looking up, red-eyed, in a sheepish manner. "Look at me! You have a new baby, *non?*"

Alain laughed, relieved to release some of his tension. "Tamson and I have always wanted a daughter, but it didn't seem, after Robert's birth, that that was to be." He pointed skyward. "That Man up there, His ways are curious, *non?*"

"That Man and Gaspar," she answered, wryly. "He has known all these years about us and never told!"

Arissa squeezed Alain's hand. She'd dreamed of such a man carrying her off romantically, but considering her circumstances of late, her knight in shining armor had arrived for just the right purpose—to replace her family. Family had always been most important to her, especially being adopted. She'd learned to appreciate family love, where others took it for granted.

"Ah yes, Gaspar," Alain agreed, taking the girl into his arms, until her shivering stopped.

He'd had no little girl of his own, and it had been years since he'd coddled one of his sisters. Annette now lived north of Albany on a big farm with her husband, Tom, and their children. Their firstborn, Jenny, came in the same year as Alain and Tamson's John. Liselle lived in Charleston with her husband, Mark Heathcote, and their offspring. Alain's baby sister had met and married a printer in Philadelphia, where Marie La Tour Beaujeu lived with her youngest daughter until her death five years ago.

"You have quite a big, natural family to meet, you know, *ma petite,*" he said, encouraging her to walk again through a muddy swath cut between campsites that led to the fort's gate. "I have three sisters, and they each have an assortment of children. I can no longer keep them straight. Then there's my wife, Tamson, and our three boys."

Arissa's gaze sparkled with heartfelt enthusiasm. "I can hardly wait to meet them!"

Alain pursed his lips to keep from grinning. "So you think you can give up your plans to save the Canadian refugees to become part of the American Beaujeu clan?"

"I know I can!" she declared, eagerly, before frowning with obvious second thoughts. "That is, if they will accept

me. I am from the enemy. I have not always supported
the Americans." She lowered her voice in honest admission. "I don't know how I feel now about this war. I only
wish it were over."

"Just give my family a chance, and you will be as great
a patriot as your husband was."

"Phillipe?" The girl was clearly taken back. Her voice
broke. "Y . . . you knew him?"

"He was a business associate and a friend. His is a great
loss to us both."

Her swollen eyes welled again, and Alain not only saw,
but felt, her pain. For all their differences in political
views, he knew then that she had loved the young man.
And now her heart and spirit were broken. He hugged
her and then fitted her under his protective arm, as they
walked through the gate of the fort. Ignoring some of
the curious stares directed at them, for he was obviously
old enough to be the child's father, he planted a kiss on
the top of her head, at a loss as to how to soothe the
wound he'd inadvertently reopened by mentioning Phillip Monroe.

"Let us not look back, *ma petitesse*. We have only a future ahead together as a family. How bad can that be?"
He pointed to the desolate camp. "The war, it comes and
it goes, but the families, they will hold together. They will
be there after the treaties are signed and the guns are
put away, until the next time. Family is foundation of life
itself and, tomorrow, we will begin our journey to Albany,
where one set of Beaujeus is waiting to welcome you."
He chuckled at her skeptical glance. "That is the way we
are. You will just have to accept our love as a matter of
course . . . not to mention a good deal of teasing. After
all, I have three boys."

Arissa digested Alain's words. "And I have three more
brothers . . . and a mother!"

Alain nodded. And a mother, but how was he going

to explain Arissa to Tamson? He took the letter Arissa
still held in her hand and shoved it back into his jacket.
He sure as the devil wasn't going to do it without that
letter. After all, Tamson would have to understand he
was not responsible for infidelities before he had ever
met her.

Nineteen

The trip from Ticonderoga to Albany had been almost as relentless as that from Montreal to the fort. However, Arissa had grown hardened to the long days on horseback and had even begun to appreciate this wilderness of massive forests and deep blue lakes—that is, when she wasn't frightened senseless worrying about Indians. They had seen several along the way, but Alain Beaujeu had been familiar with their tribes and spoken fluently with them, introducing her proudly as his daughter and a medicine woman. They'd also seen patrols on their way north to reinforce Ticonderoga, carrying much needed supplies.

Although a far cry from what she was accustomed to, Arissa adapted well to the camp life and the convenience of the trousers and shirt her new father had purchased for her. Many nights they'd spent among fellow travelers, exchanging the latest news from the north as well as the south. Word from a trapper on his way to New York from the Lake George region revealed that, with the British on the march southward, they had released the prisoners taken during the Battle of Quebec. The officers and men were being delivered to New York by ship, which amazed Arissa.

She couldn't imagine a British ship sailing into the American-held New York harbor. When her father explained, tongue in cheek, that even the royal governor still ruled some parts of the city from the same harbor, she was incredulous. Again she wondered what manner of war was this.

"The New Yorkers, they are much of the Dutch influence. Like the merchants in Montreal, they wish to trade with both sides." Upon seeing her skepticism unthwarted, he shrugged. "I imagine when General Howe is ready to make his move, and General Washington makes his stand, that will change."

"Them Yorkers ain't like the rest of us," the man who'd introduced himself as simply Egan, chortled. "The New Englanders and Quakers think they're a hair short of heathen, and the southern folks just don't trust 'em. They's a folks all to their own, liking to make money and spend it."

"And this is what *you* think of Montrealers?" Arissa demanded of her father.

"You forget, Arissa, I was one of them. They do not mind the war, so long as the trade is unimpaired. Your being in the business of innkeeping, the trade requirements do not affect you so much."

"But I need supplies, like any business."

"So you would purchase only from one side, even if that side did not have what you needed, and the other did?"

Arissa nodded in understanding, seeing for the first time the reason for the two faces of the British merchants. She bought her supplies from them, but their sources were of no concern to her. And everyone knew of the black market trade and did not hesitate to get the best it had to offer, without paying English tariffs. It was an accepted matter of fact.

They were odd, these matters the Americans were fighting for. They were an irritant to the Canadians as well, but the French had known monarchy for so long, and the English king had made things so much better than the French one, that her people were content with their improved lot—At least some of them were, she thought with a pang of regret. Stephen had not been. He had been willing to fight to make it better.

Across the campfire, the trapper rose and collected his belongings. "Well, I'd best git some shut-eye if I'm gonna be on the trail afore sunrise. Nice to chat with you folks. Keep your powder dry."

Arissa's thoughts about Stephen were unexpectedly jarred by the sight of a beaded cartridge case bearing the insignia of an eagle on it. Trailing from the leather-tassled strap were braided, multicolored ribbons, once bright before exposure to the sun. Her chest clenched with recognition and alarm, yet she said a goodnight, along with her father, and watched as the man walked away.

"What is it?"

She had gone pale. A choking feeling made it impossible to speak normally. "That cartridge case he carries. It was my brother's."

Alain glanced after the retreating man curiously. "Are you certain? He'd said earlier that he'd served no further north than Montreal with Montgomery's army."

"I know it!" Arissa swore. "An Indian squaw made it for Stephen and added her precious hair ribbons to it. I think they were sweethearts during the season he served with the voyageurs."

"That is possible," Alain agreed. He'd certainly known the favors of a particular squaw, daughter to a Menominee chief. His thoughts came to an abrupt halt. *Dieu!* Was it possible he had yet another child he was not aware of?

"What is that man doing with Stephen's cartridge case?" Arissa demanded, anger rising to deepen the sapphire of her gaze.

Alain shuddered, trying to dismiss the troubling idea. He had not been as free with the women as most of his companions of the wilds, but he'd known a few. He forced his attention back to his daughter. "If it is your brother's cartridge case, there are many explanations."

There was only one Arissa knew of—he'd killed Stephen and stolen it from him.

"If he found Stephen dead, he might have relieved your brother of all his portable gear. Equipment is dear to every man, and such a thing would have been of no use to your brother."

"But he lied. He said he'd not been to Quebec!" Arissa pointed out. "If he lied about one thing . . ."

"He may well have traded for it in Montreal with the man who relieved your brother of it. It may have changed hands even more than that, Arissa," Alain explained, aching for the girl grasping so desperately for something, someone to vent her grief upon. "Do you wish me to try to purchase it from him?"

Arissa shook her head. "I have no use for a cartridge case!" She caught the sob in her voice and mastered it. Her father was right. His explanation was logical. Besides, she wanted nothing to remind her of Stephen's death, only his life. She knew he'd died with that memento of a happier time slung across his shoulders. Phillip had carried nothing of hers, only a love that was not big enough to wish him victory. How could she have been so selfish?

Doing her best to hold back her tears, she rose from the campfire. "I am tired. If we are to ride all day tomorrow, I'd best shut my eyes up, too," she admitted, before the torment swelling in her breast gave way and she made the fool of herself. No one knew, not even her father, who had taken her to his bosom as one of her own, of the grief she felt over Phillip's departure, the denial of his last kiss. *Dieu,* but it would persecute her forever!

Annanbrae sat majestic at the top of the green hills rolling down to the Hudson, a white queen with royal pillars and glowing with grandeur from the sunlight sparkling off her many windows. It was more elegant by far than the Chateau Royale, even before she and her brothers had made the mansion an inn, Arissa thought, as she rode beside Alain Beaujeu up the locust-lined drive toward the portico. For once, Gaspar Le Boeuf had not exaggerated.

Under other circumstances, her arrival there would have been like a fairytale coming to life. She'd dreamed of Alain Beaujeu and his beautiful Tamson. He had been everything Arissa had thought and more, especially now that he was her father. So was the legendary Annanbrae to which he'd returned his war bride. As they pulled up their horses at an ornate wrought iron hitching post, she discovered that Tamson Stewart Beaujeu was no disappointment, either.

Arissa watched quietly, as a lovely lady, dressed patriotically in blue homespun, rather than the silk or fine chintz Arissa would have expected, rushed out the open door with a squealed "Alain!" that could not contain her delight. In the seconds it took for Alain Beaujeu to slide off his stallion, the woman was in his arms.

Mesmerized by the long, hungry kiss the couple exchanged, Arissa moved her hat off her forehead, so that it fell to her back. She should have looked away, but such passion for people their age was something she had not considered before. With her, Alain Beaujeu had been completely the father, but with the copper-tressed woman in his arms, he was all man. Like Phillip . . .

"They're like that all the time," a young man, whom Arissa had not noticed, remarked, as he ambled around the corner of the house. "You get used to it after a while."

The young man with dark hair and extraordinary blue eyes, Arissa needed no introduction. It had to be John Beaujeu, who was approaching her horse without trying in the least to hide his outright appraisal of her. He was as handsome as his father, she thought, and such a smile!

"I am John Beaujeu. Welcome to Annanbrae, Miss . . . ?"

From his wife's embrace, Alain finished, in a chiding tone, at his son's outright flirtation. "Mrs. Monroe. Pardon me, Arissa. It has been a long time since I have seen my lovely wife. Tamson," he said, his arm slipping possessively about Tamson Stewart Beaujeu's waist, "This is Mrs. Phillip Monroe."

"Phillip?" John exclaimed, his incredulous gaze moving to his father with curiosity. "Our Phillip?"

Alain nodded solemnly. "Arissa and Phillip were married in Montreal."

Tamson pulled away from Alain, as John helped Arissa down from her horse. "Oh, you poor dear! Would that it were under other circumstances, but welcome to Annanbrae."

Arissa was enveloped in a sincere and lightly scented hug. "Thank you, madame."

"You're French?"

"Non . . . no," Arissa corrected herself, pinkening beneath John's scrutiny. "I am English. That is . . . well, I was raised by an English father and French mother. In Quebec, it is hard to speak English without a French accent, no matter how hard I try."

"I think it's perfectly charming. No doubt, you won't be a widow long."

"John!" Tamson's horrified exclamation blended with Alain's reprimand.

At that, the younger Beaujeu turned a ruddy shade of scarlet, beneath his tanned complexion. It was obvious that, like his father, he was a man who would not remain cooped up in a house or office. No doubt, he'd been overseeing Annanbrae's rolling properties in his father's absence. *Their* father's absence, Arissa remembered, glancing at Alain Beaujeu expectantly. He had said he wanted to tell Tamson privately about her, before announcing it to the family.

"That is very flattering, monsieur, but I have no wish to replace my Phillipe. I have yet to come to terms with his loss," Arissa informed the younger man, with a sad smile.

John cleared his throat of embarrassment. "No, of course not. I only meant . . ."

At that moment, a second boy charged out of the house, leaping from the portico to the ground without touching a step. "Papa! Welcome home! Guess what? I broke the bay from Maryland. You should see her run! She'll take the fair this year. I just know it!"

"James, this is Mrs. Phillip Monroe," Alain told his second son, patiently. "She is going to be our guest for a while."

"Welcome to Annanbrae, Mrs. Monroe," James announced, with a hint of a formal bow. He, like his brother, ran the bluest of gazes over her, from head to toe. His hair, however, was the same strawberry blonde as his mother's. He was also as tall as John, but possessed of that gangly build which had not yet filled out, as his older sibling's had. His interest in his horse superseding recognition of the name, James was still intrigued by Arissa's garb. "Why are you dressed like a man?"

"Your father thought it was safer for travel," Arissa told him, adding with a chuckle, "and trousers are certainly more comfortable and practical than skirts."

James frowned. "Guess so. Never wore one though," he reflected, with a wry twist of his lips. "A skirt, that is."

"You idiot!" John admonished, tugging at the plain brown ribbon holding his brother's copper-gold queue in place.

"Just teasing!" James protested, darting out of reach. "Look. She's laughing!"

" 'Tis no wonder," Tamson averted, hands on her hips, in indignation. "The two of you are acting like fools." She reached for Arissa's arm. "Come inside, dear. I'm sure you're fairly dying to freshen up. I'll order you a bath immediately, and tonight you'll sleep in a plump feather bed."

"That would be wonderful, no more than that!" A bath and a change of clothes, not to mention a night in a real bed, would make a new woman of her, Arissa thought.

They'd stopped occasionally at inns, but those along the frontier were not very accommodating for privacy, much less bed space. She took the haversack containing her sole belongings off the hook of the saddle, as well as her dusty medical bag. The break would also give her father time to speak to his wife about her. Although he'd said nothing to indicate Tamson would be anything but gracious, she could sense that gracious was the reaction he hoped for, but was not certain of.

Upon reaching the front door, she stopped, remembering her manners, and turned toward the two boys, who nearly ran her over in their rush to take her bags.

"I have carried them these last several hundred miles," she told them, holding on firmly to all she had of her past. "Perhaps you will see to my horse. It is as worn as I."

"But you've weathered the journey better," John complimented, exacting a blush from her.

Arissa could tell this one was incorrigible and certainly a success with the ladies. "It was my pleasure to meet you, *messieurs*. Your father has told me so much about you that I feel I already know you . . . and you," she added, for Tamson's sake, as she returned her attention to her hostess and followed her inside the house.

There was a grand curving staircase which rose to a salon on the second floor. Straight through was the back door, shorter than the front and open as well to take advantage of the river breeze. A beautiful mural flowed from one floor to the other with a classical theme, weaving rich shades of greens and blues and golds.

"I cannot believe this!" Arissa murmured aloud, fascinated by the dream castle she'd heard about from Gaspar.

"We'd just had the hall done before the war broke out," Tamson told her, mistaking the source of her awe.

"Non, it isn't that, not that it is not lovely. It is just being here at Annanbrae."

"You know of it?"

Arissa grew sheepish. "A mutual friend, Gaspar Le Bouef . . ."

"Gaspar!" Tamson echoed in delight, as she paused at the top of the steps. "You know Gaspar?"

"For many years. He and his wife, Chiah, they worked for my adopted parents." Arissa winced inwardly. She'd not meant to say anything about her parentage.

"There's no shame in being adopted, dear," Tamson reassured her, noting her inadvertent dismay, and once again mistaking the source.

Arissa nodded and proceeded after her hostess down a long hall. Lined on both sides with rooms, it was painted in green a shade lighter than that in the mural. Elegant moldings crowned it, white against the white of the ceiling. Hers was a back room which overlooked the river and was flooded by the afternoon sunlight. Louvered shutters, however, filtered out the brightness and heat and let in the breeze, cooled by the tall oaks gracing the mansion at each corner. The gold-stenciled white walls gave it an even airier presence and matched the gold damask of her bedspread and drapes.

"Gaspar told me all about how you and your husband met. It was as romantic as any fairy tale told to me as a young girl," Arissa admitted, with a shy grin. "And now to be here, this house, it is like the Camelot I have read about!"

"Now there's an imagination for you!" Tamson quipped, wryly. Then slowly, her lips flushed with a full smile. "At least the house may meet that measure, but our meeting was far from romantic."

Arissa put her bag on the large, plump cannonball bed. "But you fell in love, despite all your hardships and differences."

A devilish twinkle lit in her hostess's golden brown gaze. "Aye, that we did."

The very idea brought a glaze to Arissa's eyes, born partly of warmth over the success of their love and partly of grief. She and Phillip had fallen in love too, despite the same obstacles, but the ending to their story was so very different from the Beaujeux.

Tamson was at her side instantly, a comforting arm about her shoulders. "There, dear, let's change the subject. You're worn out from all that riding, to be certain. Fatigue leads to leaky eyes, especially when the heart is sore." She pointed to a door, which Arissa had thought belonged to a closet. "There's the bathing room. It separates the master bedroom from yours. Better to have you in *our* wing than at the mercy of the boys in the other. They can be a noisy lot," she said, fondly. "I'll have the servants draw you a bath. Meanwhile, I'll send up some tea to relax you."

"That's very kind of you, madame. I mean to be no trouble."

"Nonsense! I love having guests!" Tamson protested. "You can tell me all about Gaspar and your trip, because, if I ask Alain, he'll say, *Oh, Gaspar is fine and the trip was too long.*"

Arissa laughed at Tamson's mimicry of her husband. "That would be true, I suppose."

Tamson stared curiously at the devilish twinkle in the blue gaze of her guest, startled for a moment. Then, with a swish of her homespun skirts, she marched to the door and turned in mock-indignation. "Dearie, you have been around Alain too long! You are acting just like him,"

Tamson left her new guest smiling at least, she thought, as she started for the servant's staircase leading down to the warming kitchen, rather than trek back through the salon to the center of the house. However, as she reached it, she heard a familiar whistle and turned to see her husband standing at the door of the master suite a short distance away, crooking his finger at her, mysteriously. She couldn't guess why she'd missed him. Perhaps it was the way Arissa Monroe had laughed and looked at her. It looked so familiar. Distracted from her original plan, Tamson went to Alain, a questioning look in her gaze.

"I was about to order tea and a bath for our guest . . ." she whispered, lowly, making Alain aware of the where-abouts of their youngest. Four-year-old Robert was taking his afternoon nap and would be sorely put out when he awakened to discover he'd missed his papa's arrival. Alain usually let him ride to the stables, before turning his horse over to the hands.

"I've already done so," Alain announced, herding her into the room with deliberation.

Tamson cut her eyes at her husband with a saucy slant. "Robert is in the next room, and you could stand a bit of washing yourself."

Alain met her insinuation with feigned innocence. "So he is and so I do, but that's not what I called you in here to discuss. Were you expecting more than talk?" He couldn't resist teasing her, although the mere hint of what she was insinuating made his already nervous pulse leap for another reason. As warmth generated from the blood rushing to his loins, he purposefully turned away from that intoxicating look his wife had brandished and reached in his shirt for the letter from Jeanette.

"Tamson, there is more to my bringing Arissa here than helping out the widow of a friend," he began, in a stilted tone. "And since I am not so good with words, I think this best explains her being here." He turned and presented her with the yellowed missive, as though handing away his future.

Alain drew his hand back and crossed his arms over it to contain its shaking. Upon his marriage to Tamson, he'd sworn never to lie to her again. Their love was based on trust and respect. That was why he ignored Arissa's offer to keep their relationship a secret. The girl was his own blood. He could not ignore that.

Instead of watching Tamson directly, he paced back and forth across the foot of the large poster bed, where their sons had been conceived and born, and glanced at her occasionally through the mirror on her dressing table, as she unfolded and read the contents of the letter, silently.

With her head bowed, he couldn't see her reaction, although he'd pictured several of them, since discovering Arissa was his daughter. They ranged from rage to wounded tears to cold silence, neither of which he cared to follow through enough to guess the overall effect on the marriage he cherished. His palms were wet, and he clenched his fists, wondering what was taking her so long. Or was she like he had been—so shocked that he'd had to read the words twice. He ventured another look at the mirror to see her fold the letter and hold it against her chest, her head still bowed. Silence, he thought miserably. Wounded silence.

He fought the sudden urge to take her in his arms and assuage it. Instead, he stood, feet glued to the floor, watching and waiting. The stillness in the room was so loud, Alain wondered that it didn't awaken his sleeping baby next door. He loved Tamson. He believed in her goodness. He had faith in her compassion, he kept telling himself. Fortified enough to break the dam of silence between them, he finally spoke.

"I couldn't leave her at the fort."

"Of course you couldn't."

Alain turned, as Tamson looked up at him. Her whiskey-dark eyes were swimming with emotions, too many to read.

"If I had known about her . . ." he started. "If I had known about her, I would have married Jeanette."

"So you would," she agreed, "and we might never have met." Tamson's voice was small. She cleared her throat, gaining volume. "And we'd have never had these last twenty years together and our three precious sons." Stepping closer, she went on. "And we'd have missed so very much."

Alain held his ground, afraid that one wrong move, one wrong word, might reverse the incredible response his compassionate wife was giving. Yes, compassion was strong amidst the swirl of feelings deepening her gaze, drawing him into it.

"We'd have missed this." She brushed his lips ever so softly, and a shudder of heat thawed the blood that had pounded to a halt at her first words. "And this," she went on, taking his hand and placing it upon her bosom, so that his fingers slipped beneath the soft, low collar of her day dress, resting against a breast as firm and yielding as it had been the first time he'd caressed it. "Show me more of what we'd have missed, Alain Beaujeu," she whispered, her voice catching, as his fingers found a rigid bud of arousal awaiting them.

With a darting prayer of thanksgiving, Alain covered her mouth with his in sweet worship. Relief flowed through his veins, chased by his fiery response to the sultry invitation of her parting lips and teasing tongue. She was everything to him—wife, mother of his children, temptress. Her love was as boundless and unselfish as the passion that drove her hands wildly over the tautness of his buttocks, pulling him closer to her, so that, even through her scant petticoats, she could feel his steel-hardened desire for her.

"I love you, Tamson Beaujeu," he whispered, raggedly, pulling at the endless length of her skirts, until he found warm, satin flesh beneath.

Instead of answering, Tamson planted a string of kisses down the cord of his throat, all the while working at the fasteners of his trousers. Alain felt his composure unraveling with the ties she tugged loose, freeing him to her hot, frantic touch. If she wanted him to show her anything, it would have to be fast, he thought, picking her up by the waist and lifting her lightly to the bed. With a smile that would thaw the St. Lawrence in the dead of winter, she let him go and hiked her skirts up past her stockings, only to let them linger there.

Alain tore his canvas trousers down to his knees, but the moment she revealed the strawberry blonde tuft of femininity at the juncture of her milky white thighs, he abandoned the idea of undressing. She wasn't playing fairly, teasing him, when he'd been so long without her. But then, she'd been as long without him, he thought, a rakish grin settling on his face, and two could play that game.

"Ah, but I need my bath!" he lamented, with a sigh.

"Alain!" Tamson warned, pure fire flashing beneath her dark lashes.

"Well, if you insist," he chuckled, bending over her. A long, lascivious kiss on a certain erogenous zone, and she'd be begging . . .

Thought flowed into action. With talented fingers tripping up and down her thighs, it was only a matter of time until he had to grasp her to keep her from wriggling away from his wicked assault. Her fluttering gasps coiled his own longings tighter and tighter, until he once again risked losing control. But he persisted, expecting the "Alain, please!" that Tamson whimpered against the pillow she'd used to stifle her little noises of pleasure from penetrating the bedroom wall into the nursery beyond.

"You are the most beautiful . . ." Alain broke off, as he drove home his ardor, filling her sweetness with his all.

"Alain!"

"The most wonderful . . ." He moaned, as he began to move in and out to the demands of the fingers clawing his buttocks. She clutched him, forcing the sensual pressure building within him to the brink of explosion.

"Dieu, but you are . . ."

"Now, Alain, now!" Tamson panted, thrusting upward against him in a wild, gyrating movement.

Words, thought, control—all were lost in the pagan abandonment that followed. All that existed were the two of them, bound as one, inescapably entwined in rapture's wanton dance. And when the drums of their beating hearts and pounding blood reached the pinnacle of the ancient ritual, they rocked together in each other's arms, riding the engulfing tempest, until, once again, they were conscious of their surroundings.

"Welcome home, Mr. Beaujeu," Tamson sighed, breathlessly, as Alain heaved himself to the side to relieve her of his weight.

He drew her to him, holding her in the cradle of his arms. If his life depended upon it, he couldn't speak at the moment. Too many emotions overwhelmed him, not the least of which was the unbridled love he felt for her. He blinked his eyes and turned to stare at the ceiling, until he could regain his composure.

"And congratulations," Tamson went on, allowing him his dignity. "We have a beautiful daughter."

Twenty

Dinner was served in the long dining room in the front of the house. Like the rest of Annanbrae, it was bedecked artfully, this time in a bright floral wall covering, which was broken by a massive chair rail and crowned with dentil moldings. Through the front windows and the shaded portico, the long locust-lined lane could be viewed, allowing the family warning, if more guests were coming, according to the devilish young James, who was seated next to his brother, John, across from Arissa.

To her left was an infrequent visitor to the formal dining room—little Robert. Tamson had brought him in prepared to deal with the precocious youngster at the far end of the table, while Alain sat at the head, opposite her. But Arissa begged to have her newest relative next to her. No stranger to anyone, Robert was an endless source of questions to any and all who would hear him, and the discovery of a willing ear in the pretty guest next to him delighted him no end. He hardly touched the food Tamson tried to coax him into eating.

"Did you see Injuns?" he asked, squirming in his seat, as if it were crawling with fire ants.

"Many," Arissa admitted.

"Were they friendly?"

She pointed to her hair, now neatly confined by a ribbon at the neck and hanging down her back. "I still have my scalp, don't I?"

"Did Papa have to buy you?"

"Robert, give our guest a chance to eat her food," Tamson chided, gently.

"Now you can see why we only let the little monster in the dining room on occasion. I'll bet Bess is enjoying a quiet, uninterrupted meal in the kitchen, for a change," John added, referring to Tamson's personal maid. Tamson had explained earlier that she'd have no nurse for either of her children when entertaining, only some aid from Bess, who adored all the Beaujeu boys as though they were her own.

Arissa held up her fork as Robert started another question, catching his full attention "I will tell you what. Take a piece of that meat and chew it quite thoroughly. While you do, I want you to think of another question. After you swallow your food, you may ask."

Dark, honey-colored eyes considered her proposition seriously from beneath thick black lashes, which matched his short curls. He'd had a queue, like his father and brothers, until he cut it off with Tamson's sewing scissors. With a bobbing nod, the little boy stabbed a piece of roast duckling with his fork and popped it into his mouth. That which did not go in willingly was helped by his fingers, to his mother's dismay.

Actually Robert was a welcome distraction for Arissa. Alain had told her that he was going to introduce her as his daughter at the table, and Arissa couldn't have eaten, if she'd had to. Not even the good wine served with the meal could calm her nerves or her growling stomach.

"Now that I have everyone's attention, I have an announcement to make." Alain rose at the head of the table, handsome in a bright blue dinner coat and black trousers. Everyone had dressed formally, including Arissa, who wore the rose day dress Chiah had packed for her,

the best of the only two she possessed. Making such a
formal occasion of this made her all the more nervous,
especially since formal dining was a luxury she was rarely
afforded at the Chateau Royale, after her father died and
Martin went away. She and Stephen favored informal atmosphere and transient guests over those from all the
right families.

"Gentlemen . . . all of you," he added, for Robert's
sake, garnering his youngest's attention. "One again, I
want to welcome Arissa to our home, not only as the
widow of our good friend . . ." He hesitated, glancing at
Tamson, who nodded encouragingly. "But as your sister,
as well."

"What!" John spurted, spilling his wine. He hurriedly
dabbed at the front of his coat with his napkin.

Alain gave his eldest a scowl and went on. "Listen and
learn from this, *messieurs*. When I was very young, I fell
in love with my uncle's ward. I courted her the whole
winter of my last year of schooling."

"That would be Jeanette de Montigny, wouldn't it,
papa?" James inquired. "You and mama told us about
her and how she married her way through the nobility,
all the way back to Paris!"

With an apologetic look directed at Arissa, Alain nodded. "That is our irascible Jeanette, but, you recall, she
always had a big heart and gave of herself and her money
to her people."

"Yes, she volunteered with Mama at the Hotel *Dieu*,"
James put in, unabashed.

So her mother had worked with the ill and less fortunate. The idea was reassuring to Arissa, particularly after
reading her practical, yet selfish, letter to Alain concerning her baby daughter. Arissa couldn't imagine placing
the improvement of one's station in life over raising one's
child.

"If you are through, James," Alain reprimanded. At his

son's apologetic shrug, he continued. "When Jeanette turned down my marriage proposal, I went into the wilderness. We continued to see each other once or twice a year as friends, even though she was married to the Marquis de Montigny." Alain took another drink of his wine, finding it hard to swallow. The words simply were not coming.

"Meanwhile, while Alain was away," Tamson picked up, issuing a supportive smile at her husband, "Jeanette, unbenownst to him, had his baby daughter, whom she gave up for adoption. That baby girl is Arissa, my dears. So at last, you have a sister, an older one at that," she added, seeing the mental calculation running through John's quick mind.

Not about to let the entire burden fall upon her father and his wife, Arissa joined in to answer the questions bearing heavily in each gaze fixed upon her. "I was born in 1749 and given to the physician who delivered me. He and his French wife had two sons, but wanted a baby girl, so it was best, all around. My real mother was free of scandal and to pursue her life as she chose. Your father was free to meet and marry your mother. And I had a very happy childhood with my adopted family, whom I loved very much. I hope to feel the same about my new family."

"How'd you find out all this?" John asked Alain, still in shock. "Not that I don't believe you, Arissa, it's just that . . ."

"He's sorry you're his sister!" James provided, earning a sharp elbow and a scathing look from both John and his father.

The letter from Jeanette was passed about the table to the boys, but Robert, who could care less about the stir his father's words had created, was growing impatient to pose his question to Arissa. She leaned down so that he could whisper it.

"Do you like to ride horses?"

"I didn't in Montreal," Arissa confessed, lowly, "but I do now."

"Will you take me riding while papa is away?"

"You didn't eat anything," she reminded him.

She leaned back for the servant to fill her cup with the coffee she'd requested earlier, for fear of the wine fogging her mind during this most important of all occasions. As it was, it was hard to tell just how the boys were taking it, although Tamson had welcomed her earlier in her room with an enthusiastic hug and hearty "Welcome home, daughter."

No one saw it coming. No one even suspected. With a grand sweep of his spoon, Robert swung back to Arissa, striking the arm of the servant pouring the steaming brew. It so startled the girl that she dropped the pot. It landed in the little boy's lap, spilling its scalding contents on his short trousers, before Arissa could knock it onto the floor. Tamson, Robert and Arissa's cries of alarm rose as one, as the three bolted away from the table. That which had splattered on Arissa's lap, rolled off her thick skirts and petticoats, but Robert had no such trappings, just a simple pair of short trousers.

While Tamson held the wailing little boy, Arissa stripped him of his clothes. "Go get a cold basin of water and towels!" she snapped, authoritatively to the distraught maid. "John, fetch the black bag from my room!"

Alain went to bring additional water, while James blew furiously on the scarlet marks left by the hot coffee on Robert's flailing white legs. The two women cleared away the dishes on the table, shoving them to one side without regard for what spilled or fell off to the floor, and put the sobbing child on the cloth. One by one, they emptied the wineglasses on dinner napkins and placed them on the welting burns, until Alain and the maid could return with the water.

"It's not so bad, I think," Arissa told Tamson, lifting a cloth to touch one of them. "It was the pot that burned more than the coffee that spilled. Thank God the lid remained on, until it hit the floor!"

John rushed into the room breathlessly with the dusty medical bag. "What's in here?"

Arissa flipped open the hasp and opened it. "My medicines. I'm a doctor . . . of sorts," she added, seeking Tamson's face for acceptance.

"Go on, Arissa. Alain told me about your training."

"A real doctor?" John said skeptically. It was clearly too much for him. The pretty girl his father had brought home was his half-sister and a doctor. He'd never seen such a fetching sight in trousers and a shirt before.

"I was not licensed. I apprenticed with my father, who was."

Arissa found what she was looking for and put out the bottle of glycerin water. By that time, Alain had arrived with a large basin, slushing with cold water from the well. Bess was on his heels, her face a mirror of concern.

"Good, we can sit him right in that."

Robert shivered as he was lowered into the water, all the while clinging to Tamson. Arissa looked at the scene, thinking her heart would break from her helplessness to do more to ease the little one's pain. Once he was in control of his crying and hysterics, she would clean the wounds with glycerin water and then apply poultices of bread and milk. Then they would have to wait and see just how bad it was. Perhaps it would blister and fade away, but if he lost much skin . . .

Arissa refused to consider that option. She'd knocked the pitcher from his lap to the floor. The spillage had been minimal, compared to what it could have been.

"Oh, God bless 'im," Bess prayed, wringing her starched apron in her hands, while the serving girl apologized over and over.

No longer hungry, Arissa abandoned the table and went upstairs with Tamson and Bess to finish the baby's treatment. A small dose of a pain elixir would not only help the child sleep, but lessen the chances of infection, according to her father's medical books. It would also help him to remain still, so that the poultices could do their job.

"There," she said later, tying the last loose end of the gauze she used to hold the poultice in place about the little one's legs. "I expect the burns to blister in one or two places, but, all in all, I think our little boy was very lucky."

"God bless ye, mam," Bess whispered, taking her place in the chair beside the bed, stalwart as a soldier.

Tamson Beaujeu came around from the other side of the small single bed where her son lay sleeping and hugged Arissa. "I think we all are lucky . . . to have found each other. You were so good with Robert. I know Maddie Monroe will just love you."

Arissa looked at her hostess—no, her new stepmother—blankly. "Maddie Monroe?"

Tamson put her hand to her forehead. "I'm so sorry, Arissa. There's been so much to tell you and it seems you've been doing all the talking in trying to satisfy our curiosity. My dear, you've a mother-in-law and a toddling stepson fifteen miles down the road from here. It's the Monroe summer home. Maddie goes there every summer to get away from the city heat and stench."

"Bless me!" Bess exclaimed, giving away the fact that she'd been listening to that which did not concern her.

Arissa hardly heard her. Phillip's mother! She felt suddenly weak in the stomach. And Phillip's child, the little boy he so raved about, she recalled, putting her hand to her temples where her head was beginning to ache. *Dieu*, how many more surprises were in store for her?

Tamson put her hand on Arissa's shoulder. "Phillip didn't tell you about his family?"

"Only that he was a widower with a son, whom he'd given to his mother's care until he could send for them." She shrugged, tiredly. "I'd given up hope of finding Phillipe's family. So many have abandoned their homes . . . I was happy enough just to have found my own. Everything is happening so fast, I . . ."

"I tell you what we'll do," Tamson interjected, sympathetically. "Why don't you take this one step at a time? Get used to us, if you can," she added facetiously, "and next week, we'll invite Maddie and Jonathan over and introduce you."

"Yes . . . I suppose that would be best. For an adopted child, I am suddenly finding myself with more relatives than I can keep straight!" Arissa remarked, her half-hearted laughter evident of her desperation to find the humor in the situation.

"And thank you, Arissa, for what you've done for Robert. I don't think I'd have thought so quickly."

Arissa answered with a smile. "It is what I enjoy doing—helping people." She glanced back at the sleeping cherub. "Especially little ones."

"Not that I'm trying to get rid of you, but Jonathan is a dear, as well. It's just that, considering Maddie's years, he's a bit of a handful for her, especially now that Phillip is gone, too. The poor dear's been a real soldier over the whole thing, but it's taking its toll. As for Deborah's family, they don't want the child, except on occasion. They have a social schedule to maintain," Tamson explained, laconically. "The little boy needs a mother, but that is something you can think about for a while. You've had enough surprises of late to last you a lifetime." She bussed Arissa on the cheek. "Just sleep on it, dear. You've a family behind you, no matter what you decide to do."

* * *

Sleep Arissa did, as she'd not slept since before meeting
Phillip Monroe. She worried about nothing, for her eyes
closed almost the instant she hit the pillow. She never
heard Robert awaken once during the night, when the
elixir she'd left with Bess and Tamson needed to be given
again, nor the rowdy whispers in the bath separating her
room from the master bedroom, where Alain had coerced
his wife into joining him. It was as if all her troubles had
given up and sought rest with her body.

The next day, however, they were back again, as life
resumed its normal pace at Annanbrae. John offered to
take her riding over the property, but she refused, graciously, dreading the thought of taking to a horse again
so soon. Beside, she felt obliged to keep an eye on Robert,
who was demanding constant attention whenever his
elixir wore off. James had his duties to perform, too,
among them attending the young men's school in Albany.
As for Alain, he spent most of his day sequestered in his
office, updating himself on his eldest son's progress at
the plantation. From the grim expression he wore
through the noon day meal, it wasn't what he had hoped.

As she'd passed through the hall afterward, Arissa had
overheard father and son in heated debate. John openly
admitted he was not a country squire, much less an over-
seer. Instead of following in his father's footsteps and going to the wilderness, he wanted to go to sea. He wanted
to sign on one of the Dutch-Acadie ships and work his
way up to captain.

"Turn Annanbrae over to James. He's the farmer
among us! He'd rather be out working with the field-
hands than be in school, any day!"

"Who wouldn't?" Alain's response was cryptic.

"Yes, but he likes to watch things grow. He's always
riding out, checking this field or that . . . and he can

calculate the crop into money with astounding accuracy.
It's a gift! And you've seen his eye for good horseflesh
and his way with the beasts."

"Until he finishes school, or this war ends, we'll have
to make do without his gifts," Alain responded, his tone
indicating to Arissa that perhaps John was not as far away
from the sea as he'd been when he went in to speak to
his father. Of the boys, the eldest was decidedly the most
restless. Now she knew why. He was forced to run the
family estate, while Alain did his part for the fight for
liberty, when it was clear the youth wanted to do his share
of the battle as well.

As the week wore on, the days unfolded in a similar
fashion, with the exception of Tamson attending a spinning bee and Alain taking to the fields with John each
morning. Arissa insisted on staying with Robert, since she
had more practice at tending the injured than at spinning, which also freed Bess to go. The youngest Beaujeu
actually needed no more serious nursing, for his burns
were already fading, save the few places which had blis-
tered. Those, the women kept cleansed daily, the real task
being to keep young Robert out of the dirt he was particularly fond of.

When Tamson and Bess returned home that evening,
however, they delighted Arissa with an account of the occasion. Two groups of women from different townships
met at a public building and actually had a contest to see
who could spin the most yarn. It was their way of fighting
the British by producing their own materials, rather than
buying British-made, which still managed to slip into the
mercantiles, despite the ban on enemy trade.

Although home life went on among the Americans
much as it did in Quebec, the spirit of liberty seemed to
drive it. The crops were for the armies. The mercantile
goods and weapons brought in by her father's shipping
company were for the army. Even Alain's upcoming trip

to New York was not simply business, but to ferret out the counterfeiters who had been paying the New York regiments and suppliers with useless money. That, too, was because of the war.

It consumed these people with such conviction that Arissa found herself believing more and more that there was perhaps a chance for this outlandish cause of theirs. The British army fought in a strange land with no incentive, aside from wages, to give their all. These people fought for their own land and the right to have a say in its government. Based on motivation and sheer determination alone, the Americans could well have a chance.

She'd seen both armies—one willing to sacrifice all, and one reluctant to sacrifice at all. Could that intangible factor—the fact that they fought with their hearts, as well as their bodies—offset the rebels' desperate lack of capital? Greatly affected by this strange liberty fever from her family, she was beginning to wonder.

Regardless of what Arissa thought, Maddie Monroe was certain they were going to run the redcoats out of the colonies with their "tails tucked between their legs." One look at the stalwart matron and Arissa believed the woman might be able to do it singlehandedly. Phillip's mother was tall, with expressive brown eyes framed by lines of laughter and hard times. Her bust, waist, and hips were all the same size, giving her an even more formidable appearance, like a pillar of strength.

Yet she was dressed stylishly upon arrival for her invitation to an afternoon at Annanbrae and certain to point out she'd had that gown before the hostilities broke out, absolving herself of not wearing homespun. "I save my homespun for showing off," she told Tamson upon arrival in an open carriage in front of Annanbrae's portico. Then, with a twinkle in her eye, she added, "Like at spinning bees."

After handing a round bundle of energy to Tamson,

she climbed down from the carriage she'd driven herself, without Alain's offered assistance. The Beaujeus had said Maddie was an independent sort and frugal with the use of her staff, although not with their pay. "Can't have men-folk spoiling me, when it seems I'm destined to live the balance of my days without them."

Upon seeing Arissa standing on the porch in her best rose dress, the woman sharpened her bright gaze. "Now who's this pretty lady? I don't recall seeing her around."

Despite the early summer heat, Arissa felt cold. She wasn't ready for this meeting. There had been too much to come to terms with between her and Phillip before she could meet his mother, yet time had not been on her side. She stepped forward mechanically and extended her hand.

"I am Arissa Conway Beaujeu Monroe, Madame Monroe." Arissa winced at her inadvertent French address.

It didn't seem to phase their guest, however. "Is this another of your sisters, Alain? I swear, you've got them all over the country," she teased, mischievously. "And now one of them's up and married a Monroe!" She winked at Arissa. "I can't say I blame the man. I imagine that little accent of yours would set him crazy as a bear in spring. Got that from your folks, I suppose."

Alain stepped forward and gathered up Jonathan Monroe from Tamson. The baby's sparse brown hair fluttered like down in a breeze, as the man stood back and motioned for the ladies to enter Annanbrae's hall ahead of him.

"Come into the parlor, Maddie. I've had some lemon tea cakes made just for you," Tamson told her guest, adding, "although we'll have them with coffee." Refusal to drink tea was another of the ladies' protests against the English King. They were willing to change their entire lives for their freedom.

"Sounds delightful. Where's Robbie?"

"Robert's taking his nap. He's not been well."

Tamson motioned for her to take the chair by the hearth, usually occupied by Alain, while she took the opposite one. As Alain dropped to the floor to play with the baby, Arissa found a place on the edge of the matching settee.

"What's wrong with the little fellow? I thought he'd occupy Jonathan for a while. That boy's a dear, but he's a mighty responsibility for a woman my age. Not that I'm complaining," she added, glancing affectionately at the baby boy. "But now that he's stumbling around, so am I."

Arissa laughed nervously. Tamson had told her that Maddie Monroe, despite her New York prominence, was a down-to-earth lady. She'd been raised on an Albany farm—now their summer home—and married Phillip's wealthy city father.

"Robert had an accidental burn, not too serious, and Arissa has been treating him. She's not only a doctor, but such a dear with children."

"A doctor, you say?"

"I am not licensed," Arissa pointed out, modestly, "although I am as a midwife. I studied under my father, who was an English physician."

"You're mighty young to be a midwife," Maddie observed, obviously impressed. "But medicine's good to know, especially these days. Do you have any children, Miss . . . Beaujeu . . . Monroe Conway . . ." The woman laughed at her confusion. "I've got the memory of a simpleton."

"Non, I am sad to say that I do not . . . not of my own."

The sadness in Arissa's voice touched a spark of compassion in their guest's gaze. "So what Monroe are you married to?" Maddie asked, helping herself to a lemon cake. "We might be related."

Arissa's heart lurched. Maddie Monroe seemed a fair enough lady, she thought in panic.

"If you'd stop gabbing like a silly goose and give us a chance to speak, we'd like to introduce you properly to our guest," Alain jibed good-naturedly from the floor, where Jonathan Monroe chewed vigorously on his attendant's knuckles.

With a sniff, Maddie Monroe sat back against the chair, although she was not the least put out. It was evident she thought highly of her neighbor by the spontaneous face she made at him. "All right then, Frenchie. Since it doesn't appear we're planning any more spinning bees, and you're still married to Tamson, you must have invited me over to meet the girl." She crossed her arms. "I'm waiting."

Arissa liked the woman's directness, but it was scaring her to death.

"Maddie Monroe, first I would like to introduce you to my daughter, Arissa. It is only by fate and this war that I discovered she existed." Alain caught the speculation directed toward Arissa and headed off the question. "Her mother was a French noblewoman who gave her up for adoption, without my knowledge, to the family of the physician that delivered her. This was long before I met Tamson."

"I am illegitimate," Arissa explained, with a hint of apology in her voice. "But that would not have been the case, had Alain, my real father, known about me. We met when I was fleeing Canada, and we were united by a mutual friend who had known the secret all along. Both of us were surprised."

"Alain and I have always wanted a daughter," Tamson put in, "and I don't think we could have asked for a prettier or a smarter one." She gave Arissa a sincere smile of encouragement.

"Humph! It certainly seems that way," Maddie agreed, eyeing Jonathan, who by now was toddling unsteadily toward Arissa, attracted by the bright pink pleats on her skirting.

Arissa held out a ready hand, lest the toddler take a fall toward the tea table. "One injured baby is enough for me," she explained, with a forced grin. "What are you doing, *mon petit?*"

As if he knew he was being addressed by the strange-speaking woman, Jonathan Monroe looked up at Arissa and gave her a wide, drooling smile, revealing three tiny white teeth. It was not the smile that affected her so strongly, however, as much as the eyes. They were Phillip's eyes, dark lashed, despite his lighter brown hair, and the color of deep amber or rich whiskey. There was no denying he was his father's son.

Jonathan's cherubic face blurred before Arissa, as he caught her finger and waddled up to the settee, where he could finger the neatly pressed pleats that had caught his eye. Instantly, a wad of her skirt was in his mouth.

"He is hungry!" she exclaimed, scooping him up in her lap. "Could he have a small bit of the lemon cake?"

"That youngster's always hungry, just like my Phillip was at that age. I'll wager, he'll be at least as tall as his father, when he fills out. Feed him once, and he's your friend for life."

Arissa exchanged a helpless glance with Tamson. What was she going to say? "That is how I met my husband," she blurted out lamely. "That is to say, he came to our inn looking for work, and we hired him for food and lodgings."

"You must have been a good cook."

"*Non,* my staff has a good cook. I . . . I cannot say how we fell in love. We were not even friendly, at first. My brother brought him without consulting me."

"Just like myself and Phillip's father. I thought he was a snotty city dandy, and he thought I was dumb as the dirt my daddy tilled," Maddie commented, sobered from her drift back to another, more carefree time. "So where is he? Ticonderoga? What's his full name?"

Arissa held the contented baby, her panic welling in her eyes, as she frantically sought help from her father, who seemed to have the most sway over Maddie Monroe. To her relief, Alain spoke for her.

"His name was Phillip Monroe, Maddie."

Unable to do more, Arissa merely nodded in answer to Maddie Monroe's questioning look. "We were married in Montreal, just two days before he left for Quebec City."

"That would be November last," Maddie figured, aloud. "His last letter, soldier's chest, and bed came just about that time, though the letter was dated months earlier. He didn't say where he was going, but that it would be a while before I heard from him. I could have whipped him with my lips for not writing, after that, but . . ." She swallowed hard, staring off unseeing at the panel over the fireplace. "Of course, my letters came back . . . and they didn't go safe, either," she added, stiffly. "Every one had been opened."

Arissa remained silent. Obviously Phillip's mother hadn't known he was a spy. She watched, as the woman composed herself, the crack in her impenetrable veneer hardening over, as she turned her gaze back to the girl.

"And you came to the colonies to find his family, because you had no where else to go?"

The sharpness in her mother-in-law's voice cut Arissa to the core, but she lifted her chin proudly. *"Non,* I fled Quebec in fear of my life. I did not know where I was to go, but for Gaspar. He worked for my family for years."

"My ex-trapping partner," Alain filled in.

"He took me to a father I did not know I had." Arissa drew a fortifying breath. "And he took me to a family I did not know I had."

"And now they've brought you to me," Maddie finished, flatly.

"We've introduced her, Maddie, nothing more. Arissa is a member of our family and can remain with us for as long as she chooses," Alain averred, in a stern tone. "She has no need of you or your grandson, so don't mount up on that high horse. She thought Phillip was a penniless clerk when she married him, not that she will need his money, either. If there's a need anywhere, it's yours."

"Alain!" Tamson exclaimed, offering an apologetic smile to her guest. "I am sure Maddie is in shock, just as we were. We . . ." she said to Maddie, "felt that you should at least be introduced. If your relationship is to go beyond that, that is up to the two of you. But you have a home here, Arissa," she reiterated. "Keep that in mind."

"Now you just fetch yourself off your own high horse, Frenchie. I wasn't meaning that the way it sounded. If the girl is your blood, that speaks good enough to me. Things like that happen between red-blooded men and women struck by infatuation, rather than love," she went on, referring to Arissa's illegitimacy. She appraised Arissa directly. "At least you're not rouged to the ears like I've heard most of those women up there are," she conceded. "And you seem a better package than what he shoed himself with before, at least sense-wise."

Uncertain as to what to say in response to the frank analysis from her formidable mother-in-law, Arissa remained silent.

Tamson motioned Alain to his feet. "Perhaps we should take Jonathan out to see the horses and let these two speak. They have both lost someone they loved. I think they need this time in private."

Arissa gave her father a grateful smile for his strong support, as he took Jonathan from her. It helped to be reminded she had a place to live until she could build her life back up again; that she was under no obligation to this woman, whatsoever.

Yet Phillip had expected her to be Jonathan's mother, she recalled, with a twinge of guilt. Hadn't she let him down enough without turning her back on his child? But what if she had no choice in the matter, she reflected, even if she decided that was what she wanted?

"Do you know how he died?" The words came out of the matronly pillar's throat, as if they'd been torn out, revealing that once again the crack in her veneer had opened.

"A soldier I was treating in the hospital told me," Arissa answered, stonily.

It was the only way she could maintain her composure, having to relive that horrid scene again. She could smell the stench of death and hear the moans of the dying all around her. She'd searched each pallet, hoping to find Phillip among them, since he'd been listed as missing. Perhaps he'd lost his memory and lay wounded among the masses lining the corridors and filling the wards.

"I did not know the man, but he recognized me as Phillipe's wife. He told me he saw both Phillipe and my brother lying dead in the snow, as he retreated. They were apparently felled under the first fire of the British guns along with General Montgomery. Because it was three days before the English were able to retrieve the General's body, even if they had only been wounded, they would have frozen to death. There was a terrible snow-storm," she explained, "and the soldier himself was wounded and unable to assist them, even if there had been time during the mad retreat."

Arissa started to add how foolish they'd been, but held her tongue. She despised the emotions the recollection dragged to the fore—the hatred of the two men she loved for fighting a hopeless cause and her regret over it. It would haunt her long after she'd come to accept Phillip and Stephen's loss. It was guilt that plagued her more than grief—her guilt.

"If only I had sent him off with my love."

Arissa didn't even realize she'd spoken aloud. She was back at the bedside of the injured soldier, as wounded and bleeding as he. She could no longer control the trembling of her chin any more than she could the tears that spilled down her cheeks. If only she could take back the scorn she sent Stephen and her husband to battle with. If only she'd demonstrated but a portion of the support she'd witnessed shown by the colonial women for their fighting menfolk.

She sensed, more than saw, Phillip's mother get up and take the seat next to her. The settee swayed with the woman's weight.

"Soldiers die, dear, and my Phillip was one of the best. Sounds to me as though your brother was, too, right up front with the General. They couldn't have gone in better company!"

Arissa shook her head. It ached almost as much as her stricken heart. "I am certain he died in honor," she managed. "It is this terrible guilt that I feel, which will not let me put him to rest. It is I! I did not deserve his love, much less expect his family to accept me! But it was done, and I could do nothing to change it, no matter how much I wanted to."

She could not apologize to Phillip. That chance was gone. But she could to his mother. It didn't matter whether the woman accepted her regrets or not; Arissa had held them in long enough. She would purge them and then, perhaps, she might get on with her life without such torment.

Twenty-one

Intimidation in speech and size was merely a front for Maddie Monroe among strangers. Arissa came to realize this in the hours and weeks that followed. Maddie not only welcomed Arissa to visit Blaine's Folly, the small farm where the woman had been reared, but encouraged her to spend time with Jonathan.

"I'm not looking for a nurse for Johnny, nor am I trying to make you feel you've an obligation, based on a two-day marriage, to raise Phillip's son by another woman, but the two of you sure seem to make a merry pair," her mother-in-law explained, repeatedly. "A woman needs to make her own decisions, and then live with them."

A decision was exactly what Arissa was going to have to make, and soon, she realized, upon hearing the news that the British reinforcements had landed at their stronghold on Staten Island. Maddie was ready to pack barrel and baggage to move back to the city to defend her home, despite Alain's argument against the wisdom of the idea. If their boys were going to fight the British, she intended to be there to support them, and if they lost, she was determined to make certain that the Monroe mansion would not be abused by the British occupation. She'd house the bloody-backs, keep the mansion in tact, and spy on them while doing so, she'd declared at the picnic the two families had put together to celebrate the formal signing of the Declaration of Independence in Philadelphia.

"I'm not like those faint hearts that abandoned the city by the droves after General Washington arrived, but my summer annual is over, by damn!" Maddie had sworn, in outright belligerence. "A woman can do her part as well as a man, though the manner may be more subtle."

With her feisty mother-in-law readying to leave for the city, Arissa struggled with the choice. She was welcome to go with Maddie. The woman had made that plain. However, her father was dead set against it. Arissa adored her youngest brother, Robert, who was now fully recovered from his accident, but holding baby Jonathan was like holding a part of Phillip, more tangible and comforting than her memories.

Of the Beaujeu family, only one supported the idea that she should take a stand with their neighbor at Monroe Place—her brother John.

"It's her decision, Papa," he'd argued over the supper table, the following evening. "I think you're trying to frighten her out of going, just like you're trying to keep me on a tether." Arissa had been startled when John threw down his napkin and rose, red-faced, from the table in rebellion. "I love this family as much as you do, but you have to realize that I am a man and she is a woman. We're adults, and you have to let go of us!"

At the week's end, John was packed and ready to travel with Maddie Monroe by boat to New York City. It had broken Arissa's heart to see the torment on both her father and brother's faces. To endure the emotion-filled silence between them was even worse. Unlike Tamson and James, who were caught in the middle, she was going to have to cast her lot with John, or with her father.

When Maddie's carriage arrived, this time driven by the caretaker of the farm, John's bags were on the front porch. He was going to New York with the intention of signing aboard a merchantman, if he had to go on to Philadelphia to do so. This was a real possibility, what with the gathering of British ships in the harbor. Such belongings as Arissa had were in her room. Her heart and head were torn between disappointing the new family that had welcomed her so unselfishly into their close circle and Phillip's mother and son.

Even as she went down the steps, she knew where her duty and at least half of her heart lay. All she had to do was summon the nerve to tell her father. John was on the portico, as was the rest of the family. Tamson snatched up Robert, who excitedly darted out without caution to greet little Jonathan, as the carriage came to halt.

"Blessed Savior!" Maddie called out from the hard leather seat, waving a letter in her hand. Her faced was flushed with excitement, as she began to jump up and down, rocking the vehicle, to the delight of Jonathan, who was tied securely on the seat beside her. "Arissa, child, it's Phillip! He's alive!"

"What?" Arissa's incredulous exclamation was echoed all round. She stood, riveted by disbelief, while her father took the missive from Maddie's hand and proceeded to read it.

"Mon Dieu!" he swore, when he'd finished the letter. He walked toward Arissa with it. "It is true, *ma petite!*"

As the others gathered around her, Arissa read the handsomely penned letter from one Jonathan Hale, Deborah's brother and Phillip's partner in law. Baby Jonathan had been named after him. Phillip had been taken prisoner in Quebec City and delivered by one of the recently arrived British ships, along with some other prisoners from New York, with the provision that he not bear arms against the king again! Her pulse racing, Arissa read on that he was "somewhat worse for the ordeal," but was in good health and spirits, otherwise.

"I cannot believe this!" she cried, choking on the mixture of emotions that overtook her. "This man Hale," she said, addressing her father, "he would not . . ." She broke off, realizing the folly of her ill-founded suspicion. It was true. Phillip was alive and well . . . except that he was somewhat worse for the ordeal.

"But what does this mean?" she asked, her professional demeanor rising above her excitement.

"It means my boy's lost a pound or two. Maybe they even striped his back," Maddie suggested, trying not to let concern dampen her elation, as it was doing to her daughter-in-law's. "But you're the doctor, child. Go get that black bag of yours and your things. You've got a husband waiting!"

Inadvertently, Arissa glanced at Alain Beaujeu. The time had come that she'd been dreading all week. As she groped for the words, however, he stepped forward and enveloped her in his arms.

"But of course you will go. I left my country and took great risks for my love. How can I expect my daughter to do anything less?"

Arissa sobbed in relief. "Thank you, Father!"

"We'll miss you terribly, but Phillip obviously needs you now," Tamson told her, slipping her free arm about her.

Little Robert strained to leave his mother's other arm, seeking his share of the affection. As Arissa and Alain made room for him, James reached forward and squeezed her shoulder. He didn't say anything. His expression, for once completely devoid of mischief, told his feelings. How long she basked in the warmth of her family's good wishes and love, she didn't know. When Maddie Monroe interrupted them, however, with a wry, "If it gets any wetter around here, the road'll be too bad to get to the landing," Arissa broke away.

"Well, I guess I'd better get my things."

As she started for the door, she saw Alain approach

John, who'd stood silently off to the side. She couldn't help but pause just inside to eavesdrop, despite her proper upbringing.

"And how could I expect my son to stay and run an estate, when I left my father's farm to live the carefree life of a voyageur. It seems I have overlooked a very important lesson that my father taught me in giving his blessing, even though he wanted me to stay."

Arissa blinked away tears of joy, as she tore up the central staircase to retrieve her few belongings. Providence's hand was certainly busy today, she thought. God must truly be on the side of these good people and, because of them, hope had been restored in her heart once again.

Passage for New York City on the schooner waiting at the wharf was no problem. Maddie Monroe had already booked Arissa, confident that the girl would accompany her, even before the good news about Phillip's survival came. Nor was there any problem with the other unexpected traveler going with them—Alain Beaujeu. He'd already made up his mind to go with John and, like Maddie, had anticipated Arissa's decision.

"You are a Beaujeu, *non?*" he teased, when Arissa expressed her astonishment at his perception. "You loved the father. How could you not feel the same for his son and follow your heart?" Beside, according to him, he'd not found satisfactory answers during his last trip about the fake money.

Despite her flying spirits, the sailing vessel took three long days to reach their destination. The captain exercised unusual caution, due to the reports of British warships seeking to block off the harbor. However, on the morning of the third day, they disembarked at the jagged coastline of city docks on the East River, where longshoremen unloaded goods from everywhere—Maine lumber, luxury goods from Europe, tobacco from Virginia, silk from South Carolina, rum and molasses from the West

Indies, ivory and slaves from Africa, and daily provisions
from Long Island.

Of the four travelers, her father alone seemed to be
able to contain his excitement, which was just as well, for
the rest of them were charged up to the point of giddi-
ness, each for their own specific reason. Even the baby
Jonathan, who had recovered from teething, boasted his
fourth tooth with good-natured cackles and smiles.

Yet by the time they'd hailed a coach to take them to
Monroe Place on lower Broadway, the realization that
Arissa was soon to see Phillip, face-to-face, again became
a sobering reality. A hundred questions began to plague
her, ranging from the insinuated condition of his health
to the equally paralyzing prospect that he might not have
forgiven her for her cool send off.

The magnificence of the city managed to distract her
momentarily from her increasing apprehension, as the
coach made its swaying way through the traffic, past a
procession of brick and tile buildings with the staggered
architectural lines of Dutch influence. Churches ranging
from simple to magnificent proportions with high stee-
ples—some topped with weathervanes—caused Arissa to
point in wonder to Jonathan, who was cradled comfort-
ably in her lap, unimpressed. Even the streets were lined
with lanterns every fifty feet, extending four feet or so
from the buildings, per city ordinance, according to her
father.

Further away from what had been the old part of the
city, wooden buildings became more prominent, although
brick indisputably marked affluence among the private
homes. When the coach pulled onto Broadway and
slowed before an impeccably kept cobbled drive circling
in front of one of the finest examples of elegant masonry
Arissa had seen to date, she knew instantly her father's
indication that Phillip Monroe possessed his share of
wealth was an understatement.

Unlike the sprawling farmhouse that had grown from a one-room cabin at Blaine's Folly, Monroe Place was designed from the outset to be a showplace. Constructed of brick imported from England, from the street it appeared as broad as it was long, with a hip roof boasting three dormers per side. On the front and sides were centered doors beneath a spread of five windows, each entrance accessed by a high covered stoop with steps approaching from the ground level, where windows set in small arches indicated a basement.

The moment the coach came to halt before the mansion, the door opened and a man about Phillip's age rushed out to greet them. Judging from his dress, which was of the latest fashion, this was no servant. After seeing the grandeur of Monroe Place, however, she wasn't certain that this could not be its servants' attire. The moment Maddie Monroe addressed him, however, she knew instantly who the man was.

"Jonathan! How good to see you!" Although her words were full of enthusiasm, concern emerged on their heels. "Is something wrong? Is Phillip all right?"

From the hesitation before Jonathan Hale's answer, Arissa, like her mother-in-law, knew something was amiss. The plaguing insinuation about Phillip's health immediately filled her mind.

"Not exactly," Jonathan admitted at last, as if uncertain as to how to tell his friend's mother of the problem clouding his face.

"God, he's lost a limb!" Maddie whispered, paling beneath her natural glow, as she pushed past Arissa to get out of the carriage. "Take me to him, boy."

"No, he's fit," Jonathan protested, rushing to catch up with her. "It's just that . . ."

"Well, man, who the devil are you bringing in now?"

Arissa hardly felt her father's steadying hand on her own, as she stared beyond Maddie and Hale at the disheveled man standing in the open doorway beside a clearly distressed steward. His clothes were like Hale's—of good cut and quality—but they looked as though he'd slept in them. In fact, he looked as if he'd just tumbled out of bed after a drunken revel, with his uncut hair and unshaven face. There was a wild quality about his gaze, as he stared at the older woman approaching him with open arms.

"Phillip, thank God!"

Instead of embracing Maddie Monroe, her son ducked out of her reach with a look of sheer disdain. "For what, madame?" He looked at Jonathan. "Who is this woman?"

Jonathan grabbed Phillip by the arm, steadying him, as he staggered sideways, leaving Arissa to believe her husband was still enjoying his drinking spree. She held little Jonathan's head against her bosom, as if protecting the child from the sight of his father, as Alain left her side.

"That is your mother, *mon ami!*" he called out to Phillip.

Phillip stepped back in disbelief. "So you say!" Again he sought out Jonathan. "Well, what do you say, sir?"

"This is your mother, Phillip."

The unstable man closed his eyes tightly, all the while swaying back and forth. "Strike me blue, you say I am Phillip Monroe, master of this grand palace, and this is my mother?" He opened his eyes, blinking as if to focus, first at Hale and then at Maddie.

Recovering quickly from her initial shock, Maddie Monroe stepped up to her son and seized his arm. She was equal to his height and weight, if not his strength. Regardless, she shook him soundly.

"I'll strike you blue, young man, if you don't come to your senses. I've never tolerated excessive drink in this house, and I won't now! Don't even know your own name," she snorted. "No wonder Jonathan refused to disclose the nature of your indisposition!"

With a powerful thrust, which obviously took the younger man off guard, she ushered Phillip into the house past the doorman. "Out of my way, Eugene!"

"Now look, Mother, or whoever the hell you are! . . ."

A slap, loud enough to travel out to where Arissa was being helped down from, resounded from inside, followed by an angry growl, which sent Alain and Hale both rushing in after the two.

"By God, I've been brought up not to strike a woman, but . . ."

"So you have, Phillip Monroe! It's all right," Maddie assured Alain and Hale, as Arissa hurried after them up the steps and inside with John. "I have everything under control. My son knows his manners, if he's forgotten himself at the moment. Arissa, give the child to Eugene! Eugene, take him to Anna!" the matron ordered, assuming the command to which she was accustomed.

At the mention of her name, Phillip backed against the wall, his hand resting on the polished rail of the walnut-paneled wainscot and stared at Arissa in such a way as to send chills up her spine. She hurriedly handed little Jonathan over to the doorman, eager to get the child out of the same room with his crazed father.

"And who is this?" Phillip demanded, pointing rudely at her. "Do tell me she's not my sister!"

Arissa had felt the sensation of being visually undressed before, but never had it made her feel so lowly. With a shiver of foreboding, she stepped under John's protective arm, as her father moved forward, blocking her from Phillip's liquor-crazed gaze. In the enclosure of the formal hall, the scent of alcohol permeated the air, as if the man had absorbed it, within and without. An empty bottle lay at the bottom of the steps, evidently where he'd just dropped it, for the rest of the house, from what she saw, was immaculately kept by the staff.

"You do not know her?" Alain questioned, testily.

"Nor do I know you, or the man clinging to the delicious bit of fluff, for that matter."

"Phillip! Enough!" Maddie Monroe ground out, her indignation once again overcoming her shock. "Now you either march up these steps to your room on your own two feet, or I shall have these men physically transport you!"

Arissa held her breath, as Phillip teetered, one foot on the first step, and looked at his mother in consternation. He seemed to be trying to decide whether or not to take the woman seriously. Whether it was from Maddie's size, the sight of Alain, John, and Hale moving toward him in unison, or the paltry remnants of his ingrained manners, Arissa couldn't guess. Regardless, he pivoted abruptly toward the stairwell. But for Jonathan's quick reflexes, he'd have fallen flat on his back.

"Come on, man, I'll help you back up," his friend cajoled, taking him in a firm hand.

At the top of the landing, a maid carrying the baby darted up the second section of stairwell to the next floor, as though the devil himself were approaching, and disappeared with rapid steps across the upstairs carpet. Phillip didn't appear to notice, for he was concentrating on the proper placement of his feet to keep from tumbling head over heels, forward or backward.

"Eugene," Maddie Monroe said to the doorman, who'd returned for further instruction, "see the young lady is shown to . . . to the guest room." For the first time, the older woman's voice faltered. She met Arissa's gaze with one full of apology. "I think it best, for the time being, dear."

Arissa nodded, perhaps too eagerly, in agreement. *Dieu,* but she had never expected such a reception. Was

Phillip drunk out of his mind, or had he been that way before he'd taken to drink? What had the English done to him?

"Father, will you and John be staying?"

"We'd planned on residing at the hotel further up the street," Alain answered, "but I would be more comfortable if you joined us. I am certain Maddie would understand."

"I think Papa's right. You ought to go with us. Phillip's clean out of his mind," John chimed in. "You'll be safer with us."

Of that, Arissa had little doubt. Still, she said, *"Non,* I am needed here more than ever, now. Madame Monroe and her staff, I believe, can control Phillipe. If they cannot, I can give him something that will pacify him, once I am certain the alcohol is out of his system. But . . . would you mind bringing up my bags?" As brave as her words sounded, she was still unnerved by the scene with Phillip.

"I will stay here and see your sister settled," Alain told her brother, as he picked up one of her two cases. Eugene had already taken the other in hand. "You go on to the hotel with our things and engage a room for us."

John leaned over and bussed Arissa on the cheek. "I'll be back later," he promised.

"Are you ready, Miss . . ." The manservant hesitated, realizing with embarrassment that he had not gotten her name.

"Madame . . . er . . . Mrs. Monroe, sir. Mrs. Phillipe Monroe."

It was later when Arissa had unpacked her three dresses, for she now had one of tawny homespun, thanks to her stepmother and mother-in-law. Since it was in the better shape among the three and quite in style, she donned it, after freshening up and joined the others downstairs in the parlor, where, after recovering from the shock of Arissa's introduction as Phillip's wife, Jonathan Hale told what he knew of Phillip's malady.

Phillip had been delivered to Monroe Place by one of his prison mates. According to the man, he'd been disoriented since his internment. Whether madness had come from the fever, from the flesh wound on his side or from the bullet graze on his forehead, no one knew, but the prisoners had protected his identity from the British, lest he be accused of spying in Montreal and hanged.

Jonathan had sent word immediately to Albany and summoned a physician, who resolved that there was nothing physically wrong with Phillip. He suffered from the mental illness of amnesia, the result of physical shock. Ever since Jonathan had tried to keep an eye on his friend.

"But I tell you," the young man swore, "I was at my wits' end. I could not control him, short of physically restraining him. He has the strength of a madman, despite his imprisonment. They fed him and exercised him well enough, I can tell you that! I swear, I've chased him all over the city. He takes these notions to go out and . . ." Throwing up his hands, Jonathan Hale fell back against his chair in utter resignation.

"There are some jobs best left to women!" Maddie spoke up confidently. "Men can often be gentled when they can't be overcome. He was quite manageable, once he saw that I would not back down."

"I do not imagine the alcohol is helping his madness," Arissa added. "Can we hide all the liquor from him?"

"I've already instructed Eugene to lock it all in the wine cellar," Maddie affirmed. "I've got the key."

"Are you certain he is manageable?" It was obvious to Arissa that her father was not convinced, nor was John, who'd returned, as promised, and now listened with quiet regard.

"He's sleeping like a lamb . . . a drunken one, but nonetheless, a docile one."

Arissa nearly smiled at her mother-in-law's attempt to lighten the subject. Even if her father was not, she was more reassured. "I will fix some tea for him later, to insure that he sleeps through the night. Rest is the most important contribution to recovery of any sort, but especially that of the mind."

She was even more convinced of that later in the evening, as she tossed and turned in her bed, unable to sleep. She should have been exhausted from the travel, not to mention the travail of discovering her husband's madness. It was worse than she'd imagined. She didn't have to face his contempt, for he had lost that, along with all memory of her. She was married to a crazed individual who treated everyone with distrust.

If only her father's medical books hadn't been lost in the fire, she might begin to study, to search for a way to restore Phillip to her and his family. Although her escape from Montreal had hardly allowed for a trunk full of books to be carried along, she recalled, fitfully. All she had were medical instruments and a store of knowledge which did not include much information on amnesia.

Arissa turned over again, tossing her light coverlet off, with an oath at the rampant thoughts that would give her no peace. True, an army physician had examined him, but she'd seen the results of some of the physicians employed by the Continental army, and was not impressed. A clock in the upstairs hall struck the hour of three and she started. At least Phillip was sleeping, she mused, grudgingly, jumping from the bed to walk to the window, where lamplight combined with moonlight and filtered in through the louvered shutters.

She stared out at the tiny specks of light marking the blocks on the opposite side of the street. Hugging her-

self like a lost child, she took in the strange surroundings, when she was distracted by a loud creak which cut
through the serenity of the night. A stiff hinge, perhaps,
she guessed, shivering at the raking chill it sent up her
spine. She listened more attentively. Although they were
soft, there were retreating footfalls outside in the hall,
betrayed by the faint groan of a warped floorboard.

Holding her breath, Arissa tiptoed to her door and
rested her hand on the latch. Ever so carefully, she lifted
it, certain that she was likely to see the maid, or perhaps
her mother-in-law, up and about to check on baby
Jonathan. Except that the nursery was adjoining the master suite on the opposite side of the main hall, across
from Maddie Monroe's room. There was no one, to her
knowledge, except herself in the guest wing.

Inching the door open and praying it was well oiled,
Arissa peeked out into the small hallway separating the
front and back bedrooms in the guest wing. Seeing nothing worthy of immediate suspicion, she looked around
the jamb and across the large upstairs hall to see the door
to Maddie Monroe's room close, shutting off the rays of
light from the chamber stick within. Had Phillip's mother
been checking on her, as well?

Arissa smiled. It would be like her. Just that evening,
after Maddie had returned from coaxing Phillip into taking the tranquilizing elixir, she'd gathered Arissa in her
arms and thanked her for staying, calling her *daughter* for
the first time.

For a long while, Arissa stood inside her door, her
thoughts snagged on the fact that Phillip was sedated.
That meant he could be examined. She closed her eyes
and leaned against the cool plaster wall behind her, debating whether or not to risk an encounter with the man
she'd once known as husband and lover when, out of
nowhere, he materialized.

Shock at the brief flash of cherished memory coming

to life—the warmth of his lips, the sapping strength of his embrace—thawed with the real heat of the thinly clad male body pressing hers hungrily to it. While she knew it couldn't be, that Phillip *had* to be in his room, lost in a drugged sleep, it was the man in the flesh who now ravished her mouth, waylaying any protest, with his deep, fervent kiss.

Twenty-two

"Non!" Arissa gasped, when the intruder finally granted her reprieve so as to seek her neck with an agonized groan.

"God 'Rissa!"

The use of her name halted the panicked scream in her throat, before it could gain sufficient volume to attract help.

"God!" the man swore again, his hands dropping to roam the curve of her back and buttocks over and over, as if trying to savor all of her at the same time. "I thought I was hallucinating!"

Arissa thought it was *she* who was hallucinating. But could all her senses be so deceived? Every nerve in her body had come alive at the beck and call of the one who had taught it to feel, to respond, as never before. So much reminded her of the man she'd taken as husband, rather than the madman she'd witnessed earlier—his touch, hungry, but ever so considerate, the clean scent of his talc, his desire-laden whispers. She was shaking—physically shaking—from the physical and mental bombardment of this fierce assault, her defenses thrown out of kilter.

"Please, Phillip," she implored, breathless from fear of the passion this madman was awakening. He was taking advantage of her memory of him, while he had none of her. "You . . . you are frightening me! I cannot stop you!"

Again, a tormented groan escaped the lips that had taken to her ear and with it, the encompassing embrace dissolved. Cool air rushed between them, as the ardent intruder straightened to his full height, giving her room to escape. Despite her freedom to do so, Arissa couldn't bring herself to move. Instead she stared up at the faceless stranger so very much like the Phillip of her dreams, the one who had worshiped her body with his all and yet made it his slave.

"You just did," came a hoarse reply. One of the devil's hands returned to her face, fingers caressing the taper of her cheek. "I'm sorry, 'Rissa. I . . ." Suddenly, she was in his arms again, crushed breathless against him. *"I thought you were dead!"*

Her mind reeling with the impact of his words, Arissa eventually squirmed free and moved warily along the wall. "I thought *you* were insane!"

Phillip reluctantly swung away from her, as if to convince her that she was safe. "I believed I really would go insane when I heard about the fire at the Chateau Royale. I'd had one of my prison mates, whom I took into my confidence, bribe a guard to find out what had happened to you, to see if you'd left with the troops . . ."

"What do you mean *'really would go insane'?"* His insinuation was as incredible as his appearance. "Phillipe, are you saying that you are not . . . that is . . ." She darted around the corner of the bed, as he turned back to her.

"I'm acting, 'Rissa!" he blurted out, in exasperation. "I've been acting the fool for months."

She was better now, more in control of herself with the distance between them, but no less confused. "But why?" She grabbed one of her pillows instinctively, putting it between them like a shield, in a paltry attempt at defense against her quandary. Her mind was as disconcerted as her body, torturously so.

"I couldn't risk the bloody-backs discovering I'd been a spy!"

"But you are safe now!"

"I'm not so sure about that."

More bewildered than ever, Arissa sank on the edge of the mattress. *"Non,* don't come any closer!" she warned, as Phillip started toward her. "Explain . . . please!"

"Arissa, I was shot by one of our own men. The same bastard killed Stephen when he tried to help me." Phillip put his hand to his head, as if to drag the memory from the past. "I crawled through the snow to him, but he was dead. I . . . I don't know what happened after that. They say I wandered into the fort, disoriented, and collapsed in front of the door of the blockhouse that blew us to pieces. All I can recall is waking up in the hospital with the wounded, my head and arm bandaged. I think the bandages were all that kept my brain from exploding," he added, with a halfhearted chuckle that was so like the Phillip she knew—always trying to make light of things. "Well, I sure as hell wasn't going to tell them who I was!"

Arissa couldn't believe what she was hearing, but then nothing she'd witnessed since arriving in New York was credible. It was only by keeping his wits that Phillip survived to act without them, and now he was saying that the charade continued to serve him and his country.

"New York is crawling with Loyalist informants," he told her grimly, "but worse, it's infested with counterfeiters. Remember that bad issue you received at the inn?"

"My father, he is trying to trace the bad money, too."

"Who?"

"My father." Cautiously she rose from the bed and put aside the pillow. "Phillipe . . ." She hesitated and shook her head. "I don't know which of us is insane now!"

"Me, Arissa. But I know a doctor who can cure me with

a sweet smile . . . and by telling me what this father business is all about."

She closed the distance between them and placed her hands against his nightshirt. So many thoughts, so many questions . . . "Phillipe, you must tell your mother. This is breaking her heart."

"I already did." He brushed her tumble of hair behind her shoulders, gently. "Just before I came here . . . and I promised her I'd tell you in the morning, but I was in more of a dither than she was when she left. I couldn't wait."

"*Non*, don't touch me yet," Arissa warned, as he started to place his hands on her white shoulders, bared by the sleeveless linen night shift she wore. "I can't think, and I must do so! There is so much to say."

"My God, 'Rissa, don't you think we've waited—no, suffered—long enough?"

Arissa clenched her fists against the rise and fall of Phillip's chest, wrestling with her response. His one question obliterated all of hers. When had she ever been able to think clearly this close to Phillip? Even though he respected her request and refrained from touching her, she felt as though his hands were all over her at once. Even when she'd hated him for planning to go to Quebec, she hadn't been able to refuse him her body. She'd wanted him as much then as she did now.

"You don't hate me for not saying good-bye?" Her voice broke with the sudden exonerating realization.

"Hate you? Strike me, woman, I love you so much, I . . ." He cleared his throat, huskily. "I don't want to scare you, but I don't think I can keep my hands off you a moment more, love!"

Arissa ran her own over Phillip's shoulders and down his arms to the trembling hands he referred to. Taking them, she placed them on her breasts and stared into the tormented gaze she sensed, rather than saw.

"Then don't, *mon cher.* Don't ever again!"

Tears spilled down her checks, as Phillip leaned forward and tenderly kissed away each one, as if he too, knew her pain. The anguish and hunger from months of torment and denial surged forth, making each caress, each breath, tremble with relief and anticipation. As he did for her, so she tried to do in return. Her shift had no more than touched the floor when Arissa was tugging Phillip's nightshirt over his head to have it drift down to cover hers, even as Phillip's body was now doing to hers.

No longer a dream, here was living flesh against living flesh, reveling in the wild, sensual reintroduction to all those erotic reflexes they'd scarcely come to know in one another, and yet had not forgotten. The eternity of their separation now fired the urgency of their reunion, so that neither he nor she could stand more than the most cursory of rediscoveries. Their need was as hot as their bodies, so that when Phillip took his intimate possession of her, he was received with equal passion, welcomed by her wholehearted embrace, without and within.

His breathless apology, as he vigorously took his pleasure, would have made Arissa laugh at the folly of it, were she not caught up in the throes of her own rapture. Why waste his breath on words, when there would be time for them later, as they lay in each other's arms! Somehow, for some reason, she'd been given another chance at happiness and this time, there was no holding back. She seized the moment with her lover, riding high to passion's peak and coasting back to sweet reality, still entangled in love's ultimate embrace.

It was only then that she laughed, a small chuckle which caused him to lift his head and stare into her sparkling gaze.

"What?"

"Don't ever apologize for doing that, *mon mari.*"

"My husband," he echoed, more than pleased by her

remark. His humor moved within her, making her cling all the more to the last physical link of their intimacy. "As many times as I'd imagined making love to you again, I had hardly intended it to be so . . . brief."

"But there will be more. Our time as man and wife was but a few days, yet you taught me much about the resilience of . . ." Arissa shifted beneath him, seductively. "This."

"Strike me, you are a vixen!" Phillip growled, lowering his head to attack her throat with playful nipping and kissing. He eventually worked his way up to her ear. "I can't believe I'm not dreaming!"

Arissa pulled away, sobering at the mention of slumber. "Speaking of which, how is it that you are not asleep? Your mother gave you . . ."

"That was the foulest tasting poison! I held it in my cheek so long, I thought the side of my face would go numb, but I couldn't tell her then, not with Eugene standing by, ready to pounce on me if I got out of hand." He caught her chin with his fingers, his voice suddenly quite grave. "No one must know I'm in my right mind, not even the servants! Do you understand?"

Arissa shook her head. She really didn't. So much of Phillip's story was still missing.

With a sigh of exasperation, he rolled away, relieving her of the weight she'd hardly noticed. With a moue of disappointment that their intimate tryst had ended, at least for the moment, she turned on her side to face him and raised her head up on one elbow.

"Why can I not tell my father and brother? Father is trying to find the same brigands that you are, I think."

Phillip dislodged his troubled gaze from ceiling. "What is this father talk? Dr. Conway died, didn't he?"

"Didn't your mother tell you?"

"Mother was so overjoyed that her son was in his right mind that all she managed to get out was that I had married a sweet, pretty, and smart girl—nothing I didn't already know," he added, with a lopsided grin. "I understand little Jonathan is quite fond of you, as well.

It was still unbelievable to Arissa. Phillip was here, alive and in his right mind. The sheer adoration in his voice moved her deeply, yet she tried to keep a steady voice. Desperate for distraction from the surge of emotion that was overtaking her, she brushed his long hair out of his face. "Does your charade prevent you from having a haircut? You look like a wildman."

"Your father," Phillip prompted, stubbornly.

Arissa cleared her throat. There, that was better. "He is Alain Beaujeu!"

"What?"

"He is . . ."

"I heard, it's just . . ." Phillip ran his fingers through his disheveled hair in disbelief, as Arissa placed her arm across his chest, her face a mirror of pride and joy.

"You are friends and business associates, I know!" she declared, smugly. "Oh, Phillipe, it was so unbelievable! I was told you and Stephen were dead and the American troops, they had left, and . . ."

Piece by piece, Arissa put together her story for the still man at her side: how Gaspar had saved her from a murder charge and taken her to Ticonderoga; about the letter which had revealed Alain as her father and a noblewoman, now living in Paris, as her real mother; her loving welcome into the Beaujeu family and by his mother; and, lastly, about the torment which had burdened her since their parting.

" 'Rissa, I understood," he assured her, cradling her in his arms. "I knew you were torn. You never held back your love for me, even when you hated what I was doing." He kissed the top of her head. "How could someone so smart be so silly?"

"I was not so silly until I fell in love with you," she admitted, sheepishly.

She did love Phillip, more than she had in her dreams. With him here beside her, she could well face anything—anything except his being taken from her again, she thought, his words about his attempted murder coming back to her.

"Phillip, who is it that is trying to murder you? Why?"

"If I knew that, I'd feel a lot easier, but those months in prison gave me a lot of time to think, to put things together . . . like the attempt on Stephen's life the night I brought him to the Chateau Royale."

"You think those robbers were after you?"

"I think someone allegedly on our side followed Stephen. He was wearing my cloak, remember?"

"Another spy?" Arissa suggested in alarm.

"I assume so . . . although why he tried to kill me again during the attack is a puzzle. There was no motive then, as there would have been before I began my mission." Phillip sighed in confusion. "Regardless, I still have a job to do."

"And that is?"

"Convince everyone that I'm out of my wits, all the while checking out the printing establishments we know of."

"Then you can work with Father."

Phillip shook his head. "As much as I trust Alain Beaujeu, I can't, Arissa. I'm under strict orders not to confide in anyone. I simply couldn't leave you and Mother at loose ends." He rolled over, gathering her to him. "You realize the trust I'm putting in you, don't you? I don't want anything to come between us again, ever!"

Neither did Arissa. That was why she met his kiss, rather than protesting. If she had to act the wife of a madman, then she'd do so. She'd do anything for the man who had abandoned her lips for the hardened tip of her breast, his breath warm against it.

"It won't be easy for you, 'Rissa, but I swear to you, I love you, and I'll do all I can to make it up to you when this is over."

Arissa squirmed at the quivering flutter of desire coming to life within and buried her fingers in his hair. Nothing could daunt the rise of emotion that filled her heart to overflowing at Phillip's tender vow. He loved her, she thought, dizzily, sliding the tips of her toes up the scarred, but able muscle of his leg. And he trusted her. Nothing more mattered.

Before the week was out, a freshly printed invitation arrived from Thomas and Mary Hale for a private family dinner. Arissa hardly knew what to expect, when their carriage arrived at the prestigious home on Pearl Street, for Phillip and his mother had been full of innuendo, especially about the senior Hale's second and much younger wife, who wanted nothing to do with baby Jonathan.

"It's no wonder Deborah was as frivolous as she was, the way Thomas spoiled her," her mother-in-law had remarked in disdain. "I've still got the bolts of cloth in the attic for the new curtains she wanted to use to replace these perfectly good ones with!"

From what Arissa was able to access, Thomas Hale was a fire and brimstone patriot, but indulged Mary with any favor she asked. Therefore, both host and hostess enjoyed the high life of New York society and refused to let the nuisance of a war inhibit their style of living.

That became evident immediately, when the Monroes and Alain Beaujeu were greeted in the marbled foyer of the mansion. Like Jonathan Hale, his parents were garbed in the best the world had to offer. Mary Hale, in her painted silk dress, made Arissa feel more like a servant in her plain homespun. However, Maddie Monroe had donned the same, perhaps in anticipation of Arissa's self-consciousness, for there had been little chance to expand the girl's wardrobe since their arrival, what with reopening Monroe Place for the family occupation.

Although still exercising thrift, Maddie had summoned a few of her day servants back into service to aide Eugene and Anna in the daily operation of the mansion. Some came back with considerable apprehension, for news of Phillip Monroe's dementia had traveled through circles from the highest to the lowest order. Visits had started immediately, many spurred by curiosity in Maddie's estimation, and notes of sympathy had come in daily.

New York wanted to see for itself how crazed the Monroe heir was, not to mention glimpse his poor Canadian bride, for Arissa had received her share of sympathetic expressions at having a husband who was clearly out of his head. Keeping in character with his charade, Phillip had done nothing to change the minds of the family's friends and associates. He acted totally unpredictable, although he was considerably gentled by the arrival of his mother and wife. Drugs were responsible, the rumor had spread, medication prescribed by his wife, who, quite astonishingly, was some sort of physician.

"What a lovely wife you have, Phillip! I'm certain you must be proud of her," Mary Hale said, once they'd been shown into the parlor to await the announcement of the meal.

When Phillip leaned over his hostess's shoulder to whisper in her ear, the woman started, clearly unsure of the reputed madman. "They say she is my wife and she does act the part well enough. I like a lusty woman."

Arissa lowered demure eyes. After a week's worth of such embarrassing comments, she only pinkened now. Her father, however, who had also been invited, had yet to grow accustomed to Phillip's crude behavior. Although sorry that he was no closer to finding who had passed the fake money to him than he had been on his earlier visit to the city and reluctant to see him go because of her fondness for him, Arissa was glad, for Phillip's sake, that Alain was planning to return to Albany at the week's end. She put her hand over his in an effort to calm the indignation which flushed his face and strained the cords of his neck. *He doesn't know what he's saying,* she conveyed silently, as she had done vocally many times, of late.

Thank heaven John Beaujeu was not with them! Her brother, whose temper hadn't been as mellowed by the years as their father's, had been more of a worry, but had left her in Alain's care two days go. Realizing his dream, he'd signed on one of the Dutch-Acadie ships, which had been slipping in and out of the New York harbor, despite the endless sea of British masts gathered at Sandy Hook. He departed with Arissa's prayers, for she was not so naive as to be unaware of the danger in her new brother's pursuit of happiness.

"They also tell me you are the parents of my late wife," Phillip was babbling on, "although you look to be too young to have had a daughter old enough for marriage! 'Tis a wonder I didn't choose you, madame." Slipping an arm about Mary Hale's satin-sashed waist, he ushered her over to the window away from the others, as though he had more to say for her ears only. Despite the panicked looked she cast over her shoulder at her husband and stepson, she accompanied him graciously.

"I warned you," Jonathan Hale whispered to his father. "Our rising star of a relative has turned into a blithering idiot!"

"That's why I invited him," Thomas countered, in a voice that betrayed real concern for his ex-son-in-law. "I'd hoped familiar surroundings might bring the lad back to his senses. You need help in that law office, especially now, with all the traitors in our midst."

Seven hundred had been the number circulated for men who had been enlisted in the British service right under the noses of the occupying Continentals. Arissa had hardly believed that the serious subject of the discussions could be so casually carried on over luncheons and afternoon soirees, like idle gossip. Some of the rogues had been rounded up for trial, but others were still at large, living in taverns and public houses throughout the city. All were waiting for Howe to make his move, since the British ships filling the harbor and the Staten Island stronghold itself could contain no more troops than were already there.

Even General Washington's private staff was in question. One man had already been convicted and executed publicly near the Commons for an assassination attempt. His questioning had brought forth a list of several other suspected agents for the British, including the Mayor of New York and his brother. The findings of John Jay's Conspiracy Committee had added to the rumor to fire the fuel of plans to capture a battery, cut down the king's Bridge, blow up the powder magazine, and set fire to the city, not to mention the continued plots against the general's life, as well as those of his senior officers, Greene and Putnam.

"Traitors or no, that's no reason to deny an innocent female ferry passage to her family!"

Mary Hale's dour-featured sister, Virginia Ryan, had been visiting the family from her Jersey home, when Washington issued the order that no one be given permission to leave the city without a pass from General Stirling, the commandant of New York City. The petulant woman had not smiled since their initial introductions. Even then, a grimace was as close as she came to the pleasantry.

"Oh my!"

Distracted from Virginia's quandary by Mary Hale's indignant exclamation, Arissa turned in time to see her

hostess rush to her husband's chair, her color having re
turned full force.

"I shall check on supper, sir," the woman informe
Thomas Hale, in a rush of words, as hurried as her en
suing exit.

His face a picture of innocence, Phillip ambled bacl
to the group and took up a glass of wine. Arissa glance
fretfully at Jonathan Hale, only to be met by the man'
reassuring nod. The liquor had been diluted in anticipa
tion of their arrival and would continue to be so through
out the meal, lest it compound, or worse, counter th
effects of Phillip's alleged medication.

"Jonathan tells me you're trying to trace some coun
terfeit bills, Mr. Beaujeu," their host addressed Alain
"He's had his hands full with the problem himself . .
every one of his clients has had trouble."

"I'm personally checking their transactions," young
Hale added.

"It would be most helpful if I could obtain from yor
a list of these clients. To date, I am exhausting my suspi
cions and accomplishing nothing. I understand there i
a man named Fletcher in prison now, and that he ha
mentioned some of the men who are clients of your firm
but I cannot find out their names."

"Unfortunately, our client list is confidential, as well,'
Jonathan answered. "Sometimes ethics and law protect the
bloody beggars abusing them. This bad money could forge
the collapse of our cause. We're lost without credit."

"Bad money?" Phillip echoed, his wandering attention
captured. "Why, I've never known money to be bad for
anyone. I'm rather enjoying mine!"

Thomas Hale broke the shocked silence that followed
"Someone is counterfeiting the bills, Phillip. It's British
subterfuge."

"Oh," Phillip acknowledged, turning to Jonathan.
"None of mine is bad, is it?"

"We've all had a smattering of it, I'm afraid. But nothing for you to worry about. I'm taking care of it for you until . . . until you're ready to come back to the firm."

"What firm?"

Arissa actually felt sorry for Phillip's friend. He'd come by daily to see how her husband was doing and offered to help her replace her medical supply of ingredients for the sedating elixir.

"Your law firm, lad!" Thomas Hale informed him, with a hint of desperation. "You're one of New York's finest attorneys and noblest patriots. You're as dear to me as my own son, lad. You married my daughter. You've given me a fine grandson," he added, pointing to little Jonathan, who was sleeping in his grandmother's lap.

Maddie had said that Jonathan's name on the invitation had come from Thomas Hale and not his wife. While their host had gently touched the sleeping child's face before assuming his responsibility of introductions and welcome, the second Mrs. Hale had not afforded the child the slightest bit of interest, as yet. Of course, she was decidedly disconcerted by Phillip and his malady, Arissa mused on the woman's behalf.

"Why don't you go to the office and help Jonathan? God knows the lad needs it!"

"I'm doing well enough, Father," Jonathan declared, tersely. He gave Arissa an imploring look that tugged at her heart. Here was another soul who suffered from a small degree of parental support, she observed, unless Thomas Hale was unusually patronizing of Phillip because of his condition.

"You're supposed to be a physician, madame. Don't you think the more familiar surroundings we expose Phillip to, the quicker he'll recover his memory?"

"The idea is heaven-sent!" the man in question shouted. Phillip jumped to his feet from the arm of the settee, where he'd perched next to Arissa. "I've been bored to distraction with tête-à-têtes and mother hen and her pretty chick hovering over me. I'll go to work! That's novel, at least!"

"Father, think of our clients!"

"Perhaps you are not yet up to working, Phillip," Arissa suggested, rallying to Jonathan's support. "You must have your sleep, or you shall never recover."

"You just want to keep me in your bed, my lusty little love," Phillip shot back, a lascivious look lingering on the modest dip of her neckline. "And that is a pure temptation, but, strike me, I'm all but worn out!"

Virginia Ryan audibly gasped. "I'll go see what's keeping Mary. Excuse me."

No amount of conditioning had prepared Arissa for Phillip's most blatant remark about their relationship, especially since he'd made the same comment to her that morning after their lovemaking. It had been in jest then, but here in a room full of people, strangers and family, it was embarrassing to no end. Maddie Monroe was purposely concentrating on pulling out the wrinkles in her sleeping grandson's dress, while Thomas and Jonathan Hale grappled for a means to change the subject.

With no respectable response coming to mind, Arissa's gaze once again retreated to her lap, earning sympathy from the company. Next to her, however, Alain Beaujeu had heard all he was going to and rose to speak, before she could restrain him.

Arissa was certain of a scene, but it was diffused by the appearance of a uniformed servant at the door, who made his announcement with the utmost of decorum.

"Dinner is served, ladies and gentlemen. The mistress invites you to join her in the dining room below."

Twenty-three

"Ah, there she is!" Jonathan Hale announced, when Arissa entered the Broad Street law office the following day.

The young man was perspiring excessively even for the July heat and had stripped himself of his jacket and tie. Never had Arissa seen anyone so joyous to receive her—at least, aside from her husband, she thought, glancing beyond Jonathan to where Phillip sat flipping without purpose through official looking papers. They were scattered everywhere around the front desk, as though he tested the direction of the scant breeze afforded by an open window with each carefully penned sheet he'd scanned.

"I think his medicine is running out," Phillip's partner confided, in a low tone. "And if he doesn't take it soon, *I'm* going to need it. My clerk walked out and the office is in shambles!"

"Here, here! If you say she's my wife, why are you whispering so sweetly in her ear!" Phillip challenged, noticing them for the first time. "Grant you, she's more interesting than these godawful documents, but she's mine. You said so!" He overturned his chair and strode indignantly toward Arissa, his finger shaking in warning. "If you're going to act the tart to other men, I'll pack you off to Holy Ground faster than a jackrabbit can run!"

"We were discussing your medication, Phillipe. I brought it, in case you needed it."

Phillip looked suspiciously from Arissa to Jonathan. "It's only sugar and water, good friend, but it keeps her in good humor," he relented at last.

Arissa nearly choked, as she fished the bottle from her purse, for her husband had told the absolute truth. Yet Jonathan, none the wiser, was obviously relieved after Phillip had taken two healthy swallows and a third for good measure.

"*Sacre bleu*, Phillipe! You will sleep through supper, drinking so much!" Arissa protested, with appropriate concern. Both she and Maddie had, at Phillip's request, led people to think the elixir knocked him out through most of the night. It was that concept that allowed Arissa to move safely into the master suite in order to sleep in a single bed the staff moved in there for her. At least that made her safe, in the eyes of the servants. As for the debauchery they endeavored to protect her from, her husband had her enjoying every moment of it.

"Not bloody likely!" Phillip blurted out, in defiance. "I'm fairly starving, madame! There's a fine tavern across the way that boasts good fare, judging from its sign. Let's have supper before returning to my palace. Just once, I'd like to eat without having Mother Hen hovering over us. I can believe you are my wife, much more than I can accept her as a mother. She might have been my commanding officer when I was in the army," Phillip conceded, mischievously, "but I'm damned if I sprang from that iron womb of hers."

Once they were out on the street, Jonathan closed the door behind them. It was all Arissa could do to keep from giggling when she heard the bolt click above the noise of the street. Carriages, carts, and wagons of all shapes and sizes moved up and down the thoroughfare, delaying Arissa and Phillip's crossing long enough for Jonathan to close the windows and inside shutters as well. The poor dear was taking no chances on Phillip's return, she reflected wryly. She hurried to the other side after her husband, her skirts hiked to avoid the rubbish swept to the fairway's center where dogs and an occasional pig scavenged hungrily.

However, by the time they reached their destination, she could no longer hold her amusement. "Phillipe, you must have been horrible!"

Her husband put his arm about her and leaned over, as if whispering something totally scandalous in her ear. "So what do you say? Shall we dine out? I don't think Mother will mind."

"Only if you can act civil!" Arissa countered, her humor fading, as she remembered that she was still peeved at the man.

She had not been so amused yesterday. Never in all her life had she been so embarrassed as she had been at the dining room table in the Hales' fashionable town house. Half the meal, she'd spent looking through the small ground level windows of the room at the moving legs of the passing gentry, out for an afternoon walk.

Phillip had been so obnoxious that, upon their leaving, she'd no longer been able to contain her father's wrath. Alain Beaujeu waited until they were inside the polished hall of Monroe Place and then delivered her irascible husband a smart cuff to the jaw, sending him sprawling against the stairwell.

"You will in the future watch your speech, where my daughter is concerned, monsieur, or I shall do more damage than a split lip, is that clear?" he'd ground out, furiously.

When little Jonathan started to cry at the angry outburst, however, her father caught himself. With an apology to his hostess and to her, he left, his jawline bulging with the effort to exercise the restraint it took to do so without further word.

"Arissa, I have to act the part. You know it's not really me!" Phillip protested, lowly. To her distraction, he blew lightly in her ear. "I'm hungry."

Arissa pushed him away in annoyance. "Very well, let us go in this place then. People are staring at us!"

As she scanned their surroundings, confirming her declaration, her attention was caught by a large buckskin-clad man carrying a leather haversack. He'd stopped to knock at the door of Phillip's office. She'd seen dozens of such men in the city, but there was no mistaking this one. His face, she'd committed to memory, despite her father's assurances that he was just another frontiersman.

"Mon Dieu!"

"What? What is it?" Phillip asked, tightening his hold about her, as she swayed in shock.

Arissa turned away, despite the fact that the trapper was oblivious to her existence. "That man, Phillipe! That is the man who tried to kill you!" Phillip ventured to look in that direction, but Arissa caught his face. *"Non,* do not attract his attention! He may try to kill you again. Can you not see that long knife on his leg?"

The sight of a buckskinned trapper wasn't odd, but his wife's bizarre reaction to him was enough to move Phillip. "Come inside," he counseled, ushering her to the open door of the tavern. "You need to sit down before you swoon."

"I am not going to swoon!"

Regardless of Arissa's protest, she offered little resistance, as Phillip directed her past one of the long tavern tables to a smaller one by the window overlooking the street. There he could observe the source of her distress without upsetting her further. Arissa wasn't the hysterical sort, but she'd turned ashen with alarm.

By the time they were seated, however, the man had

disappeared. Whether he'd gone inside the office or given up knocking and walked on beyond their view, Phillip couldn't tell. If he was inside, Jonathan had not opened the shutters, but was carrying on business in the dim light afforded through them. After ordering a lightly spirited punch for Arissa and a flip for himself, he covered her folded hands with his in concern.

"Are you all right now?"

Arissa nodded silently, but she had not regained her color.

"Can you tell me what that was all about?"

"That man, he is the one who tried to kill you. I know it!"

"How, Arissa?"

She inhaled shakily. "I . . . Father and I met him on the way to Albany. I think his name was Egan, although he had been drinking and slurring his words. It was hard to tell. He was traveling from Fort Ticonderoga to New York City and shared a campfire with us one evening. He had been in Canada with the Americans."

"So have a lot of men clad in buckskin."

"But this one carried Stephen's cartridge case! I knew it, because of the beaded design on it and the faded ribbons. It was a gift from an Indian squaw my brother met, when in the wilderness."

Phillip digested his wife's words thoughtfully. He knew the case. Stephen was quite proud of it. He'd once confided that he'd sometimes thought of going back to fetch the pretty Indian squaw who'd made it and possibly make her his wife.

"He could have traded or bought it from the murderer."

"That is what Father said," Arissa admitted, anxiously perusing the street, as though looking for a ghost.

Stephen had been stripped of his gear within minutes of his being shot. No one but the murderer could have

done it. That much Phillip knew. The cartridge box could
have changed hands more than once since then, but the
coincidence of the man's showing up at their law office
was too much to be totally ignored.

"Let's enjoy our meal and watch the office. Then, I'm
taking you home."

"And you are not remaining?"

Phillip's heart did a somersault at the troubled blue
gaze that sought his out. Did she even realize her power
over him, he wondered, reluctant to affirm her query.

"I need to get back to the office after dark. First, I
want to get that list for your father."

"I thought you couldn't because of ethics."

"I'm out of my mind, remember?" he quipped, in an
attempt to bring a smile to her face. It didn't work and
that bothered him. He thought he'd loved Deborah, but
Arissa had given a whole new meaning to the word. "Beside, I owe Alain something for not letting him in on
this." At Arissa's skeptical arch of the brow, he assured
her, "I'm not going to hit your father."

At that, she smiled. "Of course not. You could not
catch him off guard, the way you have been acting."

That was much better. Even Phillip had to laugh at her
rejoinder. He was damned lucky Alain Beaujeu hadn't
done more than he had. The sooner this charade was
over, the better it would be for all of them.

"Phillipe?"

"Yes?" He loved it when she said his name with that
charming accent and assumed that thoughtful purse of
her lips. They were so kissable . . .

"What is this talk of packing me off to a nunnery that
you said in the office . . . for acting the tart," she reminded him, in a derisive tone which betrayed her feelings about his unfounded accusation.

"A nunnery?" Suddenly Phillip chuckled aloud. "Oh,
you mean Holy Ground!" He lowered his voice. "That's

not a nunnery, love, it's . . ." He laughed again. "It's the district where ladies of the evening live and entertain."

"Dieu, but you *bastonnois* have strange terms for things!" Arissa sipped her drink and put it down, wiping her nose daintily with her free hand, where the froth topping the punch had spattered.

She missed part of it. Instead of leaning over on impulse and kissing it off, he reached across the table and gathered it with his finger. Then, as if savoring its flavor, he licked it off, a wicked twinkle in his gaze, as he pondered the entertainment of his wife in a slightly tipsy state. The very thought of it made his blood run warm.

"Phillipe, look! There he is again!"

Shaking himself from the intruding fantasy, Phillip followed Arissa's gaze across the street, where the trapper was leaving the office. This time he was empty-handed, obviously having left his haversack with Jonathan. This indeed needed to be looked into, although, Phillip reasoned, it was possible the man had legitimate business with his partner. They dealt with independent voyageurs.

A few moments later, Jonathan Hale emerged and locked the door. Glancing about, ill at ease, he hesitated briefly and then started down the street toward the corner. As he disappeared around it, the tavern maid returned to their table with the supper Phillip had ordered, yet he hardly appreciated her artful unveiling of the dish, nor was his appetite nearly as raw as it had been earlier.

God strike him, was it possible that the prisoner had told the truth, that Jonathan Hale *was* involved in the counterfeiting? Worse, was there a connection between the murderous attempts in Quebec and his law partner, his alleged friend? Phillip moved against his chair back, as he was served slices of the spiced pork, garnished with exotic fruit from the Indies.

More than ever, he was determined to return to the office tonight, even if it meant leaving Arissa for a few hours. She'd remained so close to him since their reunion, unselfishly making his problems her own. But he'd put his trust in her, and she was going to have to put hers in him. It was the only way their love could survive this damned war.

Although she was not fond of the idea of his leaving after the household had gone to bed for the night, Arissa did not contradict his argument of love and trust. Phillip's mention of trust doused the objection on her lips, replacing it with reluctant submission and support.

"It is only that I love you, and I will count the seconds until you are back at my side," she told him, throwing herself into his arms. "Be careful, *mon cher.* I could not bear to lose you again."

Phillip could still taste their parting kiss, flavored by the punch and her own sweetness. He'd pulled away and stopped only long enough to hug Jonathan and buss the cheek of his mother, who was also aware of his plan, before slipping out into the lamplit darkness.

As he walked the two blocks to Broad Street, he fingered the pistol tucked inside his jacket, well aware of the dangers at night in the city. Gangs were known to prey on lone figures, to rob them and beat them senseless, although Phillip had no intention of taking any back alleys. The streets themselves were adequately lighted and traveled by lantern-bearing coaches carrying late night revelers to their homes or lodgings.

The businesses on the block where the office was located were closed, however, making the distance between the corner lamplights dark and isolated. Key in hand, Phillip stepped into the shadows of the doorway Jonathan had vacated earlier, and gained entrance into the dark, deserted building. As he closed the door behind him, he thought he heard a movement in the back office, which

had served both he and Jonathan, the front being reserved for their clerk.

Belatedly, he froze. Since he'd made no effort at silence
in his entry, were there someone else there, they definitely had the advantage. After all, he hadn't expected
to encounter anyone inside. Swearing at himself for his
carelessness, Phillip made a point of walking loudly to
the clerk's desk, rattling some papers, and then returning
to the door. After opening it and closing it, as if he'd
found what he'd wanted and was leaving, he locked it,
the bolt sliding with a loud click into its keeper.

For the longest time, he waited, his breathing ever so
shallow. Had the ruse worked? The only sense detecting
anything was his nose, for the office always smelled of
tobacco smoke. Phillip even began to doubt that he'd
heard right, to begin with, and that his precautions had
all been for nothing. However, impatience was dangerous
in his profession, and he continued to listen to the quiet
above the steady beating of his pulse, his pistol ready in
hand.

Still, there was no further sign that someone lurked in
the dark office beyond. Arissa's fretting had begun to affect his work, he scolded himself, as he felt his way to
the clerk's desk and searched for the expensive musket
lighter Jonathan had won at the gaming tables of their
gentlemen's club. It had been there that afternoon, for
he'd panicked his partner by nearly setting the papers on
the desk afire, toying with the contraption. That was what
had sent the clerk rushing out of the office with his panicked, "I'll be back, sir, when he's gone!"

Just as Phillip grasped the handle of the lighter, the
floorboard behind him creaked in warning. With an in-
stinctive pivot, he fired the lighter, the resulting flash siz-
zling in the face of his stealthy assailant and blinding
them both. Out of the white and burnt-powder-scented
void, the other man pounced upon him like a big cat,

driving him back, against the clerk's desk and scattering papers, in the process. Phillip, unseeing, brought the lighter up to strike at where he thought his assailant's head should be, when a deadly cold blade pressed unerringly against his throat, freezing him in mid-strike.

A blood-stilling warning rumbled close to his face "Drop it, *mon ami!* Now!"

The stinging sensation beneath the sharp edge drove home the danger of hesitation. Certain he was already bleeding from a meticulously honed hunting knife, Phillip did as he was told and summoned his bravado.

"What the devil are you about at this hour?" he demanded. Whoever it was, friend or foe, he hoped to throw them off guard long enough to dislodge the pistol between him and the desk.

"I might ask the same of you, Phillip Monroe." This time, the voice was less threatening and disturbingly familiar. The knife, too, had eased its pressure against his pulsing throat. "I thought you slept like a lamb every night, that is, when you were not ravishing my daughter!"

"Alain?" Phillip ventured, his hand closing on the handle of the hidden weapon. "Alain Beaujeu?"

"Since I have the knife, you answer first, monsieur."

The blade's pressure had lessened, the voice had changed, but something in the coiled muscle of the man holding him at the disadvantage told Phillip he was not absolved of danger yet. It was no wonder Arissa's father thought him a raving maniac.

Training, however, kept him from taking too much for granted. "Well, I . . ." Phillip shifted subtly so that the barrel of the gun came free. "I think we are at a stalemate, sir." He pressed the barrel against his father-in-law's ribs. "Shall we put aside our weapons and discuss this reasonably; or will one of us devastate the life of a young lady we both love?"

"I am a reasonable man, which is more than you have

een, of late," Alain conceded. He removed the knife
rom Phillip's neck and, ever so slowly, backed away. A
elltale floorboard confirmed his retreat.

Yet, Phillip was not fool enough to dismiss his father-
n-law's expertise at throwing a knife. At this distance,
ither of them was impossible to miss. "I am working for
General Washington, Alain, and, I believe we are both
after the same people."

"You think Jonathan Hale is involved in the counter-
eiting?" Although Phillip could not see his father-in-law's
ace, he heard the surprise in his voice.

"There's been some testimony from one of the coun-
erfeiters in prison to that effect . . . and I think this of-
ice plays a key role in the conspiracy."

Orders be damned, there was no avoiding letting Alain
n on what he knew, at this point. Beside, he welcomed
he additional help. Although Beaujeu was not in the
army, he was a fellow patriot. Phillip briefly filled Alain
n on the outcome of Jay's inquiries, as well as the pur-
oose of his charade.

"*Sacre bleu,* someone has been trying to kill you since
ou left for Quebec?"

"If not, I've had an ungodly streak of bad luck," Phillip
emarked, in a wry tone.

"But you saw this man who shot you."

"So wrapped in furs and dusted with snow that he
ooked like most of the other riflemen. Damnation, his
ace was encrusted with ice. We'd have to freeze the black-
guard in order for me to identify him!" Exasperation in-
ected his words. "But Arissa said you two camped with
a trapper who was carrying her brother's cartridge case."

"*Oui,* but he could . . ."

"He was here this afternoon, after the office closed.
She was quite alarmed and was no less so when I left
her," Phillip added, with a pang of guilt.

"Then let us search these records and see what we can

find, so that you can get back to your wife," Alain sug
gested, clapping Phillip on the shoulder in a congenia
fashion. *"Dieu,* but you do not know how much seeing
you in your right mind has relieved me, *mon ami!"*

"I wanted to tell you . . ."

Alain cut him off. "The army must have its secrets,'
he reassured Phillip. "Now, I have a lantern in the back
so that we can see . . ."

The unmistakable turn of a key fumbling in a lock some
where in the back made both Phillip and his companior
halt just inside the other office. While they'd been talking
in the front, obviously someone else had approached the
building and was entering through the alley door
Jonathan? Phillip wondered, as he noiselessly crossed the
room on tiptoe and pressed against the wall on one side
of the door, while Alain assumed the same position on the
other.

He mentally wrestled for an excuse to be in the office
at that hour, particularly when he was supposed to be
sleeping a drugged sleep, and finally opted to continue
his charade. He could say he'd refused his nightly dose
of medication and that Arissa had sent for Alain to follow
him and bring him home. Hopefully, Alain would catch
on and pick up the hoax.

The door finally opened, admitting a tall, broad shoul
dered man carrying a lantern. Before his eyes could ad
just to the sudden burst of light in the room, Phillip was
immediately assaulted by the smell of liquor and cheap
perfume mingled with that of an unwashed body in buck
skin. Although his pistol was readied, before he could
issue a warning to the intruder, Alain Beaujeu was on the
man's back, the blade of the intimidating hunting knife
at his victim's throat, before the latter knew what was hap
pening.

With equal agility, Phillip snatched up the lantern as i
was dropped in shock and put it on the desk Jonathan

Hale had taken over in his absence, for it had once been
his. He'd only used it for a short time after his recovery
from the fire, which had destroyed his original office and
bachelor quarters on its second floor. As a junior partner,
Hale had used the second, smaller desk.

"Well, well, Monsieur Egan! Imagine meeting you
again. One does now realize how small this world is, *non?*"

"I've got him covered, Alain." Phillip held the gun on
the man, as Alain withdrew cautiously.

"When did ya take to hangin' about with a madman,
Beaujeu?" the trapper asked, eyeing Phillip, warily.

"My wife sent him after me," Phillip answered, rubbing
his thumb on the firing mechanism, in an intimidating
manner. "I escaped!"

"Now you will tell us why *you* are here, monsieur."

"Especially with a key to the office." Phillip added.

Now it was the intruder's time to think quickly. The
eyes which Phillip had not been able to see before, narrowed in quick calculation. "I dropped some business off
this afternoon with Mr. Hale. He was goin' ta read over
the contract and approve or change it, if he thought it'd
need such. A man cain't be too careful with these big fur
comp'nies."

Phillip did not miss the inadvertent glance to the desk
Jonathan had commandeered. For the first time, he saw
the fringed haversack the trapper had brought by earlier,
hanging on the back of the chair.

"Then as senior partner of the firm, I should take a
look at the papers myself."

As Phillip reached for them, Egan protested. "I don't
want no crazy man in my business!" Phillip's brandished
pistol, however, stopped the big man from making any
moves that would provoke its use.

"Strike me blue, this is a pretty heavy contract!" Phillip
remarked, lifting the leather bag.

Egan made no comment. He simply glared at the

younger man, as the haversack was emptied on the desk
Instead of papers, two ink-stained printing plates fell ou
representing the front and back of a Continental bill.

"Damn you, Monroe, ya got more lives then a passl
a' cats!"

Without warning, Egan grabbed an open box of file
on the corner of the desk and let them fly at Phillip'
gun hand. The office resounded with the explosion c
the weapon, drowning out its owner's curse. Swingin;
both fists locked together, Egan pivoted almost in th
same motion and struck out at Alain's midriff. The ex
voyageur, however, was lighter on his feet and quicke
than the larger built man. Alain easily jumped out o
reach. As Egan's knuckles brushed the front of his shir
he kept on going, making a break for the door.

Phillip started after him, when he caught the flash o
Alain's knife cutting through the air and hesitated lon;
enough for it to find its target. Egan yelped in pain, a
the knife went through his upper arm, pinning him t
the jamb. Before the man could pull the riveting blad
out, Phillip had removed the trappers own long knif
from the beaded sheath strapped to his leg and put it
tapered point to its owner's neck.

"For the love a' God, man, pull the blade out!"

"Tell us all you know, first," Phillip demanded, whil
Alain grasped the hilt of his knife, as if to guarantee i
stayed where it was. It was all falling into place now, an
Phillip was furious, furious at what this man had done
and wounded at the thought that Jonathan was someho
connected with him. "It was you that shot me in Quebec
wasn't it?"

"I told ya, ya had more lives than a passle a' cats."

"And it was you who attacked Stephen Conway on th
road, after he left the Chop House. You thought he wa
me, didn't you? *Didn't you!*"

"Hell, I ain't got no quarrel with you pers'nally! Hale hired me to do it!"

"Why?" Phillip felt as if the knife he held had been thrust into his chest—Jonathan, whom he'd tutored as a junior in law school. Jonathan, who'd stood up with him at his and Deborah's wedding and been named godfather of their child.

"He didn't say. He just paid me. Then you come back from the dead, out a' yer mind!" the man accused, with derision. "I ain't seen the like a' ya. Ya must be charmed."

Phillip mentally shook the rampant thoughts of wounded betrayal. "Tell us about the plates."

"I don't know anything about 'em. I'm just to deliver packages."

"To whom, monsieur?"

"Here and there." Alain shifted the impaling knife, and Egan shouted. "To places where presses are set up."

"How many?"

"Four, altogether. They take turns so's they won't get caught."

"Name them!"

"They's a place in White Plains, one on Murray Street in the Dutch section, another at Butler Mill, and one in Brooklyn. I cain't recall the names, I swear it," the man vowed, as he eyed the knife pinning him to the wooden jamb. "Dammit, take it out a'fore I bleed ta death!"

At Phillip's nod, Alain complied. Egan yelped again in pain and slumped against the wall, clutching his wound. Without one thread of mercy, Phillip removed his tie and bound the trapper's wrists behind his back. As far as he was concerned, the man deserved none. He'd killed Stephen Conway in cold blood—Stephen, whose generosity and thoughtfulness had led to his pointless death.

"A hangman's noose is too good for you!" Phillip averred, at the man's pained whimper.

"I can tell the army a whole lot more, if they let me go."

A twisted sneer came to Phillip's lips. "Is that so? Well, I'm certain you will." Grabbing the man's wounded arm, he hauled him toward the door. "Guess we're not going to need that list, after all," he remarked to Alain Beaujeu, who'd reloaded Phillip's gun, while Egan was being properly trussed.

"It appears we have all we need right here." Alain clapped their source on the back.

"You jackasses think you're right smart, don't ya?" Egan growled, as Phillip shoved him through the door. "Well you hear them fire bells?"

Phillip stopped and listened, aware for the first time that an alarm had been sounded. That could account for the reason the pistol shot had not summoned a member of the night watch by now. A sick wave of apprehension washed over him, for the sound was all too familiar, taking him back to another time, a nightmare Arissa had managed to all but erase.

"So there is a fire." Although he appeared unintimidated by Egan's implied threat, something in the man's gaze only added to Phillip's increasing anxiety. His control breaking, Phillip thrust the trapper up against the outside wall of the building. "Where is it, damn you? The arsenal?"

Egan smiled, his perspiration-damp face glistening in the moonlight, shafting into the alley. "You do have trouble keepin' a wife, Monroe."

Twenty-four

Arissa's head ached abominably, as she wriggled on the attic floor of Monroe Place to get to the window. She could hear the fire bells and the roar of activity outside, although she needed no confirmation that Jonathan Hale had made good his threat to set fire to the house. The smoke was drifting naturally up the attic stairwell, despite the bolted door below, and stung her eyes.

When she'd heard someone climbing the central staircase in the wee hour of the morning, she'd rushed to meet him, certain it was Phillip returning from his nocturnal prowl at the office. She'd called out his name in a whisper and waited for him to reach the second floor, before going into his arms. It was only then that she realized she'd made a mistake.

Instead of Phillip's heady scent of spice talc, she detected a stronger one, like that worn by his partner, although she did not make the connection to Hale immediately. She was distracted by yet another smell—that of lamp oil. It was as though he'd been wallowing in it. Before she could react, however, a painful blow to her temple came out of nowhere, robbing her of consciousness and casting her into darkness.

When she stirred, it was to the bite of the ribbon from her peignoir cutting into her wrists. A handkerchief had been stuffed into her mouth to keep her from crying out in warning to the others, sleeping peacefully in the large house.

"Can't have you waking up the household now, can we, madame?" Jonathan told her, when he saw her open her eyes in the light cast in by the moon through the attic window.

What are you doing? Why? Those questions, among others, swam through the agonizing jumble in Arissa's head. However, the gag kept her from expressing them.

"I truly regret your becoming involved with Monroe, but that's what you get for associating with his likes. You'll have to burn with him." He finished tying her feet in a likewise manner. "Except, I gather, from your earlier greeting, that our Phillip is not sleeping as he is supposed to be. So, I am going to remove the handkerchief and you must tell me where he is. Now, if you try to shout," he warned, "I shall put it back, if I have to knock your teeth in to do so, do we understand each other?"

Arissa refused to tell him anything. Even when he struck her, she held in her information, as well as her pain.

"So be it!" Hale declared, in resignation. "Since you were looking for him, I can assume the devil has once again evaded my plans. However, this time, I am going to kill him myself. I'm through depending on that half-witted fur trader."

Her heart cringed at the words, which confirmed her worst suspicion. The trapper *had* been Stephen's killer and Phillip's attempted murderer. But that Jonathan Hale was behind the treachery was a total shock! He'd acted so concerned over Phillip, had been there for the family. She continued to stare at him in disbelief, as he went on.

"I shall wait for him. I'm certain the fire will bring him running into the house, eager to rescue his family. Now don't worry, dear, I've allowed for the back stairwell on the south side of the house to permit escape for old Maddie and the babe. Mayhaps even the servants, if they keep their heads. After all, little Jonathan is my blood, as well. I owe that much to his mother. . . . No, I've only saturated certain rooms and the main stairwell, of course."

Considering his horrible plan, it was hard to believe Jonathan Hale felt obliged by honor to anyone.

" 'Tis you Phillip will try to rescue. But you won't be in the master suite and your room will be in flames." Hale's laugh had a sinister sound that chilled Arissa, despite the close attic heat. "Oh, he'll charge right into the thick of it. He's of that bent, as you know."

The clang of the arriving fire engine drew Arissa back to her purpose—reaching the attic window. If she could break the glass, she might use it to cut through the binding silk ribbons. Then there was a chance she might escape, although the way the smoke was slipping in around the jamb of the attic door and the heat that pervaded the planking beneath her was dissuading. Still, she gave it her every effort.

By the time she reached the window, wriggling and rolling around trunks and other dusty clutter, she could hardly see. Her eyes were stinging and blurred, and she felt giddy. It was only stubborn resolve that permitted her to carry through with her plan. The window shattered with the impact of her bound feet.

Heartened by her success, Arissa twisted, until she could back up to the ragged glass remaining in the muttons. Ever so carefully, she began to pull the ribbons between her wrists over the sharp edge, well aware that a reckless slip might cause her to bleed to death, before she was of any use to herself or anyone else. Despite the urgency of her situation, she had to keep her wits. Not only did her life depend on it, but possibly Phillip's, as well.

* * *

A great crowd had gathered on the grounds at Monroe Place, in addition to the fire engine and its crew of an engineer and four assistants. Six of the twelve citizens designated as firemen by the city were frantically pumping the water tank on the wagon, while the others manned the hose, shooting water through the broken front windows. Two more tried to break down the locked front door with axes. Neighbors and a few volunteer bystanders were circling the house, looking for other ways to gain entrance.

Such was the scene, when Phillip Monroe and Alain Beaujeu arrived. The fire, which was concentrated on the family wing where the master bedroom, nursery, and his mother's room were located, had shattered the glass on the second floor of the mansion, as well, all the while licking hungrily at the wooden frames and drapes.

Phillip blanched. Everyone of any meaning in his life had been sleeping in the inferno consuming the south wing. Throwing his prisoner—whom he'd dragged relentlessly the two long blocks to the Broadway mansion—at a bystanding officer of the military, he shouted, "This man is a traitor. Arrest him in the name of the Continental Congress!"

Without waiting for a reply, Phillip charged up to the house, as the front door gave way. The two volunteers grabbed his arms in restraint.

"Here now, what do you think you're doing?"

"My family is in there!"

The words made him sick, even as he said them. They were the same he'd shouted, as he'd tried to get into the house to get Deborah and the baby. He'd failed then, but he wouldn't, he couldn't fail now.

"Phillip, thank God!"

From the crowd, Maddie Monroe broke free, rushing toward her son in her night dress and bare feet. "I've got Jonathan! Eugene and Anna are with me, but we

couldn't get into your room!" She gasped, trying to regain her breath and enveloped him in her arms. "Dear
God, I'm sorry, son. The room was in flames. Eugene
burned his hand on the knob, trying to open it, and
when he kicked in the door . . . no one could have been
alive in there."

"She could be elsewhere," Alain suggested, as reluctant
as Phillip to accept Maddie's words. "We can go in the
north side of the house and . . ."

"Look, up there! There's someone in the attic window!"

Even as the crowd gaped upward, Phillip backed away
in time to see Arissa knocking out the remaining glass
and muttons of the window, her arm wrapped in some
sort of rag.

"Dieu, what is she doing up there!" Alain turned toward
the crowd and ordered abruptly, "Someone get ropes, as
many as you can find!

"I'm going in."

"Non, Phillipe! Stop him!"

Phillip heard Arissa scream from the window, as he
darted around the corner and to the north side of the
house, which was as yet free of the fire. He wouldn't be
stopped, he thought, snatching an ax from a fireman.

"I know how to get to her . . . my wife in the attic,"
he called back, in explanation, and he lunged inside.

"Don't go in there till the other engine gets here!
You'll be killed, mister!"

The fireman's warning fell on deaf ears. Phillip bolted
up the servant's side stairwell to the second floor, but
upon reaching the smoke-filled hall, he could see that
any attempt to use the main stairwell, which accessed the
attic on the third floor, was rendered impossible by the
raging flames racing their way toward him. There was only
one other way, he thought, glad that he'd taken the ax.

He could cut through the wall in the servant's quarters that separated the attic from their rooms.

"Welcome home, Phillip!"

Startled by the unexpected sound of Jonathan Hale's voice, Phillip squinted in the smoke-filled hallway to see the man emerging from one of the doors that opened on it.

"Jonathan!"

"You've more lives than a cat."

"So Egan said," Phillip answered, warily. Was that a pistol Hale held in his hand? He couldn't see. "He told us everything, Jonathan. The least you can do is help me get to Arissa. Things might go easier on you!"

There was a loud click—or was it the fire crackling along the walls? Time was running out. Instinctively, Phillip jumped sideways, as the gun went off. At such close range, the bullet still managed to graze his side, but he was too worried about Arissa to pay it heed. Adrenaline pumped its steeling way through him, anesthetizing and strengthening at the same time, so that he regained his balance, just as Jonathan charged him.

"Damn you, die, Phillip Monroe!"

Without thinking, Phillip swung the ax, catching his assailant full in the chest. Jonathan screamed, a blood-curdling sound that erupted in agonized coughing, as Phillip withdrew the ax from the bone and flesh, and spun toward the narrow stairwell to the third floor servants' quarters. He had to get to Arissa. *He had to!*

Taking the steps two at a time, he bounded upward and into the black smoke, his lungs aching and burning.

" 'Rissa!"

His cry was no more than a rasp, as he reached the door of the room which bordered the attic. Upon opening it, the intense heat of the flames, which met him, set the scars on his body afire with memory as agonizing as that which flooded his mind. He couldn't get to her! A solid tunnel of flame separated him from her. Perhaps Alain . . .

Desperately, Phillip turned away and stumbled down the steps, his arm over his nose to filter out the equally hot smoke that burned his lungs. As he darted across the hall, he heard Jonathan Hale call to him.

"Help me, sir! I'm dying! Don't let me burn like Deborah! I didn't know she was there! She was supposed to be with our parents!"

The admission struck Phillip still, halfway down the steps. "You bastard!" he swore, hoarsely.

His head swimming dizzily, he bounded upward and seized Hale by the collar. With him in hand, Phillip set off down the steps, dragging his late wife's murderer behind him like a sack of grain. Yes, he'd save the sniveling coward, if only long enough to hear his motive for this unfounded hatred.

Upon arriving on the first floor, Phillip plunged headlong into the reviving cold spray of the second fire engine, which had arrived from another ward of the city. Immediately, he was supported under the arm by one of the firemen, while another grabbed the bleeding Jonathan Hale.

Phillip's consciousness threatened to abandon him, but he resolutely hung onto it during the spasmodic coughing that racked his chest and sent him to his knees.

"You were always best!" Hale accused, with labored breath. "Father had even named you . . ." He coughed, bringing up blood, and collapsed against the man tending his wound. *"You* are executor of his estate . . . over me . . . his own son!"

Jealousy? Phillip thought, in disbelief. God strike him, Jonathan was jealous enough to kill his own sister?

"The rope, it's too heavy to throw up there."

Alain Beaujeu's frustrated cry dragged Phillip's wavering awareness to where lengths of hemp lay in a useless heap at his father-in-law's feet.

"Arissa, come back to the window!" Alain shouted frantically.

Phillip shook his head in an attempt to clear his mental fog, which was as debilitating as the smoke. Arissa! He tried to focus on the attic window where he'd seen his wife earlier, but now, all that was visible were the upward wisps of smoke, the forerunner of the insatiable black monster climbing toward her with its fiery companion at its heels.

"She can't get out the attic door!" Jonathan Hale called out, in a singsong voice that erupted in a fit of coughing. "I bolted her in."

But for Arissa's immediate danger, Phillip could have finished the man off with his bare hands. "Arissa!" he cried out, hoping she might appear for him.

"Put a ladder against the house. I'll try to toss the rope up from a higher point!"

Immediately the firemen obeyed Alain Beaujeu, but as the wooden ladder struck the masonry side of the building, Arissa appeared again. Phillip blanched, as she leaned out the window, gasping for breath. There had to be a way beside the brick-weighted rope, yet he was at a loss as to how. So much they'd come through together, he thought, his mind giving way to helplessness. If Arissa died, he didn't want to live.

"Father, stand back!"

Like a lifeline, Arissa's voice delved into his despair and drew him out. Clinging to consciousness, Phillip struggled to his feet and watched, as yard after yard of heavy printed material unfolded down the side of the house, moving dangerously toward an open second story window, where flames clawed upward toward it.

"Wet it down!" Phillip croaked. He cleared his voice again and shouted with renewed hope. "Wet it down!"

Catching onto his idea, the engineer and firemen turned the hose onto the material, while their cohorts pumped furiously.

"Bring the other wagon around, and be quick about it!"

Phillip's command was echoed by Maddie Monroe, who, unbenownst to him, had been attending him. He ventured a grateful glance in his mother's direction, before returning his gaze to the attic window where Arissa waited with admirable patience for the cloth to become soaked, before unfolding more of it.

"That gal's got a good head on her shoulders!"

His mother's compliment hardly registered. Phillip had grown oblivious to all but the girl unfurling drapery cloth, as though she had the remainder of the night to do so. Again, at her father's direction, she stopped lowering the material just short of the first story window directly under her.

"Now, tie it to something sturdy!" Alain ordered, the calm in his voice belayed by his anxious expression.

"Done!" Arissa shouted back, her voice strangled by the smoke.

Phillip's heart seized as the young woman started to back out of the window, holding on to the wet cloth, only to resume beating with each hand to hand that brought her closer to the second floor window, where fire lapped dangerously.

"Let's pull the cloth to the side!" Adrenaline once again surging through him, Phillip ran to the ladder Alain had abandoned and started up it. "Arissa, hold on tightly. I'm going to pull you to the side!"

With Alain and several of the men steadying the ladder, Phillip reached for the end of the cloth. Mustering his reserve of strength, he tugged it as hard toward him as he could, while water from the two engines showered both he and the girl swaying perilously above him, her arms and legs wrapped about the length of material, as though she were half-dead.

Phillip was tempted to climb up after her, but that would pull the lifeline into the fire and perhaps be too much weight for the anchor his wife had used. Instead, he waited with stinging eyes and breath, praying as he'd never done before. A single lash of a flame against her tender skin could cost her her hold and send her plunging to her death.

" 'Rissa," he muttered over and over, as she painstakingly made her way past the window, where black smoke nearly obliterated his view of her.

He heard her coughing and felt the result in the material he'd wrapped about the top rung of the ladder. Fearful of it pulling the ladder into the range of the first floor window, where the fire was barely being held at bay, he glanced below in apprehension to see what looked like a score of men counterbalancing the ladder with the once-useless ropes.

"I love you, 'Rissa!" Phillip called out, when he saw her descend from the cloud of smoke above, just beyond his reach. Suddenly her bare feet came within his grasp in a startling drop. Phillip seized them at the ankles, steadying the trembling girl above him.

"You're almost here," he encouraged, placing them firmly on the top rung of the ladder. "Come on, love. You're almost in my arms."

Whether it was the reinforcement of the solid wooden ladder beneath her or Phillip's words that gave her the additional burst of energy she needed, he didn't know, but Arissa began to descend the ladder steadily, until she was indeed in his embrace. A full head above the cheering crowd below, she hugged him joyously.

"You're alive!" she blurted out in French. *"Merci a Dieu!* I was so worried about you! Jonathan . . ."

"I know, love!" Phillip gave her a quick peck on the cheek. "But let's discuss this on the ground."

He couldn't believe it. She was in the attic of a house consumed by fire, and she was worried about *him!* Phillip reluctantly released Arissa into the arms of her father and finished descending the ladder himself. Weak with relief, he permitted the volunteers to support him, as everyone moved away from the burning house.

He hardly noticed the firemen moving the pumpers about to the northern wing under Maddie Monroe's authoritative direction. All he could see was the girl in the soaked peignoir, assuring her father that she was fine. Leaning against one of the giant shade trees garnishing the grounds, Phillip listened, as Arissa excitedly told how she'd met Jonathan Hale in the dark, thinking him her husband, and how the man had bound, gagged, and locked her in the attic.

"He was waiting to kill Phillipe!" she exclaimed, looking over her shoulder, as if reminded of him. "That was why I begged you not to go inside. I knew he was waiting," she told him, obviously dismayed that he hadn't listened to her.

With a heart-wrenching sob, she tore away from Alain and rushed once again into Phillip's arms, hugging him as though he were going to try to get away. At that moment, even if he were inclined to, he didn't think he could.

"Oh, Phillipe," she cried softly, catching his soot-smudged face in her hands. The blue eyes which had stolen his heart, long before he even realized it, were swimming with compassion. "It was Jonathan who killed Deborah."

Phillip pulled her head to his chest, well aware of the tears spilling from his own gaze. "I know, love."

"But w . . . why?" she whispered, brokenly.

So close, Phillip thought, locking his hands in her

soaked tresses. He'd come so close to losing her, too. If he had, living would have been worse than a fiery death.

"What happened to Jonathan?"

At Arissa's query, Phillip looked over to where a fireman had covered Jonathan Hale's face with a blanket. In all those years of friendship, he'd never once given Phillip a clue that he envied him. Phillip had been like a big brother to Jonathan, often intervening on the man's behalf with the stern, unbending Thomas Hale. Who'd have dreamed Jonathan resented it?

"Jealousy and greed took him, love." Upon seeing her quizzical expression, Phillip conceded, "We'll discuss it later."

Even if he wanted to spare the Hales the scandal their son had generated, he couldn't. Egan not only would incriminate Jonathan, but Jonathan himself had boldly admitted his guilt in front of the fireman attending him.

"Maaa!" Distracted by the small voice at his feet, Phillip looked down to see his son tugging on Arissa's wet peignoir. "Maaa!" the child shouted again.

"Strike me!" Phillip exclaimed, as Arissa reached down and gathered little Jonathan up in her arms. "Did you hear that? He called you mother!"

"Well, not quite," Arissa laughed, pulling away, as Jonathan grabbed at her mouth. He loved to feel her teeth and then his own. As he put his finger into his mouth and discovered a baby tooth, drool streaking his soot-stained face, she rewarded him with an enthusiastic, "Big boy!"

Happy amidst all the chaos, Jonathan cackled in delight. He loved being called a big boy.

"I think he said it, too, madame," Anna, who had been keeping the youngster in tow, told her. "You've won his little heart, to be sure."

Phillip put his arms around both Jonathan and Arissa.

"Well that settles it. You're stuck with us now, woman. You hold both our hearts in the palm of your hand."

Arissa leaned into the kiss Phillip gave her, sealing the pact. She wasn't certain what tomorrow held for them, but, considering what their love had already survived, she was no longer afraid. Her own heart, once torn, was now whole and completely belonged to her new family. Surrounded by those she loved and those who loved her, she knew no border could separate them. Not anymore.

Epilogue

December 1783

Phillip was coming home. The British were evacuating New York City. Soon the last of the forces sent to subdue the rebellious colonies would be gone from their Staten and Long Island strongholds. The preseason gaiety that filled the sprawling farmhouse at Blaine's Folly in anticipation of the homecoming could not begin to match that in Arissa's heart.

December had not been much of a month of celebration for Arissa since her marriage to Phillip. His military duties required him to almost invariably be away during the holidays from Blaine's Folly, where the family had moved after the destruction of Monroe Place and the British occupation of New York. It made for many a fretful family Christmas.

He was at Trenton in 1776, having gone in ahead of the troops for surveillance. In 1777, he was promoted to colonel, after his involvement in the prisoner exchange for General Lee. He wintered that year at Valley Forge with his fellow patriots. 1778 was service in Connecticut, while 1779 found him in Morristown with General Washington, followed by 1780 in the south, with General Greene.

Ironically, when Phillip did come home to celebrate the first public day of Thanksgiving with his family in mid-December 1781, it was Arissa who was called away from the festivities to deliver twins at the camp of Canadian refugees established at Albany, where she'd been continuing to practice medicine. Nonetheless, the two made up for loss during the rest of his leave. The following year, their new daughter Jennie—named after Arissa's real mother—helped assuage the holiday loneliness.

Now, at long last, it was over. The treaties had been signed, nearly two years after Cornwallis's surrender at Yorktown, and Phillip was coming home. The farmhouse was filled with tempting aromas of holiday baking and fresh evergreen, which Arissa and eight-year-old Jonathan had cut to decorate. Her heart filled with the spirit of peace and joy, Arissa sang along with Alain Beaujeu and his family, while Jonathan delighted his baby sister by pulling the most outlandish of faces. They were waiting, all waiting.

It was hard for Arissa, although she had complete faith in her husband's word. It felt as though she'd waited a lifetime for her husband, not that she'd ever uttered a word of complaint. His commitments were hers now. Besides, Phillip had promised to be there on the first and, even though it was approaching the dinner hour, she knew he would be. But for that trust and her undying love for the man, she might never have survived the war and their long separations.

Family had kept her occupied, involving her in all the patriotic efforts, but she'd found her niche helping the Canadian refugees, whose sole support was the Continental Congress. They'd been promised land and now, perhaps, that promise could be made good. But for the charity of the Albany citizens, she didn't know how the poor souls would have survived. Like her, they were welcomed and supported, while their husbands fought for freedom along with the colonials. There had been joyous

reunions taking place there for weeks, with the disband-
ing of the army.

"I hear something!" Jonathan shouted above the din,
startling little Jennie.

Before Arissa could reach her daughter, clad in a spe-
cially embroidered dress of red on white made by her
grandmother, Tamson had gathered up the baby and was
coddling her with affection. A baby girl in the family had
been a welcome relief, after so many boys. In a rush of
skirts, Arissa darted for the hall, after her stepson, and
arrived in time to see Jonathan throw open the door.

"Papa!"

While Arissa waited for Phillip to peel Jonathan away
from him, she glanced beyond to the two men who accompanied him. Recognition lit up her face as she saw
the eldest of the Beaujeu boys.

"John!" she exclaimed, bypassing her husband to welcome her half-brother in.

Immediately they were surrounded by the rest of the
Beaujeu clan. Tamson had handed off Jennie to Maddie
and, with tear-filled eyes, hugged her son, while Alain
clapped him heartily on the back. Arissa could not help
the gaze that stung her own, as she was finally enveloped
by Phillip's arms and kissed quite thoroughly. In the background, the younger members of the clan hooped and
shouted with glee at the reunion.

The cold air that had filled the hall before his other
companion closed the door could not possibly offset the
giddy warmth that flowed through her. Even when Phillip
pulled away, its glow continued to radiate from her face.

"I believe I haven't introduced you to my guest," he
reminded her, turning her toward the tall man standing
quietly by the door.

He was clad in the brown and buff uniform of his regiment, but it was not his Canadian uniform that com-
manded Arissa's attention. It was his face and those dear,

dancing brown eyes that belayed his otherwise stern demeanor.

"Martin!" she whispered, in disbelief.

Arissa couldn't have moved, if Phillip hadn't ushered her over to her Canadian foster brother. She'd long given up hope of ever seeing Martin again. Phillip had sent her letters to her brother, but no answer ever came.

"Oh, Martin!" It was all she could say, before sobs of joy overtook her.

"Merry Christmas, 'Rissa," her brother managed, stiffly.

He was so different from the demonstrative Stephen, yet the trembling hold that embraced her told Arissa of his true feelings. There was nothing to do but to purge their grief and spend their joy in silence.

"So much has happened!" she managed at last, backing only slightly away.

"So your letters said."

"You got them?"

"Well, they kept showing up in my quarters. You'll have to ask your crafty husband about that. He and this seafaring bloke kidnaped me right out from under the sentries' nose three days ago! I vow, I've yet to recover from it!"

Arissa looked at Phillip, a grin tugging at the corners of her lips. "He can be a rascal." She hugged her husband's arm emphatically. "But a lovable one, *non?*" Emotion crept into her voice, as she bathed in the love light of his gaze that merged with her own. "How can I ever thank you?"

"I'll think of something," Phillip answered, with a perfectly wicked twist of his lips. "In the meantime, I promised Martin here that John and I would more than make up for his inconvenience. John is going to see him safely back to Staten Island in time to sail with his troops, but for now . . . how long will dinner be? We're famished."

"I can tell my son's home!" Maddie Monroe teased at the edge of the crowd. Her only sign of emotion was her overbright brown eyes, as warm and inviting as the cinnamon buns on the sideboard in the other room. She waved one arm overhead, like a commander leading a charge, all the while playing the grandmother with little Jennie in her other.

"We eat right now, boys. Just come on in and fill up! We'll get to know who we're eating with later!"

The vertical wood-paneled dining room was crowded, but everyone managed to find a seat at the table. Maddie had explained that when her father had built it, he'd done so in order to feed his help as well as his family. It had always been an informal setting, and today was no different. Although Eugene and Anna served the meal, there was a place for them on the corner near the back kitchen. Even the children were seated with the adults, some in laps and some in chairs, although they were separated to avoid mischief's temptation.

After a reverent grace delivered by Phillip at his place as head of the house, an endless stream of platters circled the table with an assortment of meats, both roasted and boiled, as well as accompanying dishes. All the while, introductions were being made and conversation ensued, nonstop. There was much to catch up on, with family members spread throughout the new and independent country.

Arissa found that Martin was not only aware of Arissa and Stephen's fates from her letters, but had followed her advice in deeding over the Chateau Royale to Gaspar and Chiah Le Boeuf. He, now a colonel, like Phillip, intended to marry his superior's daughter in Nova Scotia and proceed on to England, where he would run the family estate.

Tamson read letters from Alain's sisters, which told that they, too, had survived the war. In fact, Phillip had worked with Mark Heathcote when he was in the Carolinas with General Greene. The hardest part on each of the girls was doing without their husbands for the cause. Now, they were looking forward to Christmas with the whole family together again.

John Beaujeu had no shortage of adventures to tell, which completely captivated young Robert and Jonathan's attention. There had been close calls with British warships and hair-raising tales of slipping past blockades under the cover of night. He'd met a young lady from Maine, whom he intended to visit when his ship sailed back to Portsmouth. Her father was a shipbuilder, he went on, ignoring his brother's teasing remarks.

As Arissa looked about the table, she was too filled with happiness to eat. All she wanted to do was study each precious face and cling to every word from those she cared for. Christmas was still weeks away, but if she never received another gift, this one Phillip and John had given her would suffice her for the rest of her days.

"You're not eating," Phillip prodded, his hand finding her knee beneath the table. "You're going to need your strength later, madame."

"I am too full of love," she told him, blushing, despite the fact that she had grown accustomed to her husband's scandalous suggestion. "Never in my life, Phillip Monroe, have I known such happiness as I am feeling now."

"Just wait till later," he whispered, surreptitiously.

"Phillipe!"

Phillipe. No matter how often he heard it, Phillip still melted when she said his name in that French manner— that is, all but that part of him which reacted with passionate steel. God, he ached for her. He knew she had been in complete earnest about her happiness, but that was not enough for him. Later that evening, after the Beaujeux had departed for Annanbrae and the children had been tucked into bed, he fully intended to make his blushing bride happier yet. That was his only assignment, now that the winds of war were spent, and borders could no longer keep them apart.